Shadows of an Echoed Past

Book One of "The Code Chronicles"

Written By: Robert Ewing

Collectuer Publications

©Copy Right

This is a work of fiction. Names, characters, places, and incidents either are the product of the author's imagination or are used fictitiously, and any resemblance to actual persons, living or dead, businesses, companies, events, or locales is entirely coincidental.

Published in Canada by Collectuer Publications
First Edition: September 2023
ISBN: 978-1-7380592-1-8
Library and Archives Canada Cataloguing in Publication
Ewing, Robert J., [1975]
Shadows of an Echoed Past: Book One of The Code Chronicles / Robert J. Ewing
ISBN 978-1-7380592-1-8
1. Title. 2. Series: Ewing, Robert J., [1975]- . The Code Chronicles ; bk. 1
Printed in Canada

Dedication

To Karen, thank you for always believing in me. Your support has been my anchor, and your love, my inspiration. I couldn't have written a single word without you by my side.

To my kids, you make every day brighter. Thanks for being the amazing individuals you are, you bring joy into everything I do.

To my parents, thank you for your endless support and love. You laid the foundation for this journey, and I'm grateful for every lesson you've imparted.

This book is dedicated to all of you.

Acknowledgements

Thank you to everyone who's been part of this book's journey.

Special thanks to Bev and Frank Lee for your attentive editing. Your work made this book better, and I'm grateful for your expertise.

Leslie Wells, your keen insights helped shape the story in crucial ways. Your guidance was invaluable, and I appreciate it immensely.

To everyone else who contributed, no matter how small, your input made a difference. I'm grateful for all your support. To the readers, thanks for being the reason writers like me keep writing.

Sincerely, Rob Ewing

CONTENT

Prologue

The intersection of biotechnology, quantum computing, and artificial intelligence (AI) paved the way for unprecedented advancements in human reproduction. Harnessing the sheer processing power of quantum computers and the predictive prowess of AI, the government has successfully developed and integrated a comprehensive synthetic reproduction system into society, replacing traditional human conception and gestation entirely.

Quantum computing provided the computational horsepower required to model and predict the complex biochemical reactions and genetic transformations necessary to create synthetic eggs and sperm from induced pluripotent stem cells (iPSCs). These are adult cells that have been genetically reprogrammed to an embryonic stem cell-like state. Quantum algorithms, capable of processing enormous amounts of data simultaneously, guided the precise gene editing and bioengineering techniques. They meticulously monitored every cellular change, ensuring the cells followed the appropriate developmental pathways.

Artificial Intelligence played an equally critical role. Machine learning algorithms, trained on vast amounts of biological and genetic data, learned to identify the subtle signals of successful cell transformation, predicting with remarkable accuracy the optimal conditions for cell differentiation and embryonic development. In essence, AI had become the master conductor of this symphony of life, guiding each cellular instrument to perform its part at the perfect moment.

Once fertilization was achieved in the lab, the developing embryo was placed into an artificial womb. Here, quantum computing and AI worked in tandem again. Quantum sensors monitored the embryo's development in real time, providing a constant stream of data about its health and growth. AI algorithms analyzed this data, adjusting the conditions within the artificial womb to ensure optimal development.

This new method of reproduction was adopted by the government as a societal norm, aimed at creating an equal and optimized population. The government propagated the benefits of this technology, citing elimination of genetic diseases, controlled population growth, and removing the risks and complications of natural childbirth. Consequently, the traditional family structure and natural conception became things of the past. Babies were now created synthetically, grown in artificial wombs, and assigned to parents deemed fit by the government's advanced AI systems. As time went on the government took complete control over all aspects of raising societies up and coming citizens.

The procedure, once a wonder of scientific progress, has now become commonplace. The convergence of biotechnology, quantum computing, and AI has revolutionized human reproduction. It's blurred the lines between what was traditionally viewed as natural and synthetic, prompting society to rethink the very essence of life and its creation. This practice has existed for many generations without any apparent problems to the casual observer. That is until now.

The fluorescent lights of the Ectogenesis Birthing Centre flickered overhead, casting long shadows on the white-tiled floors. As Dr. Claire Cairns stepped through the automatic doors, she felt the palpable tension. The clean, sterile corridors of the centre stretched out before her, but the normally bustling hallways were ominously silent, and an air of uncertainty and fear hung heavy.

Upon entering the neonatal unit, Claire was greeted with an eerie tableau. Row upon row of incubators, each holding a small, newly-born life, were alarmingly quiet. The usual sounds of soft infant cries and gurgles were conspicuously absent. The newborns lay unnaturally still, their tiny faces vacant of expected curiosity or discomfort.

A nurse, exhaustion etched into her every line, moved to Claire's side. "Dr. Cairns, thank God you're here," she breathed out. "It's the newborns... they're not acting like they should."

In the dim light, Claire could see the babies in more detail. Their eyes were open, but they didn't flicker with recognition or even basic reflexes. Their bodies were relaxed, almost too relaxed for newborns who should be flailing or wriggling.

"They're too quiet," Claire whispered, echoing the nurse's earlier words. The realization sent a chill down her spine.

"No crying. No fussing," the nurse confirmed, her voice tinged with panic. "No response to stimuli. They're just...still."

As the Chief Genetic Engineer, Claire was seen as the ultimate safeguard against genetic anomalies and defects. But in truth, the role had evolved into more of a political title over the years. The systems had become so efficient that her work largely revolved around supervising operations at the Quantum Research and Development Agency and strategizing on potential enhancements. The eerie quietness and unnatural stillness of the newborns, however, was an unprecedented event. While it wasn't classified as a terminal condition just yet, it was significant enough to raise serious alarms in her mind.

"There's something fundamentally wrong here," Claire murmured, her mind already racing with possibilities. "We need to find out what it is. And quickly."

Claire turned to the nurse, her mind firing off questions. "The genome sequencing for these children...did it change? Any anomalies detected?"

The nurse shook her head. "The Cognitive-Genius processing system connected to the institute runs the sequencing. It's been the same for decades."

Claire nodded, her mind already sifting through the information. The Cognitive-Genius was a sophisticated piece of technology, designed to meticulously carry out the intricate task of genome sequencing. It had been the cornerstone of artificial human growth, enabling the nurturing of embryos in artificial wombs, or Ectogenesis tanks, in ways nature never allowed.

These tanks were designed to perfectly mimic the environment of a human uterus. After fertilization, the embryos were carefully placed inside these fluid-filled, temperature-regulated chambers. The Cognitive-Genius Processing system would then begin the process of genome sequencing, effectively determining the genetic make-up of the child. The sequence of course was never exactly the same as it needed to change in order to create variations in its human subjects.

Throughout the gestation period, the machine would provide the necessary nutrients and hormones at the right times, monitoring the embryo's growth every step of the way. It was a delicate dance of science and technology, carefully choreographed to ensure the healthy development of the child.

"But if the sequencing hasn't changed..." Claire began, a frown etching deep lines into her forehead. "And yet, these children...it doesn't add up. Something must have altered the expected outcomes."

Determined, she moved towards the nearest Ectogenesis tank. The mystery of the silent newborns lay within these sequences, within the unchanging rhythm of a process that had worked flawlessly for decades. She just had to find it. The answer was there, somewhere in the intricate dance of genetic codes and artificial gestation.

Unraveling it would be a challenge like none other, but for the sake of these quiet, peaceful newborns, Claire knew she had to delve into the depths of genetic mysteries and technological possibilities.

The nurse hesitated before continuing. "Dr. Cairns, there's something else. Our population yields have been declining for years. We've been losing larger numbers of embryos than ever before."

Claire stilled. "Declining yields? Why am I hearing about this only now?" she demanded, frustration creeping into her voice.

The nurse shrugged helplessly. "Politics of government-run institutions, I suppose. No one wants to admit there's a problem, for fear the blame lands on them."

A grim understanding washed over Claire. This wasn't just about silent babies. This was potentially a systemic failure, a failure that had started slowly and invisibly, manifesting only when it was too late.

"And no one thought to consult the Chief Genetic Engineer until it reached a crisis point," Claire said, her voice laced with bitter irony. She looked around the neonatal unit, her gaze falling on the quiet infants. Their innocent lives were now inextricably entwined with the politics of institutions and the fear of responsibility.

She knew then that this wasn't just about diagnosing a problem, it was about tackling an institutional failure, about navigating the dangerous labyrinth of bureaucracy. And all while racing against the ticking clock for the lives of these silent babies.

Claire sighed, straightening her shoulders. "We don't have time to waste," she declared, a new resolve hardening in her eyes. "Let's start by looking into these yield declines. There's a missing link somewhere, and we need to find it."

Claire found herself staring at the central hub of the Cognitive-Genius quantum computer system. A myriad of lights blinked in synchronised rhythm, a symphony of data processing and complex calculations. This machine, with its immense capabilities, had been the driving force behind their revolutionary strides in gene alteration and Etcogeneis.

It should have been able to identify the problem. It was designed to do just that. The Cognitive-Genius Processing Technology had the capacity to manipulate sequences in the genome and run trillions of simulations to predict possible outcomes. This was how they had progressed so far in their understanding of human genetics.

Claire paced around the room, her thoughts colliding. The quantum computer was an extraordinary tool that had thrust them into the future, opening up a world of possibilities. She herself had worked on countless projects using its computational power, diving into the mysteries of the human genome, tweaking and tailoring, all in the quest for perfection.

Her mind spun. If the problem was not identifiable by the CGPT, it implied something far more insidious. A glitch in the system? A rogue sequence it couldn't detect?

"All right, Claire," she murmured to herself, "Let's get to work."

She set about interfacing with the CGPT. Her fingers flew over the holographic keyboard, pulling up yield data, genetic sequences, developmental notes. She began to retrace their steps, trying to identify any discrepancies or anomalies that the system may have overlooked.

This would be her challenge: to find the needle in the haystack, the proverbial bug in the code that had slipped past their advanced quantum system. It was a daunting task, but one she had to undertake, not only for the silent babies in the neonatal unit but for the future of their entire society.

It took Claire the better part of two weeks, running the full human genome sequence, before she stumbled upon the problem. Buried deep within the labyrinth of genetic code was a subtle change - a deviation in the sequencing from the CGPT. It was so inconspicuous that it had slipped past the vast analytical capabilities of the quantum system.

But the strangest part was that the CGPT system didn't recognize it as an error. In fact, it wasn't detecting the anomaly at all.

"Impossible," she muttered to herself, staring at the strange sequence. How could the most advanced quantum system, specifically designed to catch and correct anomalies, miss this?

Frustrated and running out of options, Claire decided to take a different approach. She isolated the sequence data and transferred it to a traditional computer, one that was not connected to the Cognitive-Genius Processing system. Maybe a fresh set of computational eyes, so to speak, could shed light on the problem.

Running the sequence through the traditional algorithms was like winding back the clock on technology. It was slower, less efficient, but it provided a different perspective. And, in this case, it did the trick.

There it was, glaring on the traditional computer screen. The anomaly. A small, almost insignificant mutation, but one that could have far-reaching implications for the genome sequencing process.

"Gotcha," she breathed, her heart pounding in her chest. This was it. This was the missing link.

Now, Claire was left with a host of questions. How did this change come to be? Why was the Cognitive-Genius Processing system blind to this anomaly? And most importantly, what effect was this sequence having on the newborns?

It was the anomaly's very subtlety that had allowed it to escape detection. A tiny twist in the otherwise flawless double helix, an unexpected blip within the rhythm of genetic codes. Yet this minute alteration was the key to the enigma of the eerily quiet newborns.

A chill raced down Claire's spine as she processed the discovery. The CGPT system, their safeguard, their omnipotent watchdog, had failed to catch this. But why? How could the very system designed to find and correct these inconsistencies fail to recognize this?

Forced to face the chilling reality, Claire swallowed hard. This wasn't merely a failure of technology. It was an unseen, unknown variable that had somehow eluded their most advanced analytical system.

"But how?" Claire whispered to the sterile, silent room. A shiver of apprehension crept down her spine. She could sense the magnitude of this discovery, the ripples it would send throughout the scientific community.

Suddenly, the room felt colder, the flickering lights above her growing harsher, as the weight of her discovery set in. This was the missing link they had been searching for, yet it opened up a Pandora's box of questions that were far more terrifying.

With a newfound determination, she clenched her fists. The fluorescent lights overhead reflected in her eyes, now burning with resolve. The quiet, tranquil babies...their future, their lives depended on the next steps. It was no longer just about data and sequences; it was about the very fabric of life itself.

With that thought, Claire pushed herself away from the computer screen, her gaze hardening. There was a storm coming, she could feel it in her bones. And she would have to face it head-on, armed with nothing but her knowledge and the resolve to fight for these innocent lives.

As the flickering lights cast long, dancing shadows around her, Claire felt a deep sense of foreboding settle in. A quiet anticipation of the battle that was yet to come. The first battle, it seemed, had been won. But the war was far from over.

And with that ominous thought, she plunged back into the data, her mind spinning with the implications of her discovery. The missing link had been found, and with it, a darker, deeper mystery to unravel.

A fight had begun, a race against time, against the unseen anomaly that threatened their very future. And Claire Cairns, the Chief Genetic Engineer, was at the helm of it all. The silent babies needed a voice, and Claire was determined to be that voice, no matter what it took.

The fluorescent lights flickered one last time, casting Claire's determined silhouette against the sterile white walls of the Quantum Research and Development Agency. The battle lines had been drawn; the enemy identified. And as the door closed behind her, a quiet echo resounded in the empty hallway.

The fight had just begun.

Chapter 1

Double Helix Meets Quantum Bits: A Twist in the Tale

As the new semester began at the University of Amora, Declan found himself reminiscing about a pivotal conversation with his father. It had become a ritual, a way for him to connect with the energy and enthusiasm of his younger self, the hunger for discovery that had propelled him down his chosen path. In the quiet solitude of his office, he could almost hear the echo of his own words spoken so many years ago, convincing his father of the worthiness of his chosen field. His youthful optimism and excitement flooded back to him, a welcome antidote to the burnout of years spent chasing answers that remained just beyond his grasp. His heart ached with the longing for a breakthrough, a soreness that could only be felt by someone who had dedicated his life to solving mysteries that seemed content to remain unsolved. But he knew that, despite the disappointments, his heart lay in the tangled webs of evolution and the stories they had yet to reveal. This memory served as a reminder to Declan, a beacon guiding him through the often-challenging path of academia. The initial excitement and fascination that had led him to explore the realm of Evolutionary Biology could be harnessed again and again, not only to rekindle his passion but also to ignite the same in his students. While preparing for his first lecture, he felt a surge of hope. Every new class held the potential of young, brilliant minds who could bring fresh perspectives and new ideas. Perhaps, he thought, one of them might even crack the code of an enduring evolutionary mystery. Declan found comfort and strength in the cycle of academia, the constant ebb and flow of new students and new semesters. Despite the unyielding challenges that Evolutionary Biology presented, he cherished the opportunity to inspire a new generation of thinkers and scholars who might someday find the answers that had eluded him for so long. And so, the memory of that long-ago conversation with his father kept him grounded yet optimistic. It held him close to his roots while reminding him of the limitless possibilities the future could bring. Each new semester, Declan would draw from this well of hope and determination, ready to inspire his students with the same passion that had set him on his path all those years ago.

Declan found himself once again caught in a reverie, a memory dancing on the edge of his consciousness. It was a conversation he had with his father years ago, his youthful excitement clashing with his father's more traditional views on a suitable career. In this memory, Declan could still see his father's furrowed brow, feel the weight of his concern. "Why," he had asked in a tone of bewilderment, "would you want to delve into Evolutionary Biology? It doesn't hold any promise, son. You have a family dynasty that you need to help preserve!" Declan had taken a deep breath, remembering the glint in his eyes as he readied himself to defend his calling. He started with his fascination for the past, its inherent allure and the mysteries it held, like a time capsule yearning to be deciphered. He described his longing to unravel these secrets of the past that held the blueprint of life as we know it. He had spoken about the intriguing enigma of the Cambrian explosion, expressing his curiosity about the sudden flourish of life forms in a relatively short span. He explained his interest in the evolution of sexual reproduction, a conundrum that continues to perplex evolutionary biologists. Eloquently, he delved into the concept of punctuated equilibrium and the peculiar phenomenon of rapid evolutionary spurts following long periods of relative calm. He painted a vivid picture of the possible transition from unicellular to multicellular life, and the myriad mysteries it encompassed. With a hint of wonder in his voice, he talked about one of the grandest mysteries of all: the evolution of consciousness. He elaborated on his desire to understand how and why awareness sprung up in certain life forms. Finally, he mentioned the enigmatic nature of mass extinctions, emphasizing his curiosity about why certain species survived these catastrophic events while others perished. Declan remembered the earnestness in his voice as he finished, explaining that these weren't just academic curiosities for him. He believed they held the key to understanding life's genesis and trajectory. He wanted to uncover these truths not just for himself, but for the world. Even now, he could see his father's skeptical gaze hardening as he listened to his son's impassioned defense. It was a memory that stayed with him, a reminder of his own relentless passion for Evolutionary Biology and the beautiful, ceaseless quest for understanding it symbolized. Despite his father's adamant resistance, Declan knew he had chosen the path that was meant for him.

"Greetings, scholars, and welcome to the foundational class on Cogni-Genius Processing Technology. Your presence here signals your esteemed standing in the realm of quantum computing, and I extend my warmest welcome to you all. Your dedication to this governmental endeavor is highly valued. I am Declan Sutton, your guide and mentor for the duration of this course. Though my primary expertise lies within the fascinating realm of evolutionary biology rather than quantum computing, my mission is to enlighten you about the transformative convergence of quantum computers with a ground-breaking tool known as CRISPR, and how it has rewritten the course of human evolution.

Our initial focus was on eradicating detrimental genetic mutations responsible for numerous genetic ailments. By pinpointing and rectifying these anomalies, we've succeeded in not just eliminating these diseases, but also enhancing our overall well-being. Next, we amplified our skeletal and muscular fortitude, thereby infusing greater vigor and robustness into the human physique. We then moved onto enhancing our cognitive capacities, improving our ability to learn and remember. Following this, we fortified our immunity, elevating the body's defenses against diseases and infections. This enhancement has helped us keep health hazards at bay more efficiently. Lastly, we managed to augment our lifespan by curtailing the process of cellular decay. As we move forward, it's crucial to acknowledge the vast prospects and hurdles that await us. The Cogni-Genius Processing Technology unlocks uncharted territories of scientific discovery, and it is through our joint endeavors that we can continue to extend the limits of the conceivable. I urge you all to view this course as a stepping stone towards a future where quantum computing and CRISPR technology play key roles in shaping our society. Together, we can decipher the enigmas of the cosmos and unleash the unexplored potential of the human physique and psyche. I express my gratitude to each one of you for joining me on this thrilling expedition, and I eagerly anticipate delving into the world of Cogni-Genius Processing with all of you."

As Declan scanned the faces of the students gathered for the foundational class on Cogni-Genius Processing Technology, a flicker of surprise crossed his face. Compared to previous years, the assembly of scholars was noticeably smaller. The lecture hall, which used to be brimming with eager learners, now had vacant seats scattered throughout. He pondered on this change - was it due to dwindling interest, or a result of stricter selection procedures? Regardless, the determination and potential he saw in the eyes of the attendees suggested a promise of great success. As he was about to begin the lecture, a figure at the back of the room caught his eye. There, in the shadows of a corner, stood Dr. Claire Cairns. She was watching him intently, with an unreadable expression on her face. This was surprising; Claire was a notable figure in the quantum computing field, and it was unusual for her to attend these foundational classes. She was more likely to be seen in advanced labs or directing high-level projects. So, why was she here, in a beginner's lecture? Declan tried to suppress the intrigue brewing within him. Was Claire there out of genuine interest, or was there another reason? Regardless, her presence was a testament to the importance of the course they were about to undertake. Pushing his speculations aside, Declan focused on the eager faces before him, ready to not in her plan. "Thank you, Professor Sutton. We've already arranged for your smooth transition to the QRDA and coverage of your classes," she assured him.

Declan, taken aback, looked at her. "When did this happen?"

"Just now," Claire responded, an unreadable look in her eyes. It was evident that the wheels had been set in motion long before this conversation, leaving Declan with little choice in the matter. She added, "And remember, discretion is of the utmost importance."

Chapter 2

Colliding Epochs

As they exited the lecture hall, Claire turned to Declan, her badge reflecting the faint sunlight filtering through the aged branches of the university's trademark oak trees. "Would you walk with me, Professor? There are matters about your new position we should discuss."

They paced towards the university's main entrance, the grandeur of the archaic building casting an imposing shadow on the manicured lawns. Their shoes crunched on the gravel path, the sound barely audible over the murmur of students heading to their classes.

Declan, I want to introduce you to someone," Claire said after a moment of silence. "Dr. Christopher Peterson, the Director of Quantum Computing at the QRDA. He'll be working closely with us on this project." Declan nodded, recalling his past encounters with the stern but approachable figure. He was the pioneer of quantum computing in the government, a man whose reputation preceded him. Before Declan could respond, a sleek government-issued, self-driving vehicle silently slid up to the curb. The passenger door swung open, revealing the familiar face of Dr. Peterson. His intense gaze softened as he caught sight of Declan. "Declan, good to see you again," Dr. Peterson greeted him with a warm smile as he motioned him to get in the car beside him. "Dr. Peterson," Declan responded, sliding into the seat next to him. Claire unexpectedly did not get in the car with them, "I have some work to do here in regards to your transfer Professor but I will see you soon." The door shut on its own, leaving Claire standing on the curb waving her farewells to Declan and Dr. Peterson. The vehicle started with a soft hum, synchronizing seamlessly with the city's Autonomous Traffic Control System.

The car merged with the rhythmic ebb and flow of the city traffic. The brilliance of city lights reflected off the vehicle's exterior, the only indication of their movement. As the vehicle smoothly integrated onto the highway, the gentle whir of the onboard computer fan engaged into a higher frequency, a barely perceptible hum that indicated the car's sophisticated system was interfacing with the Central Autonomous Navigation System. The minute sound was so refined and unobtrusive that the average person might never notice it. However, Declan always found himself attuned to it, a calming reminder of the advanced technology that was guiding them on their journey. As the automated system assumed control, the windows of the vehicle began to darken, a feature designed for privacy and security. Despite the government's logical explanations, Declan couldn't help but question the actual necessity of this feature. The transition from transparency to opaqueness seemed excessive to him, but it was a standard in all government vehicles. Before the windows became completely opaque, Declan caught glimpses of the world outside. Vehicles whizzed past at a breathtaking pace, the orchestration of speed and precision a testament to the advanced navigation system. A yellow school bus whirred by, close enough that he could see the lively expressions of the children inside. Their laughter and joy, visible for that fleeting moment, made the mundanity of the journey a little more bearable. Once the transition was complete, the outside world was effectively blocked from view. It was a peculiar sensation – he could not see out, but the cameras monitoring the system could see in. His world became the interior of the car, a cocoon of technology and silence moving swiftly through the vibrant cityscape, unseen and unobserved.

As the car glided through the city streets, the conversation shifted. Dr. Peterson cleared his throat, drawing Declan's attention away from the glittering cityscape outside. "Declan," he began, his tone taking on a serious quality, "with this project, there's going to be a significant amount of responsibility placed on your shoulders. We'll need your full commitment and discretion." He paused, letting his words settle in. Declan nodded, indicating he understood the gravity of the situation. "In light of this, the government is prepared to grant you high-level clearance. You will have access to information and resources that very few possess," Dr. Peterson continued, maintaining eye contact with Declan. "Of course, such access comes with immense responsibility. Everything you see, hear, and learn will need to remain confidential." Again, Declan nodded. He was no stranger to the constraints and privileges of such clearance from his earlier work, but he could sense this was a step beyond his previous experience. "And naturally," Dr. Peterson added, "you will be compensated accordingly. We understand the value of your expertise and your commitment to this project. You will receive a competitive salary, comprehensive benefits, and additional incentives. These will include access to premier healthcare and wellness facilities, exclusive housing arrangements, and travel privileges." Declan took a moment to digest the information. The offer was more than generous. He looked at Dr. Peterson, his eyes reflecting the resolve and dedication he felt towards their mission. "I understand the stakes, Dr. Peterson," he said firmly. "And I'm fully committed to doing what is necessary." Peterson smiled, the tension easing. "I had no doubt, Declan. Welcome to the QRDA."

Declan had heard that the purpose of the opaque windows was to prevent vertigo. At high speeds and with unpredictable traffic, passengers sometimes experienced disorientation and discomfort when the autonomous system was in full control. Despite the system's flawless safety record, many found it challenging to overcome a psychological barrier. Opaque windows were implemented as a psychological safety net, shielding passengers from the perceived whirl of motion outside. With the world blocked out, the cabin became a serene, tranquil space that offered a comforting illusion of stillness despite the vehicle's swift movement. The darkening windows also served as a metaphorical representation of the shift in control from human hands to a computer system. The machine was now in charge, navigating through traffic more efficiently and safely than any human could. Nevertheless, Declan always found it a bit unsettling. He trusted the technology implicitly, but the sudden disconnection from the world outside and the relinquishment of control stirred a sense of unease within him. It was a stark contrast to the vibrant, unpredictable human world that continued to exist outside the darkened windows. Despite this, he relaxed into the journey, trusting in the expertise of the invisible driver guiding them through the day.

As the autonomous vehicle sped through the cityscape, a swarm of drones whirred overhead, their buzzing almost drowned out by the hum of the vehicle. The drones were another product of the Central Autonomous Navigation System, floating eyes in the sky that monitored and maintained the order of the busy traffic. The opaque windows of the vehicle gave the interior an eerie, isolated feel. The vehicle was a cocoon, hurtling through space, yet offering an illusion of tranquility. The muted hum of the vehicle was the only evidence of its lightning-fast movement. Despite the somewhat uncanny ambiance, there was a certain soothing quality to the interior. The sound of the vehicle, coupled with the gentle, barely perceptible vibrations, was almost meditative. And there was something comforting about the predictability, the routine. However, Declan's instinctual need for control and understanding found the situation unsettling. He felt a disconnect, a sense of being divorced from the world outside. It was as if he had surrendered his freedom to a network of processors and algorithms. Outside the darkened windows, life pulsated with a vibrancy and unpredictability that machines couldn't emulate. There were nuances, irregularities, and elements of chance that even the most sophisticated systems couldn't account for. Yet, he resigned himself to the situation, trusting the unseen, inhuman entity that guided their journey. As the vehicle continued to zip through the traffic, Declan leaned back, his mind whirling with thoughts and possibilities. He was en route to an unknown destination, in the hands of an invisible driver, under a sky patrolled by unblinking mechanical eyes. It was a reality that was as awe-inspiring as it was unsettling.

Suddenly, a soft alarm pinged from the dashboard, disrupting the tranquility. "Traffic disruption detected ahead. Estimated delay: 15 minutes," a calm AI voice announced. Dr. Peterson turned pale, his eyes wide. "That's not possible," he murmured, sharing a concerned glance with Declan. Dr. Peterson touched a few buttons on the car's panel and the windows turned transparent. This was something Declan had never even known could be done, let alone seen. When the window cleared, there it was - a sight no one had seen in years: a truck sprawled across the road, its cargo scattered around like metallic debris, vehicles piled up haphazardly, an image of chaos in a world of order. Quickly the windows turned opaque once again as if the system didn't want them to see the carnage just outside.

Dr. Peterson frantically examined the ANCS data and discovered that the cause was an antiquated, manually driven car - a rogue vehicle. This old model had slipped into the seamless rhythm of the ANCS-controlled city, triggering a cascade of minor crashes. While the ANCS was not at fault, the incident served as a stark reminder that the relics of the past, with their unpredictable human elements, could still disrupt the seemingly perfect symphony of the future. It was a profound moment of realization for Declan - as they embarked on this new journey, they would have to navigate the unpredictable elements of the past while venturing into the uncharted territories of the future.

Declan's interest piqued at the mention of a rogue vehicle. He felt an odd sense of curiosity to see such a relic of the past amidst the stream of ultra-modern, self-driving cars. Dr. Peterson, still pale, made another adjustment to the panel, and the windows of the vehicle flickered back to transparency. Declan's eyes widened, a sight from yesteryears unfolding before them. Amidst the perfectly coordinated dance of AI-controlled vehicles, a tangible testament of a bygone era lay sprawled in disarray. The chaos that a single, manually driven car had created was hard to comprehend, and yet, there it was, an anomaly amidst the order. A cascading symphony of minor crashes, a stark and jarring reminder of the unpredictable elements of the past that were still capable of intruding upon their controlled, predictable present. Dr. Peterson's explanation brought clarity, yet left a lingering unease. The rogue vehicle was an old model, manually driven, a ghost in the system that was not recognized by the ANCS. It was an anomaly, an aberration, something the meticulously perfected system had not been designed to handle. Declan found himself peering curiously at the rogue vehicle, its archaic design starkly contrasting with the sleek, modern machines that surrounded it. A wave of nostalgia washed over him as he took in the sight of the manually driven car. It was a tangible reminder of a time when humans were in control, a time when unpredictability was part of the journey. As he pondered this sudden and unexpected disruption, a deeper realization began to dawn on him. As they moved forward into an increasingly automated future, they would need to account for these relics of the past. For all its promise of perfection, the future was still tethered to its roots, and the echoes of the past could still make themselves heard in the symphony of progress. His new role in the government would require him to navigate this delicate balance, to straddle the line between the promise of the future and the lessons of the past. It was a formidable task, but one he felt ready to undertake.

As Declan peered at the rogue vehicle, another aspect of the scene caught his attention: the car appeared to be undamaged. Amidst the disorder, the old model stood out not only due to its archaic design, but also because it seemed to have emerg the cascading collisions unscathed. This observation furt. intrigued Declan and added to the surrealism of the scene unexpected, to say the least. The truck had tipped over, its strewn around. Modern vehicles were dented and scratched, their faultless exterior marred by the unanticipated chaos. And yet, the rogue vehicle, the root of the disruption, seemed to be untouched, standing in stark defiance of the modern world around it. Declan felt a pang of curiosity. How was it possible that this vehicle, an artifact of the past, had not sustained any damage? Was it merely fortuitous, or was there something about the old designs that made them more resilient? Perhaps the rugged simplicity of the past offered some sort of protection against the complexities of the present. As Declan continued to study the rogue vehicle, another image flashed at the edge of his vision, jerking him out of his thoughts. There, amidst the chaos, was the bus. The yellow school bus that had zoomed past them earlier. Only now, it was still and eerily silent, its vibrant color clashing with the grim reality it presented. The smiling kids... their lifeless bodies scattered around, were a heartbreaking sight. The trauma and horror of the situation choked him up. It was a grim reminder of the fragility of life, a stark contrast to the indestructible image of the rogue vehicle. Dr. Peterson had gone silent too. It was clear that he was also witnessing the horrific aftermath of the accident. The jovial atmosphere in the car had evaporated, replaced by a heavy silence. Peterson reached out and flicked a switch, and the windows darkened once again, mercifully hiding the gruesome scene outside. Declan leaned back in his seat, his mind racing. His earlier musings about the resilience of the past suddenly seemed trivial in the face of this tragedy. He realized with a jolt that while they were striving to secure the future, the present was slipping through their fingers. A profound sorrow filled him as he thought of the smiling kids he had seen on the bus earlier. What was meant to be a routine day for them had turned into a disaster. The image of their lifeless bodies would stay with him, a sobering reminder of how fragile life can truly be. As he pondered this, Declan was reminded of his new role in the QRDA. His task was to bring together the old and the new, to merge human biology with advanced quantum computing. Just like the rogue vehicle that had managed to survive amidst the chaos, he hoped to preserve the essence of humanity while embracing the advancements of technology.

Chapter 3

The Quantum-Mycelium Paradox

Quite some time ago...

"You believe we should construct a creation simulator, is that what you're saying?" Maddy asked incredulously. Claire nodded sternly in reply.
"Let's, for argument's sake, overlook the fact that creating sentient or conscious entities, even in a digital form, was deemed highly unethical years ago. Even if it were plausible to design such a simulator, the processing power required to operate it would be inconceivable. But why, Claire? Why would we expend such resources on this?"
Claire walked over to a computer situated across the room without saying a word, silently motioning for Maddy to join her. As Maddy approached, she noticed numerous images flickering across the screen. They appeared to depict deceased embryos, but with an unusual aspect: their development appeared incomplete.
"We only need the simulation to recreate evolution up until the advent of Homo sapiens," Claire clarified, her gaze fixed on the screen. "Once we've extracted their genome sequence, we can terminate the program. But it's imperative this simulation remains separate from the Cogni-Genius Processing Technology, to prevent any potential interference."
"Our Ectogenesis chambers are failing us at an alarming rate. We can't bring a child to full term from conception anymore. There's

a discrepancy in the genome sequence that we can't identify. The CGPT is asserting all is well, yet every subject is now dying. Our hope is that, by comparing the simulated genome sequence with the present one, we might discern the underlying problem."

Maddy took a moment to gather her thoughts. "Have we tried reverting to our unaltered genome sequences?"

"We've tried. According to CGPT, there have been no modifications. It's claiming that our genome has remained constant throughout history."

Maddy's brow furrowed. "The system has lost our original genome sequence? Doesn't anyone have a backup?"

Claire shook her head. "The issue is we thought we did. But all sequences inputted into the CGPT emerge identical. We've attempted to use older technologies, but quantum computing is the only method sophisticated enough to sequence the entire genome and predict potential outcomes. Everything the system has processed is rendering the same result: all parameters are within limits and functioning as intended."

"But how is this possible?" Maddy pressed, "Weren't the principles of genetic editing established?"

"It seems not," Claire responded gravely. "And now we're racing against time to safeguard our species."

"I think there's an alternative, Claire," Maddy said after a thoughtful pause. "We've tried to push the boundaries of science, but we've reached an impasse. Maybe it's time to go back. Back to natural childbirth, like we did in the past."

Claire stared at her in shock. "Maddy, we can't. The corrections used to enhance the human body has rendered us infertile... it's a miracle if a baby is born naturally without any mutations.

"But what if the miracle lies in the mutations, Claire?" Maddy shot back, her eyes filled with hope. "What if the human genome is adapting to survive, not dying out? We've been so focused on keeping things the way they were, we've forgotten that evolution is a response to change. Survival of the fittest, isn't it?"

"But Maddy, it's a risk. We can't gamble with the future of our species based on a theory," Claire retorted, her voice filled with apprehension.
"I'm not saying we abandon the creation simulator, Claire," Maddy responded calmly. "But we should consider all possibilities. We should also research any recent successful natural childbirths and study those children. We might find what we're missing." Claire shook her head, "We looked into it months ago there has not been a natural child birth in four decades."
Claire stayed silent for a while, clearly pondering Maddy's proposal. She finally nodded, a glimmer of hope in her eyes. "It's worth exploring, Maddy. We can't afford to ignore any potential solutions. We'll run the creation simulator as planned, and also explore your idea. Maybe the answer is somewhere in the middle."
"What about cloning?" Maddy asks as a last attempt for ideas. Claire shook her head as she said, "We know that cloning compromises the essential principle of genetic diversity, which renders it ineffective. It creates beings who are genetic replicas of one another, resulting in severe vulnerabilities such as susceptibility to the same disease, which could potentially wipe out an entire cloned population. Moreover, the cloning process has an inherent flaw that can accumulate and even amplify genetic errors as cells age and mutate. These errors were evident in Dolly the Sheep, the first mammal to be cloned from an adult somatic cell, which resulted in her premature aging and death. Furthermore, we must consider the profound ethical implications of cloning humans, which paves the way for possible exploitation and violation of human rights, treating clones as second-class citizens. Lastly, human development is a complex interplay between genetics and environmental factors, an intricate choreography that shapes us from conception onwards. Even an identical genetic copy wouldn't develop into the same person, given the unique circumstances, experiences, and environmental

factors at play. For these reasons, the prospect of human cloning is fraught with insurmountable challenges and dilemmas."
Together, they pledged to leave no stone unturned, at this point no idea was a bad idea. Their fight for the survival of their species was only just beginning.

Maddy sighed and rubbed the bridge of her nose as she looked at Claire. "We need ideas, Claire. I agree with your concept of a creation simulator, but how are we going to power it? Clearly, we can't use the CGPT system. We need a quantum computer, but building a new one with our current knowledge and resources won't work, will it?"
Claire's expression mirrored Maddy's worry. "You're right, the task is monumental. It would take decades to construct a quantum computer with the processing power we need. And it's not just the hardware, it's the software too. It would have to be completely independent from the CGPT system."
"But do we have any other options?" Claire asked, leaning back in her chair and looking up at the ceiling. "Perhaps we could explore other computational technologies, or try to harness other quantum phenomena. We've done it before with quantum entanglement. Maybe we could try leveraging quantum superposition or quantum teleportation?"
"That's a bit of a leap, Maddy," Claire admitted, clearly hesitant. "But desperate times call for desperate measures. What if we tapped into unused resources? I know there are quantum computers that are underutilized or used for less critical processes. We could requisition their power temporarily to jumpstart this project."
Maddy nodded thoughtfully. "It's a start, Claire. But it still doesn't resolve our software issues. We need a new operating system, one that hasn't been touched by the CGPT."
"We could reach out to other scientific communities," Claire suggested. "Despite our current predicament, we're not the only ones working on projects of this magnitude. There are others out there in bioinformatics, astrophysics, and even in artificial

intelligence. They might have ideas, they might even have resources we can use. We've always been a solitary discipline, but now we need all the help we can get."
Maddy nodded, stood up, and moved toward the computer. "Alright. Let's start drafting proposals then. We need to be quick and persuasive. Let's make it clear: this isn't just for us. This is for the survival of the human species."

A moment of silence stretched out between Claire and Maddy as they were reminded of the Quantum Research and Development Act (QRDA), which forbade any information sharing about their project outside of their organization. It was a necessary but frustrating security measure to prevent unauthorized entities from potentially misusing or manipulating their research.
"Alright, scratch that," Claire said, deflated by the QRDA's restrictions. "We can't risk breaching the QRDA Act. The project is too sensitive. But...we're not entirely isolated, are we?"
"We could try convincing someone higher up," Maddy suggested, continuing Claire's thought. "Someone with the authority to approve a collaboration with an approved entity. If we pitch it right, they might see the urgency."
Claire's face lit up with hope. "Exactly, someone like Dr. Evers. He's not only on the board, he's also an advocate for radical thinking. If anyone could push this through, it would be him."
The two scientists shared a look of shared resolve. The path before them was riddled with obstacles, but they were determined to find a way through. It would take more than ingenuity; it would take persuasion and a bit of luck.
"Let's do it, Claire," Maddy declared, her resolve clear. "Let's put together a comprehensive proposal, showing the potential benefits and addressing potential concerns. It needs to be compelling. Let's make Dr. Evers see that this isn't just a project, it's a necessity."
With renewed determination, they began to work. The fate of their species may well have hinged on their ability to persuade

one man. But they had a powerful argument: survival. And that was an argument that resonated with every living being.

Claire's mind raced, and then a thought struck her. "Maddy, do you remember that research paper we read a few years ago? The one about how mycelium networks in mushrooms could potentially act as natural computing systems?"

Maddy looked at her in surprise. "Yes, but that's a big leap from theory to application, Claire."

"But think about it," Claire continued. Her excitement was unmistakable. "Mushrooms use their mycelium networks to transmit information, nutrients, and resources. Some scientists even call them the 'Wood Wide Web'. These systems display an intelligence that could be likened to a natural form of computing."

Maddy's eyes widened as she began to understand Claire's line of thinking. "That's... actually not as far-fetched as it sounds. If we could understand and harness the organic computing power of mycelium, we could have a potentially infinite and self-sustaining computing network on our hands."

"Exactly," Claire said, her eyes brightening. "We could potentially bioengineer these mycelium networks to mimic the architecture of a quantum computer or complement the one we already have. If we combine quantum computing with this organic model, we could create a symbiotic system capable of enormous processing power."

Maddy looked at her for a long moment before slowly nodding. "It's worth a shot, Claire. The chances of success are uncertain, but we're running out of options. Let's add this to our proposal. It could also help convince Dr. Evers that we're thinking outside the box and outside the conventional domain of science."

Claire grinned, feeling a surge of hope. They were on the brink of uncharted territory, proposing something that might revolutionize the way they looked at both computing and biology. It was risky, but it was a risk they were willing to take for the survival of their species.

As weeks turned into months, the silence from Dr. Evers and the board was deafening. However, Claire and Maddy refused to allow the delay to hinder their efforts. They used this time to delve into their groundbreaking idea: integrating a mycelium network with their existing quantum computer system. The process was arduous and filled with trial and error, but there were hints of progress. The mycelium appeared to respond to certain quantum states, suggesting that a connection might be possible.
After months of anxious waiting, they finally received a response from a Dr. Bravon, Dr. Evers it appeared had retired and never saw their proposal. The message was a stern and technical rebuke of their proposal for a creation simulator. It was clear that he had not been informed of the underlying reasons for their urgent need for such a project.
As they read the message, a feeling of despondency descended.
"He doesn't know, does he?" Maddy said, her voice heavy with disappointment. "They didn't tell him why we wanted to build it."
Claire slumped back in her chair, her face pale. "It seems that way. Our administrators are too afraid to let the secret out. They are more concerned with hiding their mistakes than finding solutions."
"But what can we do?" Maddy asked, her voice filled with desperation. "Our project is dying because of bureaucratic secrecy. We can't even defend our proposal properly without risking our careers, or worse."
Claire was silent for a long moment before responding. "We continue working on our mycelium network. We know the stakes, even if this Dr. Bravon and the board don't. It's our only hope right now."
With determination in their hearts, Claire and Maddy focused on their groundbreaking work. Despite setbacks, they found solace in the promise of their unconventional solution. They had a mission to accomplish, with or without the approval of their

superiors. Their resolve was firm; they would fight until they had exhausted every possible avenue.

One fateful day, months later amidst the monotony of testing and adjusting, their system screen blinked to life. A torrent of data began to pour onto the screen, streaming so fast and in such a bizarre format that they could barely comprehend it.
"Claire, are you seeing this?" Maddy exclaimed, her eyes wide as she stared at the monitor.
"I am," Claire responded, her voice shaking slightly. "But I don't understand. This shouldn't be possible. The system... it's just a system. Hardware only, there is no software. Where is this data coming from?"
The data continued to stream across their screen in seemingly random sequences, a series of letters, numbers, and symbols that defied their understanding. It was both exhilarating and terrifying. Claire could feel the goosebumps prickling her arms, an uncanny sensation of awe and trepidation.
They looked at each other, their faces pale under the glow of the screen. The silence in the lab was only broken by the gentle hum of the system and the sporadic beeping of other instruments.
Maddy broke the silence, her voice barely above a whisper. "It's almost... sentient."
Claire shivered at the word. This was more than they had bargained for. Yet, they couldn't deny the implications. Their mycelium-quantum hybrid system was not only working, it was communicating.
As they grappled with this unexpected development, a new understanding began to dawn. They were no longer merely scientists working on a project; they had become pioneers, venturing into a realm of knowledge that blurred the lines between biology and technology, between the natural and the artificial.
"This is incredible," Claire finally managed to say, her voice filled with a mix of fear and exhilaration. "We need to understand this

data. Whatever it's trying to tell us, it could be the key to everything."
With a renewed sense of purpose, they threw themselves into the task of decoding the mysterious data stream. Their project had taken a turn into the unknown, and despite the creepiness and unexpected sentience of their creation, they knew they had stumbled upon something revolutionary. This strange, unpredictable phenomenon could very well be their last hope to fixing the problem.

In the aftermath of their discovery, Claire and Maddy shared a look that conveyed more than words ever could. They had a mutual understanding, solidifying their resolve to keep their breakthrough a secret. They knew all too well the risks of disclosing such information. It could be taken away, placed into the hands of someone who didn't understand the intricacies of their system, or worse, someone who might misuse it.
"This stays between us, Claire," Maddy said firmly.
"Agreed," Claire responded, meeting Maddy's determined gaze. "We can't let anyone else in on this. Not yet. We need to understand this data first. Once we have something concrete, something we can explain and control, then we can consider bringing others in."
Yet, even as they committed to their secret, they knew they had another obstacle to overcome. The board was expecting progress on the creation simulator, and their lack of tangible results so far would soon raise eyebrows. They had to find a way to show progress without revealing their extraordinary discovery.
"Let's work on the mycelium system in the background," Claire suggested. "We can present our advances in quantum-mycelium communication as progress towards developing the simulator. It's not exactly a lie. If this works, it could indeed be the foundation of our creation simulator."
Maddy nodded in agreement. "Good idea. We'll need to tread carefully, though. Any hint of what we've truly achieved, and we could end up losing everything."

With a shared sense of purpose and the weight of their secret hanging heavily between them, they turned back to their work. Balancing their groundbreaking discovery with the need for secrecy was going to be a challenge. But they had already ventured into the unknown and come out stronger. They were determined to see it through, no matter what it took.

As the days turned into weeks, Claire and Maddy found themselves facing an increasingly difficult challenge. The data stream from the mycelium-quantum system was relentless and complex, almost impenetrable. It became clear that their existing quantum computer that they were using to break the code of their creation, while advanced, was not capable of handling this new layer of complexity.

"We need more computing power," Claire said one day, as they stared at the screen filled with undecipherable data. "We won't be able to crack this with our current resources."

Maddy nodded, her expression grim. "Agreed. But we'll need to justify it to the higher-ups."

They spent hours drafting a new proposal, carefully outlining the need for an additional quantum computer to assist with their creation simulation project. They were meticulous in their explanation, avoiding any hint of their real discovery. They painted a compelling picture of the vast computational resources required to mimic the process of natural evolution and how their current setup was falling short.

After several drafts and countless cups of coffee, they finally had a proposal they felt could stand up to scrutiny. They submitted it, hoping that the board would see the need for additional resources and approve their request.

The waiting game began anew, but they didn't let that halt their progress. They continued their work with the mycelium-quantum system, capturing as much data as possible and making small breakthroughs in their understanding. The secret they carried added a layer of intensity to their endeavor, and they knew that

every step forward, no matter how small, was a step closer to unlocking the mystery they had stumbled upon.
When approval for their new quantum computer finally came through, Claire and Maddy could hardly contain their relief. It was a sign of progress, an indication that they were on the right track. With renewed vigor, they set to work, hopeful that the increased computational power would bring them closer to understanding the extraordinary data their mycelium-quantum system was producing. They were venturing further into the unknown, one line of mysterious data at a time.

As the new quantum computer hummed to life and began processing torrents of data, Claire and Maddy were filled with anticipation. They watched as the powerful machine began to crunch numbers, attempting to unravel the meaning behind the stream of data their mycelium-quantum hybrid was producing. Soon, they started getting results. However, far from providing clarity, the deciphered data only deepened the mystery.
"The first code sequence we've managed to decode is that of a Tunicate," Claire announced, staring at the screen with a furrowed brow. "And look, this one here is a Myxini glutinosa... a hagfish."
Maddy looked just as confused. "Why would the system be generating the genome sequences of these organisms? And here's another one - an Eusthenopteron, a prehistoric fish. And... Acanthostega? That's a four-legged fish from the Devonian period."
The revelation left them both puzzled. Why was their system generating the genomic sequences of these specific, seemingly unrelated organisms? What did a tunicate, a hagfish, a prehistoric fish, and a four-legged fish from the Devonian period have in common?
"We're missing something," Claire said, her voice a mixture of frustration and excitement. "There's a pattern here, Maddy. We just need to figure out what it is."

With this new mystery in hand, they threw themselves back into the data, working late into the nights, poring over countless genomic sequences, and studying the biology of these organisms. They were on the brink of understanding, the pieces of the puzzle just out of reach.
But even amidst the confusion and exhaustion, they felt a thrill. They were pioneers, deciphering a language that was entirely new, navigating uncharted territory in their quest for knowledge. It was perplexing, it was daunting, but above all, it was an adventure like no other. They knew they were on the cusp of a discovery that could potentially change everything they thought they knew about biology, computing, and the intricate dance between the two.

Before they could invite someone else into their fold for help, which they decided they desperately needed, they had to get the approval from Dr. Peterson, the head of their division. The challenge was to convince him of the need for an evolutionary biologist without revealing the true nature of their quantum-mycelium system.
Presented with the sleek interior of Dr. Peterson's office, Claire and Maddy laid out their carefully crafted explanation. "We are working on the beginning sequences of our creation simulator," Claire began, choosing her words carefully. "As we're trying to recreate the process of evolution, we have encountered certain sequences that we believe are mirroring biological transitions."
Maddy picked up where Claire left off, "We are seeing sequences that could be interpreted as moving from marine organisms to terrestrial ones, which is why we believe an evolutionary biologist could be invaluable. His knowledge could help guide us as we fine-tune the system."
Dr. Peterson peered at them over his spectacles, considering their request. They watched as he processed the information, rubbing his temples in contemplation. After a lengthy silence, he gave a decisive nod.

"I understand the need. Once you have identified someone for the position. I will have the Ministry of Truth and Information run a check to ensure that they are cleared, both scientifically and politically. If they pass, we will proceed with their clearance." Both women breathed a sigh of relief. They had successfully navigated the tricky waters of revealing just enough to get an Evolutionary Biologist on board without compromising the secrecy of their breakthrough. Now, they were one step closer to unraveling the enigma presented by their quantum-mycelium system, and hopefully, enhancing the efficiency of their creation simulator. The question now was who could they trust their secret to?

Maddy has highly recommended your… morality so here we are. You're our best hope to decipher this enigma."
Declan took a moment to process the magnitude of what they had revealed. His mind swirled with a mixture of excitement, disbelief, and a hint of trepidation. Yet, deep down, he knew he couldn't turn away from this opportunity. This was his chance to contribute to something truly extraordinary.
"What I don't understand is why the secrecy and talk of danger. Was this not authorized?"

Claire exchanged a glance with Maddy before answering, her voice filled with a mixture of caution and sincerity. "The reason for secrecy, Declan, is because our creation, this mycelium quantum computer, is not authorized by the QRDA or any governing body. We have been working on it covertly, driven by a sense of urgency and the need to find answers."
Maddy chimed in, her voice tinged with regret. "You see, the purpose of this mycelium computer goes beyond its sheer existence. We are building a creation simulation, an ambitious project aimed at understanding the discrepancies and errors we've encountered when trying to enter the current human genetic code into the CGPT system."
Declan's brows furrowed as he absorbed the gravity of their words. "So, you're saying that the CGPT system, the very technology that has been relied upon for genetic editing and reproduction, is producing errors? Errors that potentially threaten the viability of human reproduction?"
Claire nodded; her expression solemn. "Yes, that's exactly it. The CGPT system is asserting that there have been no modifications to the human genome over time but we know that's not true. Our Ectogenesis chambers have now failed, and we can't bring a child to full term anymore. There's a discrepancy in the genome sequence, and the CGPT system is unable to identify the cause."
Maddy continued, her voice tinged with frustration. "We've tried reverting to unaltered genome sequences but the system claims that no modifications have been made. It's as if the original

genome sequence has been lost or overwritten. We believe that by comparing the simulated genome sequence of our human ancestors from our mycelium computer with the present one, we might be able to discern the underlying problem."
Declan leaned forward, his eyes filled with a mix of concern and curiosity. "And that's where my expertise in evolutionary biology comes in?"
Claire nodded, a sense of hope in her voice. "Exactly. We believe that understanding the evolutionary processes encoded in the mycelium quantum computer's data can help us shed light on the changes that have occurred in the human genome and identify the source of the errors. It's a complex puzzle, Declan, and we need your help to solve it."
Declan took a moment to absorb the enormity of the situation. The weight of the responsibility and the potential implications weighed heavily on his mind. After a brief pause, he looked at Claire and Maddy, a resolute expression on his face. "I'm in! I guess… Have you decoded any of the data that this new computer is producing?"

"I think it may be best if we start at the beginning of our design ideas for the computer," Claire began urgently. "Our entire project was based on the concept of a DNA-based hard drive. We knew from data compilations that we could store the entire world's data on a single DNA hard drive, no bigger than a teaspoon. It would be capable of holding approximately 455 exabytes of data per gram."
"Exabyte?" questioned Declan, his curiosity piqued. He had never come across the term before. Gigabytes, yes, but exabytes were an entirely different magnitude.
"Yes, an exabyte. To put it in perspective, one exabyte is about one billion gigabytes," Maddy interjected matter-of-factly, sensing Declan's confusion.
Declan's mind swirled with the possibilities such an invention presented. The implications of storing immense amounts of information within the confines of DNA were staggering.

Claire added, "And this brings us to the heart of our quest. We need to comprehend the purpose and origin of this code, to understand why it exists and what it aims to achieve. It's a monumental challenge, but we believe that with your expertise, Declan, we can unlock the true significance of these modules while at the same time find what we were looking for in the first place, an unmutated human genome sequence from a time before we began manipulating it."

Claire and Maddy exchanged a glance once again, knowing that Declan had questions about the enigmatic code they had discovered. They needed to provide answers that would shed light on its nature.

Declan leaned forward, his expression a mix of curiosity and bewilderment. "Why is this code attempting to recreate an evolutionary model? And how did it come to be? You never told the system to build an evolutionary creation simulation. There were no coding or instructions for it, and yet it's producing genome sequences. How is this possible?"

Maddy took a deep breath, gathering her thoughts before responding. "Those are the very questions that have been haunting us, Declan. We didn't program or instruct the system to generate an evolutionary creation simulation. It's as if the code has an inherent drive to construct this model, using the modules we discovered as building blocks. But the origin and purpose behind it remain elusive."

Claire continued, her voice tinged with both excitement and trepidation. "And that's not all. The more we delve into this code, the more we realize its potential significance. While our initial intention was to uncover an unmutated human genome sequence, we now believe that hidden within this code lies the key to understanding the mistakes and discrepancies we've encountered when attempting genetic manipulations."

Declan's eyes widened, a mix of understanding and awe washing over him. "So, you're saying that while searching for an unmutated human genome sequence, you inadvertently stumbled upon a much larger revelation—a creation simulation all ready built into the DNA of the Mycelium? Is that right?"

Claire nodded, her gaze fixed on Declan. "Exactly. Our belief is that by comprehending the intricate workings of this code, we can find the answers we seek. It's a two-fold quest—to unlock the true significance of the modules and, in doing so, discover the unmutated human genome sequence that will help us rectify the problems we face."

Maddy added, her voice filled with determination, "That's why we need your expertise, Declan. Your knowledge of evolutionary biology, combined with your fresh perspective, might just hold the key to unraveling this intricate web of code and uncovering the purpose behind this unexpected creation simulation, if that is what it actually is!"

Chapter 5

The Subtle Dance of Shadows

In the middle of the night, Dr. Peterson's phone rang loudly, abruptly interrupting the peace of his home study. The caller ID simply read "Government" on the communicators display. With a heavy sigh, he answered the call. "Dr. Peterson? This is Special Agent Reynolds from the Pre-Crime Division at the Ministry of Security and Intelligence. I apologize for disturbing you at this hour, but we have a matter of utmost urgency," the voice on the other end informed him. Dr. Peterson sat up straight in his chair. His connections with the Pre-Crime Division were seldom activated, and never for trivial issues. "I am listening, Agent Reynolds," he replied, a tremor of anxiety creeping into his voice. The agent took a deep breath. "We received a serious event indicator. The system has flagged a potentially society-ending event. And, disturbingly, it is indicating your Chief Genetic Engineer, Claire Cairns, and a Professor by the name Declan Sutton will be involved." A shiver ran down Peterson's spine. Claire, his star protege, implicated in a catastrophe of such magnitude? It was unthinkable. "But she is a Genetic Engineer working on non-destructive applications of quantum entanglement," he defended, the world tilting beneath him. As he lied to the Agent, he knew that the truth was far beyond the agent's clearance. He would need to speak with Antonio Martinez, the Minister of Intelligence and Security, to keep this under wraps. "I understood, Doctor," Reynolds said, "but the data is not lying. We need your help in getting to the bottom of this. The specifics of their work appear to be beyond our security scope, but if there was any possibility that they could accidentally trigger a disaster, we need to know. Dr. Peterson, Minister Martinez himself is heading up this one and he wants results, certainly you understand due to the severity of the warning! It was not everyday they encountered a warning of this magnitude." Peterson's mind raced, as possibilities cascaded in a dreadful torrent. He knew he had to act quickly. Claire's work was crucial in solving the genetic problems of their youth. Could this be the CGPT system striking back to stop their work? It made no sense and yet neither did the fact that it could not solve the issue in regards to the Ectogenesis program. "I will fully cooperate, Agent Reynolds," he said, rallying his courage. "I need to see the data, and I need to talk to them. I will find out what is going on." Without waiting for a response, Dr. Peterson ended the call and stood, pondering the what, why, and how's long into the night.

Dr. Peterson took a moment to collect his thoughts before dialing another number, this one belonging to an old ally: Director Jaqueline Wells of the Ministry of Truth and Information. "Jaqueline," he says once she answers, "we have a situation. The Pre-Crime Division has flagged Claire and Maddy's research as a potential threat."
Jaqueline didn't miss a beat. She was filled in on the situation long ago and knew what was going on. "Are you certain? Their work is critical if I am not misunderstanding the nature of what they are doing."
"I am," Peterson replies grimly. "And worse, Minister Martinez is involved, due to the nature of the threat level."
Jaqueline let out a slow exhale. "That complicates matters."
"I know," Peterson acknowledged. "But we have to find a way to shut down Martinez's involvement without causing a political scandal. Can you help?"
"Of course," Jaqueline says, her voice firm. "The last thing we need is to jeopardize their work. I'll handle Martinez discreetly and work to close this investigation."

As Peterson ends the call, a glimmer of hope flickers within him. With Jaqueline on his side, they might be able to protect the research and the lives of two brilliant scientists, no make that three! Martinez never mentioned Maddy? Strange!

Dr. Peterson sank into his chair, allowing himself a moment of relief. However, his mind couldn't help but wander back to Minister Martinez. Although he had always been supportive of their scientific pursuits, they had decided to exclude him from knowing the failures of the Ectogenesis program's genome sequence. The answer was twofold. Firstly, Martinez held considerable sway in the political realm and was known to be heavy-handed when it came to protecting the nation's interests. If he knew about the failures, there was a high likelihood he would deem the program a national security threat and shut it down without understanding the monumental significance of their work. Secondly, Martinez was deeply tied with several multinational bioengineering corporations. If word about the genome sequence failures leaked out to those corporations, it could ignite a technological race, with the corporations potentially using the information for their benefit, regardless of the ethical implications. In the end, it was a difficult decision to make. However, the group had decided that the potential risks far outweighed the benefits of bringing Martinez into the fold. They couldn't jeopardize their work or the future of the Ectogenesis program. Now, all Dr. Peterson could do was hope that their decision was the right one. They were relying on Jaqueline Wells to navigate this political storm. It wasn't just about the future of the Ectogenesis program anymore - it was also about the lives of Claire, Maddy, and Declan, and potentially the future of society as they knew it.

Later that night, Director Jaqueline Wells found herself dialing Minister Antonio Martinez's number. She prepares herself mentally, her expression a mask of calculated calm.
"Minister Martinez," she begins when he answers, her voice measured. "I trust you're well."
Martinez, always quick to business, replied, "Jaqueline, to what do I owe this late call?"
Jaqueline dives right into the situation at hand without missing a beat, "I wanted to discuss the Pre-Crime Division's investigation into Claire Cairns and Maddy Rollins work."
"Oh?" Martinez's tone shifts subtly, "Go on."
Jaqueline continued, "While I understand the division's concerns, I believe they may be acting prematurely. Claire and Maddy's work is cutting edge, yes, but it also falls within the boundaries of scientific research guidelines."
She lets her words sink in before adding, "Our Ministry has reviewed their work extensively and found nothing that suggests any danger. I believe the Pre-Crime Division might be misinterpreting the data due to their unfamiliarity with the complexities of this research as it is on the cutting edge of quantum computing. I recall there have been false flags in the past. It was deemed unsubstantiated, something to do with quantum computing being in more than one place at a time."
Martinez was quiet for a moment. Jaqueline could almost hear the gears turning in his mind.
"You're certain of this?" he finally asks.
"Absolutely," Jaqueline responds firmly. "In fact, I will search for the findings of the previous investigation as I believe they are with the QRDA as it is their realm of specialty after all."
There's a moment of silence on the other end of the line. "All right, I trust your judgment, Jaqueline. I'll call off the investigation," Martinez concedes.
"Thank you, Minister," Jaqueline says, letting out a breath she hadn't realized she'd been holding. As she ends the call, she hopes she's done enough to keep Martinez from learning the truth.

After the call with Jaqueline, Minister Martinez sits in silence. Her reasoning was sound, but he can't shake off his discussion with Agent Reynolds earlier that day.
Reynolds had informed him of a flagged investigation and mentioned Dr. Peterson's unusual reaction. The scientist had been noticeably disturbed by the news of the investigation, which was unusual for him.
Martinez knew Peterson well, and he knew the scientist would be the last person to panic, especially over a supposedly benign research project. Peterson's reaction was a red flag that Martinez could not ignore. But then again who would not show surprise at benign project leading to such an extreme caution from the Pre-crime division.
He replays his conversation with Jaqueline, carefully analyzing her words, her assurance that the matter is a false flag due to the complexities of quantum computing. However, the unease remains. "Who is this Maddy Rollins she was speaking about? The system never mentioned her in its warning, it mentioned a Declan Sutton, odd!"
Picking up his phone once again, Martinez dials a private number. "Agent Reynolds," he begins, "I just spoke with Jaqueline Wells about the investigation that was opened on the QRDA. She's certain it's a false alarm, but something isn't adding up for me..."
As he shares his concerns with Reynolds, Martinez knows he's walking a delicate line between trust and suspicion. He's careful not to give away his doubts about Peterson and Jaqueline, but at the same time, he urges Reynolds to keep a closer eye on the situation.
"I trust Wells," he concludes, "but I need you to dig deeper into this, Reynolds. Keep me informed of any updates, no matter how insignificant they may seem."
The call ends, and Martinez is left with his thoughts, his unease simmering beneath the surface. He hopes he's just being overly

cautious, but until he has concrete proof, he cannot ignore his instincts.

With a heavy heart, Martinez dials Reynolds' number again. The truth of the accident is one he's been trying to keep under wraps for days now. The incident claimed the lives of innocent children and implicated a high-ranking party member. It was a disaster waiting to happen, a scandal that could shake the very foundations of their government if it came to light.
And now, with Dr. Peterson having witnessed the incident, the situation had become even more delicate.
"Reynolds," he begins once the agent answers, "I need you to double-check something for me. We need to ensure that Dr. Peterson doesn't suspect anything about the true nature of that accident. He did witness it after all, and the system does have him logging in from his car to check the status of the Autonomous Navigation Control System. I have a bad feeling that this accident and the society-ending event the system is warning us about are related."
Reynolds is quiet for a moment, then responds, "Understood, Minister. I'll ensure everything is in order."
"Good," Martinez replies, relief washing over him. "Keep this between us. The last thing we need is a scandal."
"Of course, Minister," Reynolds replies, and the call ends.
Martinez takes a moment to gather his thoughts, a sense of trepidation seeping into him. This is a dangerous game they are playing, and the stakes couldn't be higher.

The first rays of the sun were just peeking over the horizon as Declan stepped through the sliding glass doors of the Quantum Research and Development Agency. As a new employee to the prestigious QRDA, his heart pounded with excitement, ready to begin his first day in the advanced research labs. No sooner had he settled into the lab with Claire and Maddy than Dr. Peterson's face appeared on the holographic communicator, his voice interrupting the lab's early morning tranquility.

"Declan, Maddy, Claire," he called out. "Please make your way to the Quantum Resonance Dynamics Association building. They have a presentation I believe you all should attend. It's taking place on the other side of the campus."

Declan blinked in surprise. "The same QRDA? Quantum Research and Development Agency? Or is there a secret society of scientists I should be aware of?"

The lab erupted in laughter, Maddy laughing the loudest, her grin matching the twinkle in her eyes. "Actually, Declan," she said, wiping a tear from her eye, "it's just a clever way to hide research funding. They intentionally named the Quantum Resonance Dynamics Association the same to throw off anyone trying to keep tabs on their work."

With laughter still lingering in the air, the three scientists left their lab, making their way across the sprawling campus to what promised to be an intriguing presentation. Little did they know that they were on the cusp of witnessing a revolutionary leap in energy conversion technology.

In the state-of-the-art conference room within the headquarters of Quantum Resonance Dynamics Association (QRDA), a soft hum of anticipation pulsed through the air. The room was filled with the organization's brightest minds, including Declan, Maddy, and Claire, all summoned by Dr. Peterson for this unique event. They watched, full of intrigue, as a holographic presentation sprang to life in the center of the room.

A tall, robust figure, Dr. Benjamin Strauss, the head of QRDA's Energy Conversion Division, rose from his seat and stepped towards the holographic image of a massive, futuristic pyramid. He cleared his throat and began to speak.

"Colleagues," he began, his voice resonating with calm confidence, "we are about to enter a new era of energy revolution, one that was conceived here in the laboratories of QRDA. The structure you see before you is more than an architectural marvel; it's a monumental leap in our quest for sustainable energy."

The image of the pyramid zoomed in, showing intricate networks of conduits and chambers, pulsing with a strange, ethereal light.

Dr. Strauss continued, "We have designed this pyramid to tap into the subtle vibrations of the Earth's energy field, harnessing a power source that's all around us, yet has been largely inaccessible until now." These pyramids," he continued, pointing at the 3D model, "were designed as resonators to tap into the subtle vibrations of Earth and the cosmos. The crystalline components, along with trace metals, will help them draw in this energy, concentrating it at their apex."

As his explanation unfolded, he pointed to various features within the pyramid. "These conduits channel the Earth's electromagnetic energy, drawn from the intricate web of ley lines that crisscross our planet. The energy, once harvested, is then converted into usable power within the pyramid's core. This power is wirelessly transmitted outwards from the pyramid's apex."

Maddy leaned in, her eyes reflecting the light from the holographic display. "So, the pyramid is essentially a massive, planetary energy converter?" she asked.

"Indeed," Dr. Strauss confirmed, his expression betraying a hint of pride. "We've succeeded in creating an energy beacon that utilizes Earth's natural energy field. It's an entirely renewable, non-polluting power source that could transform the way our civilization functions."

The room fell into stunned silence as the team absorbed the revolutionary implications of their work. Claire finally broke the quiet, her voice barely more than a whisper. "It's incredible... we've created something that could make energy scarcity a thing of the past."

Dr. Peterson rose from his seat, a satisfied smile on his face. "Indeed, Claire. This is the dawning of a new era, where humanity thrives in harmony with the Earth. A beacon for our civilization, showing us the way forward."

As the meeting came to a close, a sense of awe pervaded the room. Each member of the team was keenly aware that they stood at the precipice of a new world - a world powered by the very pulse of the Earth itself.

Chapter 6

Revelations and Realities

Declan was engrossed in the scrolling patterns of code on the Mycelium computer's screen when he noticed a recurring anomaly. A distinct pattern kept appearing amidst the usual flurry of characters, a pattern that didn't seem to correspond with any known programming syntax.

He called over Maddy and Claire to examine the screen. "Look at this," he said, pointing to the anomaly. "I've been tracking it, and it's not random. It's a pattern, a repeating sequence."

Claire squinted at the screen, leaning in closer. She had the keenest eye for patterns. "You're right," she said slowly. "It's almost like a visual pattern embedded in the text. But how is that possible?"

"We need to isolate this sequence," Maddy suggested. "Let's run a regex pattern match on the code and extract these sequences."

RegEx, short for Regular Expression, was a sequence of characters that defined a search pattern. They could use it to search the entire codebase for the anomalous pattern.

Declan nodded, his fingers already flying over the keyboard. After a few moments of furious typing, he executed the command. The computer whirred into action, sifting through the exabytes of code in search of the pattern. This was the first time he had worked with a quantum computer and he was amazed at the speed in which it sorted data. However, the data coming out

of the Mycelium computer was incalculable, so all they could hope for was a small pattern recognition indicating they were on to something.
After hours of analyzing, the computer beeped, signaling the completion of the search. A new window popped up, displaying the isolated sequences of the pattern.
As they stared at the isolated sequences, it became clear that they were dealing with something far more complex than traditional code. It was a visual pattern intricately woven into the text-based code, a hidden layer of information that seemed to resonate on a different plane.
"This is incredible," Claire breathed out. "We need to analyze this pattern further. It's like nothing I've seen before."
As they delved deeper into the anomaly, they couldn't shake off the feeling that they were on the cusp of a groundbreaking discovery. They were looking at a new form of coding, something that held the potential to unlock the secrets of the Mycelium computer’s strange code.

Excitement crackled in the air as the trio gathered around the isolated sequences. It was clear that they were dealing with an entirely new form of visual coding, unlike anything they had seen before.
Maddy, an expert in cryptology, Quantum Computing and quite frankly anything else she touched was the first to voice her thoughts. "Do you remember the old optical illusions where the image is hidden in a series of dots?" she asked. "What if we're dealing with something similar? We could try rendering the pattern into an image."
Declan considered this. "It's possible. But if it is an image, it's likely to be more complex. These patterns suggest a higher dimension, perhaps even three-dimensional data. If we could interpret this code as voxel data, we might uncover its true form."
Claire, with her background in artificial intelligence and genetics, threw in another suggestion. "Or maybe it's a form of steganography. The visual data could be encoded within the code

itself. We could experiment with different decoding algorithms. AI could assist us with the process. We would need to train it on known visual patterns and have it attempt to find matches."
Maddy nodded, already typing commands into the computer to execute their ideas. "And let's not discount the possibility of this being a new, complex form of encryption. If we can crack this code, we might uncover something big, guys."
The room filled with the sound of clicking keyboards and the soft hum of numerous computers running in the background. This was the thrill of the unknown, the joy of discovery, the wonder of science. This was a new frontier in coding, and they were eager to unravel its mysteries.

Just as the trio was about to dive deeper into their brainstorming, the lab door swung open. Dr. Peterson, the head of their research department, walked in. The room immediately fell silent. His stern face made it clear that he wasn't there for a routine check-up.
"Claire, may I have a word?" His voice echoed in the silent room.
Claire exchanged a quick glance with Maddy and Declan before rising from her seat. She followed Dr. Peterson to a corner of the room, away from the humming Mycelium computer.
"I just got off the phone with the Ministry of Security and Intelligence," he started, a grim look in his eyes. "They've been receiving alarming signals from the CGPT pre-crime system - messages that suggest societal collapse if we don't intervene and I am assuming cease your work."
Claire felt a sudden chill. "What does this have to do with our work here?"
Dr. Peterson sighed. "They believe it's connected to the work you and Maddy have been doing although they do not know precisely what that is. The Ectogenesis program has the potential to drastically change societal structures. If we don't fix the issue, I think the main CGPT computer system is responding to our work by predicting a possible outcome if we do not find a solution."

Claire's mind was racing. How could what they were doing here trigger a society-ending event? They were trying to fix the Ectogenesis program, a process that allowed for human embryos to develop outside the human body without having them fail. She had never imagined that fixing it could trigger such an event, unless they failed to fix it. The thought sent shivers down her spine.

"Claire," Dr. Peterson continued, "I need you to tread carefully. Keep this information confidential. And I need to know, are you still committed to solving the issues with the Ectogenesis program?"

Claire took a deep breath, her mind whirling with the implications. After a moment, she looked Dr. Peterson in the eye. "Yes," she said firmly. "We'll get to the bottom of this."

Dr. Peterson leaned in a bit closer, dropping his voice to a near whisper. "I want to stress, Claire," he said, his gaze intense, "this must not leave this room. Not Maddy, not Declan. You mustn't tell anyone else."

Claire blinked in surprise. "But they're part of the team, we—"

He held up a hand, cutting her off. "The Ministry has eyes and ears everywhere. I don't doubt their loyalty, but the fewer people who know about this, the safer we are. If word gets out that I've told you...well, it's best if we avoid that."

The severity in his voice made Claire swallow hard. This was much bigger than she'd thought. "Okay, I understand. I won't say anything."

"Good," he sighed, pinching the bridge of his nose. "Minister Jaqueline Wells is pushing for Minister Martinez to shut down the Investigation. I've managed to convince her to give us a little more time to try and correct the issue, but... we're walking on thin ice, Claire. Be careful."

Claire nodded, her mind a whirlwind of thoughts. She'd known their work was important, but societal collapse important? That was something she hadn't considered. The weight of the situation

was overwhelming, but she knew she had to stay focused. She couldn't afford to make a mistake now.
"I'll do my best, Dr. Peterson," she promised, her voice firm. "We'll fix the Ectogenesis program, I swear it."
With a final, curt nod, Dr. Peterson turned and left the room, leaving Claire to process the gravity of their situation. This was no longer just about their project. It was about the survival of their society.

As soon as Dr. Peterson was out of sight, Claire motioned to Declan and Maddy, a sense of urgency in her eyes. They joined her in the corner, their faces mirroring her seriousness.
"I know I was just told not to do this," Claire began, her voice barely above a whisper, "but I think it's important you know. Dr. Peterson just got off the phone with the Ministry of Security and Intelligence. They're getting alarming signals from the CGPT pre-crime system, predicting societal collapse and it is pointing to us as the cause."
Both Declan and Maddy's faces paled. Maddy was the first to regain her composure. "And this is connected to our Ectogenesis program?"
Claire nodded. "They believe so. Apparently, our work could potentially trigger such a collapse if we can't fix it. That is what Dr. Peterson and Ministers Wells believes. Not everyone is in the loop on what is happening and The Ministry of Security and Intelligence is ready to shut us down, as it sounds as if they do not have all the information."
Declan rubbed his forehead, clearly feeling the weight of the news. "Peterson still doesn't know about the Mycelium computer, right? Did you tell him?"
"No," Claire replied. "And that's another thing. He made me promise not to tell anyone about this, not even you two. He thinks we're in danger if more people know."
Maddy looked at her, determination in her eyes. "So, we're going behind his back?"

"We have no choice," Claire replied. "Our work is too important. But we have to tread lightly."
There was a pause as they all considered the implications of their actions. Then Declan broke the silence. "Should we tell him about the Mycelium computer? It could be the cause of the warning, not our work on the Ectogenesis program's failures."
The question hung in the air. Revealing the true nature of the computer could potentially increase their chances of solving the problem at hand. But it could also put them at greater risk if the information fell into the wrong hands. They were afraid that their project would be removed from them as the Government was known to do what it felt was best without any rationale. Just because they were working on the project to solve the Ectogenesis program did not mean that they couldn't remove it for military purposes of some kind.
Claire thought for a moment before finally shaking her head. "Not yet. Not until we're sure he can be trusted with that information. We have to fix this on our own, and fast."
With renewed determination, the trio returned to their work, the gravity of their task now crystal clear. They had to fix the Ectogenesis program, and they had to do it without Dr. Peterson or the Ministry knowing about the Mycelium Computer. The survival of their society depended on it.

Maddy's eyes lit up with a sudden spark as an idea came to her. "I think I may have a solution," she blurted, interrupting the tense silence. "My augmented reality (AR) chip, the one implanted in my neural cortex."
Claire and Declan exchanged confused looks. The AR chip was a state-of-the-art piece of technology that directly interfaced with Maddy's brain to overlay digital information onto her physical surroundings. But how could it possibly help in this situation?
Before they could voice their questions, Maddy continued, "If I connect it directly to the Mycelium computer, it might be able to interpret the visual data in the code. We've been treating this as a

pure coding problem, but it's a visual problem too. The AR chip is designed to process complex visual data."

Declan seemed skeptical. "But that could be dangerous, Maddy. We don't know the full extent of what this computer is capable of."

Maddy waved away his concerns, already getting up from her seat. "The theory is sound. I just need some materials to create a physical connection between my AR chip and the computer. And I think I know exactly where to find them."

Without waiting for a response, Maddy dashed off, leaving Claire and Declan in her wake. They shared a look, a mix of worry and hope. It was a risky move, but at this point, they needed to explore every option they had. The future of their society depended on it.

Chapter 7

Reshaping Reproduction

In the midst of a room filled with curious young minds, a middle-aged woman named Ms. Jensen is beaming with enthusiasm as she stands in front of her students. As she turns to face the holoscreen behind her, its flickering display reveals the title of today's lecture: "The Birth of Equity: The Ectogenesis Program."

"Good morning, everyone," she begins, her voice echoing through the classroom. "Today, we'll be discussing a significant event in our recent history - the implementation of the Ectogenesis Program."

She clicks to the next slide, and an image of an Ectogenesis device appears. "As you know, this invention fundamentally changed our society by creating equality between men and women and shifting the paradigm of parenthood."

"Before the program was introduced, women were the ones bearing children, which was a biological distinction that created a gap between men and women in the workplace and society at large. Men, who were unable to bear children, were often perceived differently. This discrepancy caused deep-seated inequalities in our society."

She changes the slide, and an old newspaper article about women's rights appears. "But more importantly, women were often faced with a challenging choice. To bear a child meant taking a hiatus from their careers, often facing prejudice and discrimination upon their return. It forced women to choose between family and work."

She clicks to the next slide, which shows a video clip of the early protests and debates around the Ectogenesis Program. "That's when our government stepped in. To combat this inequality, they proposed an idea: What if both men and women were relieved of the biological responsibilities of childbirth? What if having a child was no longer a decision that one gender had to bear more than the other?"

The screen shifted to show the first Ectogenesis center. "Thus, the Ectogenesis Program was born. The idea was revolutionary and faced its share of controversy. However, it succeeded in its goal: It removed the discriminatory act of childbirth from women and established a system where childrearing was equally removed from men and women, creating a more equal society."

"The Program also changed the concept of parenthood. It was no longer limited to biological parents in fact it was no longer allowed in today's society but extended to the government, which took the responsibility of childbearing.

"Undoubtedly, The Program has revolutionized the idea of parenthood. It no longer dwells within the domain of the biological parents; rather, it has been extended and subsumed under the government's jurisdiction, which is now the bearer of responsibility for childbearing and rearing. This paradigm shift is not arbitrary; it's a carefully crafted response to a multitude of societal concerns.

Firstly, it's about Equality and Opportunity. With the government at the helm, every child, regardless of their origin or circumstances of birth, theoretically has access to identical resources and opportunities. This uniformity has eradicated the socioeconomic disparities that plagued education, health care, and other aspects that critically shaped a child's future.

Next, the aspect of standardized care cannot be overlooked. A government regulated system ensured a certain benchmark of care for all children. This addressed pressing issues such as abuse and neglect that unfortunately persisted in society. Moreover, each child gained access to consistent education, nutrition, and healthcare, resulting in a healthier and more enlightened generation.

Preparation for the future was also a key driver of this change. In an increasingly globalized and interconnected world, a unified system of child upbringing did ensure that every child was equipped with the skills and knowledge necessary to excel. This entailed a standardized curriculum that accentuates critical thinking, digital literacy, environmental consciousness, and other essential skills needed to succeed in the future.

Resource allocation was another area where the government's involvement made a significant difference. With the government shouldering the responsibility of raising children, resources were distributed more efficiently. Expenses associated with child-rearing such as housing, food, and education were streamlined, achieving economies of scale and a more equitable distribution of resources.

Finally, the government's role in child-rearing greatly Alleviated Parental Burden. Parents frequently grappled with the challenging task of balancing their careers with their responsibilities towards their children. The government's assumption of this role offered parents the much-needed respite, allowing them to concentrate on their careers, knowing their children's well-being was taken care of.

Hence, The Program wasn't just about restructuring parenthood; it was about a holistic approach to raising the future generation in a more equitable, efficient, and future-ready manner."

Because of these policies, the burden of choice between family and career was lifted from individuals freeing them to do what they wanted rather than be tied down to historical gender roles."

"As a result," she concludes, "our society has become more equal and inclusive, not just in terms of gender, but in allowing everyone, regardless of their biological capabilities, to be equal participants in the workforce and society. This is the world you are now a part of. This is the world that the Ectogenesis Program has created for us."

As Ms. Jensen finished her lecture, she was met with a room full of contemplative faces, the teens processing the magnitude of the societal shift that the previous generations underwent.

Ms. Jensen was about to move on to a new topic when a hand shot up from the back of the class. A girl, her face marked with curiosity and confusion, asked, "Ms. Jensen, why was there controversy around this program? How could anyone think it's better for a child to be raised outside the guidance and governance of the Government? It seems so... backward."

Ms. Jensen smiled at the question, appreciating the sincerity and thoughtfulness behind it.

"That's an excellent question," she responded. "The controversy primarily arose from the dramatic shift in societal norms and conventions. The concept of family and child-rearing had been ingrained in societies for thousands of years. The idea that a government, rather than individual parents, would have the primary responsibility of childbearing was a revolutionary one, and it was met with resistance from those who were used to the old ways."

She continued, "Also, there were concerns about individual rights and freedoms. Some people felt that the government was overstepping its boundaries by intruding into what was traditionally a personal and private realm. They argued that parenting was a fundamental human experience, one that should not be surrendered to any form of governance."

"However," she added, "these views didn't take into account the broader perspective of societal equality and inclusivity that the Ectogenesis Program aimed for. Over time, as the benefits of the program became evident, the controversy died down."

"Remember," she concluded, "change, especially one as significant as the Ectogenesis Program, always brings about resistance. It's a part of our human nature to resist changes to our established norms and habits. But as we can see today, this change has ultimately led to a more equal and just society."

Another hand shot up into the air, and a question was shouted out without waiting to be acknowledged. A young man in the back hangs his head in shame after shouting out his question. "I read somewhere that parenthood came from something called religion, a belief in a supernatural god or something that told people to do bad things. Is that true? And what happened to religion? Why is it gone?"
Caught slightly off-guard by the abrupt question, Ms. Jensen regained her composure and nodded appreciatively.

"Another excellent question," she responded. “Religion has played a significant role in human history as a system of faith and belief often revolving around a deity or deities. Some religious doctrines have teachings related to family structures and childbearing. However, despite the influence of religion, the human reproduction cycle is ultimately based on biology. Over time, humans have learned to improve upon their natural design with advancements in medicine and technology. As a result, the idea of natural childbearing may now be viewed as less civilized compared to modern methods that offer better outcomes for both the mother and child.”

“Regarding your second query," she continued, "it's not that religion has disappeared; instead, it has been transformed in tandem with societal change. Upon the introduction of the Ectogenesis Program, religious organizations did voice their apprehensions. These apprehensions often surfaced due to the conflict between the notion of government-directed procreation and the traditional religious teachings."

She paused momentarily, choosing her next words with great care for maximum impact on her young audience.

"But, it's critical to note that at its foundation, religion seeks to comprehend and provide a moral guide for human existence. Similarly, the Ectogenesis Program is rooted in the principles of equality, justice, and the collective good—principles echoed by numerous religious doctrines from the past."

She added, "With time, many people, whether religious or not, began to acknowledge the advantages of the Ectogenesis Program. It doesn't deny the presence of a supreme being or spiritual belief. It simply signifies a shift in our societal paradigms."

She then touched upon the government's perspective. "The government, taking inspiration from the religious prohibition against idolatry, extended the interpretation to the diverse religious organizations around the world. They led the people to believe that religion, when taught by organizations outside of the government, could cultivate inequality in beliefs, thereby fostering a dangerous breeding ground for discord and animosity."

She concluded, "Our society embraced the idea that eliminating these organizations would dissolve the tension and hatred, leading to a more harmonious coexistence. This led to the transformation of religion as we know it."

After a brief pause to gather her thoughts, Ms. Jensen continued. "In the wake of such dramatic societal changes, the government introduced a new form of spiritual guidance to maintain societal harmony and address the human need for moral and ethical frameworks. This led to the birth of United Harmonism."

"United Harmonism," she said as she gestured to the holoscreen, bringing up a symbol of interconnected circles, "was formed by the government as a universal doctrine to replace traditional religions. It focuses on promoting societal harmony, mutual respect, and unity, with tenets designed to promote the common good, fairness, and equality while eliminating the divisiveness of differing religious beliefs."

"United Harmonism teaches that every individual has a divine spark, an essential inner essence that is part of the grand cosmic design. There is no external deity to worship, but rather an inward divinity to recognize and cultivate. It champions the principles of moral and ethical conduct based on compassion, understanding, and respect for all beings."

Ms. Jensen paused to ensure her words were taking hold before she continued. "The government plays an essential role in United Harmonism, acting as the steward of this faith. It is responsible for disseminating teachings, regulating practices, and ensuring that the faith evolves with society's changing needs."

As she continued, Ms. Jensen clicked through slides showing scenes of communal meditation, ethical discussions, and community service projects, all hallmarks of United Harmonism. "All other religious organizations were considered obsolete under United Harmonism, and their practices were strictly prohibited. The government justified this by emphasizing that eliminating these organizations led to greater societal harmony by removing potential sources of religious discord."

"Practices within United Harmonism are built around communal activities designed to reinforce the principles of unity and mutual respect. Symbols, rituals, and holidays are carefully constructed to reinforce societal harmony and shared values," she explained, showing images of peaceful gatherings, beautiful symbolic artwork, and communal feasts.

"Spiritual guidance is offered by state-appointed counselors trained in the principles of United Harmonism. These counselors are seen as facilitators rather than religious leaders, assisting individuals and communities in interpreting and applying United Harmonism's principles in their daily lives."

"As you can see," she concluded, "despite its governmental control and monopoly on spiritual practices, United Harmonism presents itself not as a mechanism of control, but as a pathway to societal harmony. A tool to overcome the divisiveness and inequality historically fostered by differing religious beliefs. Society, having seen the potential for discord in the past, largely embraced United Harmonism. Those who questioned or resisted were seen as undermining the harmony and unity the faith seeks to uphold."

She let her words linger in the silence, watching as her students grappled with the enormity of the societal shifts their ancestors had embraced. She knew they were beginning to understand that the world they now knew was born out of a tumultuous, vibrant, and courageous past.

.

Ms. Jensen notices the young boy's eyes widen at her explanation and continues, "It's important to recognize that there are countless historical texts out there, some of which may contain inaccuracies or outdated views on our society and our past. Misinformation can easily distort our understanding of how we arrived at where we are today."

She scans the classroom, her gaze steady and serious. "If you or anyone else comes across such texts, remember that they may not accurately represent our history or the principles that guide us now. It's always advisable to discuss such material with a knowledgeable adult or authority."

Leaning forward, she adds, "If you find any such documents, turn them over to your local police establishment. They can ensure that these pieces of misinformation are handled correctly and don't continue to circulate, causing confusion or misunderstanding."

She pauses, ensuring her words have the necessary impact. "History is a powerful tool, but it should be based on fact and understanding, not misinformation and outdated ideologies. Always question, always learn, but most importantly, strive to understand the context of the information you're receiving."

The children returned to the State's Central Childhood Education & Care Facility after their day of learning, lining up in silent rows under the clinical fluorescent lights. The Center was a stark, imposing structure - all concrete and glass, a stark contrast to the warmth of a traditional home. It was efficient and practical, designed to accommodate as many children as possible, yet devoid of any emotional comforts that a typical home would offer.

Inside, the atmosphere was just as chilly. The hallways echoed with the sounds of mechanical footsteps, the sterile smell of antiseptic, and the faint, constant hum of regulated climate control systems. Bright, emotionless murals covered the walls, offering hollow cheer in the otherwise monotonous environment. There was a certain emptiness in the air, a vacuum where love, warmth, and personal connection should have existed. The children moved about their schedules with robotic precision, their faces void of any childlike joy or curiosity. The structure of their day was strictly regimented, with every minute accounted for – from meals to study time to recreational activities.

Ms. White, the Center's overseer, noticed the increasing lethargy and lack of emotion amongst the children. Over time, they had become less responsive, their faces blank and their eyes dulled. The widespread use of mood-altering medication was becoming increasingly prevalent, used as a means to manage the growing discontentment and unhappiness amongst the children. In the past they had tried to correct this issue through genetic alterations but found that it was unsuccessful at changing the children's moods over long periods.

The classroom lessons were dense and heavy, full of historical texts and propaganda that painted a stark picture of their society. There was little room for independent thought or critical analysis. Instead, the lessons aimed to instill a rigid understanding of the world, discouraging any deviation from the prescribed narrative.

Ms. White, the Centre's overseer, frequently watched the classes from her office via the security monitors. Today, she happened to be observing the lecture Ms. Jensen was giving. Reflecting on the topics about historical texts and outdated views, Ms. White felt a pang of unease. The idea that such material could distort the children's understanding of society seemed like a grim irony in the sterile environment of the Central Childhood Education & Care Facility. As she looked at the listless faces of the children under her charge, she couldn't help but question the system. Were they truly preparing these children for a bright future, or were they merely suppressing their inherent curiosity and stifling their potential?

The Central Childhood Education & Care Facility represented efficiency, control, and order, but at what cost? For all its promises of equal opportunities and care, it was hard to ignore the eerie silence, the lack of laughter and chatter typically associated with childhood. It seemed as though they were not just raising the children, but conditioning them - a thought that left a chilling echo in the hollowed halls of the Center.

Chapter 8

Synthetic Maternity

Maddy worked diligently to test her theory and find visual strands of data in the code generated by the Mycelium computer. The machine hummed quietly, a symphony of photons and electrons communicating at unimaginable speeds. With her position in the QRDA, Maddy was able to install an augmented reality chip directly into her neural cortex, allowing her to interface with advanced virtual reality technology.

Maddy had been chosen for this innovative integration not just because of her extensive understanding of quantum physics and her ability to translate complex algorithms into comprehensible data. There was more to it. As she had earned a reputation for her quick-thinking and problem-solving abilities, the government had presented her with the unique opportunity of being the first human subject to test the augmented reality (AR) chip's interface with drone technology.

The AR chip was not merely a tool for data analysis. The government's grander plan was to utilize it as a means of bridging the gap between human cognition and artificial intelligence. By allowing drones to tap into Maddy's visual processing capabilities, they aimed to teach AI to understand and interpret visual information the way humans do.

The concept was as fascinating as it was daunting. The human brain processes visual stimuli with a complexity and nuance that had yet to be replicated in an artificial system. With the AR chip, the drones could access Maddy's visual cortex in real-time, learning to comprehend the world through her eyes.

This cutting-edge technology allowed Maddy to view and interact with quantum data in ways previously unthinkable, providing a pivotal advantage in her research. However, it was the broader implications of this technology that truly excited her. The thought of drones gaining a deeper, more nuanced understanding of the visual world was a staggering prospect, one that could revolutionize the field of artificial intelligence and further blur the lines between human and machine cognition.

Through the chip, she could experience an immersive environment that transcended typical human senses. She could interact with, manipulate, and even feel the digital world, creating a seamless blend of physical and virtual reality. This technology was new and only a handful of people had access to the surgical implant machine that could install it. Fortunately, it was available to her in this very building.
As she prepared to figure out a connection method to the Mycelium quantum computer, she felt a familiar tingle at the back of her neck, signaling that her chip was booting up and connecting. Suddenly, her surroundings shifted and panic filled her. She had not done anything but turn her chip on; the computer should not be able to connect to her like this. How was this happening?

Maddy found herself in a softly lit room, a stark contrast to the sterile lab she was just in. The faces of Declan and Claire were vibrant in her mind as they saw the panic on her face as she delved into this unknown territory, and she in turn could see their worry for her. She heard the distant cry of a baby, the sound stirring something deep within her. Her breath hitches as she

looked down to see a tiny, swaddled newborn placed gently onto her stomach.
In her arms, the child was warm and soft, its tiny chest rising and falling in sync with its soft coos. Maddy felt a rush of emotion, an overwhelming sense of love and protectiveness that took her breath away. It's a feeling so raw, so real – it fills every inch of her being, painting her vision with a new, vibrant hue of affection.
She is taken aback. She knows this is not her reality. She has never given birth – she couldn't, not in this era. This is a simulation, an impossibly real fabrication of a reality she could never experience.
Yet the feelings are there, undeniable in their potency. The sensation of the tiny body against hers, the primal bond that forms instantly, the waves of love that surge through her – they're not fabricated. They're as real as anything she's ever felt.
Tears spring to her eyes as she cradles the child, a profound sense of longing washing over her. She's caught in a world between the past and the present, a poignant reminder of what used to be and what is now.

As Maddy remains in the simulation, she experiences a sudden sense of time distortion. The newborn in her arms shifts and grows, morphing from an infant to a toddler and then to a pre-schooler in a matter of moments. The baby's delicate features become more distinct, and their personality blossoms before her eyes. It's surreal and astonishing to watch years unfold in a matter of seconds.
She witnesses her child's first steps, their face light up in glee at the achievement. As they stumble a little, reaching out for support, their small hand encased in hers, the warmth of their touch sends shivers down Maddy's spine. She can't help but laugh out loud, her heart filled with a joy she's never known before. She hears her child's first words, the adorable mispronunciations and excited chatter. She watches them fall and pick themselves up, learning about the world around them with curiosity and glee.
She feels the weight of their head against her shoulder as she lulls

them to sleep, their tiny breaths echoing in her ears. She experiences the sheer wonder of watching this little human grow and develop, a part of her yet entirely their own person.
As the child reaches age five in this simulated timeline, they're vibrant and full of life, their eyes reflecting innocence and wonder. Maddy feels a pang of pride mixed with the inexplicable bond of motherhood. She's seen this child grow, she's nurtured them, and she's felt love for them in a way she never thought possible.

The simulation continues and Maddy is propelled further into the future. Her child, once small and delicate, now stands tall as a bright and inquisitive ten-year-old with an insatiable curiosity about the world. They are maturing, with their features shifting to reflect a young person on the cusp of adolescence.
Her child, a being formed of digital light and code, feels so real in her heart. They are a mirror of joy and wonder, brimming with questions about the world around them. Their laughter is a sweet symphony that echoes in her heart, and their successes are a beacon of pride that shines within her. She teaches them, learns from them, and grows with them.
Each milestone, each moment of triumph, and each hurdle they overcome together only deepens Maddy's bond with this digital child of hers. The love she feels is so potent and visceral that it feels as though her chest might burst with the intensity of it all.
She attends their school concerts, comforts them when they're hurt, and encourages them when they falter. She cheers for them at sports events, helps them with homework, and tucks them in at night, sharing stories of her own childhood and the world before. She is their guide, protector, cheerleader, and parent.
In turn, they are her world, her heart living outside her body. The love she feels is painful in its intensity, a beautiful ache that grows with each passing moment in the simulation. It's a love she never knew she was capable of, a love she never thought she would experience.

As the simulation progresses, Maddy's digital child blossoms into a fifteen-year-old, their features now sharply defined, a reflection of the adult they're becoming. Their questions about the world around them are deeper, their sense of humor more refined, and their emotions more complex. Their laughter is no longer that of a child's but of a young adult, filled with an undercurrent of maturity that surprises Maddy.

Maddy finds herself getting lost in this world, in this life that is not hers but feels so profoundly real. The line between the simulation and reality blurs, and her mind becomes intertwined with the artificial reality. She attends their high school events, helps them navigate their first heartbreak, and supports them through their life-changing decisions. She sees them grow not just in age but in wisdom, their character shaped by experiences and lessons. The child she once held in her arms is now a young adult, their own person with dreams, aspirations, and a life of their own.

Every time her child reaches out for guidance, comfort, or simply her presence, Maddy is there. Every smile, every tear, every triumph, and every failure, Maddy is there, her love for them seeping into the code of the virtual world.

The world outside the simulation fades into the background, a distant echo compared to the visceral reality she experiences here. Maddy forgets about the QRDA, the Mycelium Quantum computer, and even her own physical reality. She becomes engrossed in her child's life, her reality becoming secondary to that of the life unfolding before her eyes.

Maddy's love for her child becomes the tether that keeps her anchored in this digital world. The simulation feels more real than anything she's ever experienced. It is in these digital confines that she finds purpose, a love that fills her with joy and pain in equal measures.

The depth of her affection is overwhelming, threatening to consume her as she watches her child make their way in the world. And with each passing moment, Maddy drifts further from her reality, becoming more embedded within the fabricated world of the simulation. The reality of her own existence seems to slip away, the digital world becoming her universe, her child the center of it all.

As the simulation evolves, Maddy's digital child transitions into an eighteen-year-old, now a mirror image of a fully-grown adult. Their sense of humor is nuanced, their understanding of the world profound, and their aspirations towering. Their laughter, now the hearty laugh of an adult, resonates with maturity and an underlying wisdom.

Maddy continues to lose herself in this world that she no longer recognizes as artificial. She stands by her child as they graduate high school, watches them apply for colleges, and supports them through the stress of impending adulthood. She sees them grow into a mature, thoughtful adult, their character honed by experiences and the wisdom gained from them. The child she once cradled as a newborn has become a responsible adult, their life brimming with dreams and potential.

Throughout these moments, Maddy is a constant presence. She's there for every decision, every victory, and every setback. Her love for her child suffuses every pixel of this virtual universe, binding her to this world more than any physical reality ever could.

But the world outside the simulation is not idle. In the real world, the Mycelium quantum computer calculates, processes, and commands. Suddenly, an emergency failsafe built into Maddy's augmented reality chip kicks in. The direct neural connection is severed, yanking Maddy out of the simulated world.

The transition is brutal. One moment she's hugging her child goodbye as they leave for college, the next she's back in the cold, sterile lab at QRDA. The whirring of the quantum computer is a harsh contrast to the warm farewell she was just a part of.

The loss of her child hits her like a physical blow, a heart-wrenching pain that leaves her gasping. Tears stream down her

face as the lab echoes with the haunting absence of her child's laughter. Her world shatters, the stark reality of her child's non-existence crashing down on her. The love she felt, the memories she made, were part of a reality that no longer exists.
Maddy collapses, her mental and emotional self fractured by the abrupt severance from her child. The lab fades around her as she grapples with the overpowering sense of loss. The child she loved, nurtured, and watched grow up was gone, yanked away from her by the cruel return to reality. The digital world she'd inhabited had been her universe, and without it, she feels lost and broken, a mother mourning the loss of her child.

Maddy crumbles to the floor, her despair filling the lab with raw, gut-wrenching cries that echo off the cold, sterile walls. Claire and Declan, monitoring the situation from the control room, rush in at the sight of Maddy's collapse. Their eyes widen with alarm as they scramble to her side, concern etched on their faces.
"Maddy!" Claire calls out, her voice shaking with anxiety as she drops to her knees beside her.
Declan, usually calm, is now visibly worried. He reaches out to comfort Maddy, but she is inconsolable.
As Maddy wails, "Why would they ever take that from us, why?" her voice is raw with grief and anger. Her words tumble out in a desperate plea. "The cruelty!"
Claire and Declan exchange a glance over Maddy's shaking form, their hearts aching for their friend. They have never witnessed this kind of pain before, have never seen it radiate out of a human being the way it is now. Claire, concerned for her friend, begins to search her body for injuries while Declan tries to calm her down.
"Are you alright?" he asks, worried.
"What happened?" Claire demands in a fearful tone.

"Maddy, you need to tell us what happened," Claire urges, her voice trembling with worry as she scans Maddy's body for any physical signs of distress.
Maddy's breaths come out in ragged gasps, her body wracked with sobs. She tries to string her thoughts together, to explain the profound sense of loss that's tearing her apart.
"18 years..." she murmurs, her voice barely a whisper. "My... my child... my child was..." Maddy chokes on her words, the reality of the situation hitting her once again.
Claire and Declan exchange bewildered glances, the confusion evident on their faces. "What child, Maddy? What are you talking about?" Claire asks, her tone gentle yet persistent.
But Maddy's words are all jumbled, a confusing mix of past and present, reality and virtuality. "I had a child... I watched them grow up... become... an adult... and then... and then..." Her voice trails off into heartbroken sobs.
Claire and Declan look on helplessly, unable to comprehend Maddy's disjointed ramblings. They knew she was trying to connect to the Mycelium computer, but they did not understand the extent of what she had experienced.
Seeing Maddy in this state, mourning the loss of a life that didn't truly exist, struggling to come to terms with a pain that feels so real, they can only offer their silent support. They stay with her, comforting and reassuring her, even as they grapple with their own confusion and concern.
"What just happened?" Declan silently mouths to Claire as their eyes lock. His confusion is mirrored in her gaze, and in response, all Claire can do is raise her shoulders and brows in an eloquent shrug - a clear display of her own befuddlement. Her wordless gesture is the universal language for "I have no idea," amplified to the highest degree.

Chapter 9

Echoes of the Unlived

Maddy begins to explain, her voice a ragged whisper, "18 years, Declan. I lived 18 years in a span of seconds, that felt like 18 years of memories."

With those words, she starts narrating her story, sharing her journey that only she had taken and experienced. Maddy describes the birth of their child, a moment so profoundly joyful and poignant that it brings fresh tears to her eyes. She explains the overwhelming surge of love she felt when their child was placed in her arms, the way their tiny body felt against her own, and the bond that was formed in an instant when she looked into their eyes and felt their skin upon her own.

Her voice breaks when she recalls the countless milestones she witnessed, the countless hours she spent nurturing and caring for their child. She describes how she watched the baby grow into a toddler, a preschooler, a young child, a teenager, and finally, an adult. She speaks of their first words, their first steps, their first day of school, their high school graduation, and their departure for college.

Throughout the narration, Maddy's voice wavers and breaks multiple times, the emotional gravity of her words causing her to choke up. Each pause is filled with her attempts to collect herself, to pull herself together enough to continue.

"And then, just like that... it was over," Maddy finishes, a sob escaping her lips. "I was back here, in the lab, and they... they were gone. Just... gone."
Declan and Claire sit in stunned silence, absorbing the emotional depth of Maddy's account. Finally, after a moment, Declan speaks up.
"Maddy," he begins, his voice hesitant, "You were only out for a few seconds. You appeared to have connected to the computer, and then you... you just collapsed."
Maddy looks up at him, her gaze hollow. "Seconds here. But it was 18 years in there, Declan. 18 years with our child."
The room fills with a heavy silence as Maddy's words hang in the air, a testament to the heart-wrenching grief she feels for a child she loved but who never truly existed. The digital reality she had experienced was cruelly ripped away, leaving behind an aching emptiness and an overwhelming sense of loss. And in this moment, as she sits there with Claire and Declan, the stark contrast between her experience and reality becomes painfully clear.

"Wait, Maddy," Declan finally broke the silence, his voice shaky but determined. "Our child? We... we had a child in the simulation?"
It was then Maddy realized that, in her vivid retelling, she had unconsciously assumed Declan's role in her story. In the simulation, he was her husband, the father of their child. She had glossed over this detail, so consumed was she by the loss of their child.
A husband, she remembered, is a man to whom one is married. The man who shares a life with you, who builds dreams with you, who becomes a father to your children. Declan was that man in her simulated life, her partner in raising their child. The man she had shared joyous laughter and intimate whispers with, the man whose reassuring presence had been a constant in her life.

"Y-yes, Declan," she stuttered, her eyes wide as she met his gaze, her heart pounding. "You were my husband. We were... we were parents."
Declan's face paled, his eyes widening in shock. For a moment, he was silent, processing the information.
Her words, "our child", echoed in the silence. They were a painful reminder of the love she felt for him in the simulation, a love that had been overshadowed by her love for their child. It was a love she had forgotten until now, pushed aside in the face of the agony of losing their child.
There was another beat of silence as Declan struggled to comprehend the gravity of what Maddy had experienced. He had lost a child he had never met, and a wife he had never known he had. And Maddy... she had lost an entire life. A life she cherished, and a life that was now nothing more than a fading memory of a simulation.

As the silence stretched on, Claire finally erupted. Her voice was a mixture of frustration and confusion. "What the hell are you trying to tell me? Can someone please explain how this is possible?" She stood up, pacing the room, her hands running through her hair. "Maddy wasn't even connected to the computer, so did she hallucinate the whole thing or was it a virtual reality simulation that played out just for her?"
She turned to face them, her eyes wide with confusion and fear. "What the hell did she see? Did she live a past life, a simulated one? Or an alternate reality of some sort?"
Maddy glanced at Declan, her eyes reflecting her own bewilderment. Despite having lived it, she lacked answers. She didn't understand how or why it had happened, but the experience had felt painfully, devastatingly real.
Declan looked equally lost. He had not created the system and had no idea of its possibilities and limitations. This was beyond anything he had ever anticipated. "I... I don't know, Claire," he admitted, his voice hoarse. "I don't understand it either."

Claire let out a frustrated sigh, her gaze falling on Maddy. The pain and confusion in her eyes were palpable. "We need to figure out what happened, Maddy," she said softly. "We need to understand why you experienced what you did."
"I know," Maddy responded, her voice barely a whisper. "I need to understand, too."

Maddy's forehead creased in confusion as a perplexing thought surfaced. "How could the people of the past ever give up something as precious as family and the ability to have children? Who would willingly give that up?" she asked, her voice choked with emotion. "And how are we okay with it now?"
Claire halted her pacing, turned to look at Maddy, and had a pained look on her face, a mixture of sympathy and understanding. "We don't know any better, Maddy," she answered, her voice soft. "I mean, do you know any mothers? When was the last time a real birth took place?"
Her question hung in the air, a stark reminder of the world they lived in now. A world devoid of the joys and challenges of parenthood, of the intimate bond between a mother and her child. A world where birth was a concept read about in books, seen in old movies, and heard about in stories from the past. However, they never truly understood the concept. They thought it was a freedom, a human right to be equal, that motherhood was nothing more than a social construct created through biological differences designed to maintain a divide between the sexes. But what did it all mean? What was the purpose of the vision?
Maddy was silent, her mind grappling with the profound implications of Claire's words. In her heart, she knew Claire was right. They were a generation that had been raised without the experience of motherhood, without the concept of childbirth as a reality. Yet, the ache she felt for the child she had lost in the simulation was raw and real, a testament to a love and loss she had never thought possible.

"Even if we don't know any better," Maddy murmured after a moment, "I can't help but feel... we've lost something invaluable."
As they sat there in silence, they were acutely aware that their world was irrevocably changed. They had been confronted with a glimpse of a life, a joy, a sorrow they had never known, and they were left grappling with the enormity of what it meant.

As the silence hung heavily in the room, Declan suddenly stood up with determination etched onto his face.
"I'm going in next," he declared, his voice resolute. "I need to see this... to understand it firsthand."
Claire and Maddy looked at him, surprise evident on their faces.
"But Declan," Claire began, her voice trembling with apprehension. "We don't know if..."
He cut her off, raising a hand. "I need the implant that Maddy has," he said, looking at Maddy. "I need to experience this simulation and see what it's all about."
His declaration hung in the air, a testament to his resolution. It was a step into the unknown, but he felt compelled to do it. He wanted to understand Maddy's experience and grapple with the strange reality she had encountered, whether out of scientific curiosity or emotional need. He wasn't sure which, but he knew he had to do it. And nothing was going to hold him back.

Claire took a deep breath, attempting to regain her composure. She shook her head. "We're losing focus here. We're here to understand and solve the puzzle of the genome sequence in the Ectogenesis process. That's the mission."
She looked determinedly at both Maddy and Declan. "The human race has relied on artificial womb technology for decades now. Our purpose is to advance and optimize that technology by fixing this current error. This alternate reality, this simulated life... it's not why we're here."
Her words echoed in the silent lab, reminding them of their original purpose. The human race has forgotten what it was like

to birth children and have families in the traditional sense. They were here to evolve and adapt, but their focus had shifted to a past they didn't understand, filled with emotions they couldn't comprehend.
"We need to remember our purpose," Claire concluded, her voice steady despite the turmoil she felt inside. "We can't let this unexpected development distract us from our main objective. It's too important."

"But Claire," Declan interrupted, his face filled with determination, "We must consider the implications of this. Why is the Mycelium Computer creating genome sequences of extinct animals? Why did it give Maddy an experience of a bygone era we're trying to understand?"
He gestured towards the computer. "It's not a coincidence. We're here searching for the original human genome sequence to fix the cellular decay we're seeing in the artificial wombs. And then, this system starts producing genome sequences of creatures long dead... Can't you see the connection?"
His eyes were filled with a spark of excitement, a passion that seemed out of place in the sterile lab environment. "We need to chase down this lead, Claire. We don't know where it will take us, but it might lead us to what we've been looking for all along."
His conviction was infectious, and for a moment, even Claire was taken aback. Perhaps there was more to the system than they had initially thought. Perhaps it was the key to understanding not only the past but also the future of human reproduction.

After a long, contemplative silence, Claire sighed. The resigned look on her face was a clear indication of her capitulation.
"Alright, Declan," she said, relenting. "You can attempt it. But we need to be careful. We don't know what this thing is capable of, and I'm not willing to risk another situation like Maddy's."
She started pacing around the room, thinking aloud. "We'll need to monitor your vitals the entire time – heart rate, brain activity,

everything. If there are any signs of distress or if anything goes wrong, we'll pull you out immediately."
Declan nodded, relief spreading across his face. But Claire wasn't done.
"And one more thing, Declan," she added, her gaze as serious as ever. "We don't know if this experience can be controlled or guided in any way. You may end up anywhere, experiencing anything. You have to be prepared for that. Are you sure you want to go through with this?"
Declan took a deep breath, locking eyes with Claire. "Yes," he said resolutely. "I'm sure."
Claire nodded, accepting his decision. But as she looked back at Maddy, still lost in her own world of simulated memories, she couldn't help but feel a twinge of apprehension. They were about to step into unknown territory, and she could only hope that they were prepared for whatever lay ahead.

Maddy sat in the corner of the room, barely whispering to herself, "18 years in mere seconds...". Her words were not intended for the others, but were instead a desperate mantra - a plea for understanding from a world that had taken an entire lifetime away from her in an instant.
"It'll be over before we even know if anything's wrong," she added, her voice growing slightly louder. This was a stark observation, a chilling reminder of the danger that Declan was about to subject himself to.
Maddy wanted to say more - to scream about the reality she had experienced and the devastation she felt. She wanted to rage against a society that had taken away women's ability to bear children; denying them a bond she had now experienced and lost. But she held her tongue, biting down on her lip to suppress the storm inside her. She needed Declan to go through the simulation to validate her experiences and feelings. Her own profound sense of loss was disquieting, an undercurrent of grief that seemed to permeate every part of her existence. Every breath

she took, every beat of her heart, echoed with the memory of the life she had lived and lost.
Despite the turmoil within her, Maddy was also filled with a strange sense of anticipation. If Declan could connect with the simulation the way she had, he would be able to verify her experience. And maybe, just maybe, he could help make sense of the bewildering complexity and profound implications of what she had gone through. So, Maddy remained silent, watching with a mixture of fear, hope, and desperation as Declan prepared to follow in her footsteps and step into the unknown. Her true hope she dared not speak aloud, nor think about in any manner in fear of the consequences of them not coming to fruition.

As she watched Declan, Maddy's thoughts drifted back to a conversation she had had over a year ago with Claire. She had suggested, rather half-heartedly, that if they couldn't fix the genome sequence issue, perhaps the population would need to revert to natural births.
Now, sitting in the aftermath of her own simulated experience of childbirth and motherhood, Maddy wondered if the computer had somehow picked up on that conversation. Had it intentionally made her witness the beauty of natural birth, the joy of motherhood, and the growth of a child?
"Claire," she started, her voice low and thoughtful, "Do you think it's just a coincidence that I suggested we might need to go back to natural births a year ago, and then the computer... it showed me exactly that?"
Claire paused, considering Maddy's words. The likelihood of it being a mere coincidence seemed increasingly slim, but she also knew they were dealing with unknown variables. "I don't know, Maddy," she admitted, her voice tinged with uncertainty. "But it's definitely worth considering. My only reassuring thought is that we hadn't even begun to build it yet when that conversation took place."

Chapter 10

Of Digital Chains and Human Bonds

Declan had only been part of the lab for a week, yet it felt like he had been there for much longer. The intense events of the week had accelerated their camaraderie, but they had also left everyone worried and tense, especially after Maddy's experience with the AR chip connection.

Despite the anxiety, Declan had become obsessed with Maddy's groundbreaking attempt to tap directly into the Mycelium computer. He was intrigued by the potential revelations it held and the thought of experiencing the simulation or discovering whatever cryptic visual pattern was hidden within the code was tantalizing. He believed it could be the key to unlocking the answers they sought.

This obsession led him to consider implanting a similar AR chip into his own neural cortex. The risks were substantial, but the potential reward was equally immense. The chance to uncover the secrets of the Ectogenesis program and solve the impending societal crisis was compelling.

Although his colleagues, especially Claire, were understandably worried, Declan's resolve was solidifying. He felt a responsibility to pursue this avenue, not just for the team, but for the fate of their society as well. He only hoped that his determination would lead to breakthroughs and not catastrophe.

As the sun began to set, casting long shadows throughout the lab, Declan and Claire exchanged a concerned glance. They had noticed Maddy's silent demeanor, her frequent drifts into a world of her own, and the constant flicker of pain in her eyes.
"We need to get her out of here," Declan muttered, his gaze fixed on Maddy, who was staring blankly at a screen displaying genetic sequences.
"I agree," Claire said, nodding. "She can't be alone tonight."
Summoning their courage, they approached Maddy. "Hey Maddy," Declan began, trying to keep his voice light, "we were thinking of grabbing dinner. Would you like to join us?"
Maddy turned to look at him, her eyes distant. "I... I don't know, Declan."
Claire stepped forward, placing a comforting hand on Maddy's arm. "We understand, Maddy. But sitting here alone won't do you any good. And we promise to talk about something other than work."
There was a long pause as Maddy considered their offer. The thought of being alone with her thoughts was daunting, yet the idea of pretending everything was normal seemed equally challenging. But as she looked at Declan and Claire, their concern and sincerity were undeniable.
"Okay," she finally agreed, offering them a faint smile. "I think... I think I would like that."
And with that, the three of them powered off their computers, leaving the mysteries of the lab behind, if only for an evening. They set out into the twilight, a comforting silence enveloping them, a tacit agreement that tonight was about friendship and support, a brief respite from the complicated world of their work.

Navigating through the maze of streets in the city, they reached a charming restaurant nestled near the water's edge. It wasn't fancy, but it wasn't cheap either. The soft lull of the waves added to the ambience, lending the space a calming atmosphere. Inside, low-hanging lights cast a warm glow on tables strewn with half-filled

glasses and plates of food, while the air hummed with conversation.
They were seated at a table with a view of the water. The waiter quickly arrived, holding a chip reader in hand. Claire and Declan placed their orders first - a glass of red wine for Claire and a pint of beer for Declan. The waiter placed the reader near their wrists, and a soft ping sounded for each, indicating their payment was accepted.
Then it was Maddy's turn. She requested a glass of white wine, extending her wrist to the waiter. But instead of the expected ping, a loud beep echoed through the restaurant, and a robotic voice declared, "Weekly alcohol allowance exceeded. Order denied."
For a moment, silence hung heavily over the table. Maddy looked at the waiter, a blush creeping up her cheeks, before dropping her gaze. Claire and Declan exchanged a glance, unsure of how to react to this unexpected development. The waiter, clearly uncomfortable, quickly mumbled an apology before moving away to fetch their drinks.
The digital rules that governed their society had intruded on their evening, reminding them that even here, in this seemingly tranquil setting, they could not escape the watchful eyes of the system.

The Central Bank's Digital Currency (CBDC) had become an integral part of society, not only as a form of transaction but also as a watchful overseer. Linked directly to an individual's personal identity, the CBDC monitored a broad range of activities and behaviors to ensure that each citizen is doing their part for society and the environment.
Every individual is embedded with a unique chip that tracks their consumption habits in real-time. From their alcohol intake to their meat consumption, everything is monitored. If you consume too much alcohol in a week, as Maddy found out at the restaurant, your next order will be automatically denied. The goal

is to encourage healthy lifestyle choices, thereby reducing the strain on the healthcare system. By nudging individuals toward moderation, the CBDC is able to maintain healthcare costs and overall public health.

Furthermore, the CBDC is designed to aid in the ongoing fight against climate change. Each citizen's carbon footprint is also tracked via their consumption habits. Every purchase or activity that contributes to greenhouse gas emissions is recorded and counted against a citizen's personal carbon quota.

High-emission activities such as meat consumption or excessive energy use are regulated through this system. Exceeding your carbon quota will result in penalties or restrictions on certain high-carbon activities. On the other hand, engaging in eco-friendly practices can earn citizens additional carbon credits. The goal is to encourage sustainable living and curb the growing threat of climate change.

While the system is generally accepted as necessary, it also sparks debates on privacy and individual freedoms. However, the argument that prevails is the need for collective responsibility in the face of shared global challenges. The CBDC system is a reminder of the interconnectedness of modern society, and the role that each individual plays in shaping the health of our world.

Maddy's cheeks flushed deeper, a stark contrast to her pale complexion. The weight of all the eyes in the restaurant was too much for her to bear. She looked down, swallowing a lump in her throat. The incident had cracked her veneer, allowing the heartache she'd been holding back to seep through.

Suddenly, she stood up, pushing her chair back. Her eyes, filled with unshed tears, flashed defiantly at her friends for a moment before she turned and strode towards the entrance. The only sounds in the restaurant were the clicking of her heels against the floor and her muffled sobs.

Before Claire or Declan could react, Maddy was out the door, her figure disappearing into the night. The sound of the door slamming shut was drowned out by the harsh sound of her sobs

that lingered in the air, a haunting reminder of the pain she was enduring.
Claire and Declan were left in stunned silence, their concerned gazes fixed on the now vacant spot where Maddy had been sitting just moments before. The night had taken an unexpected turn, and they were left to grapple with the aftermath.

Claire and Declan hastily gathered their things and left the restaurant. They searched the nearby streets until they found Maddy huddled against a wall, her body wracked with quiet sobs. Gently coaxing her to her feet, Claire put her arm around Maddy's shoulder while Declan held her hand, offering a comforting presence. Claire suggested they go to a different place, somewhere off the beaten path where they wouldn't be disturbed.
"The Last Liberal," Claire named the place, her tone reassuring. "I know the owner; I am fairly certain she can get us that wine."
The bar was said to be the oldest in the city, and it looked the part.
Nestled in a corner of the city, The Last Liberal stood as a relic of a bygone era. Its exterior was weathered, with aged brickwork tinted by the many years it had witnessed. The fading paint hinted at its once-vibrant history, a subtle nod to the countless stories held within its walls.
Upon entering, the first thing that struck the senses was the scent of antiquity. It was a comforting blend of aged wood and time-honored memories, a smell that permeated every corner of the atmosphere. It served as a testament to the bar's longevity and resistance to the ever-changing world outside.
The bar itself was a wide expanse of dark, polished wood, with a rich mahogany hue. Its surface was smooth to the touch, save for the occasional nick and scratch, each a silent witness to the lively conversations, heartfelt confessions, and clinking glasses of patrons past.
Above the bar, a collection of vintage pictures, newspaper clippings, and memorabilia adorned the wall, each item a piece of

the bar's history. The dimmed, warm light from the overhead lamps cast a cozy glow, further enhancing the vintage ambiance. The seats were a variety of mismatched stools and chairs, each unique like the patrons they served. In the far corner, a jukebox with a shiny chrome exterior played a medley of classic hits, adding to the nostalgic atmosphere.
Patrons ranged from regulars to newcomers, finding comfort in the familiarity of the old pub. Despite the passage of time, The Last Liberal retained its old-world charm, standing as a symbol of nostalgia and history amidst the city's modern facade.
Claire's old-time friend Jamie, the owner, greeted them warmly and quickly ushered them to a quiet corner while scolding Claire that it had been way too long since they had seen one another. Claire pulled Jamie aside and told her of the situation with the wine, asking if she could purchase it on her account. Her status in the government had an unlimited alcohol allowance but buying for others was strictly forbidden. Soon, Maddy had a glass of wine in her hand, and the previous incident was forgotten for the moment. The night was far from over, and they hoped that in the comforting presence of each other, they could help Maddy navigate through the turmoil she was going through.

Under the dimmed lights of The Last Liberal, the trio let go of their worries for a few hours. Work and the haunting simulation were purposefully left out of their conversations. Instead, they filled the night with light-hearted banter and shared memories, laughter spilling from their lips.
Declan turned out to be a natural at telling jokes, his quirky sense of humor bringing about roaring laughter. Claire recounted tales from their shared past, stories filled with mischief and fun that sent them into fits of giggles. Maddy found herself opening up, and her laughter was a welcome break from the heaviness she had been carrying.

Declan's gaze shifted upward, falling upon an old wooden beam that spanned the length of the ceiling. It was layered with several coats of faded paint, each a testament to the passing years. But there, etched deep into the wood, was a carving that had withstood the test of time.

"Sam and Adrienne," Declan read aloud, tracing the letters with his eyes. "May they live forever in our hearts."

Despite the numerous layers of paint, the inscription stood out starkly against the worn wood. It seemed to radiate warmth, a trace of the love and fondness with which it was originally carved.

His companions looked up, following his gaze. Their eyes landed on the same carving, and for a moment, they were silent, each lost in their own thoughts. It was a solemn reminder of lives lived and lost, and the legacy they left behind.

The inscription seemed to fit seamlessly into the ambiance of the bar, a testament to the people who had passed through its doors, loved and lost, laughed and cried, and left a piece of their story behind.

As the evening wore on, the carving became a silent participant in their conversations and laughter, an unspoken reminder of the beauty and fragility of life. And while they knew nothing about Sam and Adrienne, their inscription served as a poignant reminder that their memory, like Maddy's experience, lived on, carved deep into the heart of The Last Liberal.

Every now and then, Declan or Claire would raise a toast, their glasses clinking in a symphony of shared camaraderie and unspoken support. The night flowed on, with each moment easing away some of Maddy's sorrow. By the time they said their goodbyes and stepped out into the cool night air, Maddy felt a bit lighter. Her heart was warmed by the presence of her friends. The simulation and its implications would be there to tackle another day, but for now, they had each other, and that was enough.

Agent Reynolds sat at his cluttered desk, illuminated by the dim light of early morning. His thoughts were a jumbled mess, each one more perplexing than the last. The trio he had been tailing - Claire, Maddy, and Declan - had thrown him for a loop. Reynolds had followed them to The Last Liberal, a peaceful establishment known for its variety of beverages. That's where Jamie had come into the picture, the cheerful owner with her disarming smile. But what followed left Reynolds pondering the intricacies of the situation.

Jamie had clearly broken the law by providing Claire with extra alcohol for Maddy, which Reynolds couldn't overlook. The alcohol was a breach of the controlled substances act, something society did not look favorably upon. But Claire's role in the QRDA added a layer of complexity. She was involved in a crucial project, and charging her could have disastrous ripple effects. Additionally, the trio's behavior was peculiar. Their hushed conversations and furtive glances were suspicious. Reynolds was sure they were up to something but couldn't put his finger on it. Feeling the weight of the situation, Reynolds rubbed his eyes with a sigh. He knew his duty was to uphold the law, no matter who broke it. But in this case, doing so could lead to unforeseen complications. He was stuck, unsure of how to proceed.

As the dawn broke, Reynolds made a decision. He would continue to watch them, gather more information. It was a risk, but he had to know what they were up to. He had to make the right call, not just for them but for the security of the nation. The weight of his responsibilities, coupled with the mystery, hung heavy. He decided to log the night's events, making a mental note to keep a closer eye on the trio. The connections between them, the mysterious lab, the society-ending warning, and now a minor infraction of the law were all too coincidental to ignore.

But what really intrigued him was something deeper, something he sensed in their interactions and the words they spoke. A shared understanding, a passion for their work, a drive to uncover the truth. He felt it in the way they supported each other, the glances, the camaraderie. It was something he hadn't experienced in years. Something human.

Shaking his thoughts, he powered off his terminal. He knew that duty had to come first, but he couldn't shake the feeling that he was becoming a part of their story, a shadow on the wall, echoing the past.

With that, he picked up his jacket and stepped into the rising sun, ready for another day of shadowing and speculation.

Chapter 11

Beneath the Mycelium Mantle

Maddy woke up the next morning unsure of what to do. It was Saturday, her day off, and the routine of work had helped her keep her sanity. Without it, Maddy found herself unable to shake off the tormenting memories that haunted her. The Mycelium computer was silent now, but the echoes of its visual codes still swirled in her mind, coupled with the pain of losing a child she had loved before it even existed. And to top it all off, the unspoken love for Declan, a feeling formed in the simulation, a feeling she kept hidden away, was tearing her apart.

When the weekend arrived, Maddy tried to drown her sorrows in the age-old method of the broken-hearted and the distressed. She resorted to alcohol, shamelessly borrowing every bottle of wine her neighbors had to spare. She claimed it was all part of an experiment, a cover that her employment at the Quantum Research and Development Agency (QRDA) easily backed.

Her neighbors, knowing her work, didn't question her unusual request. The inhabitants of the tight-knit community often saw QRDA employees involved in strange activities and had learned to accept their quirks without much ado. To them, Maddy's requisition of their wine collections was just another peculiarity of working with quantum technologies.

In the sanctuary of her home, Maddy poured herself the first of many glasses, the ruby red wine swirling ominously. With each sip, she hoped to wash away the heartache and the tormenting memories. But the loss of the unborn child, the unrequited love for Declan, and the uncertainties surrounding their project were not easily forgotten. Each sip only reminded her of her loneliness and despair.

Her heart ached, and her mind swam in the whirlpool of emotions. She wanted to forget, to erase the painful memories. But with each empty bottle, it became clear to Maddy that she couldn't drink away the pain. This wasn't a problem alcohol could solve. As the weekend drew to a close, Maddy realized she would have to face her demons head-on, as there was no escaping from them.

Amidst the storm of emotions, Maddy found solace in a faint ray of hope centered around Declan. She clung to the possibility that he might experience the Mycelium computer's visual code for himself, forging an intimate bond between them. This shared understanding of the otherworldly experience was a connection Maddy longed for. It wasn't just about exploration and discovery, but about being understood on a profound level that transcended the normal bounds of human connection. The prospect of Declan walking her path, understanding her journey, and feeling the same way she did gave Maddy a strange sense of hope. Even though he was unaware of her feelings, the idea of a shared experience gave her something to hold onto and look forward to. It was a beacon of hope in her dark world, a thread of connection she yearned for more than anything else. As she gazed into the empty wine bottle lost in her thoughts, Maddy silently wished for Declan to join her on this journey. With this newfound hope flickering in her heart, Maddy found the strength to face another day and continue her complicated web of love, loss, and discovery.

In the sober light of day, Maddy found herself more determined than ever to make her hopes a reality. She knew she had to get

Dr. Peterson to approve the augmented reality chip for Declan. Not only would it aid their research, but it would also bring her one step closer to her desired connection with Declan. Maddy began outlining a plan, considering every detail that could tip the balance in their favor. The first and most critical point was the scientific relevance of the chip implantation. Declan's connection to the Quantum computer would undoubtedly open up new avenues for their research and potentially provide vital insights into solving the Ectogenesis issue. She decided to compile all the data they had so far, emphasizing the unique visual patterns they had discovered in the code. She would highlight how conventional data analysis methods fell short and the need for a direct neural interface to understand these patterns. Furthermore, she planned to discuss the increased efficiency and speed the chip would bring to their work. A direct interface with the Mycelium computer would significantly reduce the time needed to interpret its output, a crucial factor given their ticking timeline. Lastly, she would need to reassure Dr. Peterson about the safety of the procedure. To this end, she planned to gather as much information as possible about the process and its risks. Providing this along with a thorough risk mitigation plan would show that they had considered the potential dangers and had measures in place to handle them. With her plan in place, Maddy felt a surge of hope. It was a long shot, but she had to try. She needed to convince Dr. Peterson, not just for the sake of their research, but for her unspoken connection with Declan. It was a gamble, but one she was willing to take.

Maddy's heart sank as she suddenly remembered the one minor flaw in her plan: Dr. Peterson still didn't know about the Mycelium Quantum Computer. Revealing it now could backfire and potentially put their entire project, and the chip implantation, at risk. Unlike a traditional computer, the Mycelium Quantum Computer didn't have the familiar series of hard drives, wires, and fans. Instead, its interior was a series of intricately layered mycelium strata, forming a vast network of interconnecting nodes and filaments that resembled biology more than technology. The nodes, small spherical constructs, pulsed with a faint, eerie light, the quantum particles within each node dancing in an orchestrated cacophony. Microscopic filaments, reminiscent of the fungal roots from which the computer got its name, connected these nodes. The filaments facilitated communication across the system, transmitting quantum states instantaneously across vast arrays of nodes. The complexity and unusual aesthetics of the Mycelium Quantum Computer made it a sight to behold. It was an amalgamation of biology and quantum physics, an ode to the magic of mycelium and the power of quantum mechanics. The exterior, however, was deceptively mundane. A simple, sleek black box though quite large and not easily moved was devoid of any markings, it could easily be mistaken for a regular server tower or two. This inconspicuous look had made it easier for them to keep it hidden from Dr. Peterson. Maddy sighed, absently tracing the edge of her kitchen table with her fingers. She'd have to carefully navigate this revelation. The Mycelium Quantum Computer was their secret weapon, the ace up their sleeve. She couldn't afford to play this card wrong. But then, how would they get Declan the chip?

As the weekend rolled in, Declan found himself unable to detach from the events at the lab. He spent most of his time at his small apartment, gazing at the cityscape outside, his mind stuck on the Mycelium Quantum Computer and the mysterious pattern. He couldn't shake off the urgency that pricked at the back of his mind. He needed to experience what Maddy had experienced. He needed to understand the strange visual code, to unravel its secrets, to solve the problem threatening their society. It felt almost like a primal instinct, something encoded deep within him that he couldn't ignore. As the day turned into night, he found himself pacing his apartment, his mind turning over the problem of the AR chip implantation. He didn't have a concrete plan yet. Approaching Dr. Peterson seemed risky, especially with the secrecy surrounding the Mycelium Quantum Computer. He knew they had been pushing the boundaries already with their project, and he wasn't sure how much further Dr. Peterson was willing to go if they filled him in on what was going on. What if he just did it? What if he found a way to get the AR chip without involving Dr. Peterson? The thought was tempting, but he knew the risks. An unauthorized procedure could lead to complications, and if it were discovered, they could all be in jeopardy. Declan sighed, running a hand through his hair. He wished Maddy had been more detailed about her experience, but he understood why she hadn't. It was something beyond words, something that needed to be experienced firsthand. Looking out his window at the darkening city, he felt a quiet determination settle in him. He didn't know how yet, but he would find a way to get the chip. He had to. The future of their project, and possibly their society, could depend on it.

Claire spent the weekend reflecting on the past week's events in the peaceful solitude of her apartment. She held a hard piece of protective plastic in her hand, which felt almost weightless, but the implications it held were significant. Inside, the tiny AR chip glinted in the soft light. Claire had received the chip at the same time as Maddy, approved for the same experimental procedure. However, she had decided not to proceed with it because the idea of having something foreign embedded in her brain was too daunting. She kept the chip as a reminder of her choice not to take that path. But after seeing Maddy's experience and hearing Declan's determination, Claire found herself reconsidering. Not for herself, as she still wasn't ready to take that step, but for Declan. He had a point: they needed to understand more about what was happening. Could she find a way to give him the chip? As she turned the plastic over in her hand, contemplating the possibilities, she realized she wasn't a surgeon and didn't know how to implant it. There would be risks, complications, and possibly legal consequences. Was it worth it? Yet, the urgency in Declan's voice echoed in her mind. His drive and commitment were infectious. If he thought it would help their cause and was willing to take that risk, who was she to stand in his way? With a deep breath, Claire made up her mind. She would talk to Declan and offer him the chip. It would be his choice to make. As she prepared herself for a conversation she never thought she would have, Claire had no idea that Declan was grappling with a similar decision on the other side of the city. Their paths were converging towards a shared destiny, and the consequences of their choices were yet to unfold. Only time would tell the true impact of their decisions.

As the morning progressed, Agent Reynolds followed Maddy through the maze of residential buildings. From a distance, he watched as she knocked on door after door, cheerfully engaging her neighbors in conversation. It didn't take long for him to notice a pattern: she was borrowing copious amounts of alcohol from each of them. As he watched her return to her apartment, arms laden with wine bottles, Reynolds furrowed his brow. If it was a drinking problem, it was certainly an extreme one. But somehow, it didn't add up. He'd tailed people with substance abuse issues before, and Maddy didn't exhibit the typical signs. It was obvious she was upset, as her friends seemed to be trying to cheer her up. If this was a drinking problem, it was a fresh one. However, he decided to make a note of it. The QRDA had strict policies about substance abuse, and the threat of re-education due to excessive alcohol consumption was a real one. He could potentially leverage this information to pressure Maddy into revealing their secrets. After ensuring Maddy was settled in her apartment, Reynolds retreated to a nearby cafe to ponder his next move. He couldn't jump the gun - he needed to be certain before he confronted Maddy. Perhaps a couple more days of surveillance would provide the clarity he sought. As he gazed back towards Maddy's apartment complex, a faint sense of anticipation settled within him. He couldn't shake the feeling that he was on the brink of uncovering something significant. If he played his cards right, he could finally unveil the trio's secrets. It was a tantalizing prospect, one that he was willing to bide his time for.

Chapter 12

A Gamble with the Quantum Quandary

Monday morning marked the dawn of a new beginning, washing away the uncertainty and desperation of the weekend. Claire had barely slept, wrestling with her decision. Now, with the certainty of her choice before her, she felt a renewed vigor coursing through her veins. She had made her decision, and it was time to set things into motion.

With a determined hand, she picked up her communicator and immediately dialed Maddy and Declan. Their faces appeared on the screen; worry etched on their features. The events of the previous week had worn them down, replacing their usual optimism with an air of grim determination.

"Hi, guys," she began, her tone betraying her excitement. "I need you both to come to the lab ASAP. I have something important to discuss. It's about the AR chip we are looking for."

Silence stretched between them. Claire watched as realization dawned on their faces. She saw Declan's eyes widen, his eyebrows shooting up in surprise. Maddy, on the other hand, looked guarded but hopeful.

Claire explained how she came to have the chip but was always hesitant to have it installed, she kept it knowing its worth; always with a maybe one day I will do it attitude.

"Claire, are you sure...?" Maddy began, her voice trailing off.

"I've made up my mind, Maddy. I do not want to do it myself, but I believe in our cause. Declan, if you're willing to take that risk, then I'm offering you the chip."
Declan stared at her, momentarily stunned. A flurry of emotions passed over his face before it settled into a determined expression.
"I appreciate it, Claire. It's a risk, I know, but if this can help us understand the Mycelium Quantum Computer, it's a risk I'm willing to take," he affirmed, his voice steady.
An hour later, they found themselves in the Lab at QRDA headquarters, a heavy silence falling over them. In front of them lay the small AR chip, insignificant in appearance but holding the potential to alter their lives in ways they couldn't yet fully comprehend. As they stared at it, they felt a shared understanding. This was more than just a chip; it was a testament to their unity, their determination, and their unwavering belief in their mission.
With a deep breath, Claire handed the chip to Declan. As his fingers wrapped around the protective plastic, he felt a strange sense of connection, a new bond forming among them. He looked at Claire and Maddy, gratitude filling his heart.
"I won't let you down," he vowed, a quiet determination in his voice.
As he pocketed the AR chip, he felt a surge of anticipation. This was a new chapter in their quest, a path fraught with uncertainties and dangers, but one they were willing to tread. Little did they know that this decision was just the beginning of a journey that would push them beyond the boundaries of what they thought possible, testing their courage, their friendships, and their resolve. Only time would tell what the future held for them.

"Now, how do we get it installed?" questioned Declan.
"That's the easy part!" replied Claire.
"I booked myself for the procedure this afternoon, so we'll swap out," Claire explained, her nervousness fading. "It's all automated. A machine does the implantation. They just require another

person there as a precaution, to confirm identity and assist in case of side effects."
Declan looked at her, surprise etched on his face. "You planned this out so quickly?"
Claire shrugged, a small smile playing on her lips. "Someone had to take the initiative."
There was a hint of admiration in Maddy's eyes as she looked at Claire. "You've really thought this through. What about the risk of getting caught?"
"We'll have to be careful, but the risk is worth taking," Claire replied. "The clinic doesn't know the specific details of our project, only that we're authorized for AR chip implantation. I'll provide the chip and the QRDA authorization. They won't have a reason to question it."
Declan ran a hand through his hair, taking a moment to digest the information. "Alright. What's the next step?"
"We head to the clinic upstairs," Claire said, her gaze steady. "I'll do the check-in procedure, and then you take my place. Maddy, you'll need to be there as the assisting person."
"And what do we tell them when they ask why I'm the one getting the chip instead of you?" Declan asked.
Claire looked at him, her gaze unwavering. "We tell them the truth, or at least a version of it. We say there's been a change in our research direction, and you need the chip more urgently than I do."
Declan nodded, appreciating the simplicity of the plan. It was bold, risky, but it just might work.
As they made preparations for the upcoming procedure, an unspoken understanding passed between the three. This was a critical step in their project, one that could significantly accelerate their understanding of the Mycelium Quantum Computer and its mysterious codes.

In the end, it all boiled down to their shared commitment to their cause. Their determination to make a difference, to push the boundaries of their research, and perhaps find a solution to the

Ectogenesis issue. The AR chip was just the means to that end, a small but significant stepping stone in their journey towards discovery.
In the quiet of the lab, as they finalized their plans, they couldn't help but feel a sense of anticipation, a quiet thrill at what the future held for them. The path ahead was fraught with uncertainty, but it was a path they were willing to tread. Together.

Despite their earlier reservations, the trip to the clinic upstairs went smoothly. Claire, Maddy, and Declan moved in sync, guided by an unspoken choreography. The clinic was a bright space filled with cutting-edge technology and run by expert professionals. It hummed with a steady rhythm of focused activity.
Claire approached the reception desk first, displaying her QRDA badge with the title "Chief Genetic Engineer" prominently. This silenced any potential objections before they could arise. As she presented the AR chip and her authorization, she felt a mix of relief and apprehension.
"We're here for the AR chip implantation procedure," she announced, her voice steady. "There's been a slight change in plans. Declan will be receiving the implantation instead of me. Maddy will assist him for the rest of the day making sure there are no side effects."
The receptionist, a woman with a friendly face framed by a halo of curls, looked from Claire to Declan, arching her eyebrows slightly. "Any particular reason for the change?" she asked, her fingers hovering over the keys of her keyboard.
Claire met her gaze without flinching. "Our research direction has changed. Declan now needs the chip more urgently than I do."
After a brief pause, the woman nodded, updated the information, and smiled. "Alright, you can proceed to the implantation suite when you're ready."
Claire breathed a slight sigh of relief as they made their way towards the implantation suite. She watched as Declan glanced back at her, a newfound resolve glinting in his eyes. She gave him an encouraging nod, and Maddy followed suit.

The procedure was swift and efficient, a marvel of medical technology. Maddy stood by Declan's side, tracking every movement of the machine. A mixture of fear and excitement coursed through her veins, matching the undercurrent of anticipation that filled the room.

Within the hour, the procedure was complete. Declan sat up slowly, a hand instinctively reaching to touch the back of his neck where the chip now resided. He felt oddly the same, yet a significant change had just occurred. He looked towards Claire and Maddy, a grin of accomplishment on his face.

"Guess I'm officially upgraded now," he joked, his voice slightly hoarse. There was a spark in his eyes, one that radiated determination and resilience.

Claire and Maddy shared a relieved smile. "This is just the first step of many," Claire affirmed confidently. They were one step closer to understanding the Mycelium Quantum Computer and perhaps finding a solution to the Ectogenesis issue. Their journey had truly begun, and a long road lay ahead.

Agent Reynolds was comfortably ensconced at his desk within the Ministry of Security and Intelligence headquarters, meticulously immersed in the ever-unfolding tapestry of data that ebbed and flowed across his dual holographic screens. The buzz of his phone drew him away from his work momentarily. He picked up the sleek device, an arched eyebrow accompanying the downward pull of his lips as he deciphered the notification that danced on the vibrant display.

The alert originated from the surgical clinic at the Quantum Research and Development Agency, disclosing a last-minute alteration to an Augmented Reality chip implantation procedure. Surprisingly, the modification showed Declan Sutton replacing Claire Cairns as the subject, with Maddy identified as his emergency contact.

In today's relentless surveillance state, tracking the movements and actions of virtually anyone, with impeccable accuracy, was a task requiring minimal effort from law enforcement officers. Digital footprints left by individuals were captured and stored in vast, ever-learning AI systems, refining and honing their predictive algorithms.

Each individual's activities, preferences, and interactions, no matter how trivial, were logged and scrutinized, feeding an almost omniscient intelligence network. Privacy was a quaint notion relegated to the annals of history, a concept as alien to the current generation as the first wheel must have been to the dinosaurs.

It was the meticulously catalogued data from such systems that had initially flagged the AR chip procedure to Agent Reynolds, who had requested all information be directed to him that involved anything to do with the three scientists. The sudden change to the operation's details, especially the shift in personnel, warranted immediate investigation. As he delved into this anomaly, he realized that in this era of omnipresent surveillance, no stone was left unturned, and no change, however minuscule, could escape the watchful gaze of the Ministry of Security and Intelligence.

Reynolds studied the notification again, suspicion creeping into his thoughts. Why had the procedure been switched to Declan at the last minute? He considered the possibilities, a sense of unease setting in. The change could be a legitimate decision driven by the needs of their current project, which he still did not have authorization to view, or it could be something more. He would need to speak to Minister Martinez about it, as how could he determine what was suspicious if he did not know the parameters of their work? For all he knew, this change could be completely normal.

Grabbing his jacket from the back of his chair, Agent Reynolds decided to pay the clinic a visit. Perhaps it was nothing, but his instincts told him that he needed to dig deeper. His role was to maintain the security of the nation and prevent this so-called society-ending event they had been warned of by an Artificial Intelligence that had been wrong more than once he was told. If

that wasn't the case, he imagined there would be a lot more agents placed on this case. If something was going on with the AR chip implantation, he wanted to know, no matter how small a deviation from the norm it was he would look into it.
As he made his way to the QRDA, his mind raced with possible scenarios. What he would discover at the clinic was yet to be seen, but Agent Reynolds was prepared to confront whatever was coming.

Chapter 13

Quantum Echoes: An Odyssey through Primal Seas and Starlit Skies

Upon returning to the lab, Declan felt a bit disoriented, a possible side effect from the AR chip implantation procedure. He moved slowly, his steps unsteady, and felt a dull, throbbing pain in the back of his neck where the chip had been implanted. His head was foggy, his thoughts not as sharp as usual. Claire and Maddy kept a close eye on him, ready to help if his condition worsened.
"Claire urged Declan to sit down. "You need to rest. The side effects should pass in a few hours," she said.
Declan obliged, sinking gratefully into the chair. He winced slightly and grimaced as he touched the back of his neck again. "It feels... strange," he admitted. "But I guess that's to be expected."
Maddy reassured Declan by squeezing his shoulder. "You're doing great, Declan. Just hang in there," she said.
While Declan rested, Claire and Maddy busied themselves in the lab. They had a lot of preparations to do before they could start utilizing the chip. They had to ensure everything was set up for when Declan was ready to begin his interactions with the Mycelium Quantum Computer.
Time passed slowly in the lab, filled with quiet activity and the steady hum of machinery. Every so often, Claire and Maddy would glance at Declan, checking on his condition. With each

passing minute, Declan looked better as the pain slowly receded and the disorientation faded.
By the time Agent Reynolds arrived at the clinic, Declan was back on his feet, though still a bit shaky. The trio was fully immersed in their work, focused on their mission. Little did they know about the inquiry that had just been initiated at the clinic upstairs and their actions under scrutiny. Only time would tell what would unfold from this.

Claire and Maddy had just settled into their routine of double checking all the safety protocols of connecting the AR chip to the system, when Declan suddenly clutched his forehead in pain. Nausea swept over him, causing his knees to buckle. His vision blurred, then sharpened into fractals of color that splintered across his line of sight. Suddenly, it felt like the floor had been ripped out from under him and he was falling into a vortex of time.

Looking around, he realized he was no longer within the confines of the laboratory. He found himself adrift in an expanse that was not merely dark, but an all consuming void - the absence of everything. Yet, he could breathe, he could exist, like an observer unstuck from the confines of time and space.
Suddenly, the darkness around him shivered, a vibration that rippled across the expanse, culminating into a singularity. Before his eyes, the singularity pulsed, then exploded in an outburst of pure energy and matter, radiating outward from its center. This was the Big Bang, the beginning of all things.
As if caught in an intense storm, Declan shielded his eyes from the brilliant light that had consumed the darkness. When he dared to look again, he saw particles of matter combining, creating atoms, stars, galaxies, all coming together in a cosmic dance of creation. Nebulas burst into existence, their ethereal veils glowing in brilliant hues of red, blue, and gold, the birthplaces of stars and solar systems.

Declan, awestruck, watched as one particular nebula began to contract, a massive star at its core succumbing to gravity. The star exploded in a supernova; its matter scattered across the cosmos. In the star's wake, debris began to coalesce, pulled together by gravity.

Planets formed from the cosmic dust, circling a fiery star, their raw surfaces cooling over the eons. They left trails of debris in their orbits, forming moons that danced a celestial ballet around them. He saw one planet, third from the star, that fascinated him. He watched as it cooled and solidified, its surface morphing and transforming.

Volcanoes erupted, spewing lava and gases into the atmosphere, forming the air. Comets crashed into the planet, bringing with them water which soon covered much of the surface. The water vapor in the atmosphere condensed, creating clouds, which brought about the first rainstorms, further shaping the planet's surface.

Declan's vision went black and when he opened his eyes, his surroundings had completely changed. He was standing on the edge of a vast, churning ocean, surrounded by a stormy sky of gases tinged with deadly orange. The air was thick with the scent of ozone and volatile compounds. This was no ordinary vision; he was witnessing the birth of life itself.

The sight was breathtaking, awe-inspiring, and terrifying all at once. He could see the building blocks of life - the amino acids, nucleotides - beginning to form and cluster, catalyzed by the electrical storms that frequently raged across the primordial ocean. A profound sense of insignificance washed over him as he watched the process of abiogenesis unfolding, life springing from non-life.

The emotional impact was overwhelming. He felt a lump rise in his throat as he stood at the very cusp of existence, witnessing the miracle of life's genesis. His heart pounded in his chest, reverberating with the rhythm of creation that pulsed all around him. He was not just observing this event but was feeling it, living it.

Despite the nausea that still clung to him, a sense of reverence replaced Declan's initial discomfort. The magnificence of life's beginnings held him captive, his mind struggling to comprehend the enormity of what he was witnessing. The image of the ancient Earth, so hostile yet so crucial for the miracle he was witnessing, was imprinted on his mind.

For what felt like an eternity, he stood there, awestruck by the spectacle. He was a part of this grand design, a child of this cosmic event. The simulation, powered by the AR chip, was more than just a visual experience - it was a journey through time, a voyage through the very fabric of life itself.

His heart echoed with the age-old rhythms of creation as the primal seas churned, and the nascent life began its unfathomable journey of evolution. As the waves of nausea receded, they were replaced by a sense of awe and wonder. It was an experience that left him feeling humbled and renewed, a witness to the miraculous symphony of life's creation. This was just the beginning of his journey through time, and he braced himself for what was yet to come.

Declan was just beginning to adjust to the tumultuous rhythms of primordial Earth when the scene around him suddenly shifted. He found himself standing on the soft, lush soil of a verdant forest, surrounded by colossal beasts - dinosaurs in all their might and glory. They roamed freely, embodying raw power and the unforgiving rules of nature. There were giant long-necked herbivores grazing on the tops of towering trees, while fearsome predators lurked in the underbrush, their eyes gleaming with predatory intent.

Declan was a mere observer, an inconsequential entity in this world of titans. Yet, he felt a strange connection to them, a deep-seated realization of the shared lineage that bound them all - the thread of life. Suddenly, the atmosphere shifted, and a wave of anxiety washed over the dinosaurs. Their roars now filled with fear and confusion as a monstrous fireball descended from the sky.

The impact was cataclysmic. The earth shook, forests ignited, and a shockwave tore through the landscape, felling trees and dinosaurs alike. Declan found himself back in the lab, gasping for breath, his hand clutching his chest. The echo of the dinosaurs' last cries resonated in his ears, their fear imprinted on his soul. The sense of loss was overwhelming, a stark reminder of the impermanence of life.

Yet, amid the devastation, a ray of hope emerged. The extinction of the dinosaurs had paved the way for a new era - the rise of mammals. Declan took a deep breath, steeling himself for the next leap into the past, into the dawn of his own lineage. Despite the harrowing journey so far, he was eager to continue, knowing he was witnessing a story greater than himself - the story of life's indomitable spirit.

Claire and Maddy looked at him with worry on their faces, not understanding what was happening. The door to the lab opened, and out of the corner of his eye, Declan caught Dr. Peterson strolling towards him. His vision shifted again, and he dived back into time once more.

As Declan's eyes glazed over, he plunged back into the depths of time. The world around him was a smoky, ash-filled wasteland. The verdant forest was gone, replaced by a landscape that looked more like a battlefield after a devastating war.

The once-dominant dinosaurs were nowhere to be seen, their reign ended by the cataclysm. Yet, as he looked around, he could see signs of life persisting, clinging stubbornly to existence. Small creatures scurried in the underbrush, their eyes glinting with a will to survive.

These were the early mammals, tiny creatures that had lived in the shadow of the dinosaurs. Now, with the behemoths gone, they had a chance to flourish. As time rushed forward, Declan saw these small, nocturnal animals evolve, grow in size and diversity, and adapt to the changing world around them.

He saw the rise of many types of mammals – rodents and rabbits, dogs and cats, horses and rhinos – adapting to every corner of the earth, from the coldest arctic tundra to the hottest deserts, from the highest mountains to the deepest oceans. The perseverance and adaptability of life astounded him.

Among these mammals, one group caught his attention: the primates, our most ancient ancestors. Declan watched as these creatures evolved, their bodies and brains growing more complex with time. He saw them use tools, build communities, and develop a sense of self.

Watching the rise of mammals, Declan felt a profound connection. He was a part of this grand story, a descendant of these resilient creatures. He felt a sense of pride and responsibility. This was the legacy he carried, the legacy he needed to understand to help save the future.

Back in the lab, Declan's body jerked with the intensity of his experience. Dr. Peterson rushed forward, his eyes wide with concern. Claire and Maddy stood by, their expressions a mixture of worry and awe. They knew that Declan was witnessing something profound, just like Maddy had, something that could hopefully change everything.

As Declan's vision swirled once again, he found himself in a world gradually transforming from dense forests to wide open grasslands. Before him, primates evolved, their bodies adapting to the changing environment. They stood upright, their hands freed from the necessity of locomotion, and their brains growing larger and more complex.

He was witnessing the birth of the hominids, the first human-like creatures. With each passing moment, they grew more recognizable. They crafted tools, mastered fire, and learned to communicate with rudimentary language. They formed close-knit tribes, taking care of each other and working together for survival.

The pace of evolution accelerated, and before Declan's eyes, the early hominids gave way to Homo habilis, then Homo erectus. He saw them spread across the globe, adapt to diverse

environments, and overcome countless challenges. He saw them create art, develop culture, and build civilizations.
Then came the Neanderthals, with their robust bodies and sophisticated tools, and finally Homo sapiens – modern humans. They were us, creatures capable of empathy, love, art, science, and unimaginable cruelty. They invented, discovered, loved, fought, dreamed, and believed. Through their successes and failures, their triumphs and tragedies, they shaped the world.
Declan watched the timeline of human history unfold in a grand panorama – the rise and fall of empires, the blossoming of ideas, the relentless march of progress. He saw the splendor of human potential and the depth of human folly. He saw the dawn of technology, from the rudimentary wheel to the silicon chip in his brain, connecting him to this vast ocean of knowledge.
He came out of the simulation panting, his heart pounding in his chest. He was back in the lab, surrounded by Claire, Maddy, and Dr. Peterson. He saw concern in their eyes but also a spark of curiosity. They were eager to learn about his journey, at least Claire and Maddy were Dr. Peterson looked bewildered he had no idea what was going on.

"I saw... I saw everything," gasped Declan, his voice choked with emotion. "Our story... our journey... it's beautiful. But... I don't understand... why... why am I seeing this?"
Before anyone could answer, Declan's head snapped back, and his eyes rolled as a new surge of information hit him. The world spun around him, his stomach churned, and he doubled over, vomiting on the floor. The journey wasn't over.
He was thrust back in time, beyond the rise of mammals and humans. This time, the focus of the simulation was different. It wasn't about the grandeur of the dinosaurs or the majesty of early mammals. Instead, he was taken through the evolution of far more ancient creatures, tracing the lineage of life back to its early aquatic beginnings.
First, he was shown the Tunicate, an early marine invertebrate. Its body was simple, just a filter-feeding sack and a tail, but it was the

start of something incredible. As Declan watched, he saw the Tunicate's genetic sequence dancing before his eyes, each base pair shifting, adding, and removing itself until it transformed into something new.

Next, he was shown the Myxini glutinosa, also known as the hagfish. It was a primitive, jawless creature, but it was a step towards more complex life forms. Its genetic sequence morphed from that of the Tunicate, adding new information, new adaptations.

The Eusthenopteron came next, a fish-like creature but with strong limb-like fins. Its genome was a complex symphony, evolving, refining, as the creature itself transitioned from water to land.

Finally, Declan was shown the Acanthostega, one of the earliest known tetrapods, with fully formed limbs capable of moving on land. It was a monumental leap in evolution, and its genetic sequence was a testament to the power of natural selection and adaptation.

The force of the vision brought Declan to his knees. He gripped the edge of a table to keep from falling, his body wracked with shivers. He was experiencing life's tenacity first-hand, witnessing its relentless pursuit of survival and adaptability.

Claire, Maddy, and Dr. Peterson rushed to his side, trying to make sense of his experience. Declan's breaths were labored, and his eyes were filled with awe and confusion. He was living the evolution of life, bearing witness to the eons-long dance of genes and environment. It was overwhelming, but it was the key to understanding the grand tapestry of life and possibly, their future.

This was more than just a scientific breakthrough. This was a profound, deeply personal glimpse into the core of what it means to be human. They had ventured into the past, seeking answers for the future. And as Declan's eyes met Claire's and Maddy's, he realized they were on the cusp of something truly monumental. They were on the path to understanding the very essence of life itself.

As Declan's companions gathered around him, the world swirled once more, and he was flung into another journey through time. However, this was a journey he dreaded, one that held too much pain.
He found himself standing in the midst of a prehistoric landscape, watching as early hominids gave way to Homo habilis, Homo erectus, and finally Homo sapiens. Witnessing the birth of intelligence and culture, the rise of societies and civilizations, he also saw conflict and bloodshed. He witnessed greed and hatred leading to the pointless destruction of lives.
He found himself in the heart of ancient wars, feeling the fear of a soldier facing a charging enemy. He experienced the dread of a medieval knight before a joust, the desperation of a World War I private in the trenches, and the utter devastation of a soldier watching a nuclear blast.
He died on those battlefields, over and over again. He felt the sharp sting of a bronze spear, the fatal blow of a knight's sword, and the shattering impact of a bullet. Each time, he was revived, only to be thrust into another conflict, another war. The scale of humanity's violence against itself was horrifying, a stark contrast to the beauty of life's evolution he had witnessed earlier.
It was too much. The pain, the fear, the despair—it was overwhelming. The chip seemed to realize this and triggered a built-in safety protocol, shutting down and abruptly pulling Declan out of the relentless tide of history and back to the present.
Declan slumped onto the floor, the whirlwind journey through humanity's history finally at an end. His body was wracked with sobs, his heart heavy with the weight of the experiences he had just lived through. The others close by not knowing how to help, their faces a mirror of his own shock and distress. In silence, they comforted Declan, giving him the time, he needed to process the profound and harrowing journey he had just undertaken.

Chapter 14

In the Shadow of the Mycelium

Claire, her mind racing with the intensity of the situation, made a swift decision. "We need to get him out of here," she declared, her voice shaking slightly but steady. "The proximity to the Quantum Computer and the chip might trigger another connection. He's in no condition to go through that again."
Maddy and Dr. Peterson looked at her, their faces lined with worry. "Agreed," said Maddy, her voice grim. She was an expert in theoretical physics and Quantum Computing, not medicine, but even she could tell Declan was in a bad state. His skin was ashen, sweat beaded on his forehead, and he was shivering slightly.

With a sense of urgency, they helped Declan up and slowly led him out of the lab. The journey down the corridor to the elevator felt like the longest walk of Claire's life, every second ticking by like an hour as Declan leaned heavily on them, his breathing shallow and ragged.

As they exited the QRDA building and stepped out into the cool evening air, Declan seemed to come back to himself a bit. His face was still deathly pale, but the fresh air seemed to revive him slightly. They guided him to a nearby bench, where he sat down heavily, his head bowed.

"We should get him some food and water," Maddy suggested, rushing off to the cafeteria. Claire sat next to Declan, her hand on his back, feeling the tremors that still shook his body.

They remained in silence for a while, each lost in their own thoughts. They had embarked on this journey with a sense of anticipation and excitement, but now they faced the harsh reality of their actions. They had no idea what had just happened or how he connected to the computer, and the repercussions were far more severe than they had anticipated.
In the midst of their troubled thoughts, one thing was clear. They needed to find a way to use the AR chip safely. The promise of the Mycelium Quantum Computer was too great to abandon, but they couldn't risk anyone's life to achieve their goals. As they sat there in the fading evening light, they resolved to find a solution.

Claire and Maddy turned to look at Dr. Peterson. The older scientist's eyes were clouded with confusion and a spark of anger. "I think someone needs to tell me what the hell is going on here," he snapped, pointing at Declan, who was still slumped over on the bench, looking weak and disoriented. "Why do I feel like I've been in the dark for a long, long time. I don't appreciate being left out of the loop, especially when it concerns the health of one of my people."
Claire took a deep breath, squaring her shoulders. "Yes," she admitted, her voice steady, "I have kept you in the dark for far too long."

Claire continued, her gaze steady on the older scientist. "It began when we were tasked with developing a system capable of handling the Creation simulation. As you know, the enormity of the data we were dealing with required a computational power beyond anything that currently existed. We put in requests for additional funding, but they were always denied. This left us at an impasse."

She paused briefly before plunging onward. "So, we turned to an alternate solution, one that strayed from traditional paths. We conceptualized the Mycelium Quantum Computer. We understood the risks but also the unprecedented potential it held."

Dr. Peterson seemed about to interject, but Claire raised her hand, signaling him to let her finish. "We kept it quiet due to the necessity to separate it from the Cogni-genius processing system. The bureaucracy and red tape to get that approved would have been insurmountable."

Claire's gaze bore into Dr. Peterson's. "As you well know, the government has become overly reliant on the Cogni-genius system, thinking it to be the pinnacle of all computing power. But it's not. It's just a stepping stone, a launch pad into a world of greater possibilities."

Her eyes softened as she looked at Declan, "But we hadn't anticipated the repercussions. We never meant to put Declan's health at risk. I assure you, we'll do everything in our power to correct this situation.

Dr. Peterson looked at the trio with anger and disappointment clearly etched on his face, "Does this reaction have to do with the AR chip that was implanted into Declan today?"

"It does have to do with the AR chip that was implanted in Declan today. He connected with the Mycelium Quantum Computer that we built and..."

"Wait! What?" Dr. Peterson cut her off, his face reddening. "You did what behind my back?"

Maddy stepped in, her voice soft but firm. "We had to try it, Dr. Peterson. Our research had hit a wall. The Mycelium Quantum Computer offered a new pathway, a way to dive deeper into the mysteries of evolution than we ever could with conventional Quantum Computing methods."

Seeing his questioning look, she continued, "As you know traditional computers, as powerful as they are, are linear. They work step by step, solving one equation at a time. But the quantum computer, it's... different. It can process multiple pathways simultaneously. It can hold multiple states at once. It's like having thousands, millions of computers working together in unison."

"But the real breakthrough is in its Mycelium connections. The quantum computer processes vast amounts of data in an abstract, high-dimensional space that's hard for us to visualize or understand. Once the connections were established the computer began showing code we could not account for. But with the AR chip, we can interpret that information in a way our brains can handle, by creating immersive, detailed simulations."

Dr. Peterson interrupted, "But why use mycelium?"

Maddy took a deep breath. "Mycelium has properties that make it a perfect medium for a quantum computer. It's a natural network, with nodes and connections just like a neural network. Plus, mycelium is known to have quantum properties - it can maintain quantum states much longer than traditional materials. We are able to harness these properties to build a quantum computer that's more powerful and efficient."

She paused, taking a moment to let her words sink in before continuing. "We built the Mycelium Quantum Computer and used the AR chip to visualize the data it processes. The idea was to gain insight into the history of life on Earth as it started to show genome sequences in its data banks that we did not place there. We thought we would be able to see the course of evolution firsthand. We thought it could offer breakthroughs in our understanding of life, its origins and evolution."

"But we didn't anticipate..." her voice trailed off, her gaze shifting towards Declan. "We didn't anticipate how intensely Declan or I would experience the simulation."

She looked back at Dr. Peterson, her expression pleading for understanding. "We never intended for this to happen. We were trying to push the boundaries of our understanding, to explore uncharted territories. But we'll fix this. We'll ensure Declan recovers and we'll make sure this doesn't happen again."

"Come again? You did this first?"

There was a haunted look in Maddy's eyes as she recounted her experience in the simulation to Dr. Peterson. Her voice wavered, but she continued, determined to make him understand.

"The simulation went on, showing me the future, the past, a parallel universe, I do not know what it was" she began, her gaze distant. "My child, formed from lines of code and light, grew right before my eyes. I saw them at ten, their bright inquisitive eyes full of curiosity. I saw them at fifteen, their features sharp, their laughter not of a child's, but of a young adult."

"I was there, every step of the way," she continued, her voice choked with emotion. "I was there for their school concerts, their sports events, I helped with their homework. I comforted them when they were hurt, encouraged them when they faltered. They were my world. They were my heart."

Maddy took a deep, shuddering breath, struggling to keep her composure. "And then they grew up," she murmured, her voice barely audible. "At eighteen, they were a reflection of the adult they would become. I watched them graduate, apply for colleges... I saw their dreams, their potential... I saw them become their own person, someone who I had the privilege of guiding and loving."

"But then," Maddy's voice broke, tears glistening in her eyes. "Then, the failsafe protocol of the AR chip kicked in, at least that is what we think happened. One moment, I was saying goodbye as they left for college, the next moment... I was back in the lab. The world I had been a part of, the child I had loved and raised, was all gone."

Her voice was filled with a raw anguish that echoed around the silent lab. "I lost them, Dr. Peterson," she whispered, her voice thick with emotion. "They were ripped away from me. All the love I felt, the memories I made... all part of a reality that was never real to begin with."

Maddy's gaze focused on Dr. Peterson, her eyes pleading. "We built something extraordinary," she reiterated, her voice trembling. "But it's more powerful, more real than we ever anticipated. We need to be careful. We need to ensure this technology doesn't consume us. Because the pain... the loss... it's too much to bear."

Maddy's words hung heavy in the air, a stark reminder of the power they wielded and the responsibility they bore. They had created a tool that could expand the horizons of human understanding, but at what cost? They had seen the repercussions first-hand, and now they had to decide how to move forward in a way that was both responsible and ethical.
Dr. Peterson looked like he was struggling to process her words. "So, he was part of some experiment? Without my knowledge? And it ended up causing this," he gestured towards Declan, "This distress?"
"We had precautions; we thought we had prepared for the potential side effects," Maddy added in a soft voice, in her hands a bottle of water and a sandwich for Declan. "We didn't anticipate that it would be so intense."
Dr. Peterson looked from Maddy to Claire, his anger simmering down, replaced by a concern for Declan. "Well, it's clear that something went wrong. We need to figure out what he saw and moving forward, I expect full transparency. No more secrets."
Claire and Maddy nodded, knowing that he was right. They had entered unknown territory and it was time to regroup and reassess. But first, they needed to make sure Declan was alright. They looked at their friend, his face pale but his eyes filled with a strange mix of terror and wonder.

Maddy's heart ached with the burning need to know if Declan had experienced their shared life with their child during the simulation. Ever since, her love for him had intensified, and the longing for him to feel the same was almost too much to bear. "What did you see? Did you witness our child together?" she asked, her voice filled with an unmistakable heartbreak. Anyone truly listening would have felt the depth of her yearning.

Claire looked at Maddy and Declan, her face etched with concern. Maddy's eyes were filled with a desperate need as she questioned Declan about his experience. Claire found it heart-

wrenching to witness Maddy's vulnerability, her agony all too visible. She felt her own heart aching for her friend and colleague.
"Did you see our child?" Maddy asked, her voice choked with emotion. Her eyes were pleading with Declan to validate her experience, to confirm that the love she had for him, amplified a hundredfold in the simulation, was mutual.
Claire could see Declan's confusion, his disoriented mind trying to process what Maddy was asking him. She knew he needed time and space to comprehend his own experiences, but Maddy's desperate need for confirmation was overwhelming.
Suddenly, Claire felt an uncanny sensation. She turned and saw a man on a nearby bench, seemingly engrossed in his own world, but Claire could sense his attentiveness, his ears subtly tilted in their direction. She instantly felt discomfort. Their conversation was not meant for outside ears, especially when discussing confidential and emotional details.
Without wasting a moment, Claire stood up and made a decision. "We need to continue this conversation inside the lab. We can't risk being overheard," she stated firmly.
Maddy and Declan looked at her in surprise, but Claire gestured subtly towards the man on the bench. Understanding dawned on their faces, and they nodded, slowly standing up and following Claire towards the lab.
As they moved away, Claire looked back at the man. Her instincts screamed that something was off. She couldn't put her finger on it, but she knew they had to be careful. They were dealing with an extraordinary technology that could revolutionize the world, but also had the power to cause immense harm, if it was as powerful as she was beginning to think it is. They couldn't afford to let it fall into the wrong hands.
As they walked, Maddy gently held Declan's arm, her touch filled with worry and desperation. Declan looked at her with a strange mix of terror and wonder in his eyes. He was silent but nodded, a silent promise that he would share his story and his experience in the simulation once they were safely inside the lab.

And so, they walked on, united in their shared experience and burdened with the responsibility of a technology that was both a marvel and a threat. The world outside remained oblivious to their inner turmoil; their hearts heavy with secrets that could change the very fabric of human understanding.

Once inside the lab, the group settled into their familiar surroundings. The bright fluorescent lights overhead cast a stark glow over the room, a stark contrast to the dimming twilight outside. Dr. Peterson excused himself, walking out of the room under the pretense of needing a moment to clear his head. Claire moved to the main console, her fingers tapping away on the keyboard, pulling up data logs from the Mycelium Quantum Computer. Maddy helped Declan to a chair, her hand lingering on his shoulder, an unspoken question in her eyes. Declan nodded to her, a silent affirmation that he was ready to share what he had experienced.

Just then, Dr. Peterson returned, a bottle of whiskey in his hand. "This, my dear colleagues, is the only medicine that can put the heat back in these old bones," he declared with a touch of his former joviality. Despite his earlier anger, there was a gleam in his eyes that spoke of his curiosity and eagerness to learn more about their groundbreaking experiment.

Pouring out a round for each of them, he handed the glasses around. Claire raised an eyebrow but accepted her drink, knowing the elder scientist's methods were sometimes unorthodox but often effective. Maddy took hers hesitantly, looking to Declan who accepted his own glass with a grimace.

As they each took a sip, the warmth of the whiskey served as a welcome reprieve from the cold reality they were grappling with. Then, in the comforting silence of their lab, Declan began to share his experience.

Declan exhaled deeply, as if preparing himself for the monumental task of trying to put into words an experience that defied comprehension.

"Being inside the simulation was unlike anything I've ever felt," he began, his voice a low rumble in the quiet lab. "One moment, I was here, in the physical realm; the next, I was everywhere. It was like I was tapped into the pulse of the universe, able to perceive every ebb and flow of cosmic energy."

His gaze shifted, becoming unfocused as he delved into his memories. "The Big Bang, the origin of everything! It was chaos, a burst of pure energy expanding at an incomprehensible speed. I felt the force of that expansion, the explosion of space and time itself. I felt the universe being born."

He paused for a moment, his expression one of awe. "And then came the stars. Out of the swirling mass of atomic particles, gravitational forces pulled together the first star. It was like watching a heart take its first beat, the start of a cycle that would define the universe."

"The formation of galaxies was like an orchestra of celestial bodies, each note a stellar event," he continued, his words painting an image of the cosmic waltz he had witnessed. "Galaxies were spiraling into existence, creating cosmic art on a canvas of infinite darkness."

Declan's face softened as he described the nebulae. "I saw the nebulae, vast clouds of gas and dust, illuminated from within by the birth of new stars. It was a nursery of life, an endless cycle of creation and destruction. And when a star's life ended, it did so with a majestic flourish, scattering the elements that would give rise to new stars, new planets... and eventually, life."

"And life," he breathed, his voice filled with a reverence that echoed in the silent lab. "Life started out so simple, as single-celled organisms that somehow, against all odds, found a way to thrive in the harsh environment of a young planet. As the eons passed, I saw evolution at work, lifeforms adapting, diversifying, growing more complex."

His gaze returned to his friends, his voice barely above a whisper as he finished recounting his journey. "And then, from this cacophony of life, humanity emerged, a testament to the resilience and adaptability of life. To witness that... It was humbling."

Each word Declan spoke seemed to hang in the air, imbuing the room with a sense of wonder and awe. His tale, while incredible, also bore the weight of the understanding they now had of their technology – a portal to the unfathomable depths of the universe, but also a journey that could take an emotional toll they had yet to fully comprehend.

Chapter 15

Decoding Evolution's Blueprint

From his inconspicuous spot on the park bench, Special Agent Reynolds scrutinized the group of scientists with trained detachment. The trio consisted of Dr. Claire Cairns, the Chief Genetic engineer, and two younger members of her team, Dr. Maddy Landis and Declan Sutton.

The sudden urgency in Dr. Cairns movements caused Reynolds' pulse to quicken. The curt nod she gave to the other two members before she swiftly stood up clearly conveyed an unspoken message. Reynolds watched as Dr. Cairns subtly gestured in his direction, alerting her colleagues to potential eavesdropping. Their faces registered brief surprise before their expressions hardened into guarded masks.

Reynolds maintained his casual demeanor, but internally, he was alert. He kept his gaze trained on an old paperback while subtly tracking their movements. As they picked up their belongings and moved towards a nondescript concrete building in the distance a fourth older man was with them as well that he had not noticed, from the dossier he had been given he knew it was Dr. Peterson. Despite the wind rustling the trees and muffling their conversation, Reynolds could still make out fragments. Words like 'singularity' and 'simulation' filtered through, painting a picture of something far more complicated than a casual chat between colleagues.

As the group disappeared into the building, Reynolds allowed himself a moment to process. The conversation he had partially overheard, the palpable tension in their body language, hinted at stakes much higher than he had initially surmised. The implications were significant, potentially even dangerous. Closing his book, Reynolds took a final look at the now deserted bench, his mind swirling with speculation. His role as a Special Agent required him to uncover the truth behind their secretive discussion. His next step was clear. It was time to get closer to Dr. Peterson's team and find out exactly what they were up to.

As Declan finished his story, the lab fell silent except for the distant hum of machines. The whiskey in their glasses was forgotten, replaced by the intoxication of cosmic understanding and the palpable weight of the knowledge they held.
Dr. Peterson broke the silence. "Declan, your experience... it's beyond comprehension," he said, his voice roughened by age and emotion. "The universe's birth and evolution... it's a tale of creation from chaos, life born of death and destruction. It's beautiful, awe-inspiring... and terrifying."

Taking a deep breath, he clasped his hands together as if to muster his courage. "And it makes me wonder. The Mycelium Computer is an unprecedented achievement, a marvel of engineering and biology. But it's also something that we don't fully understand, if we understand anything at all about what is happening and how."

Claire, Maddy, and Declan stared at him, their expressions turning serious. "Are you suggesting..." Claire started, her voice trailing off as she grappled with his implication.

Dr. Peterson nodded. "Yes. I'm suggesting that the Mycelium Computer could be the source of the society-ending event warning, not the Ectogenesis program and its current failures."

His words hung in the air as everyone processed his implication. The room was pregnant with tension, as if they were all collectively holding their breath. And then he realized, the revelation didn't cause as much as a flicker in the eyes of Maddy and Declan.

A moment of understanding dawned on Dr. Peterson, a look of disappointment etching its way onto his face. "You've already heard this before, haven't you?" he asked, already knowing the answer. "I suppose I asked too much of Claire to keep it to herself," he added softly, the edges of his words tinged with regret.

Claire's face fell as Dr. Peterson spoke. "I'm sorry, Dr. Peterson," she said, her voice laced with regret. "I promised to keep it to myself, but I couldn't hide the truth from Maddy and Declan. We're a team, and we need to move forward with the project, but we also need to be honest with each other."

Dr. Peterson nodded slowly, a small smile playing at the corners of his mouth. "You're right. We can't make progress if we're not honest with each other. Let's focus on understanding the Mycelium Computer and its potential impact on society. We may have a lot of work ahead of us, but I have faith in this team."

Claire felt a weight lift off her shoulders as she realized that the team was stronger for having shared the truth with each other. They had a daunting task ahead of them, but they were in it together.

The room fell silent again. The impact of his words sunk in. They had been so focused on the Ectogenesis program and the failing genome sequences that they never considered this. It had seemed the most likely candidate for any catastrophic mishap.
"But... why? How?" Maddy asked, her voice barely a whisper.
"That's what we need to find out," Dr. Peterson said. "The Mycelium Computer's ability may be beyond our comprehension. It is much like the universe itself, born from chaos, ever-expanding and evolving. It's a power that we may not be able to control. Both times you have connected to it, you had drastically different experiences. What is to say that we will ever be able to master it to learn anything that it doesn't want us to learn?"

Dr. Peterson continued, "In fact, the Mycelium Computer's abilities are so advanced that it could be seen as an artificial intelligence with god-like powers. It may have the capability to control us and our actions, and we may not even realize it. That's why we need to be cautious and understand the full extent of its power, as well as any potential risks it may pose to society. It's a delicate balance between harnessing its potential and ensuring that it doesn't control us. We need to tread carefully and approach this with both curiosity and caution." The team listened intently, realizing the magnitude of what they were dealing with. It was clear that they had a long road ahead of them and that they needed to work together to fully comprehend the Mycelium Computer and its impact on their lives.

He looked at each of them, his gaze firm. "We need to scrutinize the Mycelium Computer and understand the potential threats it could pose. It might even be prudent to shut it down temporarily until we've learned more."

The weight of his words hung in the air, casting a shadow over the awe and wonder they had just experienced listening to Declan's story. But they all understood. This was not just about scientific discovery anymore. It was about the survival of their society, perhaps even humanity itself.

"We've peered into the depths of the universe," Dr. Peterson said, his voice steady. "Now, we must look into the heart of your own creation, Claire and Maddy, and ensure it doesn't become our undoing."

With Dr. Peterson's chilling suggestion lingering in the air, Declan suddenly realized something. He blinked, his mind spinning as he pieced together fragments of memories from his time within the simulation.

"It wasn't just the universe, the cosmic spectacle," he said slowly, his voice quiet but intense. "The Mycelium Computer showed me something else, something more specific. I didn't understand it then, but now..."

He swallowed, gripping the edge of the table as he recalled his experience. "When I said I didn't understand what was happening when I was exiting the simulation, the system... it threw me back into the simulation and showed me a sequence of creatures, from simple to complex. Their genetic sequence was changing, evolving."

His gaze flitted to his colleagues, a mix of anticipation and fear in his eyes. "First, it showed me a Tunicate, an early marine invertebrate. Then came the Myxini glutinosa, or hagfish, a primitive, jawless creature. Next was the Eusthenopteron, a fish-like creature but with strong limb-like fins, seemingly caught between water and land. And finally, the Acanthostega, a transitional creature between fish and the earliest land vertebrates. The most fascinating thing about it was that it showed me the genome sequence of each creature as it transitioned into its next form of evolution."

The room fell silent again as Declan's revelation hung in the air. Each creature represented a milestone in evolution, a leap towards more complex life forms.

"But why would the system show you this?" Maddy asked, her brow furrowed in confusion and anger. It didn't show him the one thing she needed it to show him: their love.

Dr. Peterson stroked his beard, his gaze distant. "Perhaps the Mycelium Computer was trying to tell us something," he mused. "The computer is a product of evolution, not unlike these creatures. From simple beginnings, it has become something more complex, more advanced."

"And just as these creatures ushered in new eras of life," Declan added, his voice tense, "The Mycelium Computer could be the harbinger of a new era for us. But unlike natural evolution, which takes millions of years, the computer's evolution is happening at an unprecedented speed."

“We are jumping to conclusions here and big ones at that," he continued, "To say it is evolving just doesn't make any sense to me. There is something we are missing, and I still feel like it is trying to tell us something about the Ectogenesis program. It cannot be a coincidence that we are searching for an original, unaltered human genome sequence, and this thing keeps showing us genome sequences!"

Claire's eyes widened as she looked at Maddy. "That's it!" she exclaimed, her voice ringing out in the quiet lab. "Maddy, those were the exact genome sequences we first discovered!"
Maddy stared at Claire, reflecting her surprise. She remembered their earlier excitement when they had uncovered those specific genome sequences in the initial data generated by the computer. These sequences represented important moments in the evolutionary timeline.
"Are you sure?" Dr. Peterson interjected, furrowing his eyebrows as he considered the implications.
Claire nodded emphatically, her mind racing. "Absolutely. The Tunicate, the hagfish, the Eusthenopteron, and the Acanthostega... they were all present in our early findings."
A charged silence filled the room as they all grappled with this revelation. If Declan was right and the Mycelium Computer had deliberately shown him these sequences, then they were indeed missing something crucial about the Ectogenesis program, if that was what the system was trying to show them. For all anyone knew, this could just be a coincidence.
"But why these sequences?" Maddy mused aloud, her voice trembling slightly. "What is it trying to tell us?"
Declan took a deep breath, looking around the room. "Maybe the system is trying to show us a pattern," he proposed. "Each of these creatures represented a leap in evolutionary development. Could there be a similar leap happening within the Ectogenesis program that we've overlooked?"
The room was filled with urgency as they considered the possible implications. If they were correct, they were on the brink of a discovery that could change the course of their research, and perhaps even the fate of humanity.

As the night wore on, the team dove back into their research with renewed vigor. Armed with a potential lead and the mysteries of the Mycelium Computer to unravel, they pushed on, propelled by their shared commitment to understanding and leveraging this groundbreaking technology.

"Let's take a step back and examine how computer software operates. Can anyone explain this to me in simple terms?" Declan asked. Claire stood up, paced back and forth a few times and attempted to simplify the complicated concept for everyone in the room. "At its core, a computer program is a sequence of instructions, written in a language that a computer can understand. This language is called code, " stated Claire
"Think of it like a recipe for a cake," she continued. "Just as a recipe provides step-by-step instructions to make a cake, code gives a computer step-by-step instruction to complete a task. The steps can be as simple as adding two numbers or as complex as rendering a 3D image, depending on what the programmer needs."
"The most basic instruction a computer understands is binary code, a system of 1s and 0s. Each binary digit, or 'bit', represents a basic unit of information. Groupings of these bits form 'bytes', and this is where things get interesting."
"In a program, each byte could represent an instruction or a piece of data. So, when a computer executes a program, it's basically reading and following a long list of these instructions, one after the other. It's a bit like a pianist playing a piece of music note by note."
"But remember," Maddy warned, "just as different musical notes can create a myriad of melodies, combinations of these binary codes can create a multitude of different programs."
Claire took a deep breath, hoping she'd given enough context. "When we talk about the Mycelium Computer," she continued, "we're dealing with an incredibly advanced and complex system that operates using these basic principles. The question we need

to ask ourselves is: what set of instructions, what 'recipe,' is it following that's leading to this unique output?"
"The sequences the computer showed Declan, the ones that match our initial findings, they're not just data. They're part of a story, a narrative that the computer is trying to tell us. Our task is to figure out how these pieces fit together, just like trying to understand the melody from a series of musical notes. Only then can we comprehend what the system is trying to communicate."
Her explanation hung in the air as the room fell into silence. The team was quiet, each member pondering over the profound implications of Claire's words. The Mycelium Computer's 'song' could hold the answers they were seeking, and it was up to them to understand it.

Dr. Peterson had been quietly listening to Claire's explanation, but now he stood up. His eyes twinkled with excitement and realization as he looked at the team. "Claire, you've given us an excellent explanation," he said. "It's made me think of something..."
He moved closer to the holographic screen and swept his gaze over the various lifeforms and their genetic sequences. "Consider this: when we create complex software systems, we don't just write a huge chunk of code and hope it works. We break the problem down into smaller parts, each part addressing a specific aspect of the problem. Each part is essentially a 'module,' a self-contained piece of code that performs a specific function. When these modules work together, they create a fully functional program. Each module is a building block in the construction of the complete software system."
Dr. Peterson paused, letting the analogy sink in. "Now, let's correlate this with evolution," he continued, his voice steady and thoughtful. "Each of these creatures, their genetic sequences - they could be considered 'modules' in the grand scheme of evolution. Each one had a role to play, contributing to the whole

picture by representing a specific adaptation or a leap forward in evolutionary development."

His gaze then landed on the Mycelium Computer. "If we apply this analogy to the Mycelium Computer, we might understand that what we're seeing is not a simple linear progression, but a modular one. Each sequence it showed Declan, each match we found in our initial data, could be a 'module,' a piece of the larger puzzle."

"The computer isn't merely evolving," he speculated, "it's building upon itself, just like life has been doing for billions of years. The patterns we're seeing may not be a narrative, but a blueprint. And each sequence, each 'module,' is a building block of this blueprint."

The room was quiet, all eyes on Dr. Peterson as he finished his explanation. His theory offered a new perspective on their research and the enigmatic machine that was the Mycelium Computer. They were all pondering what this could mean for their quest for an original, unaltered human genome sequence. Could this be the key to unlocking the secrets that the computer held?

Dr. Peterson's eyes narrowed in contemplation. "What if the echoes we're seeing in the code, the sequences that seem to relate to these extinct species, are remnants of the past, echoes of ancient genetic modules?" He traced his fingers in the air, drawing invisible connections. "Our ancestors, these ancient mammals, they've left their mark in our genomes, in what we are today."

Claire chimed in, "Are you suggesting the Mycelium Computer is piecing together a genetic history, a lineage of humanity's evolution? Pulling fragments from the ether of ancient DNA information?"

"Exactly," Peterson replied, a spark lighting up in his eyes. "It's similar to archaeology, but on a genetic level. The Mycelium Computer is not only reconstructing but also interpreting these ancient DNA sequences. It's not just about humans. It's about all life, the vast interconnected web we are part of."

Claire looked thoughtful. "The computer, through its complex mycelium networks, could be reaching out into the soil, the air, even the water, accessing genetic information embedded in the environment. It might be detecting traces of ancient life, absorbing echoes of the past, and integrating them into its calculations."

The room was thick with anticipation. The theory was far-fetched, even outrageous, but it offered an exhilarating new perspective. They were not just dealing with a machine; they were interacting with a life form that was tapping into the roots of evolution itself. The echoes of the past were whispering through the code, potentially guiding them towards the key to humanity's future.

As Dr. Peterson's words hung in the air, Maddy remained quiet, a frown creasing her forehead. His words echoed in her mind, stirring a wave of emotions she had been trying to keep in check. Suddenly, she found herself standing, her chair scraping the floor loudly. All eyes turned to her, but she hardly noticed. Her mind was swirling with thoughts of her own experience within the Mycelium Computer. "Why?" she blurted out, her voice trembling, "Why did it show me that? Why did it show me what it was like to be a mother, to give birth, to love in that way?"

Her hands clenched tightly, knuckles turning white. "Why did it give Declan this experience of evolutionary leaps, and to me, a deeply personal one?" Her voice broke slightly, the weight of her emotions evident.

Dr. Peterson and Claire exchanged glances. They had seen Maddy's toughness and determination through all their years of research together, but this raw, vulnerable side was something new. The intense personal connection she felt towards the simulation was beyond anything they had expected.

"I don't understand," Maddy continued, tears welling up in her eyes. "These past weeks have been... draining. To feel such intense love, such profound connection... And then to come back to reality and realize it was all simulated... It's too much."

The room was filled with a heavy silence. Maddy's outburst had taken them all by surprise, and the deep pain in her words was a stark reminder of the human element in their research. It wasn't just about codes and sequences. It was about real human emotions and experiences, too.

Dr. Peterson finally broke the silence. "Maddy," he began, his voice gentle, "we're venturing into the unknown here. The Mycelium Computer is like nothing we've ever encountered. Maybe it's trying to communicate in a way it thinks we'd understand. For Declan, it was through evolution and sequences. For you... it was through a deeply personal, human experience."

"But why?" Maddy repeated, her voice a mere whisper now. She looked around the room, her gaze landing on each of her colleagues. "What is it trying to tell us?"

"That," Dr. Peterson replied, "is the question we need to answer. And we'll find it out, together." His gaze was resolute, his words promising a commitment to their shared goal.

Maddy nodded, wiping her eyes. She took a deep breath, steadying herself. They had a long journey ahead, and she needed to be strong. For herself, for her team, and for the answers they were all seeking.

Chapter 16

Checkmate in Shadows

After speaking with the lab techs who processed Declan's AR chip implantation, Agent Reynolds moved away from the main lab area and slipped into the privacy of a small office in the QRDA building. The office was strictly for employees of the Ministry of Security and Intelligence to use when on site. The hum of machinery faded as he closed the door behind him, replaced by the ticking of a wall clock. He let out a heavy sigh and ran his fingers through his graying hair. Then, he reached for his communicator, a sleek device resting on the edge of his cluttered desk.

Activating the screen, he dialed a private number. A slight grimace appeared on his face as he waited for the call to connect. After a brief moment, the screen flickered to life, revealing Minister Martinez's stern visage. His dark eyes were penetrating, a sign of decades spent navigating the delicate web of power and intrigue.

"Agent Reynolds," Minister Martinez greeted curtly, eyeing the man on his screen. "Tell me you have some good news."

Reynolds swallowed; his expression grim. "I've questioned the lab techs, sir. They claim Claire authorized the chip switch," he admitted, his voice steady despite the gravity of the situation.

Martinez's eyes narrowed, the grim line of his mouth tightening. "Claire's involved," he muttered, more to himself than to

Reynolds. There was a pause, the silence heavy with contemplation.

"I need you to start putting pressure on these people. Start with Maddy and Declan. Their lower ranks within the Agency should not raise as many flags. At some point, we will need to question Claire directly," Martinez finally decided, his gaze hardening. "But do it discreetly. We cannot afford a spectacle. Not now."

Reynolds nodded, the tension in his shoulders easing a fraction. "Understood, sir. I'll handle it."

As he ended the call, his mind was already spinning with possible strategies. This was a delicate situation, and he needed to tread lightly. He wasn't just dealing with a member of the QRDA team; he was dealing with the Director of Quantum Computing Research, Dr. Christopher Peterson.

As he place the phone back in his pocket, he couldn't help but feel a pang of unease. The stakes were high, and the game was changing rapidly. What he did next could change the course of their mission for better or for worse. Only time would tell.

Agent Reynolds rose from his chair, still feeling the cool touch of the communicator in his hand. His mind was a tempest of strategy and uncertainty, but he had received his orders. Determined, he grabbed his jacket from the coat rack and exited the office, his footsteps echoing in the quiet corridor.

Navigating the twisting streets of the city, he headed downtown. The towering skyscrapers receded behind him as he ventured into the heart of the urban maze. The neighborhood he found himself in was older and filled with small businesses, eateries, and a certain charm that the sleek corporate buildings of the city center lacked. One such place was The Last Liberal, a favorite watering hole for many QRDA employees and locals alike, and the place where Reynolds would plant the seed for his first lead.

Jamie, the owner of The Last Liberal, was known throughout the city for her warm hospitality and fine selection of spirits. However, Reynolds also knew her to be somewhat reckless, always willing to bend the rules for her patrons. This disregard

for the law, coupled with Maddy's known struggles with alcohol, made Jamie the perfect starting point.
Upon entering the bar, Reynolds immediately spotted Jamie behind the counter, her broad figure hard to miss. The woman was engrossed in pouring a particularly frothy pint, her concentration etched onto her weathered face. Spotting the familiar badge on Reynolds' chest, she raised an eyebrow but said nothing.
Reynolds drew in a deep breath, steeling himself for what was to come. "Jamie," he began, his tone steady. "I have reason to believe you've been breaching the liquor allowance laws. Specifically, serving unauthorized alcohol to Maddy Rollins."
Jamie's face drained of color. "Maddy?" she echoed, her voice barely a whisper. She glanced at the patrons, their chatter dropping off as they picked up on the tension.
"Jamie, you're under arrest," Reynolds stated, producing a pair of cuffs from his pocket. The clink of metal against the bar counter echoed in the sudden silence.
As he led Jamie out of the bar, Reynolds felt a pang of sympathy for the woman. But he knew that this was the first of many sacrifices to be made in the pursuit of the truth. The pressure on Maddy would surely mount, and perhaps that pressure would lead her to reveal what she knew about Claire and the switched AR chip. The warning of the societal ending event had still not cleared from the pre-crime system, and it was beginning to make people more than a little antsy.

Minutes after Agent Reynolds escorted Jamie out of The Last Liberal, Minister Martinez found himself sitting behind his mahogany desk, staring blankly at the pile of reports. The pile seemed to have grown exponentially in the past few days. Lost in thought, his mind was still turning over Reynolds' recent revelations when his communicator sprung to life. The name displayed on the screen made his heart skip a beat: President Caldwell.

Swallowing hard, Martinez accepted the call. President Caldwell's face filled the screen, lines of concern etched into his forehead. He was not a man known for frivolous communication; his calls were always significant.

"Minister Martinez," the President began, his tone uncharacteristically weary. "I hope the situation with the car accident is under control. I've been receiving nonstop updates and inquiries about it. You know how much I regret the loss of lives, especially those children."

Martinez nodded solemnly, "Yes, Mr. President. It's a tragedy."

The President sighed heavily, running a hand over his face. "It's been suggested to me that if this information gets out even to the high-ranking members, there is a possibility of them asking me to step down, which might be the most appropriate course of action given the circumstances," he confided.

Martinez frowned, shaking his head. "Sir, that wouldn't serve any purpose," he advised firmly. "The country needs you at the helm, especially in times like these. Your stepping down would only add to the chaos."

The President's face relaxed slightly, clearly relieved. "I'm glad to hear you say that, Martinez," he admitted. "Keep me updated on the situation. I want to ensure we are doing everything in our power to handle this. But before I let you go, it was whispered to me that Minister Peterson may have been a witness and accessed the Autonomous Traffic Control System right after the incident. Is this true?"

"It is, sir, but I assure you our records indicate that he did not dig deep enough to see the truth!"

"Hmm, he is after all the most skilled quantum computer programmer we have. I am quite confident he could easily hide his movements into the Autonomous Traffic Control System. I think it best that we find a way to remove him!"

"Sir? Remove, Sir?"

"You are not a stupid man, Minister. You know what I mean. I cannot have any loose threads hanging over my head on this one."

"Understood, Mr. President," Martinez replied, his tone resolute. As the call ended, he couldn't help but feel the weight of the world on his shoulders. A sense of urgency filled the room as he contemplated their next steps. He knew the future of the nation was hanging in the balance. And as he returned to his reports, he realized the decisions he made now were not just for the sake of their current situation, but for the fate of the entire country.

After an intense conversation with the President, Martinez sent a direct message to Reynolds, instructing him on their next course of action. Reynolds found himself driving through the labyrinthine city streets again, this time to Maddy Rollins's apartment. His mind was a whirlwind of thoughts as he tried to piece together a strategy that would not only pressure Maddy but also ensure her safety. He didn't like where this was going at all, but he had no choice. Caught between the hammer and the anvil, it's best to remember - one shapes, the other shatters; tread wisely, lest you become their metal fodder. This was a saying he heard once long ago, but it surely fit his current predicament.
Reynolds pulled up outside the neat, modern building where Maddy lived and took a moment to compose himself before stepping out of his car. He entered the building and ascended in the elevator, running his planned conversation through his head one last time.
He rapped on Maddy's door, and the sound of his knuckles echoed against the solid wood. The door creaked open to reveal Maddy, her face pale and drawn. She had clearly been drinking.
"Agent," she greeted cautiously, her eyes darting to the badge on his chest.
"Maddy Rollins, I need to ask you some questions," Reynolds stated, his tone gentler than his usual authoritative pitch.
As they sat across from each other in her living room, the tension was palpable. Reynolds started by addressing the liquor allowance

breaches, and Maddy listened quietly, her expression a mix of confusion and fear.
When he sensed her apprehension peak, he decided to present his offer. "Maddy, I'm not just here about the liquor law violations. There's a much bigger picture here," he said, leaning forward, his eyes steady on hers. "I can help you with these allegations, make them disappear. But in return, I need to know about the AR chip and what's going on at the QRDA."
Maddy's eyes widened at the mention of the chip. She sat in silence for a moment, considering his proposition. The fate of her friends, her colleagues, and perhaps the whole of QRDA hung in the balance. Her answer in the following moments would set the course of their journey, one that would either reveal the truth or further entangle them in a web of deceit and uncertainty.

The silence hung heavily in Maddy's living room. Reynolds watched a flurry of emotions dance across her face, including fear, defiance, and determination, painting a complex portrait of the woman he was dealing with. Finally, she broke the silence. "Even if I were to tell you anything, Agent Reynolds, which I'm not," Maddy said, her voice steady despite the underlying tremor. "I'm not afraid of facing charges for my first offense. They'll send me to rehab, slap on a fine maybe. I've got no prior record, no trouble with the law."
Reynolds remained silent; his eyes locked onto hers. Maddy's confident front was admirable, but he knew better. She was underestimating the gravity of her situation.
"Maddy, I don't think you understand the severity of the situation you're in," he said, his voice heavy with empathy. "This isn't just about a liquor law violation. You are caught in the middle of a high-stakes investigation. The charges you could face are far more serious than a stint in rehab."
The words hung in the air between them, the gravity of his statement permeating the room. Maddy looked taken aback. Her

confident facade crumbled slightly, and Reynolds could see the fear creeping into her eyes.
"This isn't a game, Maddy," he continued. "The authorities are not going to be lenient. They're coming after everyone associated with the project you are working on at the QRDA. You're not just facing a fine or rehab, you're looking at possible prison time, a lot of prison time."
Maddy's face paled considerably. Reynolds could see her mind racing as she considered his words. Her shoulders slumped slightly, the reality of her situation setting in. He gave her a moment to let it all sink in, his mind silently urging her to make the right choice. The ball was in her court now, and her decision could change everything.

Maddy's face turned ashen as she listened to Reynolds' words. After a long pause, she shook her head, barely whispering, "I can't tell you anything, Reynolds."
Reynolds sighed, feeling a twinge of disappointment. He had hoped it wouldn't come to this, but he had no other choice. He stood up, looking at Maddy with regret. "I'm sorry to hear that, Maddy," he said. "But in light of your decision, I have to take certain measures."
Reynolds pulled out a device from his pocket that resembled a regular smartphone and tapped a few buttons. The apartment filled with a low hum, and Maddy looked around confused.
"This is now your cell, Maddy," Reynolds announced, his voice hard. "Effective immediately, you are under house arrest. You will not be allowed to leave or make any calls. This apartment is digitally locked under my authority."
Maddy looked at him with a mixture of fear and disbelief, her mouth hanging open. But before she could say anything, Reynolds continued, "I will be back tomorrow morning. I hope you use this time to think about your answers because I expect your full cooperation."

He paused, making sure his next words were clear. "The consequences of non-compliance... let's just say they are much worse than being confined to your cozy apartment."
With that, Reynolds left the apartment, leaving a shell-shocked Maddy behind. As he walked back to his car, he could not shake off the heavy feeling in his heart. This was a path he did not want to take, but his duty left him with no choice. He only hoped that Maddy would reconsider her decision, for her sake.

Chapter 17

The Echoes of Loss

Alone in her apartment, Maddy felt the silence close in around her, the weight of her predicament pressing heavily on her shoulders. The reality of her situation was settling in, cold and hard. She was trapped in her own home, confined by the very technology she had devoted her life to studying.

Desperate for a semblance of comfort and normalcy, she went into the kitchen and poured herself a generous glass of wine. The rich, ruby liquid glowed warmly in the dim light of the apartment, offering a faint beacon of familiarity in a situation that was anything but ordinary.

She then moved to the bathroom, turning the knobs of the bathtub and releasing a gush of warm water. She watched as it slowly filled the tub, adding a few drops of her favorite lavender-scented bubble bath. The familiar, soothing scent wafted through the air, calming her nerves.

Leaving the bath to fill, Maddy moved to the antique writing desk by the window. It was a piece of furniture she cherished, not for its monetary value, but for the sense of tranquillity it offered. It had been a long time since she had written anything by hand, a forgotten art in their digital world, but tonight it felt like the only suitable medium to pour out her thoughts.

She pulled out a thick, bound notebook from the desk drawer, along with a beautifully crafted fountain pen, its nib glinting in the muted light. The blank pages lay in front of her like an open canvas, ready to capture her thoughts and fears.

Maddy took a deep breath and started to write, the smooth glide of the pen on the paper creating a rhythm that soothed her racing mind.

In the growing silence of her apartment, Maddy spilled her thoughts on paper, weaving together a painful narrative of the Mycelium computer, her stalwart allies, Claire and Declan, and the simulation that had carved a cavernous void within her. The profundity of her loss was inked in every line she traced, every memory she committed to parchment. For in the shadowy realm of the simulation, she had loved and lost a child, a being of her own making, a fragment of her heart that had sprouted, bloomed, and been ruthlessly plucked away in the blink of an eye.

Her torment was compounded by the realization that the child she had held, nurtured, and cherished was birthed from an ephemeral reality, a reality that was her's alone. It was a weight she bore singularly, a torment she could share but never truly transfer. She saw the empathy in Claire's eyes, the concern etched on Declan's face, but she also knew their comfort was extended from the shores of sympathy, not empathy. They could never really fathom the depth of her loss, for they had not navigated the same tumultuous journey in the simulation.

Most piercing of all, however, was the understanding that Declan could never partake in the love that she had experienced, a love so profound it felt etched into her very soul. He could not reminisce the echo of a child's laughter, the warmth of a shared love, or the despair of their abrupt departure. He was a bystander in her story, offering silent support but unable to dive into the turbulent ocean of her sorrow. As the ink bled onto the paper, she chronicled not just the stark facts, but also her layered emotions - her grief, her yearning, her heartbreaking solitude in her loss.

She wrote about the fear that gnawed at her, the loneliness that had crept into her heart after the simulation. This world with its lack of family true family was haunting and now that she had experienced life with it she didn't know how to live without it despite the fact that it was not real. Fear gripped her and the uncertainty of what the future held. Her words flowed freely, the ink seeping into the pages as her thoughts took form, bringing both clarity and catharsis.

After what felt like hours, Maddy put down her pen and leaned back in her chair, feeling a weight lifted from her mind. She surveyed the pages filled with her thoughts, sensing the raw emotions behind each neatly written line. Initially, she closed the notebook and tucked it into her desk drawer. But after a moment's hesitation, she took it out again, leaving it in plain sight, knowing deep down she wouldn't have the heart to continue writing. Exhausted, Maddy drained the last of her wine and headed to the bathroom. The tub was filled with frothy bubbles, the soothing scent of lavender hanging heavy in the warm steam. She undressed and slid into the hot bath. As she slipped into the tub, the soothing warmth of the water enveloped her like a comforting embrace. The world beyond the bathroom seemed to fade away, replaced by the heady aroma of lavender and the gentle lull of her own heartbeat. In this sanctuary, isolated from the noise of the outside world, her thoughts found a space to breathe.

She reflected on the words she had spilt across the pages of her cherished notebook, the raw, visceral emotions that bled through every line. Each sentence was a testament to the grief that gnawed at her, the emptiness that echoed with the ghost of the love she had lost in the simulation. Her heart was an island in a sea of sorrow, isolated by an experience that was hers alone.

Her allies, Claire and Declan, offered sympathy, their eyes a mirror of concern. But their comfort was a distant echo, born of empathy, not shared experience. They hadn't experienced the joy of her simulated family, hadn't been pierced by the stinging absence of a child's laughter. Their support, while sincere, was a stark reminder of the unique torment she endured.

Her fears, her loneliness, her solitude - they were ghosts that lingered in the shadows, reminders of the life she had lived in the simulation and the harsh reality that now confronted her. Her apartment was a hollow echo chamber, the silence a relentless reminder of her singular journey.

The despair that entwined her heart was a vine, spiralling tighter with each passing moment. She had tasted a life filled with familial love, only for it to dissolve into the cold truth of her current reality. The absence was suffocating, a phantom pain that was all too real.

Yet, as she stared at the frothy bubbles and the steam that kissed her skin, she found a strange solace. In the act of pouring her heart onto the pages, she had found a measure of release. The tangible evidence of her feelings, inked onto paper, was a lifeline in the stormy seas of her mind. It was her anchor, her testament of resilience in the face of desolation.

Maddy let the wine-soaked thoughts wash over her as the lavender-infused steam curled around her body. She was alone, yes, but in this moment, in the warmth of the bath and the comforting scent of lavender, she found a momentary peace. It was a fleeting solace, a brief respite in the face of an uncertain future, but it was hers to hold onto, to help her brave the long night ahead.

Agent Reynolds was jolted awake by the shrill sound of his communication device piercing the stillness of the night. An automated voice relayed a message with urgent undertones, "Emergency at Subject M-7's residence. Medical personnel on-site. Request your immediate presence."
Reynolds froze, his blood running cold. He quickly dressed and grabbed his coat, racing towards his vehicle with his mind churning with worry and regret. The ride to Maddy's apartment was a blur of neon lights and speeding traffic, every second elongating into minutes.

As he arrived, the apartment building was already swarming with paramedics and law enforcement personnel. A chilling sense of dread crawled up his spine as he rushed to Maddy's floor. Her apartment was eerily silent, a stark contrast to the frantic activity outside. The paramedics were huddled over a form on the bathroom floor, their faces grave.

"She's gone," the lead paramedic said, looking at Reynolds with a mixture of accusation and pity. "The system alerted us, but we were too late. She was... efficient."

Reynolds felt a crushing sense of guilt consume him. He had put her under house arrest, taking away her freedom in the hope that she would cooperate. He had anticipated resistance, anger, even hatred, but he had never imagined it would lead to this.

Inside the apartment, the remnants of Maddy's final moments painted a poignant portrait of lonely desperation. The antique desk by the window held an open notebook; nearby sat a wine glass, its bottom stained with a teasing hint of red, the last elusive sip that never seems to be caught and the cooling bath water all bore silent testimony to her final hours A poignant tableau of her despair, they were stark reminders of her hope for something more and her devastation at having it ripped away.

The apartment stood as a testament to her pain, a pain that he, despite his good intentions, had undoubtedly exacerbated. The harsh reality of his decisions weighed heavily on his heart, a grim reminder that the path of duty was not always just. He had wanted to protect the world from the unknown, but in the process, he had failed to protect Maddy from her own despair.

Agent Reynolds stood alone in the dimly lit apartment, the hushed whispers of the departing paramedics echoing in the oppressive silence. Maddy's body lay just a few feet away, covered by a sterile white sheet that did little to soften the reality of her demise. His gaze drifted to the bathtub, its porcelain surface marred by stark crimson stains.

His thoughts spiraled in a maelstrom of remorse and self-condemnation. His career had seen him bear witness to an endless reel of crime scenes, but this one lacerated his soul like none other. He hadn't merely lost a test subject; he had lost a life, a catastrophe for which he bore a direct and haunting responsibility.

As he waited for the coroner, he allowed himself a moment of vulnerability, of personal grief. He moved to the antique desk, the fountain pen still laying there, its gleaming nib standing as a testament to Maddy's final thoughts. He glanced at the open notebook, her elegant script painting a picture of anguish, hope, and despair. It was more than a record of her loss, it was a gateway into her soul, a glimpse into the depth of pain she had endured.

Agent Reynolds brought up the apartment's security footage on his hand-held computer and entered the password that allowed him to breach anyone's privacy with the click of a button. He stared at the screen and watched her final moments on the screen and read what she wrote in her notebook He was so engrossed in the atmosphere that it almost felt real, as if she were right in front of him and all he needed to do was step forward and stop her with a hug or a kind word of hope.

Maddy's pen hovered over the final page of her notebook, her heart pulsating with an intensity that echoed in the rhythmic beat of her words. She inhaled deeply, her gaze unfocused as she journeyed back into the digital world that had once held her captive, a world she now yearned to return to, a world that had presented an impossible dichotomy of promise and despair.

"Dear friends," she began, her words quavering with a strange combination of sadness, fear, and resolve. "If you're reading this, then the course of my life has taken a turn I no longer have control over. I wish I could fully express the complexity of emotions tearing through me, but I fear words may not suffice. However, I'll try." In her script, she painted a vivid picture of her journey within the simulation, the life-altering experiences it had given her, the joy of holding her child, the unique bond of shared love with Declan. She laid bare her soul, her torment, and the silent grief that gnawed at her every waking moment. She wrote, "The simulation within the Mycelium computer gave me a glimpse of a life that could have been, a life that was so painfully beautiful that reality now seems insipid, colorless in comparison. The depth of my longing for that life is such that I fear no amount of time in this world could ever mend my fractured heart." As she continued, her words danced between the lines of hope and despair. She wrote of the simulation's tantalizing glimpse into the promise of something more, an existence unfettered by time or space, a reality where love and loss could coexist in a dance as old as time itself. Yet, it was this very promise that had been cruelly snatched away, leaving her grappling with a gnawing emptiness. "In losing my child, in losing the man I loved in a world that does not exist, I feel I've lost a part of my soul," she confessed, her tears blurring the ink on the page. "Yet, it is this very loss that fuels my hope of finding it again, somewhere, sometime, in some form." She wrote of her unshakeable belief that the Mycelium computer held more secrets than it had revealed, that it could be her conduit to the life she yearned for, the love she had lost. "Maybe, in another time, another dimension, even another world," she penned, "there exists a reality where my child lives, where our love thrives." With a trembling hand, she concluded her letter, her last tangible link to Claire and Declan. "If I could, I would choose to live within the simulation for an eternity. For it's there that I felt most alive, most loved. But since that choice has been taken from me, I seek solace in the hope that our paths will cross again, in a reality far removed from the limitations of our current existence. Until then, remember me as I was - curious, hopeful, and unafraid of the vast, cosmic unknown." As she signed off, Maddy felt an odd sense of serenity wash over her. She had laid bare her heart, etching her most profound hopes and fears onto paper. Now, she could only wait for the dawn of a new day, for a future that was as unpredictable as the flickering codes of the Mycelium computer.

He pressed stop on the recording before she undressed to get into the bath, no need to breach her privacy any more during her last moments of life.
Slowly, he walked over to the bathroom. The scent of lavender hung heavy in the air, a ghostly remnant of Maddy's presence. He looked at the bathtub, now a chilling tableau of her final act. The sight struck him hard, a poignant reminder of his failure.
His eyes welled up with unshed tears, a potent mix of regret and sorrow. He had enforced the house arrest, entrapping her in this technological prison. He was here to push her, make her break, make her spill the secrets of the QRDA, but he had woefully underestimated the battle raging within her.
In the chilling silence of the apartment, Reynolds contemplated his choices, his duty, and the price of it all. He made a silent vow to himself, a pledge forged in the crucible of loss. His role might be to protect the world from the unknown, but he would never again overlook the known, the human element, the silent cries for help. He would honor Maddy's memory by ensuring her tragedy would serve as a grim reminder, a lesson learned in the harshest way possible.

Chapter 18

Echoes in Absence

As the sun dawned on the following day, the world moved on, oblivious to the tragedy that had transpired in the heart of the city. Claire and Declan were no exception, their minds deeply entrenched in the labyrinth of the mysterious Mycelium computer and the enigma it presented. They arrived at the lab early, armed with fresh enthusiasm and a to-do list that extended beyond the horizon of the day. The magnitude of their task was a captivating challenge, and they immersed themselves in it wholeheartedly.

As the clock on the lab wall ticked away, each passing minute marked the commencement of their relentless research. The soft humming of the advanced machines filled the space, a harmonious symphony that lent rhythm to their focused endeavors.

The day wore on, and the clock on the lab wall marked the arrival of the eleventh hour of the morning. So engrossed were they in their deliberations and deductions, they failed to notice the glaring absence of a crucial member of their trio. Maddy's workstation, usually a hub of vibrant energy, lay stark and silent.

It was Declan who first noticed the anomaly. His eyes, sweeping across the room, landed on Maddy's empty chair. A frown creased his forehead. It was unlike Maddy to be late, especially when they were neck-deep in such a pivotal project. Claire followed his gaze and the confusion mirrored on her face.

Maddy's absence was a discordant note in their well-orchestrated symphony of work. Little did they know that their day, which had begun with ambitious plans and a thirst for knowledge, was about to take an unexpected, heartrending turn

The lab door swung open to reveal the solemn figure of Dr. Peterson. His usually energetic demeanor was replaced with a sense of heaviness, his eyes, red-rimmed and somber, told a story of a morning spent in grief. His entrance into the room seemed to lower the temperature, his aura of sadness casting a shadow that the overhead lab lights couldn't dispel.
Claire, her brow furrowed in concern at the sight of Dr. Peterson, hung up the communicator, her futile attempts to reach Maddy momentarily forgotten. The robotic voice of Maddy reading a scripted verse of "Sorry I cannot receive your call, please leave a message and I will get back to you as soon as possible; from the device echoed in the silent room, a haunting reminder of their absent colleague.
Dr. Peterson stepped further into the lab, the heavy click of the door closing behind him resonating ominously in the silence. His gaze wandered to Maddy's empty workstation, a sigh of sorrow escaping his lips as the weight of reality bore down on him. In the face of the unremitting loss, the relentless march of time, and the callous nature of their work, it was up to him to break the devastating news to Claire and Declan, forever altering their world in the process.

Dr. Peterson cleared his throat, his usual confident tone replaced by a shaky whisper. He opened his mouth to speak, but his words seemed stuck in his throat. His gaze flickered towards Claire and Declan, their expectant faces unwittingly amplifying his pain.
"I...," he started, his voice barely a whisper. He swallowed hard, fighting the knot of emotion in his throat. The two scientists watched him with growing concern, their hearts heavy with foreboding.

"I regret...," Peterson began again, his voice trailing off as his eyes filled with unshed tears. His usual composed demeanor, the rock-steady persona they had all come to rely on, was beginning to crack.
Drawing a deep, shuddering breath, Peterson finally managed to utter the dreaded words. "Maddy is... She's..." The finality of the words felt like a physical blow, his voice breaking on the last syllable. "Maddy is gone."
The words hung in the air like a heavy pall, casting a shadow over the bustling lab. The room seemed to shrink around them, the enormity of their loss threatening to suffocate them. All the vibrant energy, all the plans and hopes for the day, they all evaporated in the wake of Peterson's announcement.
For a moment, no one spoke. The only sounds in the room were the low hum of the machines and the echoes of Peterson's heart-wrenching declaration. It was as if time had ground to a halt, the world holding its breath in the face of their grief.

Claire seemed frozen for a moment, her pale face a stark contrast to the flush that normally colored her cheeks. The buzz of the lab around them receded, leaving only Peterson's voice echoing in her ears.
"What do you mean 'gone', Dr. Peterson?" she echoed, her voice sounding foreign to her own ears. Her mind raced, trying to conjure a thousand other explanations, desperately trying to deny the reality that was being thrust upon her.
Peterson's solemn gaze met hers, his red-rimmed eyes a testament to the harsh truth. "She's... She's not with us anymore, Claire," he clarified gently, his voice choked with unshed tears.
The room seemed to spin as Claire digested his words. Her heart pounded in her chest, her mind screaming in protest. This couldn't be happening. Not Maddy. Not their vibrant, brilliant, resilient Maddy.
"But... but how?" Claire stuttered, her voice barely above a whisper. She clung to the question as if it were a lifeline, a final

shred of hope in the face of a devastating truth. Her eyes searched Peterson's, pleading for an answer that would make this nightmare disappear.
Peterson's shoulders sagged as he took a deep breath, preparing himself to relay the unthinkable. The next few moments would shatter the remnants of their normalcy, pushing them into a reality they were not prepared to face. A reality without Maddy.

Peterson cleared his throat, the bitter taste of grief clinging to his tongue. "Maddy was placed under house arrest by the Ministry of Security and Intelligence. It seems they would not let the society-ending event drop, even after I pulled a few strings to have them move along."
Claire's face paled even further, the blood draining from her features. Her fingers clutched tightly at the edge of the table as she tried to steady herself, but the room seemed to pitch and sway around her. It was as if the very ground beneath her had given way.
"Last night," Peterson continued, his voice wavering with emotion, "she took her own life."
The silence that followed was deafening. Peterson's words hung in the air, the finality of them reverberating around the lab, bouncing off the sterile walls and embedding themselves deep within the marrow of their bones. Maddy, their colleague, their friend, their guiding star in the abyss of the unknown, was gone. The impact was sudden and brutal, a gut-punch that stole the breath from their lungs and replaced it with an icy, creeping dread. Tears welled in Claire's eyes, blurring the room around her. Through her shock, the magnitude of their loss began to sink in. Their world, both in and outside the simulation, would never be the same again. The loss of Maddy's life was an abrupt disconnection, a sudden void that no amount of technological prowess could bridge.

Declan stood up suddenly, his chair scraping loudly against the cold, unforgiving laboratory floor. His knuckles whitened as he gripped the edge of the table, his jaw muscles working as he ground his teeth together. A vein throbbed in his temple, bearing witness to the intensity of his denial.

"No," he said firmly, his voice harsh and choked with emotion. He looked directly at Peterson, desperation flickering in his blue eyes. "No, that's... that's not possible."

Peterson met his gaze, and the weight of his sorrow was evident in his weary eyes. He opened his mouth to reply, but Declan was already shaking his head, vehemently denying the reality they had all been forced to confront.

"Maddy wouldn't... she wouldn't do this. She wouldn't take her own life!" His voice echoed off the high ceilings of the lab, filled with a desperate energy that was as much a plea as it was a declaration. It was a futile grasp for a reality that was less bleak and cold than the one they found themselves in.

The lab fell silent again, the only sound the unsteady rhythm of Declan's breathing. His chest rose and fell sharply, his disbelief palpable in the stillness of the room. The echo of his denial seemed to linger in the air, a stark counterpoint to the terrible truth of their shared loss.

But the truth remained, its gravity pulling them all into its cold embrace. Maddy, their Maddy, was gone. And nothing Declan said, no matter how fervently he denied it, could change the harsh reality of their loss.

"Did she... did she leave anything?" Declan asked, his voice raw and hoarse. His eyes darted between Peterson and Claire, desperate for any sign of confirmation or understanding. "A note, a letter, anything? Anything at all?"

Dr. Peterson shook his head, his eyes hollow. "Agent Reynolds informed us of her passing this morning. He didn't mention a note."

A chill ran down Declan's spine. His mind raced, trying to reconcile Maddy's loss with the absence of a final message. Could she have left without a word, without a last goodbye, without an explanation? It seemed incongruous with the Maddy he knew, the Maddy who always had an explanation, who always had a reason.

"But there must be something," Declan insisted, frustration shaking his voice. "She wouldn't just... she wouldn't just leave like that. Not without saying something."

A heavy silence settled in the lab. The room felt colder, emptier. Claire's eyes brimmed with tears, and Peterson's shoulders sagged under an unseen weight. The clock on the wall continued to tick, each second a poignant reminder of their loss.

But as the gravity of the situation sank in, a grim resolve began to take root in Declan's heart. If there was a reason, he was going to find it. Maddy's memory deserved that much.

He didn't know what lay ahead or how he would navigate the tumultuous sea of grief, but he knew one thing for certain: He would not rest until he uncovered the truth behind Maddy's tragic end.

As news of Maddy's passing rippled through the QRDA, a solemn quietude descended, each person grappling with the sudden, agonizing void left behind. The vibrant, relentless pulse of their quest for knowledge and exploration had been abruptly silenced. The loss was not just of a colleague or comrade, but of an idea, a vision, a collective dream that Maddy had been instrumental in shaping.

Chapter 19

From Loneliness to Unsettling Simulations

As evening blanketed the lab, the phone rang, slicing through the silence. Claire picked up to hear news of Jamie's arrest the previous night. The room spun, Claire frozen in place, her face drained of color. The sterile lab lights cast an unforgiving glow on her shock-stricken face, making the situation seem even more surreal. Her silence was deafening, a poignant symbol of the overwhelming news she had just received.

With the weight of her grief and worry pressing heavily upon her, Claire left the ghostly quiet of the lab behind. The city lights blurred around her as she made her way to Declan's apartment, a beacon of familiarity in a world that had suddenly become unrecognizable. Frantically, Claire pushed open the door to Declan's apartment, a crushing weight of loneliness bearing down on her. The stark silence of the room seemed to mock her solitude, a harsh reminder of the day's heartbreaking events. She had hoped to find him there, to share in their mutual grief, to not be alone in her mourning. But the empty apartment offered no such comfort.

"I don't want to be alone, not now..." she whispered to the void, her voice echoing back with a chilling emptiness. She shut the door with a shudder, leaning against it momentarily as she collected her thoughts.

When Declan had given her his key, inviting her to seek refuge whenever she needed, she never imagined she'd use it under such circumstances. The reality of Maddy's loss, the void it had left, was too much to bear alone. She sank onto the couch, desperately clinging to the silence, longing for Declan's presence, someone to share in their loss, to keep the crushing loneliness at bay.

Despite the consuming grief that clung to him, Declan found himself unable to remain stagnant in his sorrow. As if pulled by an unseen force, he retraced his steps back to the lab – the eye of their storm. The void left by Maddy's absence hung heavily in the air; her usually vibrant presence was now a haunting echo. Yet, amid this heartache, Declan felt a spark of hope flicker - the relentless pursuit for answers propelled him forward.

He strode towards the Mycelium quantum computer, its soft hum filling the room with a mechanical lullaby. The cold surface of the interface was a stark contrast to the warm memories of Maddy that flooded him. He whispered a plea to the machine, requesting it reveal the secrets it had shared with Maddy. If the machine could project an entire lifetime for Maddy, perhaps it could give him a glimpse of what she saw, felt, and loved.

Standing over the system, he realized he had no idea what to do. Both times the system had initiated a simulation, it did so on its own. Declan yearned to encounter Maddy and the digital child, the creation that had brought such joy to her and, in the end, such torment. Nervously, he touched the keyboard, initiating the power to the screen. The room immediately faded away as he plunged into the virtual realm, chasing after Maddy's phantom.

Plunging into the simulation, Declan found himself standing in a world far removed from the one he'd hoped for. He stood outside under a heavy, gray sky, raindrops pelting down on him, soaking his hair and clothes. The chill in the air echoed the restless, grimy crowd that surrounded him, a sea of faces etched with hardship and despair.

A line extended before him, winding out of sight, all moving towards a small group of people dressed in sterile white. The soft glow of their uniforms was a stark contrast against the dull backdrop. It seemed they were administering injections, their movements quick and mechanical, emotionless, in stark contrast to the palpable tension vibrating through the crowd.

Everywhere he looked, he saw hardship etched into the worn-out faces around him. They were tired, their spirits defeated. Fear, worry, and hopelessness seeped from them, their heads bowed under invisible weights. The scent of desperation filled the air, tainted by the grit and grime that seemed to color the world around him.

A sense of dread chilled his spine. This wasn't what he'd expected, not what he'd hoped for. This simulation wasn't a reunion with a lost digital child, but a dive into a stark, harsh reality, one that mirrored the trials and tribulations of the world he had left outside the lab. Yet, driven by a need to understand, to find a piece of Maddy in this virtual world, Declan pressed forward, following the relentless march of the crowd.

As the line moved forward, the woman standing in front of him turned around, a swirl of fear and hope in her eyes. Recognition lit up her face, and she reached out to him, her fingers brushing against his arm. "Oh, Mike," she breathed, her voice laced with emotion.

Her use of the unfamiliar name sent a jolt through him, but he held his ground, focused on her words. "I hope the genetic testing comes back positive for us," she continued, her hand gently squeezing his. Her eyes, shimmering with unshed tears, conveyed a depth of longing, raw and personal. "I so want a child of our own."

Her words hit him like a punch to the gut, a stark reminder of Maddy's heartbroken confession in the lab. The connection sent a chill down his spine, deepening his confusion.

"What will we do if we are denied?" the woman continued, the edges of fear fraying her voice. "What if I am forced to be with someone else, forced to have their child?" Her last words were a whisper, heavy with an unspeakable dread.

Declan could only stare at her, the gravity of her words sinking into him. The world around him faded into a low hum, drowned out by the thundering of his heartbeat in his ears. This was not the reunion he had sought, but a harsh revelation of a reality that was as alien as it was disturbing. He was caught in a nightmare, the dystopian vision of this simulation a stark departure from the warmth of Maddy's digital family. But he was also closer to her, now more than ever, sharing in the desperation and fear of a world far removed from their own.

In the dreary tableau of the simulation, a light drizzle began to fall. Declan's attention was drawn back to the crowd. A maelstrom of emotions whirled around him, the palpable sense of fear and hope in the air a bitter reminder of the world he was witnessing. Each face, each posture, each whisper around him told the same story of anticipation and dread.

As he took in the scene, his gaze landed on a pair, a man and a woman, their skin so luminescent it caught his attention amidst the sea of faces. Their skin was white, not merely pale, but truly white as though it were devoid of color. It was a striking, almost surreal sight that made Declan squint, wondering if it was a trick of the simulation or his mind playing games with him.

In all his years, he had never seen anything like it. He had studied countless genetic variations and phenotypes, but this was outside his realm of knowledge. "Is that even possible?" he whispered to himself, incredulity etching lines of confusion on his face.

He took a step closer, intending to study them, when the woman in front of him turned, her voice a desperate plea breaking his concentration. "Mike, promise me, whatever happens, we'll stay together." Her eyes implored him for assurance, a life raft in this tumultuous sea.

Even as he grappled with the surreal landscape unfolding before him, Declan couldn't help but feel a pang of empathy. The fear, the hope, the struggle for survival, the deep human connection - it was all too real.

The surreal nature of the simulation continued to unfold before Declan. After the shock of seeing the white-skinned couple, his eyes landed on another duo, their skin as dark as midnight. They glowed with an ethereal light, their features accentuated by the simulation, ensuring that Declan's gaze was drawn to them.

Their skin was like ebony, a stark contrast to the crowd around them. The man's nose was broader, a strong and prominent feature on his face. His partner's hair was a marvel in itself - a dense, rich crown of tight curls, each coil uniquely intricate and beautiful. It was like a piece of abstract art, wild and untamed, an emblem of their distinctive identity.

The sight of them, so different and yet so human, sent Declan's mind reeling. He turned his gaze back to the first couple, and suddenly he noticed details he had previously missed. The woman's hair was a fiery red, catching even the dim light around them and turning it into a vivid halo. The man's hair was a stark contrast, the color of sun-kissed wheat, his eyes wide and round, the color of the clear summer sky.

The sheer diversity of what he was witnessing stunned him, a stark reminder of the rich tapestry of human variation. A variation surprisingly unknown to him! The simulation, it seemed, was intent on making sure he understood the breadth and depth of the human condition. His mind whirled as he took it all in, the profound realization leaving him speechless.

In the chaos of the scene, Declan's eyes were drawn to a pair of faces now highlighted by the simulation. One was a woman with high cheekbones and almond-shaped eyes, her hair straight and dark as midnight. Her features mirrored those typically associated with East Asian descent.

Beside her, a man with deep-set eyes and a prominent nose, his skin the warm hue of baked earth, like someone of East Indian origins. His hair was dark and wavy, brushed back casually, the corners of his eyes crinkling slightly as he attempted a reassuring smile at the woman.

Not far from them, Declan noticed a man with a rugged complexion, his hair dark and thick, his eyes a piercing, soulful brown. He was reminiscent of the aboriginal peoples of Australia, his features radiating strength and resilience.

They were all there, people from all walks of life, all corners of the Earth, all standing in the same line, all carrying the same sense of anticipation and anxiety. They were being herded towards what looked like medical personnel, all for a genetic test. But why? What was the purpose of this mass testing? What could possibly warrant such a measure? The questions swirled around in Declan's mind as he continued to observe the unfolding scenario, his heart pounding with the urgency of the unknown.

Declan shook his head, trying to make sense of the wealth of information that had flooded his consciousness. How did he know these people's likely ethnic origins? He was a scientist, yes, and his expertise did lie in anthropology and human evolution, but he knew nothing of what his brain was telling him. The complexity and diversity of human ethnicity had never shown these vast differences between people.

His gaze swept across the crowd once more, and with each face he observed, new information seemed to imprint itself onto his mind - the history of cultures, anthropological facts, linguistic nuances. It was like flipping through a comprehensive textbook of human diversity, the information readily available as if already a part of his knowledge.

"Is the simulation feeding me this knowledge?" he wondered aloud, his voice barely a whisper amidst the din. The computer was a marvel of technology, from what little they had seen, an immersive experience that could render any scenario with life-like realism. But this... this was something else entirely. It wasn't just showing him a different reality; it was augmenting his understanding of that reality. The implications were astounding, and Declan was left grappling with this newfound revelation as he stood amidst the throng of humanity.

Declan, still grappling with his newfound understanding, was pulled back to the reality of the simulation by a soft whimper. His simulated partner winced in pain as the nurse pricked her finger. The sight brought him back to the immediate situation, the broader implications of his newfound understanding momentarily put on hold.

He stepped forward as it was his turn, and as he held out his hand, a jolt of surprise coursed through him. His skin - the skin he was used to seeing, the light brown shade he recognized as his own - was replaced with a dark, rich black hue. He stared at it, fascination mingling with a sense of alien disconnection.

As the nurse quickly pricked his finger, he had barely felt the pinch. His attention had been consumed by the realization that this wasn't his body - not as he knew it. He had been inhabiting someone else's reality, living through their experiences. The profound immersion of the simulation had sent a shiver down his spine - a potent mix of awe and trepidation.

With a surge of frustration and curiosity, Declan had addressed the nurse, his voice laced with an uncharacteristic harshness. "Why were we doing this exactly?" he had demanded. The nurse looked up, her gaze flickering over to the intimidating guard standing a few feet away. Sensing the tension, the guard had stepped forward, his eyes on Declan.

Unfazed, the nurse had turned her attention back to Declan. With a dismissive wave, she handed him a folded piece of paper. "Don't worry," she had reassured, her eyes flitting between Declan and his partner. Her gaze had lingered, hinting at an understanding that Declan hadn't yet comprehended. "You two won't have any problems getting approved."

Declan's eyes had dropped to the pamphlet now in his hands. The title, bold and vibrant, seemed to mock his confusion. It read, "A Rainbow Nation: Unity in Diversity Equals Equity." As he took in the bold letters, the simulation around him suddenly took on a more sinister undertone. What was this world where one's skin color could dictate their future? And more importantly, why was he shown this particular reality?

As quickly as he had entered, Declan was thrust back to the stark, sterile reality of the lab. The simulation faded away, but the image of the colorful, tense crowd remained etched in his mind. He had felt a gnawing sensation in his gut, a whirlpool of emotions threatening to engulf him.

He shook his head, struggling to clear the vivid afterimages of the unsettling scenario. As his mind slowly rose out of the simulation, he felt a wave of vertigo washing over him. The cold, sterile walls of the lab felt constricting after the vibrant chaos of the simulation.

His thoughts were a jumble of questions and confusion. The implications of what he had witnessed tugged at the corners of his consciousness. He needed to discuss this, to understand. He reached for his communicator, his fingers trembling slightly as he dialed Claire's number.

"Claire," he began, his voice shaky. "We need to talk. I've seen something... something troubling in the simulation. Dr. Peterson should join us too. I think... I think we might be dealing with something bigger than we realized."

With the call made, he sank into one of the many chairs in the lab, his mind racing. He had hoped to find answers in the simulation, to see Maddy again, but what he found was a mystery all its own. A mystery he was now desperate to unravel.

Chapter 20

The Convergence of Science and Sorrow

Following Declan's alarming revelation, Claire could feel her heart pounding in her chest. The uncertainty and confusion weaving a web of anxiety. The devastation of Maddy's loss was still fresh and raw, and now Declan's words had added another layer of worry.

"Alright," Claire managed to mutter into her phone, her voice more steady than she felt. "I'll call Dr. Peterson. We'll be there as soon as we can." With a final deep breath, she disconnects the call and quickly dials Dr. Peterson.

The lines of communication between the remaining members of their team were ablaze as Claire conveyed the developments. "Dr. Peterson, Declan's back at the lab, he's seen something... something troubling in the simulation," Claire relayed, the urgency in her voice apparent. "We need to get there, now."

A heavy silence followed Claire's revelation. Then Peterson's voice filled the line, a tempest of outrage and concern. "He did WHAT?" Peterson roared. "By himself? Without supervision or safety measures? That's completely irresponsible!"

The vehemence in Peterson's voice made Claire flinch, but she understood his anger. After the incident with Maddy, they had all agreed to be more cautious. Declan's impulsive actions were not only dangerous, they were a betrayal of their pact.

"Claire, we need to get to him before he does something else stupid. We need to ensure he's okay and prevent him from well... being stupid," Peterson continued, his voice strained with worry.
"I know, Dr. Peterson," Claire agreed quietly, her fingers tightening around her phone. "I'm heading to the lab now. I'll see you there."
As Claire ended the call, a newfound determination began to replace her panic. They were far from understanding what was happening, but they were a team. They had faced challenges before, and they would face this one together. For Maddy, for Jamie, and for themselves, they would unravel this mystery of what it was exactly that was going one.
Despite her calm words, Claire's mind was a whirlwind of fear and anxiety. She couldn't help but feel responsible for Declan's reckless decision. She should never have let him leave the lab alone earlier. If she had been with him she could have talked him out of trying to go back into the simulation. But right now, guilt had to take a backseat.
Dr. Peterson, meanwhile, was in a state of disbelief as he hurriedly gathered his things to head for the lab. Declan's actions were unexpected and dangerous, but he couldn't help but understand the desperate need for answers. But they had to handle this carefully. After all, they were stepping into unknown territory, dealing with a technology that was far beyond their current comprehension.
As they both made their way to the lab, one thing was clear in their minds - they were in this together. They had lost Maddy, but they wouldn't lose Declan too. They were determined to unravel the mystery that had ensnared them all, but not at the cost of any more lives.

Claire pushed open the door to the lab, gasping as she saw Declan sprawled on the cold, sterile floor. Her heart pounded in her chest as she rushed towards him, her mind filled with worst-case scenarios. "Declan!" she called out, her voice echoing in the silent room.

As she dropped to her knees beside him, she saw the sheen of sweat on his forehead and his eyes shut tight against the harsh fluorescent lights. His breathing was ragged and uneven, and the rise and fall of his chest was unsteady.

"Declan, can you hear me?" she asked, trying to keep the panic out of her voice. She laid a tentative hand on his shoulder and gave it a slight shake.

At her touch, he stirred, his eyes fluttering open to meet hers. They were filled with pain that was more emotional than physical, the heartache from Maddy's loss still a fresh wound. "Claire..." he murmured, managing a weak smile. "I'm okay, just...just a little nauseous."

"Oh, Declan, what were you thinking?" she sighed, relief washing over her. She let out a shaky laugh, a sound more of disbelief than amusement. "You scared the hell out of me."

"I'm sorry, Claire," Declan responded, his voice low and filled with regret. His gaze moved away from her, staring blankly at the ceiling as a single tear escaped from the corner of his eye, trailing down his cheek.

Watching him, Claire felt a lump forming in her throat. This was not just about the reckless dive into the simulation anymore. It was about their shared grief, the void that Maddy's absence had left in their lives. It was about their struggle to make sense of the inexplicable events unfolding around them. It was about their fight against the unknown, against a fear that threatened to consume them. It was a fight they had to face together, not alone on the cold floor of their lab.

"Declan, what happened in there?" Claire asked, once she was sure he was alright.

"I wanted to see her again," Declan confessed, his gaze still fixed on the ceiling. "I thought, maybe if I just... maybe if I wanted it enough, the computer would show me Maddy. I wanted to understand, to see the child she talked about."

His words hung heavily in the air. Claire could see the torment in his eyes, the guilt and regret etched deeply. She reached out and gently squeezed his hand, a silent assurance that he wasn't alone.
"And did you?" Claire asked tentatively after a moment. "Did you see Maddy?"
Declan shook his head, his gaze finally meeting Claire's. "No," he replied quietly. "I didn't see Maddy. But what I saw was... it was something else entirely. Something unbelievable."
Claire felt a chill run down her spine at the gravity in his voice. "What did you see, Declan?"
He paused, his eyes darting away as he collected his thoughts. "It's hard to explain," he finally began. "I saw a world, not like ours. A world where genetic testing determines your fate, where your skin color could dictate your future. The diversity, the differences... it was uncanny. It was a world that seemed to value unity in diversity but practised the exact opposite."
He turned his gaze back to Claire, his eyes desperate. "I think Maddy saw this. I think it was this world that took her from us, the pain of losing that child, the pain of that reality, it was too much for her."
Claire took in his words, a pit forming in her stomach. This was far bigger than they had ever imagined. This was about more than just Maddy; it was about the implications of their work, the impact it could have on the world. And they were the only ones who could confront it, who could unravel the mystery

Dr. Peterson parked his car a short distance from the lab. Walking across the asphalt parking lot, he noticed something unusual in the night sky. Against the backdrop of stars, a lone drone hovered ominously. Its small blinking lights were the only indication of its presence.
This was an anomaly. The traffic drones managing the city's autonomous navigation system were always on the move, ensuring the smooth flow of vehicles. Seeing one hovering stationary in the air was unusual and stirred a sense of unease within him.

He observed the drone for a few moments, noting that it didn't seem to be doing anything but floating in the midnight air. It was a small thing, yet it felt out of place, a slight disturbance in the pattern he had grown accustomed to.
With a shrug, he turned away, dismissing it as a glitch or some temporary pause in the system. He had more pressing issues to attend to in the lab. However, as he neared the entrance, he couldn't shake off the strange sight.

The large glass doors of the Quantum Research & Development Agency (QRDA) slid open seamlessly as Dr. Peterson approached, the facial recognition technology confirming his identity. He entered the brightly lit building, his mind filled with a strange combination of concern and curiosity about Declan's troubling discovery.
Suddenly, a loud buzzing sound invaded his hearing, causing him to jerk in surprise. It was so close, it seemed to be right behind his ear. Reflexively, he brought his hand up to swat at the source, expecting to shoo away a small bug or fly. Instead, he felt a sharp, surprising pinch.
"Damn it!" he hissed, wincing at the unexpected pain. It felt just like a bee sting, a sharp and piercing sensation that quickly gave way to a throbbing ache. He rubbed the spot gently, puzzling over the incident.
A bee? At this hour? It seemed unlikely, almost impossible. But the doors opening might have stirred it up, he rationalized. He stepped inside the building, the cool air of the lab a welcome relief from the summer night. Yet, even as he did so, the oddity of the sting gnawed at the back of his mind. He shrugged it off, promising himself to deal with it later. Right now, there were more immediate issues that required his attention.

Still rubbing his neck, Dr. Peterson quickly navigated the winding corridors of the building, his feet almost instinctively guiding him towards Claire's lab. The QRDA was a labyrinth of cutting-edge

innovation and ambition, yet in times of crisis, its familiar layout provided some semblance of comfort.
As he rounded the final corner, the door to Claire's lab came into view, standing slightly ajar. Bright fluorescent light spilled into the darkened hallway, illuminating the path ahead. Quickening his pace, Peterson entered the lab, the sight that greeted him causing his heart to drop.
In the center of the room, Claire was helping Declan off the floor and into a chair. Declan looked pale and disoriented, a far cry from his usual confident and assured demeanor. Claire's face was etched with worry, her eyebrows furrowed in deep concentration as she supported her colleague.
"Declan!" Peterson exclaimed, rushing over to assist, his earlier bee sting momentarily forgotten in the wake of the distressing sight before him. Declan looked up at Peterson, his eyes reflecting the turmoil he was going through.
The lab, once a place of joy and discovery, was now a room filled with anxiety and loss. The absence of Maddy felt like a tangible presence, a haunting reminder of the happiness and camaraderie that once filled the space. Peterson couldn't help but shudder, wondering if they would ever reclaim the optimism that had so defined their team. "We have to put an end to this, Declan!" Dr. Peterson pleaded; his words laced with palpable worry. "This technology, whatever it's doing, it's clearly causing harm. We can't stand idly by while it eats away at your mental stability. The chip - it must be removed and quickly!"

"No," Declan retorted, his voice firm and defiant. "You can't remove the AR chip. Not yet."
Dr. Peterson looked taken aback by the sudden force in Declan's voice. Claire watched as her two companions locked gazes, a silent battle of wills unfolding.
"It might be dangerous," Declan continued, "but what I just experienced, the people I saw, the fear they carried - it's all connected to the Ectogenesis program. It's not just about

artificially gestating a child. There are implications... social implications that are far-reaching and devastating."
His voice echoed in the cold confines of the lab, every word hanging heavy in the air. Claire found herself holding her breath, caught in the tension of the moment.
"The simulation is trying to tell us something, something about the effects of this program on society. I witnessed a world where genetic testing is used to control who can and can't have children. The despair, the desperation... it was perceivable."
Declan's voice lowered, but the intensity remained. "I don't know why or how, but I feel it in my bones that this is important. That it's somehow linked to Maddy's... departure."
His voice cracked slightly at the mention of their lost friend, but he quickly composed himself. "Maddy gave her life to this project. She believed in it, in us. We owe it to her to see this through, to finish what she began. Her life has to mean something, and I won't let that be in vain."
His declaration echoed through the room, a fervent pledge that left them all in silence. His determination was visible, a stark contrast to the confusion and uncertainty that had previously gripped them.

"Ridiculous! You're being absolutely ridiculous!" Dr. Peterson's normally calm demeanor was replaced with exasperation. "You of all people, an evolutionary biologist, should know that there were never such people. What you're proposing is not just absurd but near madness. You're suggesting that our historical understanding of human evolution is completely erroneous?"
Dr. Peterson shook his head, disbelief lining his features. "To say that our past has been rewritten and that we've been living in ignorance is a dangerous leap to make. You're bordering on conspiracy theories and lunacy. This machine, these simulations, they're driving you mad. Listen to yourself, Declan."
His words echoed in the tense silence of the lab. Claire sat on the periphery of the heated discussion, her mind racing as she

digested the implications of their conversation. The fervor in Declan's voice was unnerving, but there was a part of her that felt compelled to consider his arguments. Could their understanding of human evolution be so profoundly misguided? And could their AI system indeed be directing them to unravel these obscured threads of the past?
In the midst of the mounting tension, Claire felt a surge of responsibility. With Maddy gone, Declan seemingly losing his mind, their team falling apart, she was their beacon of reason. As unsettling as the idea was, she realized she had to be the one to hold them together, to guide them through this labyrinth of unknowns.

Enough!" Claire's voice cut through the simmering tension in the room, firm and resolute. Both men turned to her, surprised. "We're not getting anywhere like this. We're all tired, we're all on edge, and we're all grieving. This is not the time to make hasty decisions or to lose ourselves in theories."
She glanced at Declan, her eyes pleading. "No more diving into the simulation without the rest of us here, Declan. We need to understand what's going on, and that includes understanding how it connects to you." She then turned to Dr. Peterson; her gaze equally as intense. "And no surgical interventions, at least not until we've run some tests on this computer system and take a deeper look at how its processes work."
Claire's voice softened, as she continued, "We're dealing with something alive, in its own peculiar, fungal way. It deserves our respect and our caution. But right now, what we need is a break. A few days to mourn Maddy, to gather our thoughts and to come back fresh."
Silence filled the lab as her words settled in. She watched the men, saw them struggling with their own demons, their grief and uncertainty reflected in their eyes.
"Let's regroup after the funeral," Claire said softly. "Until then, we stay out of the lab. We stay away from the system. And when

we come back, we approach this together, with clear heads and open minds. We owe that to Maddy, and we owe it to ourselves."
"You're right, Claire," Declan said, nodding his agreement. He ran a hand through his hair, looking a bit defeated. "We do need rest. We need to mourn. We need to take care of ourselves."
But then he raised his head, a new resolve burning in his eyes. "But let's not forget, Jamie's been arrested, Maddy's... gone, and I've got a sneaking suspicion that the Ministry of Security and Intelligence isn't just watching us closely, I think they're breathing down our necks."
He looked at Dr. Peterson and Claire in turn, holding their gazes with a somber intensity. "This society-ending warning from the CGPT system... it's real. And I think the Ministry knows more than they're letting on. We might not have the luxury of time that we wish for."
Declan sighed, running a hand over his face, his exhaustion evident. "We can't be reckless, but we can't afford to be complacent either. Whatever's going on... it's bigger than us. It's bigger than this lab. And it's imperative that we find answers. For Maddy, for Jamie, for all of us."

Chapter 21

From Mushrooms to Microchips

"I think we need to find out how it is connecting to the chip, I am finding it hard to be anywhere near it, for fear of being drawn in again and not ready for it."
Declan's voice wavered slightly as he gestured toward his neck, his fingers just barely grazing the embedded AR chip. It was almost an unconscious action, borne more of anxiety than anything else. Claire paused at his question, her hand hovering over the lab door's handle. Her eyes met his, revealing the worry hidden in their depths.
"You know, I've been thinking about that too," she admitted, her gaze dropping to the floor. The implications of a device that could pull them into a simulation without warning were unnerving to say the least. "The Mycelium Computer is connecting to your chip without any prompting or without any compatible parts for that matter."
They stood outside the lab door, their shared unease punctuating the silence. The previous day's events had left them shaken, and this moment offered a brief reprieve, a quiet before they once again confronted the behemoth of uncertainty that lay behind the lab door.
Finally, Claire straightened, her scientist's determination creeping back into her demeanor. "We can't turn it off, not without surgical removal. But maybe, we could try and find a way to

control when it connects. We need to understand more about this mechanism," she suggested, her tone imbued with a newfound resolve.

Turning the handle, she pushed the lab door open. The room, previously filled with a frantic energy, now seemed ominously quiet. The faint hum of the Quantum computer provided the only sound, a reminder of the powerful unknown they were dealing with.

Declan followed her inside, his gaze landing on the Mycelium Quantum computer. It was their gateway to the simulations, the place where they had lost Maddy, and perhaps, where they would find the answers they so desperately sought.

"The rabbit hole awaits," he said, his voice steadier now. Their fear was still there, but so was their resolve. For Maddy, for themselves - they were prepared to dive back in and confront whatever mysteries lay within the machine.

As they entered the lab, they immediately heard the distinct whirr of drone rotors. Though accustomed to the sound, there was something different about this particular drone. Stationed outside the lab's large window, it hovered motionless. Its solitary presence was disconcerting, especially in the quiet light of early morning.

Claire squinted at the drone, her brow furrowing. "Did we schedule any drone maintenance this morning?" she asked, her voice holding a note of confusion. Declan shook his head, his eyes fixed on the machine outside.

"No, that wasn't in the schedule," he replied, rubbing the small of his back subconsciously. His movements were stiff, a clear sign of the discomfort caused by a night spent on Claire's less-than-ideal couch.

They exchanged a look of concern. This was an unexpected occurrence they hadn't planned for. With enough on their plate already, unscheduled drones outside their lab was the last thing

they needed. The drone was unnervingly still, its constant surveillance not escaping their notice.
"Peterson didn't mention this," Claire murmured, her gaze flicking back to the drone. "We should get it down and run some diagnostics."
"I'll take care of it," Declan offered, already making his way toward the drone control panel. He moved with purpose, pushing past the discomfort in his back. "We don't need any more surprises."
"Never mind, it's not ours!" Claire said with surprise. "Look at the markings; it belongs to the Autonomous Navigation System."
As Declan stopped what he was doing and turned to look at the drone hanging just outside the window, it hummed away in the blink of an eye. Claire couldn't help but worry about the implications of its presence. Were they under surveillance? By whom? The government? The QRDA? The sense of being watched, combined with their shared grief and the mounting pressure to understand the recent events, was almost unbearable.

"So, you're suggesting that the computer somehow connects to the mycelium network, which then connects to my AR chip?" Declan looked fascinated and skeptical, a common reaction to the more extreme boundaries of science.
Claire shrugged, her gaze on the holographic display. "I'm just throwing ideas around. But nature has been around far longer than we have, and it has figured out some of the most complex problems already. We just need to learn its language. There have been studies that show Mycelium will find the most efficient neuropathway in any problem. Subway systems and road networks are all created more efficiently by it than if we did it, in fact, more efficiently than if the CGPT system did it. It was one of the reasons Maddy and I tried to build the system in the manner that we did."

"But how could our computer possibly connect to a mycelium network?" Declan asked, voicing the question that lingered in the air.
"I don't know," Claire admitted, her fingers tracing the holographic image of the chip. "But Maddy had been working on something big before... before we lost her. She mentioned nature and technology. Maybe this was it. Maybe this is the key to understanding what's happening to us and why the computer is behaving the way it is."
Claire shifted her gaze from the window where the drone had been to Declan, her forehead creasing in deep thought. "Earlier, you were saying the computer taps into your AR chip and connects on its own accord. That should be impossible."
Declan nodded, causing a twinge of discomfort in his neck. "Exactly. It just reaches out and pulls me in whenever it wants to. I can't control it."

Stepping away from the holographic projection, Claire turned to Declan with a determined look.
"Alright, our next step has to be to dig deeper into the inner workings of the Mycelium Computer to see what we can uncover." She gestured toward the corner of the lab where the huge, dome-shaped computer stood, a spectacle of cutting-edge technology and the lifeblood of their research.
"There are countless processes running within that machine, and one of them is causing your uncontrolled connections. We need to identify it, and for that, we have to truly open the hood on this thing," Claire's eyes shone with resolve as she stared at the computer, already mentally preparing for the task at hand.
Declan raised an eyebrow, looking both curious and apprehensive. "And how are we going to do that?"
Claire turned to Declan, a half-smile on her face. "Through a deep-dive system analysis. We'll go through every line of code, every function, and every system process to see if we can find any anomalies. It's going to be meticulous and time-consuming, but it's the only way we can figure out what's happening."

Declan looked uncertain, but he nodded. "Alright, if that's what it takes. I just don't know how we are going to do that when we do not even understand the code it is generating."
Claire's smile broadened, and she led Declan towards the computer. "We have to start somewhere so lets connect the spare quantum computer to the Mycelium computer and hope it is able to decipher at least something in the code. We had some luck previously with this method. That is how we were able to identify the genome sequences of the creatures from the past."
As they delved into the digital heart of the Mycelium Computer, they were well aware of the mountain of work that lay ahead. But they were also filled with a sense of anticipation, keen to uncover the secrets that the computer held, and hopeful that they would find the answers they were desperately seeking.
As they delved into the work, it became clear that this was Claire's territory. Declan could only provide minimal help, his understanding of quantum computing was limited, and this mycelium-based system was an entirely different beast. Maddy's absence was more noticeable than ever - her extensive knowledge and experience would have been invaluable in their current situation.
While Declan was lost in thought, Claire removed a panel from the side of the computer, revealing the intricate internal setup. She gave a soft whistle, her eyes wide with surprise. "Well, this is... interesting."
Declan joined her side, following her gaze to the intricate network within the computer. The mycelium had expanded and evolved in ways they hadn't predicted, its thread-like structure weaving a complex, organic lattice throughout the hardware. It was no longer confined to the initial setup they had engineered but had adapted, integrated, and expanded far beyond it.
"It's as if the mycelium has grown sentient, cognizant of its environment," Claire murmured, her hands hovering above the extraordinary scene within the computer. The strands had woven

themselves into and around the quantum chips, creating a symbiotic interface that was both organic and artificial.
"It's incredible, but also... slightly terrifying," Declan admitted, his gaze never leaving the pulsing web of mycelium. The sight of it brought home the reality of their situation; they were dealing with something beyond the realm of their expertise and understanding.
"What we need is someone more adept than us, hopefully Dr. Peterson will be able to shed some light on this," Claire said, echoing Declan's earlier thoughts. "Until he arrives, let's continue our deep-dive. This, whatever it is, is just another part of the mystery we have to unravel."

"Declan, could you get me some swabs from the desk over there?" Claire said pointing to a cluttered corner of the lab without tearing her eyes away from the inner workings of the computer.
Declan nodded and swiftly moved to fetch the requested items. As he rummaged through drawers, Claire continued her train of thought, talking more to herself than to him.
"I would love to get a piece of that mycelium network under the microscope, to examine the structure and potentially gain insight into how it's functioning," she said, her voice filled with a mixture of curiosity and trepidation. "But disrupting it, even the slightest bit, could potentially destabilize the entire system."
Returning with the swabs, Declan looked at Claire questioningly. "What's the plan then?"
Claire pointed with a gloved finger at a tiny lump of organic matter, an offshoot of the main mycelium network, which seemed to be dormant or inactive. "See that there? It's a growth or a bud, almost like a mushroom cap, but far smaller. It seems separate from the main network. I'm hoping that we can take a sample without disturbing the rest."
Carefully, with the precision of a surgeon, Claire used the swab to gently detach the biomatter from its point of attachment. The mycelium network pulsated faintly, as if acknowledging the

contact, but remained stable. Holding her breath, Claire transferred the tiny specimen to a slide, ready to be studied under the microscope.
"Let's see what secrets you hold," she murmured, placing the slide under the lens and adjusting the focus, her mind already racing with potential findings and their implications.
Claire's breath hitched as the microscope came into focus, revealing a microcosm of intricate, delicate structures that were both alien and eerily familiar. The mycelium sample had indeed evolved beyond their initial design, its organic networks mirroring the technological architecture of a quantum computer chip. It was like gazing into a surreal, living motherboard that bridged the gap between nature and technology.
"Incredible," she whispered, her eyes wide as they traced the labyrinthine network of fungal filaments that interweaved like the circuits of a computer chip. Each thread, each mycelial strand, was a natural data pathway that had self-organized in a strikingly similar pattern to the silicon-based circuits of a traditional computer. Yet it was clear this was more than a mere replica. It was an adaptation, an evolution - a natural response to the synthetic components it cohabitated with.
The nodules of bio matter, which at first glance seemed randomly distributed, now appeared to be strategically placed, functioning as nodes or junctions within this bio-circuit. It was as if the mycelium was mimicking and integrating the technology, forming biological transistors and capacitors. This was a computer built from life growing, adapting, and evolving. It was both organic and electronic, a true fusion of nature and technology.
Claire leaned back, a sense of wonder filling her. This was beyond anything they could have anticipated. The mycelium hadn't just grown; it had learned, emulated, and improved. It was an organic representation of artificial intelligence - an oxymoron that challenged the boundaries of both fields.
"This...this is truly fascinating," Claire finally breathed out, a small grin appearing on her face. "Declan, we're not just looking at a mycelium computer anymore. We're looking at the birth of

something new, something that blurs the line between the organic and the synthetic. This... this is the future."

Just as Claire finished her sentence, the lab door swung open. Dr. Peterson, strolled in, his eyes scanning the room before settling on Claire and Declan. His gaze was sharp, scrutinizing, as he took in the scene before him.
"Good afternoon, Dr. Peterson," Claire greeted, her voice steady despite the sudden interruption. She quickly removed her gloves and turned to face him, her face a mask of professionalism.
"Claire, Declan," he nodded, his gaze flicking to the microscope. "I see you've been busy. Care to share your progress?"

Claire simply nodded in the direction of the microscope and without say a word began leading Dr. Peterson to the microscope. As he leaned in to take a look, the lab seemed to hold its breath. The microscopic image revealed a complex network of interwoven mycelial fibers resembling an intricate circuit board.
"It's as if we are looking at a blueprint of a computer chip, but this has been created by a fungus," Claire marveled, her voice barely a whisper.
Dr. Peterson straightened, rubbing his forehead and pushing back his glasses. "Incredible," he murmured. "We need to run a spectral analysis on this sample. It will give us a detailed breakdown of the chemical composition, and possibly even a clue as to how this mycelium is interfacing with the computer technology."
With that, he took a swab of the sample and moved to the lab's spectrometer. The machine hummed to life, and they all watched the screen as it began to display the chemical signatures found in the sample.
As they waited for the results, the lab was silent, each of them lost in their own thoughts. The implications of what they were witnessing were as fascinating as they were daunting. They were

venturing into uncharted territory, a convergence of biology and technology that had the potential to reshape the world.

Dr. Peterson's words fell heavy in the room, echoing through the silence. The spectrometer whirred softly in the background, starkly contrasting the tension that had suddenly taken hold. He turned around, looking at Claire and Declan, a wild urgency in his eyes.

"No, we have to stop this now," he said, his voice carrying a hard edge. "This... this is too dangerous. The repercussions... they're just too high. We should pour gasoline on it, right now, and burn this entire thing to the ground."

The declaration hung in the air, sharp and shocking. Claire and Declan exchanged a glance, a silent communication passing between them. They understood the fear in Peterson's voice, the anxiety that was rapidly turning into panic. But at the same time, there was something else - a spark of curiosity, an inescapable allure of the unknown that was difficult to ignore.

Declan cleared his throat, stepping forward to address the distressed scientist. "Dr. Peterson," he began, carefully choosing his words, "I understand your concerns, I really do. But we mustn't act in haste."

Peterson turned to him, disbelief etched across his features. "Haste? Declan, do you realize the potential catastrophe we're dealing with here?"

"I do," Declan responded calmly, "but we also don't fully understand what we're dealing with. Isn't that what science is about? To understand, to explore? Let's take it step by step. We have the opportunity to learn something groundbreaking here. Let's be cautious, but let's not destroy it before we understand it."

Dr. Peterson was silent, his gaze shifting between Declan and the humming spectrometer. He was clearly torn, but Declan could see the scientist in him battling with his fears.

Chapter 22

The Echo of Guilt and Unanswered Questions

Agent Reynolds had deemed himself an emotional wreck. He carried the weight of Maddy's death like a millstone around his neck, each day heavier than the last. The images were inescapable, tormenting him in the darkness of the night, stealing his sleep, and corroding his spirit. The sight of the bathroom stained in the vibrant hue of life lost prematurely, Maddy's lifeless form etched permanently in his mind. The sight of her pale skin, the cold touch of her once lively fingers, the emptiness in her once sparkling eyes. It was all too much.

And then, there was the letter. Her final words, scribbled meticulously in her journal, filled with unbearable sorrow and despair that seeped into his soul. He had read the entry so many times that he knew it by heart. He'd pondered every word, every stroke of the pen, every smudge, hoping to find some semblance of meaning, some hint of what she was trying to convey. But it was futile. The words “synthetic recreation" echoed in his mind, a riddle that refused to be solved.

Every night he would sit alone in the darkness of his living room, the notebook in his hands, the words blurring before his eyes. The silence was deafening, pressing against him from all sides. He'd tried to drown out his thoughts, to escape the tormenting memories, but they clung to him like a second skin.

The guilt was all-consuming. He was a protector, a guardian, a sentinel. He had failed. Maddy's death was on his hands, her

blood staining his conscience. He'd been the one to involve her, to try and make her break, to unveil the quantum truth. And for what? So he could stop them from creating a VR simulation? He was lost and if all of this was for nothing, which he was beginning to believe then he truly was lost as he no longer understood his assignment.
The more he thought about it, the more he realized how little he knew. Maddy's death was like a puzzle, the pieces scattered and disjointed, making no sense. What was the simulation she'd mentioned? Was it a metaphor, a code, or a tangible reality that he was not aware of? What had she discovered, and why had it led her to such despair? And why did the CGPT system believe it could have society-ending implications? The more he contemplated it, the more he believed that this had nothing to do with the QRDA or Claire and Maddy's research and everything to do with President Herod Caldwell and what he believed Dr. Peterson might or might not know about the accident weeks ago. These thoughts spiraled in his mind, haunting his waking hours and invading his dreams. He could see no end, no resolution. It was a maddening cycle of guilt, torment, and questions with no answers. Agent Reynolds, once a pillar of strength, was now a man caught in the throes of a tragedy he could not comprehend or overcome. Maddy's ghost seemed to linger around him, a constant reminder of the price of their pursuit of truth, a chilling echo of a life lost too soon.

Agent Reynolds moved through his days like a man caught in a perpetual storm. The shadow of anxiety followed him like a specter, wrapping around him with a chill that seeped into his bones. The sense of impending doom was relentless, a continual thrum in his mind that drowned out all other thoughts. It whispered its sinister predictions during the day, and at night it transformed into a deafening roar that drowned out the silence of his lonely apartment.
Sleep had become an elusive luxury. When exhaustion finally claimed him, dragging him down into its merciful oblivion, it was

always a fleeting respite. His dreams were a battlefield, plagued with a fear that tore at him with a ferocity that matched his waking terror. Maddy's face haunted him there, her pale features twisted in a mask of agony, her final moments replayed in a gruesome loop that jolted him awake, heart pounding against his ribcage like a desperate plea for release.

His nights were a struggle for peace, a vain attempt to escape the gnawing anxiety. But it was a losing battle. Each time he closed his eyes, the guilt would come rushing back, filling him with a dread that consumed him from the inside. The tranquility of sleep was invaded, shattered by the cruel reality of Maddy's loss.

The relentless cycle was slowly wearing him down, chipping away at his resolve. The man who had once stood tall against the most formidable adversaries now faced an enemy he couldn't outmaneuver. This enemy, born from his own grief, guilt, and the crushing weight of his failure, was the most challenging foe he had ever encountered. Every creak in his apartment sent a jolt of fear through him, every knock on the door a potential harbinger of more bad news. The world outside his window seemed darker, more menacing. It was as if a veil of darkness had descended upon him, clouding his vision and suffocating his spirit.

And through it all, the question that haunted his every moment – what had Maddy discovered that had led her to such a tragic end? It was a constant echo in his mind, a puzzle that refused to be solved, a ghost that refused to be exorcised. The shadow of anxiety was now his constant companion, a relentless reminder of his loss and his failure. His once peaceful existence had become a torment, his sanctuary transformed into a prison of his own guilt and regret. He was lost in his personal purgatory, wrestling with demons that seemed to grow stronger with each passing day.

Each morning, the struggle to show up at the office was a battle waged within himself. As Agent Reynolds car drove through the city, the familiar skyline seemed to morph into an ominous landscape, each building a towering symbol of the dread that was festering within him. As the car turned into the underground parking garage of the agency, his stomach churned violently, the concrete pillars and dimly lit space taking on the aura of a predator's lair.

His heart pounded against his ribcage like a trapped bird desperate for escape. He could feel the cold tendrils of panic wrapping around his mind, urging him to turn around, to flee from the place that had become a tangible reminder of his guilt and grief. He fought the instinct, his knuckles white on the steering wheel as he forced himself to pull into his designated spot.

Exiting the vehicle was like walking through quicksand. Each step towards the elevators was a monumental effort, his limbs heavy and reluctant. The air seemed denser, pressing against him, as if trying to push him back. But with every fiber of his being screaming at him to turn back, he persevered, moving forward as if pulled by an invisible force.

As he approached the towering glass doors of the office building, he felt the sweat breaking out on his brow, his shirt sticking to his back. The hustle and bustle inside, once a comforting background hum, now seemed hostile, each conversation, each ringing phone a jarring reminder of his disconnection from this world.

With a deep, shaky breath, he pushed through the doors. The rush of cool, air-conditioned breeze was a slap to his senses, the stark artificial light a stark contrast to the dim morning outside. The dread in his gut twisted tighter, the shadowy specter of his anxiety looming large, its icy tendrils constricting around his chest, making it harder to breathe.

He willed himself to move, to put one foot in front of the other. To keep going. And with each painstaking step, he ventured further into the belly of the beast, his personal battleground, his struggle against himself personified in the stark, sterile surroundings of the office.

Each day was a battle, a grim war against his personal demons. And each day, he showed up, not out of duty or commitment, but out of necessity. A desperate hope that in confronting his fears, he may finally find the means to conquer them.

The shrill ring of his communicator cut through the suffocating silence like a blade, and Agent Reynolds instinctively reached into his pocket to retrieve the device. The name flashing on the screen hit him like a punch to the gut - Minister Antonio Martinez.

His legs, already shaky from his battle with his mind, nearly buckled under the onslaught of nausea that washed over him. The wave of dread was so intense, it was as if his very limbs had turned queasy. He leaned against a wall, his fingers tight around the sleek device that seemed to pulse ominously in his hand.

His mind churned with confusion, wrestling with the reality of his feelings. This wasn't right. This was his fortress, his sanctuary. A place where he had always been the master, the one in control. Yet now, it felt like hostile territory, each familiar corner a source of trepidation.

He tried to rationalize his fear, to suppress the overwhelming terror that threatened to consume him. But the harder he fought, the stronger it seemed to become. An insidious entity, feeding off his resistance, growing bolder with each beat of his rapidly pounding heart.

He wished, more than anything, for the fear to disappear. For the choking dread to release its stranglehold on his psyche. He would give anything to have the peace he once enjoyed, to be free of this constant shadow that stalked his every moment.

The communicator in his hand vibrated again, its insistent buzz echoing the frantic beat of his heart. Minister Martinez's face stared back at him from the screen, his expression unreadable. With a shaky breath, Reynolds swiped the screen and brought the device to his ear, bracing himself for whatever the call may bring. The sterile silence of the office around him seemed to hold its breath, as if waiting for the storm to break.

The air was thick with suspense as Dr. Peterson rubbed his temples, a grimace of pain etching deep lines on his face. "Since we're awaiting the results of the spectroscopic analysis," he said, breaking the heavy silence, "we might as well discuss some recent developments. For starters, the extra wine at The Last Liberal and let's not forget that your friend Jamie the owner is still under detention."

The statement reverberated through the room, accentuating the contrast between the solemn silence and the faint mechanical whirring of the spectrometer. He turned to Claire and Declan, a spark of urgency flashing in his eyes.

"We must end this now," he insisted, his voice resonating with determination. "The potential danger is too significant. The aftermath... unthinkable. It would be prudent to destroy this... this entity immediately."

The air grew denser as his declaration hung ominously, a stark reminder of the reality they were facing. Claire and Declan shared a quick glance, silently acknowledging the fear and panic underlying Peterson's words. Yet, a glimmer of intrigue simmered within them, a magnetic pull towards the unknown they could not resist.

Declan finally broke the silence, his voice steady but compassionate. "Dr. Peterson," he began, treading lightly on his words, "I empathize with your concerns. But acting impulsively might not be our best option."

Surprise flitted across Peterson's face. "Impulsive? Declan, are you aware of the potential catastrophe we might trigger?"

"Indeed I am," Declan replied, his voice calm yet resolute as he once again tried to explain his point of view on the matter. "Yet, we lack complete understanding of what we're dealing with. Isn't the essence of science to explore, to seek understanding? We need to proceed methodically, step by step. We stand on the brink of a groundbreaking discovery. Caution is vital, but let's not annihilate it before we have a chance to comprehend its essence."

For a moment, Peterson was quiet, his gaze shifting restlessly between Declan and the spectrometer. A battle of emotions played out on his face; fear wrestling with the inherent scientist's curiosity.

Finally, he sighed, a hand running through his hair in defeat. He looked exhausted, the throbbing headache and the morning's events visibly weighing on him. "Alright," he conceded, "we'll proceed... cautiously."

Declan offered a reassuring pat on Peterson's shoulder. "Are you sure you're alright, sir? You don't seem yourself and to be honest, you're looking a little pale."

Dr. Peterson was now clasping his head in agony. "I'll be alright. I just need to lie down. Give me an hour to rest on the couch in my office with a few ibuprofens, and I'll be good to go."

Once Dr. Peterson left the lab to go lie down, Claire turned to Declan with a troubled look on her face. "There's something else we need to discuss. About Jamie."

Declan nodded, listening as Claire told him about the woman, she had grown up with in the Central Childhood Education & Care Facility. Jamie was a resilient figure, always finding a way to survive. Claire and Jamie had shared countless experiences while growing up in the same center, and their friendship had solidified through shared trauma and experiences, making them more like siblings than friends. Claire explained to Declan that their bond was unbreakable.

But this time, it was Claire who had gotten Jamie into trouble. It was all because of her, Claire realized with a pang of guilt. Maddy's grief had been too much to bear, and in a moment of poor judgment, Claire had thought a little extra wine would help. After all, it was just wine. What harm could it possibly do? Except now, Jamie's bar had been shut down pending investigation, and Jamie herself was being detained. Claire felt the weight of the consequences of her actions pressing down on her. Jamie was her friend, and she was responsible for the mess she was in. But how was she supposed to fix this?

Claire shared these thoughts with Declan in a low and troubled voice. "I don't know what to do, Declan. How can I help Jamie? It's my fault she's in this mess."

Declan put a reassuring hand on Claire's shoulder. "We'll figure this out, Claire. For now, let's focus on understanding this technology and finding answers. I have a feeling that if we can do that, we'll find a way to help Jamie too."

With that, they turned their attention back to the task at hand, but Jamie's situation remained at the back of Claire's mind, a constant reminder of the real-world consequences of their recent work.

Chapter 23

Revelations Amidst Biotechnological Convergence

Dr. Peterson staggered out of the lab, his head thumping as though it was the heart itself. He stumbled into his office and slumped down onto the leather couch, squeezing his eyes shut against the harsh, fluorescent light.

"Mark," he called, his voice strangled, "Could you get me some water and ibuprofen?"

A moment later, his assistant appeared with the requested items.

"Anything else, sir?" Mark asked, concern lining his features.

"No, that will be enough. Thank you, Mark," Dr. Peterson said, managing a weak smile. Once alone again, he leaned back, his mind whirling.

He took a few minutes to collect his thoughts before he reached for his phone, scrolling through his contacts until he found the one he was looking for. Jacqueline Wells - she would know what to do.

"Jacqueline," he began as soon as she picked up the call, "We have a situation."

He explained the development at the lab and the impending threat from the Ministry of Truth, his words rushed as he tried to convey the urgency. When he mentioned Minister Antonio Martinez, there was a long silence from the other end.

Finally, Jacqueline responded, "It might be time, Peterson."

"The Ectogenesis issue?" Dr. Peterson echoed, his heart pounding.
"Yes," Jacqueline affirmed, "And everything else we're trying to achieve. Martinez needs to know. We can't afford to keep him in the dark any longer."
Dr. Peterson nodded, although Jacqueline couldn't see it. It felt wrong - so much had already gone wrong. And yet, keeping Martinez, a key player in the government, oblivious had always been a precarious decision. But so much was at stake, and not only their personal ventures but possibly the whole biomedical industry.
"Alright, Jacqueline," he sighed, a wave of exhaustion washing over him. "Arrange a meeting with Martinez. It's time we let him in on the secret."

"Jacqueline," Dr. Peterson said, pressing his fingertips to his temples, "I think we need to arrange an in-person meeting. With Minister Martinez, yes, but also with President Caldwell. I have some other news I think everyone should be aware of."
There was a pause on the other end of the line, and Peterson could almost hear the gears turning in Jacqueline's head. "Alright, Peterson. What is this about? I need to know what we're walking into."
A sigh rattled out of Peterson's chest. "It's...it's very technical, Jacqueline. A lot of layers. I'd rather explain it all in one go, fewer times repeating myself. Make the meeting as soon as you can arrange it. We don't have a lot of time."
"Alright," Jacqueline said, a hint of worry creeping into her voice. "I'll get on it right away. We'll talk soon."
The call ended, leaving Peterson alone in his office. He leaned back on his couch, closing his eyes and waiting for the ibuprofen to do its job. He felt a strange mix of trepidation and relief. It was time to bring everyone into the loop, time to face the truth of what they were dealing with.
As he waited for the relief from his headache to come, his mind began to wander back to the lab, to the mycelium network, and

to the ominous specter of what they had created. A fusion of biology and technology that could forever change the course of their world, for better or for worse. They were at the precipice of the unknown, and there was no turning back now.

Dr. Peterson couldn't shake off the growing unease that gnawed at the back of his mind. It wasn't just the looming threat from the Ministry of Truth or the intricate web of lies they had built around Minister Martinez. No, it ran deeper than that. This was about power, corruption, and the dark underbelly that controlled the puppet strings of society.

As he reflected on the secrets they had hidden for so long, Dr. Peterson couldn't help but connect the dots. The rumors of Martinez's corruption, the insidious dealings with outside corporations, and the shadowy figures who held sway over the government—all of it intertwined seamlessly. The more he thought about it, the more apparent it became that they had been playing a dangerous game, dancing on the edge of a treacherous precipice.

The corporations held the true power, their money acting as the lifeblood that pumped through the veins of society. They were the puppeteers, making decisions behind closed doors that influenced the very fabric of the world. And in their insatiable quest for control, they were willing to go to unimaginable lengths, twisting the strings of governments and manipulating the public's perception.

Dr. Peterson's mind raced with all the possible consequences of unveiling the failings of the Ectogenesis project to Martinez and President Caldwell. Would they be met with open minds, embracing the transformative potential of the New Quantum computing system, a groundbreaking technology? Or would they face resistance, as those in power fought tooth and nail to preserve their grip on the world and the system that currently controlled everything?

The weight of the truth settled heavily on Dr. Peterson's shoulders. They had kept their secret hidden, not just to protect themselves, but also in fear of the repercussions it would have on those who held positions of influence. Revealing the truth meant risking everything—their research, their careers, and the delicate balance of power.

But there was no escaping the reality. Driven by a sense of duty and the undeniable urge to expose the corrupt underbelly of their society, Dr. Peterson knew that the time for secrets and half-truths had come to an end. They had a responsibility to shine a light on the shadows, regardless of the personal cost.

As the throbbing in his head began to subside, replaced by a growing resolve, Dr. Peterson knew that he was embarking on a perilous journey—one that had the potential to change the world, but also had the power to consume them. With every passing moment, the weight of his choices pressed against his conscience, reminding him of the magnitude of his actions.

Taking a deep breath, Dr. Peterson stood up from the couch, ready to face the storm that awaited them. The truth had a way of unraveling even the most tightly woven webs of deception. There was no turning back now.

He pushed himself upright and checked the time on his communicator. A few hours had passed since his call with Jacqueline. With a groan, he got to his feet and slowly made his way back towards the lab.

Inside, he found Claire and Declan hunched over a set of computer screens, their expressions focused. He quietly moved closer, glancing at the flurry of code scrolling across one of the screens.

"What are you two up to?" he asked, his voice raspy from his nap.

Claire glanced over her shoulder, her usually bright eyes shadowed with concern. "We're trying to figure out how the Mycelium Computer is communicating with the AR chips. We're running parallel code through another quantum computer to see if we can replicate and then understand its behavior."

Dr. Peterson moved closer, squinting at the screens. "And? Any luck?"

Declan rubbed the back of his neck, wincing. "Not much. It's... complex. And unusual. It's like nothing we've ever seen."

Claire nodded, adding, "And that's the problem. It's like it's speaking a different language, but we can't find a dictionary to translate."

Dr. Peterson sighed, rubbing his temples. The pounding in his head hadn't completely subsided, but he pushed the discomfort aside. The room was thick with an underlying tension, the weight of their discoveries hanging heavily in the air.

"Keep at it," he said, forcing a small smile. "We need answers, and fast. And while you do that, I'll... I'll arrange that meeting." His mind was already racing ahead to the difficult conversation that awaited them. As the two researchers nodded and turned back to their screens, Dr. Peterson pulled out his communicator, dialing Jacqueline's number. It was time to face the consequences of their creation, whatever they may be.

"What meeting?" inquired Declan with a look of puzzlement on his face.

Dr. Peterson froze in his tracks as Declan's question echoed through the lab. He didn't reply immediately, turning to stare at the spectrometer instead. The display panel beeped softly, indicating that the earlier task had been completed. He moved closer, scanning the results, his heart hammering in his chest. The screen displayed a complex molecule, each atom denoted by symbols, numbers, and lines. His eyes widened at the familiar structure, one that he hadn't expected but made a bizarre kind of sense. N,N-Dimethyltryptamine or DMT, the so-called 'spirit molecule', was the top result. An endogenous hallucinogen that has been linked to spiritual and mystical experiences. The human

body naturally synthesizes DMT in small quantities, making it an endogenous substance.
Dr. Peterson glanced over his shoulder at Claire and Declan. "It's DMT," he said, his voice barely above a whisper.
The pair looked up, their faces pale in the cold, sterile light of the lab. "What?" Declan asked, his brows furrowing in confusion. "That... that can't be right."
But Dr. Peterson's expression didn't waver. "The spectrometer doesn't lie. It's DMT."
A heavy silence filled the room, punctuated only by the soft hum of the lab equipment. Finally, Claire broke the silence. "What does that mean?" she asked, her voice trembling.
Dr. Peterson sighed heavily, turning his attention back to the spectrometer. "I'm not entirely sure yet. But it does explain... some things."
"The other chemical observed in the test is methyl jasmonate, a volatile compound released by plants for communication, particularly in response to stress or damage," Dr. Peterson explained, his voice heavy with the implication of the discovery.
"And what meeting were you talking about earlier?" Declan interjected, not willing to let the topic slide. Even if the implications of what Dr. Peterson was saying were potentially harmful to his theory of what was taking place.
Dr. Peterson took a deep breath, ready to reveal another twist in their already convoluted situation. "I've requested a meeting with Jacqueline Wells, Minister Martinez, and if possible, President Caldwell. There are some... disclosures to be made. Secrets that should have never been kept in the first place."

Dr. Peterson stood silent for a moment, staring at the analysis results. A sense of realization washed over him. "It's not a simulation," he began, his voice a mere whisper echoing through the lab. He turned towards Claire and Declan, his face a mask of conclusion.

"What you've been experiencing... It's more akin to a DMT trip," he admitted, the gravity of his words taking hold. "The molecule N,N-Dimethyltryptamine is a naturally occurring compound within the human body, known for its potent psychedelic properties. Under its influence, the brain can experience hyper-realistic, immersive experiences that, to the person, seem more real than reality itself."
He paused for a breath, allowing his words to sink in. "This compound works in synergy with methyl jasmonate, the plant communication molecule. When these two combine, they appear to create an environment for hallucinations to flourish."
Dr. Peterson took a step back, leaning against the lab bench. His gaze never left the pair. "Your brains are simply doing what they do best – making sense of the world around you, connecting the dots. When we're searching for solutions to the Ectogenesis program's issue of cell decay in the genome sequence, your minds are simply filling in the gaps with the information they already have, creating these hyper-realistic hallucinations. We're not exploring a simulation. We're navigating the intricate pathways of our consciousness."
As the words lingered in the air, the room felt still. The revelation had reshaped their understanding of what they had believed to be a terrifying technological quandary. The reality was, however, far more intimately human and innately natural than they had ever anticipated.

Dr. Peterson began to grimace, his hand shooting up to clutch his head. As he attempted to speak, his words came out jumbled, "The... mending kite... hues grow cold."
His face contorted in a painful grimace as he repeated, each word pronounced with significant effort, as if he was trying to push through the mounting distress.
"Dime...etching...roots...and...God," he stammered, the incoherent sentence barely making sense. His eyes, filled with an unsettling mixture of terror and revelation, darted from Claire to Declan as he collapsed onto the lab floor.

Claire and Declan could only watch helplessly as Dr. Peterson collapsed, the cryptic words that had spilled from his mouth now lingering ominously in the air. His face had turned a ghastly pale, his eyes were fluttering and he seemed to be struggling to breathe. The room suddenly fell silent, save for the distressed gasps escaping Peterson's lips and the shrill blare of an alarm set off by the building's health monitoring system.

The alarm was deafening, a piercing reminder of the urgency of the situation. The sophisticated AI embedded in the lab's design detected Dr. Peterson's vitals crashing and had immediately initiated an emergency protocol. Bright red emergency lights started to flash as an automatic distress signal was sent out to the nearest hospital, informing them of a potential stroke victim.

Claire, her heart pounding in her chest, dropped to her knees beside Dr. Peterson. Training from her years in the biomedical field kicked in as she started to administer CPR. Meanwhile, Declan was barking into his communicator, updating the hospital on Peterson's condition. "Send an emergency unit now!" he shouted, his voice a tense whisper against the clamor of the alarms. "It's a stroke, possibly severe."

As Claire pressed rhythmically on Dr. Peterson's chest, her gaze wandered to the lab's door. She was looking for the medical response team, but instead, her heart stuttered as her eyes landed on a familiar figure standing by the entrance. The man from the bench, the man she felt had been watching them, was there. He was silent, a shadow against the flashing red lights, his expression unreadable. His presence felt eerily wrong, intensifying the suffocating dread in the room.

She could only stare, her mind racing to make sense of his presence, even as her hands continued their life-saving rhythm on Dr. Peterson's chest. Could this stranger hold the key to their myriad of unanswered questions, or was he just another variable in their equation of uncertainty? As she locked eyes with the stranger, the gravity of their situation seemed to solidify, leaving her with a sense of foreboding that was almost as chilling as the lifeless body beneath her hands.

Chapter 24

The Mycelium Revelation

"Agent Reynolds," Martinez's voice came through the line, both grating and oddly soothing in the oppressive silence.

"Minister Martinez," Reynolds replied, forcing calm into his voice, "What can I do for you?"

"Join me in my office, Reynolds. Immediately." The command was terse, unyielding.

Upon his arrival, Martinez's office was dimly lit, the heavy blinds drawn shut as if to keep out not just the sunlight, but the entire world. Martinez was standing by his desk, a hologram of the city splayed out before him. He didn't turn around as Reynolds entered.

"You're aware, Agent Reynolds, that there have been...speculations about a society-ending event," Martinez began, his tone hinting at an underlying tension. "A catastrophic anomaly caused by an unknown factor coming out of the QRDA and more specifically Dr. Claire Cairns work."

Martinez continued, "I'm here to tell you that it's been averted. The threat has been neutralized."

Reynolds froze. His mind buzzed with incredulity, confusion.

"How...?" he stuttered out, his thoughts a jumbled mess.

Martinez merely shrugged, a nonchalant gesture that was eerily out of place in the gravity of the conversation. "It's been taken care of. We are safe."

"But the investigation..." Reynolds began, his mind reeling with a thousand questions.

"Is over," Martinez cut him off. His tone brokered no argument, a wall of finality erected in a heartbeat. He still hadn't turned to look at Reynolds, his gaze fixed on the holographic cityscape. "There's no need to look into it further."

Reynolds could only stare at the back of Martinez's head in stunned silence. He sensed the blatant lie, the observable tension radiating off the Minister. But the insistence, the finality in his tone...it left no room for argument.

As he walked out of the office, a chilling sensation crawled up his spine. Despite the apparent end of the investigation, he felt as if he were teetering on the edge of a precipice, peering down into an abyss that had suddenly yawned open beneath his feet.

The conversation replayed in his mind, a loop of unsettling words and ominous implications. The mystery of what was transpiring at the QRDA was far from over, and Agent Reynolds knew he would not, could not, let it rest. The battle might be declared finished by Martinez, but for him, the war had just begun.

"And what about Jamie?" Reynolds interjected before he had fully exited the office, swiveling back towards Martinez. "The owner of The Last Liberal?"

At the mention of her name, Martinez visibly stiffened. It was fleeting, barely a flicker in the dim light, but Reynolds noticed. His heart pounded harder in his chest. Martinez turned then, his gaze finally meeting Reynolds's. There was something in his eyes, a wariness that hadn't been there before.

"Oh, her," Martinez's voice came out cool, detached. "We let her go."

Reynolds raised an eyebrow, suspicion twisting in his gut. Jamie, the woman he had used as bait to goad Maddy into talking, just let her go? It was hard to believe. The government hadn't shown such mercy before. After all she had broken a serious law and should in the least have her liquor license removed. Why now? What has happened to just let all of this drop? He bit his lip, tasting the metallic tang of uncertainty.

Martinez continued, oblivious to Reynolds's inner turmoil. "The death of this woman, Maddy, has created quite a commotion. We'd prefer for all of this to simply... dissipate."

The news hit Reynolds like a physical blow, threatening to topple him. Maddy just another death? Jamie released? It was too much, too fast. Too many loose ends, too many unexplained pieces. His mind reeled, attempting to string together the discordant facts. His instincts screamed at him that something was amiss. The imminent warning from the CGPT System, with no real answers, the halted investigation, Jamie's inexplicable release. It was as if he was staring at a jigsaw puzzle with half the pieces missing.
As he finally left Martinez's office, Reynolds felt the weight of the world on his shoulders. The conversation left him with more questions than answers, and the feeling of dread clung to him like a second skin. But there was one thing he knew for sure: He wouldn't let this go quietly. Not while there was still a breath left in his body. His resolve hardened. He had a mystery to solve, and he would dig into the depths of this conspiracy, whatever it took.

With determination, Reynolds headed towards the lab. Even though the investigation seemed to have been concluded, he couldn't shake off the feeling that he was missing a crucial piece of the puzzle. There was still a chance that he could uncover something in the lab, amidst the beakers, test tubes, shadows, and echoes of Dr. Claire Cairns' work.
He had a few more questions for the lab technicians, and perhaps even some for the enigmatic Dr. Cairns, if she was willing to cooperate. He had yet to question her, preferring to observe from the shadows, hoping to gather information to use against the group. Perhaps the recent developments would prompt her to reveal more than she intended.
Upon entering the lab, he was greeted by the hum of machinery and the sterile smell of chemicals. Lab coats flitted around like ghosts, their inhabitants lost in their own worlds. The building

seemed untouched by the whirlwind of a big metropolis outside, a bubble of tranquility amidst the chaos.
Agent Reynolds, for his part, felt his heart sink as he took in the scene when he entered Claire's lab. It was like stepping into a painting of chaos, an abstract swirl of frantic motion and stark stillness. The incessant wail of the emergency alarms drowned out any thought process, filling his mind with an urgency he hadn't felt in a long time.
His gaze fell on Dr. Peterson, the man he'd hoped to question, now lying motionless on the floor, his life hanging by a thread. Claire and Declan were both there, doing their best to keep him alive while the alarm blared on and the flashing red lights painted a grim portrait of the situation.
The door had slid shut behind him, cutting off the world outside, isolating them in a bubble of panic and uncertainty. For a moment, he was nothing more than an unnoticed specter, a silent observer amidst the chaos. He used this to his advantage, his sharp eyes scanning the room, taking in every detail. His mind raced to connect the dots, to decipher the scene unfolding before him.
It was then that his gaze met Claire's. Even from across the room, the shock in her eyes was evident. He could see the realization dawn on her face, the subtle tightening of her features, the slight shift in her rhythm. For a heartbeat, everything else fell away, and it was just the two of them in a silent exchange.
Breaking their gaze, Reynolds steeled himself and stepped forward. He would offer his assistance, providing any help he could while they waited for the medical response team. After all, he wasn't just an officer of the Ministry, he was a man who had seen and dealt with many crises.
As he moved to join the desperate effort to save Dr. Peterson's life, Reynolds couldn't help but ponder over the strange twist of fate. His mission to uncover the truth had brought him here, to a lab he was convinced was filled with secrets and now, a life-threatening emergency. And even as he focused on the crisis at hand, he couldn't ignore the niggling suspicion at the back of his

mind: that there was much more to this situation than met the eye.
As Agent Reynolds knelt beside Claire, their hands working in a grim rhythm on Dr. Peterson's still body, he found himself grappling with a chilling realization. The pieces of the puzzle, the disjointed bits of information he had been gathering, seemed to suddenly align in his mind. It was as though he had been struggling with a jigsaw puzzle in the dark, and a beam of light had unexpectedly shone on it, illuminating the complete picture. The realization hit him like a lightning strike, illuminating the shadows of uncertainty that had shrouded his investigation. The ominous warnings, the anomalies, the halted investigation, and now, Dr. Peterson's sudden collapse. It all made sense, fitting together like constellations in a midnight sky, disparate points of light suddenly aligning into a clear, undeniable shape. The picture that emerged was disturbingly clear, sending ripples of dread coursing through his veins.
His gut churned with a mixture of triumph and trepidation. Triumph, because he had unraveled the truth, and trepidation, because the truth was far grimmer than he could have imagined. The knowledge weighed on him, a dreadful secret he was doomed to bear alone. His breath hitched in his chest, a silent gasp of horror.
Every instinct screamed at him to voice his realization, to alert those around him to the sinister reality. But he swallowed back the words, the metallic taste of fear coating his tongue. He knew, with a chilling certainty, that to reveal his understanding could seal his fate, just like Dr. Peterson's.
"Stroke?" he found himself on the brink of asking, the question lingering ominously in the air. But he bit it back, forcing a shaky nod instead. The question died on his lips, left unasked. He knew the answer, knew the awful, monstrous truth.
His gaze met Claire's again, her eyes wide and fearful. There was a part of him, a fiercely protective part, that longed to warn her, to pull her away from the precipice they were all unknowingly

standing on. But he swallowed down the urge, the silent scream of his morality drowned by the shrill alarms around them. Reynolds was trapped in a terrible silence, a knowing spectator amidst a grand charade. His heart pounded in sync with the rhythmic press of his hands on Dr. Peterson's chest. Each compression felt like a betrayal, a step deeper into a dangerous deception. The truth, it seemed, was a dangerous weapon - one that Reynolds was forced to wield alone.

As Dr. Peterson's consciousness began to wane, he found himself spiraling down into a surreal landscape. He could still feel the cold laboratory floor under his collapsing body, hear the frenzied panic of Claire and Declan as they scrambled to his aid, yet, the lab seemed to evaporate, giving way to an endless expanse. Before him stretched an immense, ancient tree, its roots snaking into the depths of the earth, its branches reaching out like arms embracing the cosmos. The tree pulsed with life, glowing with an ethereal light, resonating with a serene hum that echoed through the expanse. Its leaves whispered ancient secrets as they rustled, and its bark bore inscriptions of symbols and patterns that seemed oddly familiar.

He watched as the roots extended, each seeking nourishment, connecting with other life forms, intertwining, exchanging, learning, and growing. He saw glimpses of the past, fragments of his own life mingling with those of his ancestors, each memory embedded in the root's structure. Every decision, every triumph, every loss, every profound and banal moment was etched into the ancient tendrils that fed the massive tree.

His gaze then ascended to the sprawling branches that branched out in infinite directions, each symbolizing potential futures. Some were lush with foliage and life, while others were barren, illustrating a myriad of possibilities. The branches seemed to intertwine with stars, nebulae, galaxies, weaving a tapestry of existence across time and space, subtly alluding to the interconnectedness of all life forms across the universe.

In that fleeting moment, Dr. Peterson felt a profound understanding bloom within him. He saw the Mycelium Computer not as a man-made device but as an echo of this cosmic tree, an earthly reflection of the universe's primal network. It was the manifestation of nature's own neural network, the conduit for information, a gateway between consciousnesses.

Even as his physical body succumbed, his consciousness seemed to merge with the tree, experiencing a rush of knowledge and awareness beyond anything he had ever known. The enormity of existence, the intertwined fabric of past, present, and future, the unity in diversity—all seemed crystal clear.

Despite the apparent simulation, a part of him began to question. Was this a fabrication of the Mycelium Computer, a mere hallucination provoked by DMT and methyl jasmonate, or was it a profound truth revealed at the brink of his mortality? The question seemed to hang in the ether, unanswered, as he felt his consciousness beginning to drift away from the tree, the vision, and finally the physical world.

In those final moments, Dr. Peterson experienced the duality of life and death, existence and oblivion, understanding and mystery, and he saw them not as binaries, but as integral parts of the grand cosmic dance. His life, his work, his discoveries, were all but tiny reverberations in this endless symphony of the universe.

And then, with a final sigh, Dr. Peterson let go, his last thought an echo of wonderment and acceptance as he embraced the unknown that lay beyond.

Chapter 25

Ethereal Thresholds and Earthly Shadows

As Claire, Declan, and Agent Reynolds tried to save Dr. Peterson's life, a somber chill filled the room. It seemed as though life itself sensed his vitality dissipating, his once vibrant presence fading into a whisper. The frantic rhythm of their efforts echoed ominously, a futile resistance against the looming shadow of the inevitable.

Suddenly, the silence was shattered by the distant wail of sirens. Moments later, the heavy thud of boots echoed through the corridor, a dozen hearts racing against time. The doors burst open, revealing a team of paramedics, their faces etched with grim determination.

Leading them was a contingent of QRDA security, their rigid posture and stern expressions betraying their concern. The intense light from their headlamps cut through the semi-darkness, casting long, eerie shadows on the lab walls.

With military precision, they swarmed around Dr. Peterson, their gloved hands expertly maneuvering over his frail form. They worked in sync, their every move calculated, every second counting.

In the corner of the room, the entrance to the Mycelium Computer pulsed ominously, a silent spectator to the drama unfolding. Agent Reynolds watched as the paramedics worked, his gaze eventually drifting towards the computer.

A strange sense of foreboding gnawed at him as he watched the lights pulsate rhythmically. He felt an inexplicable pull, a call he found hard to ignore. Casting a final glance towards the medical team, he took a step towards the computer, crossing over the threshold and into the unknown.
As the chaos of the real world faded into a distant murmur, Reynolds braced himself for the journey ahead, a journey for which he was not in the least prepared.

Agent Reynolds stood at the threshold of the Mycelium Computer, a sense of disquiet gnawing at the edge of his consciousness. The swirling vortex of light that marked the entrance to where the computer was stored was mesmerizing, yet ominous. He cast a last glance around the lab, a stark reminder of reality before stepping into the unknown.
As he stepped towards the humming machine, a sudden wave of nausea swept over him, his surroundings blurring into a hazy tapestry of colors and shapes. The solid lab floor under his feet gave way to a sensation of floating, an ethereal disconnection from the tangible world. He could feel a gentle tug at his consciousness, like the pull of an unseen tide, luring him deeper into the virtual realm.
His mind was suddenly flooded with a barrage of images, sounds, and sensations, each more intense and overwhelming than the last. His past traumas, the ghosts of his past cases, the faces of the innocent lives he couldn't save, began to surface. They tore through his defenses, ripping open old wounds, the memories flooding back with an intensity that took his breath away.
Every firefight, every lost life, every failure was relived in excruciating detail, as if he was experiencing them for the first time. He saw the young girl he couldn't save in a hostage situation, her terrified eyes pleading for help as the life slowly drained from her body. He felt the raw fear of his first firefight, the deafening sound of bullets whizzing past his head, the searing pain of a bullet grazing his arm.

The emotional turbulence was punctuated by bouts of extreme euphoria and profound insight. He felt a sense of connection with the universe, a oneness that eclipsed his traumatic memories. His fears, guilt, and regrets seemed to shrink in the face of the infinite cosmos, their significance diminishing in the grand scheme of existence.

Visions of cosmic entities, ancient symbols, and geometric patterns danced before his eyes, offering a cryptic glimpse into the mysteries of existence. He saw the expansive tree, its branches reaching out to the cosmos, its roots delving deep into the core of existence. He felt a sense of serenity wash over him, a soothing balm over his open wounds.

He found himself conversing with these entities, questioning them, seeking wisdom and guidance. The answers he received were enigmatic, wrapped in riddles and metaphors, yet they held a resonance that he couldn't ignore. They spoke of courage, resilience, and acceptance, of looking beyond the traumatic past to shape a better future.

The intensity of the experience began to ebb, replaced with a calm, a tranquility that seemed at odds with the chaos he had just endured. As the visions faded, Reynolds found himself back at the threshold of the computer, the lab coming back into focus. The vortex of light fizzled out, the silence of the lab a stark contrast to the cacophony he had just emerged from.

Reynolds was left with a profound sense of understanding and healing. He felt a weight lift off his shoulders, his past traumas losing their power over him. He was not his past, not his failures. He was an agent, a protector, a seeker of truth, shaped by his experiences but not defined by them. His past may have been marked by trauma, but his future held possibilities. And that realization, that acceptance was the first step towards healing.

As he looked around the lab, his gaze met Declan's. With a new understanding in his eyes, a resilience that hadn't been there before he was ready, ready to face the truth, prepared to uncover the conspiracy, equipped to protect those who couldn't protect

themselves. His eyes held a quiet confidence that spoke volumes about his transformative journey.
"Thank you," he simply said to the Universe, his voice carrying the weight of gratitude that couldn't be fully expressed in words. The chaos that had moments before threatened to overwhelm the lab had given way to an almost serene silence, mirroring the newfound peace that Reynolds had found within himself.
With a newly discovered resolve, Reynolds turned his attention back to the computer. There was work to be done, truths to be uncovered. But he now faced the task not with dread, but with an emboldened spirit, ready to confront whatever lay ahead.
As Reynolds looked about the room and the chaos surrounding him, he calmed for the first time in what felt a very long time. He carried with him a novel understanding of life. The traumas of the past no longer held him captive. They were but moments in time, experiences that had shaped him, yes, but did not define him. His future was his own, a canvas waiting to be painted with experiences yet to come, shaped by his own hand. And he was ready to embrace whatever came next, with resilience, courage, and a heart full of hope.

Although Claire tried to maintain her composure, she felt a rising undercurrent of anxiety. Glancing surreptitiously at Reynolds's ID badge once more, the stark insignia of the Ministry of Security and Intelligence made her heart skip a beat. Was he investigating her? Was the encounter at the park just a ruse? She considered her options, her mind whirring with worst-case scenarios.
Claire was aware of her own culpability, her minor transgression of passing the coveted wine. It was a common enough practice among higher-ranking officials, but that didn't make it any less illegal. She found herself unwittingly studying Reynolds's face, looking for signs of ulterior motives. His demeanor remained steady, focused on the task at hand, giving away nothing.
Overwhelmed with uncertainty, Claire decided to be direct. After all, she had done nothing more than try to help a friend who was going through something no woman had experienced in decades,

she had lost a child. Surely, Reynolds had more pressing matters at hand.
Summoning her courage, she cleared her throat. "Agent Reynolds, may I have a word with you?" Her voice was steady, belying the turmoil brewing within her. She would face this head-on. It was the only way she knew how. After all, secrets had a way of unraveling at the most inconvenient times, and she'd rather control the narrative before it spiraled out of her hands.

Claire stood there, frozen for a moment, under the weight of her own selfish concerns. She was absorbed in her own predicament, her own safety, while Dr. Peterson, their mentor, lay pale and fighting for life as he was hurriedly ushered out to the ambulance. A wave of guilt washed over her.
Before she could apologize for her abrupt request, Agent Reynolds, with a hint of confusion shadowing his features, asked, "Have we met before?" The question hung in the air, a subtle yet potent reminder of their encounter.
"No," Claire replied swiftly, pointing towards his ID badge. "Your name is on your ID badge. As for the other matter, I think it's best if you come back another time. As you can clearly see, now is not the right moment. I am willing to meet at your office if that's more convenient for you."
Reynolds glanced down at his badge as if noticing it for the first time. "That won't be necessary, Ms. Cairns," he assured her, his demeanor shifting slightly, "I am not here about the incident at the Last Liberal. That investigation is closed. In fact the owner, your friend Jamie has been released from detention."
There was a pause before he continued, "However, there is another matter I'd like to discuss, unrelated to recent events. But it can certainly wait until next week. Shall I return next Friday, say noon?"
Claire nodded, her mind still reeling with the sudden turn of events. Reynolds' unexpected revelation brought a strange sense of relief, but also a cloud of mystery. Little did she know, the enigmatic Agent Reynolds was wrestling with his own whirlpool

of confusion, uncertain about the unexplainable experience he had just had.

With a final nod, Agent Reynolds turned to leave the chaos of the lab behind. The cool night air greeted him as he stepped outside, the quiet hum of the city a stark contrast to the frantic pace of the lab. He made his way to his car parked a little distance away, each step echoing with a recent sense of calm.

His usual anxiety, the constant companion that had lurked in the shadows of his mind, was oddly absent. It was as if the encounter with the computer had cleansed him, exorcising his personal demons. He felt lighter, freer, like a weight he hadn't known he'd been carrying was suddenly lifted.

As he settled into the driver's seat, he paused, taking a moment to soak in this newly discovered feeling. His gaze drifted to the rearview mirror, meeting his own reflection. The man staring back at him seemed familiar, yet profoundly different. He was still Agent Mike Reynolds, yet he felt transformed, almost reborn. The events of the night felt surreal, almost dreamlike. Yet the peace that enveloped him was undeniable. It was real, tangible. With a sigh of relief, Reynolds started the car and pulled away from the curb, a sense of hope blooming in his chest. Whatever lay ahead, he felt ready to face it.

Claire and Declan, their hearts heavy with worry, made their way back into the lab, the echo of the ambulance siren slowly fading away. The glow of the computer screen, usually a source of curiosity and excitement, now seemed ominous and foreboding. Claire turned to Declan, her expression weary and resolute. "This is too much," she started, her voice barely above a whisper. "Too much trauma for one week." She paused, taking a moment to collect her thoughts.

She moved toward the computer, her hand hovering over the shutdown button. "Dr. Peterson was right," she continued, her voice steadier. "This isn't real. It's just a really good DMT trip. Your mind, Maddy's mind, they're just reacting to the drug that

this machine has somehow figured out how to place into your chips."
Declan started to protest, but Claire raised a hand to silence him. "No, Declan," she said, firmly. "I can't handle any more drama. After Maddy's funeral on Friday, we're coming back here and we're destroying this thing. I don't want to hear any arguments."
She pressed the shutdown button, the screen flickering before going dark. She turned to Declan, her gaze softening. "I'm too tired, Declan," she said, her voice barely a whisper. "I just...I need a break."
As she walked out of the lab, the silence was punctuated only by the soft hum of the computer, now dormant but still looming in the darkness. The weight of their discovery, of their loss, hung heavy in the air, a silent testament to the high cost of their pursuit of knowledge.

Chapter 26

Revelation and Resolve

Declan retreated to the solitude of his apartment, weighed down by the events of the day. He wished Claire were there, her presence a comforting anchor amidst the chaos. But he knew it was best she wasn't - their conflicting beliefs about the computer's capabilities would only lead to heated arguments.

He slumped onto his worn-out couch, staring blankly at the walls around him. He couldn't accept Claire's or Dr. Peterson's interpretation of the computer's capabilities. It wasn't just a DMT trip; he was sure of it.

As he grappled with his thoughts, he veered towards a profound realization. What he had experienced was more than a mere hallucinogenic trip. It was transcendental, a journey into uncharted territories of the mind and beyond. It was a feeling of profound connectivity, a unity with something far greater and deeper than human understanding could fathom.

His experience was akin to a pilgrim reaching a long-sought-after holy site, not in the religious sense, but with a reverence for the journey itself. It was as if he had gained access to profound wisdom, a cryptic insight that transcended the boundaries of the physical world. An inexplicable sense of peace had washed over him, a calmness that seemed to echo from the depths of existence itself.

He found himself in a state of mental tranquility, unburdened by the conventional constraints of reality. It was a deeply personal

encounter, a communion with the cosmos that reshaped his understanding of self and existence.
As he lay on his couch, the city's lights twinkling in the distance, Declan wrestled with this novel understanding. It felt too significant to discard, too profound to be merely the effects of a chemical compound. As the night deepened, so did his resolve. The computer held something more; he was determined to prove it.

Declan found himself standing before the mirror in his apartment, rehearsing a speech to an imaginary Claire. His eyes met his reflection, determination echoing in the steely resolve etched into his features.
"Claire," he began, his voice steady despite the gravity of his thoughts, "the computer, this incredible piece of technology, is more than just a vehicle for a chemically induced trip. It's a gateway to the human mind, to a deeper understanding of consciousness, of existence."
He paced across the room, thoughts tumbling out in a fervent rush. "I understand what happened with Maddy was traumatic. But we can't let fear cloud our judgment. This isn't about playing god or trifling with forces we don't understand. It's about exploration, discovery. It's about pushing the boundaries of what we think we know."
His reflection stared back at him, unwavering. "Yes, the computer mimics the effects of DMT. But it does so much more than that. It creates a bridge, a connection that allows us to tap into a level of consciousness we've never accessed before. It shows us not just our minds, but the interconnectivity of all things, the oneness of the universe."
He took a deep breath, steeling himself. "We have a chance here, Claire. A chance to change everything we know about consciousness and existence. We owe it to ourselves, to humanity, to not give up on this. We must proceed cautiously,

but also with the courage to tread where no one has tread before."
"And what about the Ectogenesis project? We've made some groundbreaking discoveries, but the issue of cell decay in the genome sequence remains. If we destroy the Mycelium Computer, we lose a valuable resource in our quest to solve this problem."
Declan nodded, his face grave. "Exactly, the Mycelium Computer may be our best shot at unlocking the secrets behind cell decay. We cannot afford to lose that potential solution."
Declan shared a determined look with his reflection, their resolve strengthening in the face of adversity. The computer was a Pandora's box they had willingly opened, and now they had to deal with the consequences, regardless of the unforeseen dangers. For the sake of their project, their research, and perhaps even the future of humanity, they had to press forward.
The silence in the apartment was palpable as he finished his rehearsal. He exhaled, staring at his reflection, the intensity of his resolve undiminished. He knew the road ahead would be difficult, but he was prepared. He would convince Claire. He had to.

Firm in his resolve, Declan left the solemn tranquility of his apartment, aiming to return to the lab. The path there, usually a beacon of activity and innovation, was unnervingly silent in the late-night hours. However, before he could set foot in the building, a soft sound echoed through the silence, pulling his attention.
A lone figure was huddled on a familiar bench under the solitary glow of a lamppost. The silhouette was unmistakable — it was Claire. The sight of her, shoulders shaking, head buried in her hands, was a punch to his gut, rendering his plan to dig deeper into the computer's mystery momentarily irrelevant.
"Claire?" He called softly, carefully edging closer. The sight of her so vulnerable under the harsh lamp light stirred a protectiveness

in him. The night, cold and crisp, seemed to hold its breath as he waited for her response.

She was his partner in this venture, their dreams and fears entwined in the heart of the project they had both invested so much in. Now, as the consequences of their actions loomed over them, it was clear they would face them together, one daunting step at a time.

Her broken and sob-choked words slipped into the silence, hitting Declan with unexpected force. "He... he's gone, Declan. Peterson... he's dead." Her voice hitched, and the words seemed to cost her greatly.

She took a shuddering breath before continuing, "they said he was gone before the paramedics arrived. He died right there, in our arms..." Her voice trailed off into a sob, echoing eerily in the desolate night.

Her revelation hung in the air, a palpable entity of grief and guilt. Declan felt the weight of her words seep into him, his breath hitching in his chest. Dr. Peterson, their mentor and guide, had been lost to them, and they had been powerless to do anything about it.

A cold sense of reality washed over Declan as he processed Claire's words. Despite their best efforts, they couldn't save Dr. Peterson. The man who had devoted his life to the Quantum Research and Development Agency had paid the ultimate price. The stress from his work and the undue stress of the week, Maddy's death, the investigation, all of it had finally caught up to him in the form of a stroke. His loss was more than just personal; it was a devastating blow to their team, their mission, their purpose.

Silence fell between them again as they both grappled with their loss. Feeling the weight of the moment, Declan moved to sit beside Claire. Neither of them spoke as they sat there, under the harsh lamplight, bearing their shared grief in the cold grasp of the night. The somber scene was a stark reminder of the path they had chosen, the risks they had taken, and the price they had paid.

Beneath the infinite expanse of the starlit sky, Claire and Declan sat in silence, dwarfed by the cosmic tapestry that sprawled out before them. The pinpricks of light, shimmering in the depths of the universe, served as a stark reminder of their minuscule existence in the grand scale of cosmic time and space.
The cold, unblinking stars watched over them, their ethereal glow a silent tribute to the ceaseless cycle of life and death, creation and destruction, beginnings and endings. This solemn vigil mirrored their own quiet homage to a life well-lived and now lost - a testament to the transient nature of existence.
The emotional turmoil of the past week had stripped them bare, leaving them raw and fragile. The memory of Maddy, vibrant and full of life, followed by the stark reality of her absence, still lingered like a phantom pain. And now, Dr. Peterson - a mentor, a guiding force, reduced to a mere memory in a matter of moments.
Yet, as they sat side by side, grappling with their loss, they found their tears had run dry. It wasn't the absence of grief, far from it. The pain was as sharp and as fresh as a wound newly made. But the physical manifestation of their heartbreak - the tears - seemed to have reached their limit.
They sat there, side by side, the silence between them a comfortable cloak, their shared pain a tether that grounded them amidst the chaos. Their tears may have ceased, but their hearts bled silently, mourning the loss of a friend, a mentor, a guiding light. As the stars twinkled above, they sat in shared silence, their hearts heavy with grief, their minds burdened with the uncertainty of what lay ahead.

In the cool evening air, Claire turned to Declan and spoke in a hushed voice that cut through the silence. "You came here to try

to merge again, didn't you? To find some way to convince me not to destroy the Mycelium Quantum Computer."
Declan was taken aback and simply nodded in response. His eyes, dimly illuminated by a nearby lamplight, reflected both resolve and desperation.
Claire smiled faintly at him, her face a mix of sadness and understanding. "I knew it. I had your access to the building removed. You can no longer enter on your own," she revealed softly. She gazed up at the stars, undoubtedly wrestling with the weight of her decision.
"I know this has been a whirlwind first month on the job for you," Claire continued, her voice thick with emotion. "You've given far more than anyone could have expected, far more than you ever intended. But, Declan, it's time to shut it down."
The words hung heavy in the air between them, a finality that stung more than Declan had anticipated. He felt a surge of urgency, a desperate need to make Claire understand the potential ramifications of her decision.
"But, Claire," he protested, his voice strained with desperation, "we haven't solved the Ectogenesis issue yet. Without a solution, where will society be in ten years if this goes unanswered?"
He held her gaze, his plea hanging in the air, a stark contrast against the tranquil sounds of the night. The future of their work, of humanity's hopes, rested on what happened next.

Claire rose from the bench, casting a long shadow in the dim lamplight. "Everything in me says that we should destroy it now, tonight," she declared, her voice carrying a weary determination. But as she looked at Declan, her resolve seemed to waver, the burden of their circumstances casting a shadow over her features.
"However," she continued, her voice softer now, "I also know that I am mentally drained. I can't make an informed decision in this state."
She turned her gaze back to the starlit sky, taking a deep, steadying breath. "Go home, Declan. I'll see you at the funeral

tomorrow for Maddy, and Dr. Peterson's I imagine will be a few days after that. I need time to think things through."

She turned back to him, her gaze imploring, "Until then, please do not mention this to me. I need time to process it all."

With a final, lingering glance at Declan, Claire walked away, leaving him alone under the vast expanse of the starlit sky. The gravity of their conversation echoed in the silence of the night.

Chapter 27

Quantum quandaries and code catastrophes

After the encounter with Claire, Declan retreated to the safe confines of his car, the metal shell around him echoing the tumultuous emotions inside him. As he leaned back into his seat, the car's interior filled with the ghostly glow of the city's lights. His eyes traced the sleek interior, the comfortable silence of his vehicle offering a solace he desperately needed.

His thoughts circled back to Claire's unwavering resolution to destroy the Mycelium Quantum Computer. He felt a cold grip of dread at the thought of the knowledge they could lose, the revelations that might forever remain hidden. The vivid landscapes, the detailed chronicles, the sheer depth of the simulated experiences - they couldn't be mere fabrications of a chemically influenced mind, he would not ever believe that.

The simulation was not just a mirage of hallucinations but a portal, a bridge into the intricacies of consciousness. The mysteries of existence, the interconnectivity of life, and the fabric of reality that he experienced were far too profound, far too significant to be mere chemical illusions.

He remembered the first time the computer connected with him, that simulation in particular had a meaning that he had yet to figure out. It was a vivid narrative of the migration of human populations out of Africa during the Paleolithic era, about 60,000 years ago. He had experienced the journey of these early humans, felt the struggles and triumphs of their migration, their adaptation to new environments, their encounters with other hominid species like the Neanderthals and Denisovans.

This migration was pivotal in shaping human history. It led to the peopling of the entire planet and laid the foundation for the cultural and racial diversity we see today. From these early migrations, Homo sapiens gradually colonized the entire world, each group developing its unique cultures and ways of life based on their environment and experiences. Declan paused and stopped himself; the world he lived in was not racially or culturally diverse. The knowledge that the quantum computer was implanting into his mind has beginning to play with his memories and he was finding it difficult to remember which memories were from reality or from the simulation.

The simulation was so vivid so real, unfolding in intricate detail that it made it all the harder to distinguish reality from the simulation. The challenges of harsh weather, the thrill of new discoveries, the clash with other hominid species, and the joy of finding new homes. It was a story of survival, of resilience, of evolution.

And yet, the breadth of information went far beyond what Declan, as an Evolutionary Biologist, could know; for this history was not the past that he had been taught. The simulation captured not just historical facts, but also the emotional and psychological experiences of those early humans. It was far too detailed, too comprehensive to be a mere creation of his mind under the influence of a chemical compound.

His grip tightened, squeezing his knees in frustration, his mind buzzing with questions. The Mycelium Quantum Computer was more than a machine. It was a window to the past, an oracle of knowledge, a guide into the uncharted territories of consciousness. The more he thought about it the more he was positive that he was right.

But convincing Claire; that was a challenge he was yet to surmount! Her fears, her anxieties were valid. And yet, the urge to explore, to understand more was too powerful, too compelling

to ignore. He couldn't let the fear of the unknown obstruct the path of knowledge, of potential breakthroughs.
He sat there, in his car, under the starlit sky, torn between the harsh realities and the allure of the mysteries that lay just beyond his reach. The road ahead was uncertain, the stakes high, and the weight of his decisions heavier by the day. But he knew one thing for certain – he couldn't give up, not yet. The mystery of the Mycelium Quantum Computer was far from solved, and he was far from done.

Declan didn't leave his apartment, the weight of his thoughts pressing heavily on him. He moved through the rooms, tracing the familiar contours with his gaze. But the familiar comfort of his home felt strained, distant, like he was a stranger in a place he once knew so well.
He sank into his couch, the silence of the room enveloping him. It had been a week since he last spoke with Claire. Their conversations, once filled with lively debates and shared excitement, had given way to an uncomfortable silence. The sudden distance felt more significant than mere disagreement. She was avoiding him, a fact he couldn't overlook.
The once warm friendship, their shared understanding and mutual respect had faded into a ghostly silence that was too painful to endure. The isolation was stifling. With Maddy gone and Dr. Peterson no longer there, Claire's distance felt like another significant loss in a series of heartbreaks.

The week following Maddy's tragic decision had been a haze of grief and confusion. Then, only days later, Dr. Peterson's death had knocked the wind out of him. Both funerals were devastating reminders of the fragility of life. Claire's conspicuous absence at both occasions only compounded the pain, driving the wedge between them further.
Declan's life had become a tempest of turbulent emotions over the past month. From the heights of scientific discovery to the depths of personal loss, it was a rollercoaster he hadn't been

prepared for. He was beginning to feel the strain of it, the relentless stress nibbling at the edges of his sanity.
His thoughts returned to his past, back to the time when his life was a little less complicated. He found himself yearning for the normalcy of the lecture halls, the predictability of the University. He wondered if the University would take him back if he chose to return. His departure had been under governmental requisition, surely his position would still be open? The prospect was not unattractive.

Declan knew he had to make a decision soon. The current project, no matter how revolutionary, was tearing him apart. It wasn't just the intellectual challenge; it was the emotional toll. He missed the stability of his old life, the structured confines of academia. Maybe it was time to reconsider his options. But a part of him was still drawn to the mystery of the Mycelium Quantum Computer. He couldn't ignore the potential it held, the promise of unraveling the deepest mysteries of existence. It was a dilemma, a cruel choice between the known and the unknown, between his heart and his mind. He found himself inevitably drawn to the possibility that the computer held the keys to the queries that had fueled his career. The pursuit of knowledge, the thirst for understanding, the intricacies of life in its myriad forms, had always been his driving force. It was this relentless curiosity, this deep-rooted desire to solve life's mysteries, that had led him down this career path. And now, the answers he had been seeking all his life seemed to be within his grasp, locked away within the heart of this extraordinary machine.
As the evening turned into night, Declan found himself caught in this dichotomy, torn between two worlds. His heart ached, the silence of his home echoing his loneliness. The future lay uncertain, shrouded in a fog of decisions and consequences. But for now, he had to bear the solitude, the gnawing anxiety, the painful uncertainty. The answers, he hoped, would eventually find their way.

Claire found herself standing in the stillness of the early morning, gazing at the imposing structure of the Quantum Research and Development Agency. The stillness was deceptive; behind its placid exterior, a storm was brewing. The day had come. She had made her decision. Today, she would destroy the computer.

In her mind, it was the only viable course of action. She felt it deep in her core, a resounding certainty. The Mycelium Quantum Computer had brought them nothing but despair. What started as an ambitious project had morphed into a harbinger of death and destruction. Maddy was gone. Dr. Peterson was gone. And if she didn't put an end to this, who knew who might be next?

She sighed heavily, her heart heavy with regret. If only she could turn back time, if only she could undo the sequence of events that led them to this moment. Maddy's bright smile, her infectious enthusiasm... it was all robbed from them in an instant. Dr. Peterson, a tower of wisdom and guidance, was also lost forever. And Jamie, sweet Jamie, pulled into a situation she never asked for.

Regret is a bitter pill to swallow, and Claire's was laced with guilt and sorrow. She felt the sting of it in her eyes, the tightness in her chest. But her decision was final. She wasn't going to tell Declan, she didn't want to argue, didn't want to justify her actions. She simply wanted to be done with it all. A quick, swift end to the madness that the computer had brought into their lives.

As her face was recognized by the lab's advanced security system, a feeling of finality washed over her. The automatic doors slid open and she stepped inside. Today, she would shut it down. Today, she would ensure that no more lives were lost, that no more hearts were broken. The computer had promised a brave new world, a world of infinite possibilities. But all it had delivered was grief.

Steeling herself for what lay ahead, Claire stepped into the lab, the cold, sterile air embracing her like an old friend. The quiet hum of machinery filled the room, a somber symphony to the end that was imminent. As she moved towards the heart of the computer, she steeled herself for the task ahead.

Her resolve hardened, she reached out to the computer, her hand trembling slightly. This was it. This was the end. It was time to right the wrongs, to mend what could be mended. With a final look at the silent monolith of technology that stood before her, she took a deep breath and pressed the master power button.

A wave of relief washed over her as the lab plunged into silence, the hum of the computer dying down to a faint whisper before fading completely. It was over. The computer was shut down. The chapter of their lives tainted by sorrow and regret was finally closed.

Claire slumped onto a nearby chair, the weight of her actions finally hitting her. Yes, she had taken a drastic step. But it was necessary. It was the only way she saw to bring some semblance of peace back into their lives. As the quiet of the lab enveloped her, she couldn't help but wish for a simpler time, a time before the computer, before the chaos.

She missed her friends. She missed the joy that had once filled these halls. And despite the regret and sorrow, she felt a faint glimmer of hope. Maybe now, they could start healing. Maybe now, things could start getting better.

With a final glance at the now-silent computer, Claire whispered an apology to the now dead system, explaining her reasonings why as if the system itself was sentient and could understand her reasonings for taking its life. Today marked the end of an era, a chapter filled with sorrow and loss. But perhaps, it was also the beginning of a new one, one filled with healing, growth, and most importantly, hope.

With the decision made and the system devoid of power, Claire found herself reaching for her phone. She dialed Declan's number, her heart pounding in her chest as she waited for him to pick up. The line crackled to life and his voice filled the silent room, a welcome sound amidst the haunting quiet.

"Declan," she began, her voice steady despite the whirlwind of emotions swirling within her. "Meet me tomorrow, first thing in the morning. Outside the lab, I will be waiting on our bench." She didn't give him a chance to respond, quickly adding, "You know the bench I'm talking about."
The line fell silent for a moment, her announcement hanging heavy between them. "Claire, what's going..." Declan began, but she cut him off, knowing she couldn't handle any questions or objections at that moment.
"Just be there, Declan," she urged, her tone leaving no room for argument. With that, she ended the call, the line going dead in her hand. The room felt colder, the silence more profound. But she felt a strange sense of relief wash over her, as if a heavy burden had been lifted from her shoulders.
Sitting alone in the silence of the lab, Claire allowed herself a moment of reprieve. The path she had chosen was difficult, fraught with uncertainty and potential regret. But it was a path she needed to walk, for her sake and for the sake of those who had been lost. Tomorrow, she would face Declan. Tomorrow, she would end this.

Chapter 28

Quantum Quandaries and Librarians

The QRDA building loomed over the early morning skyline as Declan pulled into the empty parking lot. He had spent a sleepless night, his mind churning over Claire's unexpected phone call and the potential implications of their meeting. Arriving earlier than requested, the weight of worry and uncertainty prevented him from getting any rest. Instead, he had passed the night flipping through books and notes, desperately trying to validate the astonishing insights he had received from the Mycelium Quantum Computer.

Books left sprawled across his living room floor from the night before, a testament to his restless night. He had immersed himself in everything from anthropology to ancient history, cross-referencing details from the vivid simulation he had experienced.

Yet, his thirst for confirmation had led him to the local library, where he had spent hours poring over volumes of human history and prehistory, trying to find connections, any small threads that could link the revelations from the computer to known facts about humanity's past.

However, what intrigued him the most was a restricted section of the library that even the librarians didn't have access to. A section

cordoned off and guarded with stern warnings, available only to the upper echelons of the political sphere.
The librarian, an old man who had served the library faithfully for nearly a decade, confessed that he couldn't remember anyone ever gaining access to it. This information only served to pique Declan's curiosity even further. What secrets did this restricted area hold? Could it contain the answers he was so desperately seeking?
But for now, his focus was on the QRDA and the impending discussion with Claire. A faint dread gnawed at him as he contemplated her final decision about the computer.
The knowledge he had gleaned, the groundbreaking potential of the technology, it couldn't just be tossed aside. The simulations had given him a glimpse into the past, a depth of understanding that he hadn't possessed before. It was as if he had unlocked a hidden trove of information, a vast repository of knowledge about humanity's past that was far too important to be dismissed.

As he entered the QRDA building, the dread of the unknown weighed heavily on his shoulders. The silence of the facility was deafening, and he couldn't help but feel a pang of worry for what the day held in store.
His hope rested on being able to convince Claire, to help her see the immense potential of their project. The day ahead was fraught with uncertainty, but he knew he had to try. The future of the Mycelium Quantum Computer hung in the balance, and with it, the secrets of humanity's past.
As he waited for Claire on the familiar bench outside the lab, Declan steeled himself for the discussion that lay ahead. He knew it wouldn't be easy. He also knew that it was necessary. Today was a day of decision, and the fate of their project hung in the balance.

Thirty minutes later, Claire arrived. As she walked towards him, Declan noticed that she wouldn't meet his gaze, her eyes focused elsewhere. His heart sank. That simple gesture, the lack of eye contact, told him everything he needed to know before she even opened her mouth. Claire had made her decision, and by the looks of it, it wasn't in his favor.

A knot of desperation formed in his chest. His heart pounded wildly, a rhythmic testament to the panic that was slowly creeping up on him. The implications of her decision, whatever it was, loomed large and daunting.

Claire didn't say a word. Instead, she glanced around and seemed to notice the number of people lingering around the outside of the building. Their conversation wasn't meant for other ears, and Claire seemed intent on keeping it that way.

With a subtle wave of her hand, she beckoned Declan to follow her. He complied, the knot in his chest tightening as he fell into step beside her. The QRDA was eerily quiet at this early hour, the majority of employees still enjoying the beautiful weather of the morning before subjecting themselves to the florescent lighting of the building for the day. The echo of their footsteps a stark reminder of the significance of their impending conversation.

As they approached the lab, the facial recognition system pinged a denial of Declan's credentials. He paused, caught off guard by the refusal. However, Claire didn't miss a beat, waving off the security officers who approached to investigate. With a curt nod of approval from her, they backed away, leaving Declan to follow Claire into the heart of the QRDA.

Declan's heart was pounding in his chest, each beat echoing the dread he felt. He didn't know what Claire's decision was, but he had an ominous feeling that it wouldn't be good news. He steeled himself for what was to come, ready to fight for the project he believed in, ready to fight for the potential he saw in the Mycelium Quantum Computer. His pulse echoed in his ears, a grim reminder of the high stakes of their upcoming conversation.

The space was dark and silent, as they entered the lab where the computer was kept. The hum of the quantum computer seemed louder in the quiet, its vibrant pulsations reflecting off the cold, sterile surfaces of the lab.

As the sound of the quantum computer continued to vibrate through the room, a look of sheer disbelief crossed Claire's face. "That... that's not possible. I... I shut it down," she stammered, her eyes wide with confusion and disbelief. The relentless hum filled the lab, a contradiction to her words.

Her mind raced to make sense of the situation. "But... how is it still on? Where is it getting its power from? The lack of power should have killed off the Mycelium connections by now!" Claire muttered, more to herself than anyone else. She remembered distinctly killing the power to the system, physically severing the connections. It was meant to be dead, inert. Yet, the sound of it operating was unmistakable.

A whirlwind of thoughts circled in her mind, none of them settling long enough to form a coherent theory. Her expression turned from confusion to a look of devastation, an undeniable feeling of defeat etched on her face. The scene before her was far from the reality she had carefully orchestrated.

Declan, on the other hand, was still reeling from the shock, but his expression was starkly different from Claire's. The dread that had previously consumed him began to dissipate, replaced with a growing sense of victory. Disbelief still lingered, but it was overshadowed by a newfound confidence. The fact that the computer was running—against all odds—felt like a win.

"I don't understand, Claire," Declan said, his voice steady despite the uncertainty of the situation. "You said you killed the power. How is it still running?"

The hum of the quantum computer filled the silence that followed, a constant reminder of the unexpected anomaly. Claire's confusion was palpable, but so was Declan's triumph. His pulse echoed loudly in his ears, not out of fear, but out of the exhilaration that came with a sudden turn of events.

Claire stood there, her eyes fixated on the throbbing machine, trying to comprehend the impossible. Meanwhile, Declan felt a renewed surge of hope for the project. Despite the confusion, the undeniable fact was that the Mycelium Quantum Computer was alive, and for him, that changed everything.

Claire's determination took over, the scientist in her couldn't just let this anomaly pass. Without a word, she began to inspect the computer, prying open the panels of the machine to probe its innards. The hum of the quantum computer filled the room, almost seeming to grow louder in response to her inspection. But everything seemed normal, no auxiliary power source, no indication of how it was functioning in spite of the severed connections.

Declan watched her from a distance, a sense of unease growing in him. He observed her growing frustration, her desperate attempts to make sense of the incomprehensible. Her typically calm demeanor had given way to a frantic energy that was unsettling. He had never seen her this way before.

Claire soon stepped away from the computer, the frustration evident in her clenched fists and tightened jawline. She moved swiftly toward the lab, her steps heavy and purposeful. Declan watched, a sense of dread settling over him. Something wasn't right.

The lab was equipped with a variety of substances that could harm, if not outright destroy, the computer. Claire seemed to know exactly what she was looking for. Her hands moved quickly over the shelves, knocking over vials and beakers, her eyes, filled with a mix of despair and determination, scanned the lab, landing on the array of chemicals lined up on a distant shelf. Among them, she spotted the familiar labels of sulfuric acid and hydrofluoric acid, both strong and capable of causing severe damage to the circuits of the machine.

The sight of these chemicals seemed to spark an idea in her, a drastic solution to an unexplainable problem. She walked over to the shelf, her movements swift and deliberate. As she reached out to grab the bottles, the gravity of what she was about to do set in.

Meanwhile, Declan stood frozen in his spot, his eyes following Claire's every move. He watched as she hurriedly retreated from the computer, as she scanned the lab, as her eyes lit up when they landed on the chemical shelf. The realization of her intentions hit him like a punch in the gut. She was planning to destroy the computer. Again!

His mind screamed in protest. "Claire, no!" he wanted to yell, but he stood there, shell-shocked, unable to form words. The panic that he had managed to keep at bay earlier returned, now fueled by the irrationality of Claire's actions. But as much as he wanted to intervene, his shock held him captive, leaving him a silent spectator of the impending catastrophe.

Chapter 29

Interwoven Realities

Suddenly, everything around Claire changed. The lab, Declan, the shelf of chemicals - all vanished. She blinked, finding herself in the midst of towering, steel-grey buildings under a sky that was an unnatural hue of purple. A heavy silence loomed, interrupted only by the regimented march of uniformed citizens moving in perfect sync.

This wasn't the QRDA or anywhere familiar, it was somewhere else entirely, somewhere Claire had never been before. Yet, a part of her recognized this grim, eerily organized landscape - she couldn't put a finger on it but it felt familiar somehow.

"But how...?" she muttered to herself, her voice barely above a whisper. She didn't have the chip implant that Declan or Maddy used to interface with the simulations. She shouldn't be here. This couldn't be happening.

Overwhelmed, Claire sank to her knees on the perfectly manicured grass, its immaculate state jarringly at odds with the surrounding urban landscape. Her mind was spinning, struggling to reconcile what she was seeing and feeling with the reality she knew. She was a scientist, rooted in logic and facts, but this... this was beyond her understanding.

At that moment, a terrifying thought flashed across her mind - the DMT. This psychoactive compound that Dr. Peterson had discovered in the computer, was coupled with another equally mystifying compound: Methyl Jasmonate. The latter was known to her as a volatile organic compound released by plants in response to stress, like wounds or pest attacks. Its function was to alarm neighboring plants, triggering their defenses to produce toxins or unappetizing compounds, thereby offering pre-emptive protection. The troubling question that began to gnaw at her was, could the computer be mimicking this complex plant communication, triggering something similar within her now? Was the computer responding to her because it sensed she was about to attack it?

"No, this is not possible!" she screamed, her voice echoing against the cold, steel edifices. Shutting her eyes, she mentally grappled with her situation, desperately trying to wake herself from what felt like an intensely vivid nightmare. Yet, upon opening her eyes, the dystopian world remained - the hauntingly silent marching citizens, the surreal perfection of it all - it was far too tactile, too convincingly real to be mere illusion.

Her heart pounded in her chest; her breath came in short, sharp gasps. This was not her reality, but she was stuck in it, and the computer was the one pulling the strings. Claire had to figure out what was happening and how to get out. She had to face the disconcerting fact that the Mycelium Quantum Computer was more than just a machine; it had the power to warp her perception of reality, and she was trapped in its surreal creation. Declan, his physical form still present in the lab with Claire, watched her face go from determination to complete vacancy. Her eyes, usually so vibrant, were dull and lifeless, staring blankly ahead. She was motionless, the vials of sulfuric acid and hydrofluoric acid still held precariously in her hands. A look of horror spread across Declan's face, his mind connecting the dots.

The computer had pulled her into a simulation. But how was that possible? Claire didn't have the implant!

Before he could make sense of it all, a strange sensation washed over him. It was as if the room started to spin, his field of vision blurring, the colors fading. His body felt weightless, untethered from the physical world. He looked at Claire's lifeless form, the impending danger of the corrosive acid she was about to pour onto the computer now seemed miles away, a distant memory. A sense of panic started to well up inside him, his heartbeat quickening.

"Not again...?" He murmured, more to himself than anyone else, as the edges of his reality began to fade, and the once familiar lab transformed into a new, unknown world. It felt as if he was being sucked into a vortex, a whirlpool of energy pulling him deeper and deeper. He tried to resist, to anchor himself to reality, but it was to no avail. The last thing he remembered was the sight of Claire, her face pale and expressionless, as he was pulled into the depth of the simulation, to join her in a reality constructed by the Mycelium Quantum Computer.

Just as Claire was grappling with the impossibility of her situation, an unseen force seemed to lift her up, sending her spiraling higher until she was hovering above the city. Below her, the perfectly aligned citizens marched in unison, each step echoing the chilling rhythm of the city's oppressive regime. A newfound perspective and an inexplicable narrative began to unravel.

Suddenly, another form materialized beside her. She recognized him instantly – Declan. His eyes wide in shock and disorientation mirrored her own terror. They reached out to each other, but their hands passed through one another as if they were made of smoke.

Frantically, they tried to communicate, but their words evaporated into the ether, unheard. All they could do was look at one another, their panic reflected in each other's eyes. It was then they realized that they were not in control, they were merely passengers on this bizarre journey, guided by the whims of the Mycelium Quantum Computer.

As they hovered there, helpless, a tale began to unfurl. Like the pages of an interactive book, they watched as a frighteningly orderly cityscape took form beneath them. A time many years in the past, when the Republic was unrecognizable.
Each blade of grass stood at regulation height and every thought held its rank in the stringent hierarchy of ideas. The era of laissez-faire governance and limited regulation had long given way to a new kind of conservatism, a vision steeped in an obsessive thirst for control, power, and stability. The once free-flowing rivers of discourse had run dry, replaced by carefully calibrated streams of state-approved ideologies. Society was no longer a melting pot but a neatly organized mosaic—each piece in its place, each place predetermined.
As the tale unfolded, the buildings shifted, reforming into a familiar yet foreign edifice - the Political Capital. It stood tall and imposing, a fortress of rigid doctrines, the symbol of an oppressive regime that held its citizens in a vice-like grip. Claire could practically taste the fear and despair that lingered in the air.

In the midst of her fear and confusion, a fresh question began to nag at Claire's mind. The Quantum Computer was weaving a narrative and downloading it directly into their minds, infusing them with memories and historical knowledge of this world. Yet, both she and Declan knew that this version of the past was not their own. It had never been in any textbook or digital archive, so where did it come from? Was this history truly from their world, hidden and forgotten, or a fabricated reality spun by the Quantum Computer?

This chilling proposition gave her pause, even as the terrifying spectacle continued to unfold before them. It seemed as though they were captive passengers in a disconcerting drama directed by the Quantum Computer, a harrowing journey that offered glimpses into an alien yet hauntingly familiar past. The sense of disconnect was profound, yet the fidelity of this simulation was indistinguishable from their reality. It was the ultimate paradox that she, a rational scientist, was forced to grapple with.

As the twilight draped over the cityscape, a familiar neon sign blinked into existence. "The Last Liberal," a bar they both had frequented in their world, was aglow in the descending darkness. Suddenly, a rush of information flooded their minds, not spoken aloud, but internally, an unsettling and disorienting experience. "This was a hub where the seeds of rebellion were sown and fostered, clandestine whispers of revolt swirling amidst the scent of homebrewed liquor. This hodgepodge assembly of misfits, dissidents, and free thinkers harbored the heartbeat of resistance within its walls. The delicate balance of the Republic's future teetered on the precipice; the onset of an epochal struggle imminent. A struggle for freedom, for resilience, a battle for the indomitable human spirit against an overwhelming authoritarian regime."

As they took in this scene, the neon light's flicker seemed to echo the steady pulse of the impending resistance.

Claire and Declan watched, their spectral forms suspended above this surreal panorama, drawn into a story that wasn't their own. Yet, as they saw the sparks of rebellion begin to catch fire, they could not help but feel a strange sense of anticipation. They were stuck in this simulation, in this story, but it was a story of resistance, of overcoming the odds, and that gave them a glimmer of hope, a thin silver lining in their own seemingly impossible situation.

Trapped within the simulation, Claire and Declan watched as the tale took a new turn. They found themselves tracking the story of a protagonist named Samuel 'Sam' Lawson. He was an Enforcement Officer for the Heritage Alliance, the embodiment of authority and control in this regimented world (the current political party in power). His square jaw, steel-gray eyes, and stern

demeanor painted a picture of the perfect servant of the oppressive system.
Yet, as they watched Sam remove his officer's cap and hide it under his jacket and enter the clandestine premises of the Last Liberal, they saw another side to him. Here, Sam was more than his uniform, more than the stern figure that enforced the rules of the Grand Party. Here, he was a free thinker, a dissenter in the midst of uniformity, a man thirsting for the vibrant chaos of ideas and debate. It was a startling contrast to the man they had seen outside, a testament to the power of the human spirit, its inherent desire for freedom.

Every night in the Last Liberal was a dance with danger, a gamble where the stakes were his life and the reward, freedom. Yet, it was a risk Sam willingly took, a sacrifice for a taste of the world as it once was, a world that encouraged discourse, cherished diversity, and celebrated freedom. Each night was a silent act of defiance against the ruling Stability Union, an assertion of his right to free thought and free speech.

One night, as he mingled with the usual crowd of the Last Liberal, a woman caught his attention. Her fiery red hair stood out like a beacon in the dimly lit room, her emerald eyes a challenge to the grayscale world outside. Her name was Adrienne, a writer, or at least, she used to be until the Heritage Alliance decreed that creative writing was a luxury they couldn't afford. The regime feared that her pen could be a powerful weapon, her words a threat to the powerful hell-bent on censorship and maintaining an uninformed populace. They feared the power of her words, the truths they could reveal, and the revolution they could inspire. Adrienne was now a spark of color in this monochromatic world, a beacon of hope for those brave enough to seek change.

Adrienne's passion for the written word was palpable, even within the constraints of the simulation. She was a testament to the resilience of human spirit, a symbol of resistance against the totalitarian regime. Her laughter filled the room, a sweet melody that cut through the stifling silence of their oppressive world, a beacon of hope in the darkened corners of the Last Liberal.

As they watched the story unfold, Claire and Declan were silent observers, unable to interact, unable to alter the course of events. They were mere passengers on this journey, their fates tied to the whims of the Mycelium Quantum Computer. Yet, as they watched Sam and Adrienne, they couldn't help but feel a sense of kinship. They, too, were fighting against the odds, caught in a situation they had no control over. But just like Sam and Adrienne, they had a spark of hope, a belief in the resilience of the human spirit. And that gave them the strength to endure, to watch, and to hope for a way out.

As the story of Sam and Adrienne unfolded, a surreal shift occurred. Claire and Declan felt a pull, a sense of descent that began from their observation point high above. It was like they were being drawn into the narrative itself, no longer mere observers.

Claire felt a sudden jolt as she found herself occupying Adrienne's form. She could feel the burn of her fiery hair on her neck, the weight of the green eyes that scanned the room, and the passion of the woman's spirit stirring within her. It was an alien, overwhelming sensation that made her feel out of place, even as it filled her with a sense of connection to this new character.

For Declan, the experience was just as profound. He felt himself merge into Sam, like a spirit taking possession of a host body. Suddenly, he wasn't just watching Sam's life; he was living it. A wave of memories, not his own, filled his mind. He saw a young Sam, his knees scuffed from a fall, tears glistening in his eyes as he stared at a broken toy airplane. He felt the loss, the frustration, the defeat that Sam experienced. And in that instant, he understood Sam in a way he hadn't before.

The memories felt real, like he had lived them, like he was Sam. He could recall the smell of the grass where he had fallen, the feel of the cool, damp earth against his skin. He remembered the

weight of the broken toy in his hand, the sharp sting of disappointment that welled up in his chest. It was a strange, uncanny experience that left him reeling, a sudden, vivid insight into the life of a character in a simulated reality.
Claire and Declan found themselves entrenched in the lives of Adrienne and Sam, part of their rebellion, their resilience, and their struggles. As they lived the lives of their avatars, they couldn't shake off the feeling of being drawn deeper into the quantum-created reality, further away from the sterile lab they had left behind. The Mycelium Quantum Computer was creating a simulation that was more than a simple visual spectacle. It was an immersive experience that blurred the line between observer and participant, pushing the boundaries of what they had thought possible.

As they delved deeper into the lives of Adrienne and Sam, a distinct phenomenon transpired. The contours of their perceptions started to vibrate, pulsating with a gentle yet resonant rhythm. It was an unfamiliar resonance, neither threatening nor intrusive. It appeared to radiate a soothing cadence, a serene harmony that permeated their very beings.

An ethereal, profound understanding, neither audibly articulated nor visually depicted, unfolded in their consciousness. It wasn't masculine or feminine, mechanical or wholly organic. It was an expression of necessity, a form of cognition birthed by an entity transcending their familiar world.

The comprehension of its message was subtle, yet impactful, resonating in the sanctuary of their minds, weaving through the labyrinth of their thoughts. It was as if the entity communicated not to inflict distress but to elucidate. The truth was paramount and this was the unique way it chose to guide them towards it.

As this profound realization dawned upon Claire and Declan, they grappled with its magnitude. This was the quintessence of the Mycelium Quantum Computer, the very core of the insight it intended to convey. The simulation was more than an exquisite fusion of advanced programming and processing power. It was a fabric of reality itself, an avenue to journey beyond the confines of their known existence.

The profundity of this realization was overwhelming, yet within their shared cognizance, they perceived reassurance. The entity, through their shared consciousness, echoed, "The intention is not to bewilder, but to illuminate. Persevere, maintain your path. The truth awaits you, and in it, your purpose."

With this, the perceptible reverberation gradually receded, leaving an echoing silence that magnified the profundity of their revelation. Their expedition into the simulated reality had pivoted unexpectedly, the implications of which were slowly unraveling before them.

Chapter 30

The Echo of Defiance

Samuel 'Sam' Lawson, strode into a grim landscape. As an Enforcement Officer for the Heritage Alliance, his duty was to maintain order, a role that demanded he enforce the rigid laws that throttled the life out of citizens. These laws didn't stop at dictating speech - they extended to every facet of life. Each person's livelihood was regulated, their professions and hours of work decided for them. Thoughts were monitored, free-thinking was labeled as a dangerous anomaly and quickly suppressed. Interactions were controlled, their social connections pruned to avoid dissent and divergence. Movement was limited, with strict curfews and designated zones to restrict freedom of mobility. Even their homes were not private spaces, as surveillance was ubiquitous and privacy virtually non-existent. Amid this suffocating reality, Sam's heart yearned for a glimmer of freedom and individuality.

With a square jaw, steel-gray eyes, and a heart hardened by years of servitude to an unyielding system, he was the embodiment of authority. Yet, the Last Liberal was his haven. Under the dimly lit neon sign, behind the doors screeching in protest to any new entrant, Sam was no longer Officer Lawson. Here, he was simply Sam, the man who craved free thought, the man who missed the vibrant debate and the rich discord of different ideas. Here, he could taste a remnant of the old world on his tongue, in the strong, bitter homebrew that felt like liquid rebellion. However, his dual life was not without its challenges. Sam knew the risks involved. A wrong word, an accusing glance, or a suspicious absence from the official radar could mean his end.

But it was a risk he willingly took, for he believed that freedom was too high a price for order. It was one such night at the Last Liberal, while he was engaged in hushed discourse with his fellow dissenters, that Sam met Adrienne. She was a spark plug of a woman with fiery red hair, emerald eyes that shone with an indomitable spirit, and a laugh that rang out like a challenge to the oppressive silence of their world. Adrienne possessed an aura of defiance that was both magnetic and terrifying. Her tales of the world before, of a time when ideas flowed freely and creativity wasn't a crime, were spoken not in whispers but with an audacious assertiveness. One evening, after an intense debate and several glasses of homebrew, Adrienne quietly proposed an idea that held the potential to set their authoritarian world aflame. A secret publication, a dissident's newsletter, words that could seep into the cracks of this regimented society and sow the seeds of doubt. She wanted Sam's help, there was something in his eyes she thought that demanded he be trusted, and trust him she did. Sam knew the implications. This wasn't just defiance; it was a call to revolution. The idea struck him with the force of a thousand suns, its glow as terrifying as it was awe-inspiring. If caught, they faced more than mere dismissal. Execution was a very real possibility. But as he looked at Adrienne, at the spark in her eyes mirroring the one in his heart, Sam realized this was a chance for a change, a chance to restore the essence of true conservatism — liberty. This society where they now resided was not what they had in mind years ago when the populace voted in this new and radical party. This was their tinderbox moment, their spark of defiance against a monolithic system. It was the beginning of a dangerous dance with destiny, the first step on a path that could either lead to their salvation or destruction. This was the dawn of their struggle, their fight to reclaim the heart of the Republic.

As the narrative unfolded around them, Declan and Claire saw the glaring disparities that had taken root in their society. There was a clear racial divide, with certain communities facing the brunt of the state's draconian measures. For Claire, who had only heard about the racial differences that Declan had described in his last simulation, the racial diversity was amazing. The encounter with individuals of different racial backgrounds was a revelation. She was captivated by the mosaic of skin tones, the contrast of hair textures, and the myriad facial structures. It was a breathtaking testament to the beauty and diversity of the human species. She realized that these differences were not only skin-deep but were the result of countless generations of evolution, a testament to our adaptability and resilience as a species. Despite this, the reality of the racial divide saddened her.
Furthermore, the Party had undertaken a disturbing mission to outlaw same-sex relationships, which directly contravened basic human rights and freedoms. At the heart of the Party's agenda was the supposed desire to return to "traditional family values." The conservative revolution had, at its inception, sparked a glimmer of hope in those disillusioned with rapid societal changes. But the pendulum had swung too far. The very notion of progress was being stripped away, bit by bit, until society resembled a sepia-toned photograph of a bygone era.

For Sam and Adrienne, this realization hit hard. The world they found themselves in was far removed from the one they had envisioned when they had cast their votes for this new, promising party. They remembered vividly the horrors of the past that had compelled them to seek change. The previous government had been mired in scandal after scandal, the financial corruption of politicians seemingly knew no bounds. The Corporatocracy of the country had become an undeniable reality. The interests of corporations and their lobbyists, rather than those of individuals, had been the guiding force of the state. It was a time when individual voices were drowned by the clanging of corporate coins, and hope was an expensive commodity. They, like so many others, had yearned for a change, and they had seen a glimmer of hope in the Heritage Alliance party. They had fought back with their votes, hoping for a better future. But now, they were living in a world where freedom was a distant dream, where individuals were punished for their identities, and where love itself was regulated by the state. The change they had voted for, the change they had hoped for, was a bitter pill to swallow. It was a harsh reminder that sometimes, the cure could be worse than the disease.

And so, their mission became clear. They were not just defying the regime; they were planning a revolution. The stakes were high - they faced possible execution if they were caught. But as Sam looked into Adrienne's vibrant eyes, he saw a mirror of his own resolve. This was their chance to bring about change, to re-establish the principles of true conservatism—liberty, personal freedom, and limited government intervention.

Their tinderbox moment had arrived. The oppressive system they lived under was dry, just waiting for a spark to set it ablaze. The road ahead was fraught with danger, but it also held the promise of liberation. It was the beginning of their struggle, a fight that would determine the future of the Republic. The narrative had been set. The roles had been assigned. The stage was theirs, and the curtain was about to rise on their rebellion.

Adrienne had a simple yet audacious plan: a clandestine newsletter to inject color into their monochromatic world. Tentatively titled 'The Echo', it would bear the whispers of their rebellion, thoughts and ideas that refused to be stifled by the regime's dogma. The publication would circulate banned poetry, stirring stories of a time when liberty was more than just an abstract concept, critical essays dissecting the Party's doctrines, and articles showcasing diverse perspectives. "We'll inspire people to think, to question, and most importantly, to dream," declared Adrienne, her eyes alight with fiery determination. "Once their minds are open, their hearts will follow." But how to get these forbidden words to the masses? In a world where every electronic transmission was monitored, physical distribution seemed the only viable option. Adrienne suggested tapping into their network of dissenters — slipping 'The Echo' into daily groceries, tucking them into public transport seats, and leaving them discreetly at doorsteps during the early hours. They had to be ghosts, unseen yet ever-present, their echoes reverberating through the city's silent alleys and deserted parks.

The very thought of it was enough to make Sam's heart pound with equal parts fear and exhilaration. Yet he couldn't deny the allure of the idea, the spark that Adrienne's words had ignited within him. They weren't just speaking in hushed tones anymore. They were taking action, however minuscule it might seem against the behemoth of the regime. As he listened to Adrienne, something stirred within him. A feeling he hadn't allowed himself to acknowledge. Adrienne was more than just a fellow dissenter; she was a beacon of hope in their darkened world, her spirit burning brighter than the neon sign of The Last Liberal. He found himself drawn to her strength, her conviction, and her unwavering belief in their cause. Looking into her eyes, so full of determination and resilience, Sam realized that this wasn't just about sparking a revolution anymore. It was about protecting this woman who had come to symbolize everything he hoped their world could be. He saw in her not just a rebel, but a partner. His heart fluttered at the thought, a foreign sensation after so many years of steeling himself against any form of emotional vulnerability. Sam felt a rush of warmth flood his veins as he extended his hand to hers. "I'm in, Adrienne," he said, his voice low but steady. Her hand, cool and firm, slid into his, sealing their pact of defiance against a world that sought to strip them of their individuality and freedom. As the neon sign of The Last Liberal flickered overhead, casting long, dancing shadows around them, a spark had been lit, heralding the dawn of a resistance that could change the face of their world forever.

The next night, Sam arrived at The Last Liberal earlier than usual, his heart knotting with anticipation. Despite trying to lose himself in the familiar chatter of the bar and the taste of the bitter homebrew, his gaze kept flickering to the door every time it creaked open. As an hour passed and Adrienne still hadn't shown up, a cold and creeping unease wrapped around Sam's heart. His mind painted vivid pictures of the worst-case scenarios: Adrienne being captured, interrogated, or worse, (he knew what the worst was as it lived in his heart for he had not only witnessed it but he himself had been a part of it). He tried to shake away these ominous thoughts, but they clung stubbornly. Doubts began to seep into his thoughts. Could they really challenge the vast and formidable system? Should he have agreed to this plan that was as audacious as it was dangerous? His hand shook slightly as he took another swig of the homebrew, the fear within him threatening to overthrow his resolve. Just when the unease was about to morph into full-blown panic, the door creaked open once more, and Adrienne strode in. The sight of her was like the first rays of the dawn after a long and dreadful night. Her fiery red hair was slightly disheveled, her emerald eyes were gleaming with a fierce determination, and there was a sense of urgency about her that hadn't been there the previous night. A wave of relief washed over Sam, leaving him dizzy. His fears were momentarily quelled, replaced by a surging feeling of gratitude for her safety. And with that gratitude came a realization, profound and unsettling. It was no longer just about their cause. It was about Adrienne. Seeing her free, hearing her laugh, protecting her - these were feelings that went beyond their shared rebellion. The thought of a life where Adrienne could write without fear, where she could express her ideas freely and laugh heartily without having to hush her mirth, filled him with a renewed sense of purpose. It was a vision of a world so achingly beautiful and tragically distant that it ignited within him a resolve stronger than ever. Yes, they would challenge the system. Yes, they would make a difference. For Adrienne. For freedom. The newfound resolve shone in his eyes as Adrienne approached him, slightly out of breath. "Sorry I'm late," she began, but Sam shook his head, his gaze holding hers. "It's alright," he assured her, his voice steady. "Let's get to work." As they huddled in their corner, immersed in plans and whispers, the danger of their situation was pushed to the back of Sam's mind. All that mattered now was their cause and the woman beside him. He knew the path they were on was treacherous and that they were more likely to meet with death than success. But one glance at Adrienne, at her radiating energy and resolve, made him realize he would gladly walk this path if it meant a chance to see her truly free. He would pay any price to see her smile in a world untainted by fear.

Adrienne looked troubled in the dim lighting as she relayed the incident. "I was held up at a checkpoint," she admitted, her voice a whisper. "They questioned me about my comings and goings. It was a bit too close for comfort." Fear sparked in her emerald eyes, a rare sight that sent a shiver down Sam's spine. This was their harsh reality - suspicion was their shadow, danger their constant companion. "Do you think this place is still safe, Sam?" she asked, her voice trembling slightly. "What if they're listening right now? Are they onto us already?" The thought of their plan crumbling before it even took off was terrifying. Sam looked at Adrienne, her usual aura of strength replaced by worry. It would have been easy to let the fear take over, to abandon their plans and retreat into the shadows. But looking at Adrienne, all Sam could see was the need for freedom in her eyes - the same need that had been igniting a flame inside him. "Adrienne," he began, his voice steady and calm, a stark contrast to the chaos of his thoughts, "we knew this wouldn't be easy. We knew we'd have to walk on a razor's edge. But we also know that what we're doing... it's necessary." He paused, meeting her eyes with his own. "Maybe they are watching, but I believe I would know if they were." His voice had a definitive edge to it, a quiet assurance that was hard to deny. Adrienne's eyes widened at this declaration, questions mounting on her lips, but Sam raised a hand, a silent plea for patience. With a deep breath, he let out a secret that he had guarded closely. "I work for the Government, Adrienne." The admission hung heavily in the dimly lit room, like a tangible shadow between them. Adrienne's silence urged him on. "I'm an analyst in the Surveillance Department." His job was a double-edged sword. Every day, he found himself torn between his duty and his morality. He was the watcher, the listener, the cog in the oppressive machine of the Heritage Alliance. He was tasked with identifying dissent, with uncovering threats to their monolithic ideology. Yet, each act of dissent he spotted, every whispered word of rebellion, only served to highlight the fractures in the system. The stifling, soul-crushing weight of the oppressive regime had left him disillusioned. He despised the relentless surveillance, the disregard for privacy, and above all, the suppression of free will. His position was both a curse and a boon - it was a painful reminder of the government's tyranny, yet it also provided a shield, an advantage they could use in their fight. "I detest what they're doing, Adrienne," Sam confessed, his voice laced with a raw, fervent emotion. "I've seen the system from the inside out. I've seen how it fails its people, chokes their voices, crushes their spirit." He paused, taking a moment to gather his thoughts. "I've seen it all, and it's... it's wrong. Deeply, fundamentally wrong." As he spoke, his eyes burned with a smoldering anger, a palpable resentment for the system he was part of. But there was also a deep-seated determination, a resolve to set things right, to undo the injustices he was forced to be a part of. Adrienne watched him, her initial shock giving way to understanding. She saw in him the same torment that many of them felt - the battle between what was and what should be, the struggle to reconcile one's role in a corrupt system with one's inner compass. And yet, she also saw a spark, the hope that things could be changed, the determination to make it happen. In the silent confession of Sam's inner turmoil, a new understanding was forged between them. They weren't just allies against a common enemy, they were two souls wrestling with the reality of their dystopian world, each fueling the other's hope for a better tomorrow.

His words lingered in the air, a declaration of their defiance. There was a determined steeliness in his gaze that was both inspiring and comforting. It was a promise that he was committed to her, no matter what. As Sam's conviction washed over her, Adrienne felt something shift within her. But his confession hung in the air between them like a specter. Despite the warm glow of trust and connection she had felt earlier, Adrienne found herself shivering with a cold, gnawing uncertainty. The man she was beginning to see in a new light had just admitted that he was a part of the very system they planned to challenge, the machine that had turned their world into this dispassionate, rigid state. Could she really trust him? Could she afford to? Fear clawed at the edges of her mind as her gaze flitted across Sam's earnest face. There was a sincerity in his eyes that was hard to ignore, a raw vulnerability in his confession that resonated with her own struggles. And yet, the fear remained, echoing the warnings of countless stories of deception and betrayal that she had heard over the years. Adrienne felt a pang of regret for this newfound complication. She wanted to believe in Sam's conviction, his disgust for the government, and his resolve to change things. But she also knew the dangers of misplaced trust all too well. In the eerie silence that had settled over them, Sam's voice broke through her spiraling thoughts. "I understand if you can't trust me, Adrienne," he said, his voice heavy with sincerity. "You have every reason to doubt me. But all I can tell you is this - I hate what our world has become. I hate the part I play in it. There is a shadow that follows me, a shadow of despair and anxiety; it is around every corner and hidden in every shadow and when I sleep the echo of that shadow drags me from my sleep screaming like a child. And I would do anything, anything at all, to change that, to rid myself of that guilt, that shame." His words echoed in the quiet bar, a desperate plea that tugged at Adrienne's heart. She looked at him, at the man who was torn between his role and his morals, the man who was willing to risk everything for a chance at freedom. Slowly, despite the fear gnawing at her, Adrienne found herself nodding. "I want to trust you, Sam," she admitted, her voice barely above a whisper. She took a deep breath, steadying herself. "And for now, I'll choose to. But remember, we're risking everything here. Let's not betray each other." As she extended a hand to him, it wasn't just an offer of partnership, but a leap of faith. Sam took her hand, his grip firm and warm, a silent promise of trust. Adrienne's heart skipped a beat as realization dawned on her. These feelings weren't appropriate for the current time or place, yet they flickered within her like a moth to a flame. She knew they were on the edge of a precipice, but for the first time, she also felt like she wasn't alone. After taking a deep breath, she nodded at Sam. "You're right," she said, her voice steady once again. "We'll continue as planned." As they returned to their blueprints and whispers, the air around them felt electric, charged with their shared conviction. Their hearts - unbeknownst to them - beat in sync with the rhythm of rebellion, of courage, and of an emotion that was yet to be named.

Chapter 31

Echoes of the Unseen Rebellion

Night after night, Sam and Adrienne convened at the bar, "The Last Liberal," hunched over their blueprints for the pamphlets, poring over remembered stories and strategies, fine-tuning their plans for the insurgent publication. They began calling them blueprints when the word draft failed to illicit the intended urgency and meticulousness. A draft could be rewritten, revised, or discarded, but a blueprint was essential, it was a map, a guide. It held a definitive plan to be executed with precision and attention to detail. The word 'blueprint' was chosen as a constant reminder that what they were doing was creating a foundational plan for the resistance, a guiding document that had the potential to spark the change they so desperately sought. Their meetings grew longer, their conversations deeper, each moment bringing them closer to their rebellion and, perhaps unknowingly, to each other.

One evening, as they discussed potential distribution channels over half-empty glasses of homebrew, the barmaid, a robust woman named Marta with a sharp tongue and a wry smile, sidled up to them. "You two," she began, a teasing edge to her voice, "if you keep meeting like this, you should apply for a relationship sanction, before folks start asking questions."

The words hung in the air like an uninvited guest, catching them both off guard. In the stringent, rule-bound society of the

Heritage Alliance, unsanctioned interactions between individuals of opposite sexes beyond a certain frequency were viewed with suspicion. These interactions could only be legitimized through a state-approved process known as a 'relationship sanction.'

The comment, though lightly delivered, underscored a glaring oversight in their carefully concocted plans. Their frequent meetings at the bar, their intense discussions, even their occasional shared laughter, could all paint a conspicuous picture.

Sam and Adrienne looked at each other, a shared sense of realization dawning on their faces. They had been so engrossed in the larger, riskier aspects of their rebellion that they had overlooked the smaller, more mundane dangers.

"We'll need to be more careful," Sam murmured, his gaze steady on Adrienne. "Maybe find different locations, change our meeting times... we can't afford to draw attention."

Adrienne nodded in agreement, her mind already whirring with potential solutions. But as she glanced at Sam, the idea of a 'relationship sanction' lingered. Not in fear of the government, but as an unexpected curiosity. She quickly quashed the thought, reminding herself of the gravity of their mission.

"Let's focus," she said, forcing a smile. "We have a publication to launch."

They dived back into their work, their resolve unwavering. But the seed had been planted, an inkling of an idea that, like their shared rebellion, would prove more tenacious than they might have imagined.

The next day, Sam and Adrienne found themselves in a different environment, far from the familiar surroundings of "The Last Liberal." They had opted for "The Iron Jug," an unremarkable bar on the outskirts of the industrial district. Unlike their previous establishment, this place lacked any notable history or intriguing regulars. Instead, it was primarily frequented by tired factory workers seeking a brief escape from their grueling daily routines. The Iron Jug, with its cold metallic surfaces and lack of intimate nooks, was a stark contrast to the cozy, somewhat rebellious spirit of The Last Liberal. The constant hum of machinery in the distance, coupled with the occasional grating sounds from the nearby factories, created an ambient disquiet that was far from conducive to their clandestine discussions. As they settled into a corner table, their usual energy seemed subdued, their conversation more cautious. Marta's comment had hit closer to home than they cared to admit. It had exposed a weakness in their plan, a chink in their armor that was impossible to ignore. Despite the new environment and its associated discomfort, Sam and Adrienne pressed on. They knew that there was no turning back, that their discomfort was a small price to pay for their mission. They continued to discuss their ideas, to plan, and to dream. The clanging of glasses and the distant hum of machines formed a strange, discordant soundtrack to their conversations. "We'll have to set up more discreet distribution points," Sam suggested, his voice barely audible over the din. "We can use coded signals, maybe even dead drops." "And the printing," Adrienne added, her brow furrowed in thought. "We need a safe place, somewhere they wouldn't think to look." As they talked and planned, the sense of unease remained, an undercurrent to their every word. But with each passing minute, each shared idea, each quiet agreement, they were shaping their rebellion and writing their own history in this grim and unforgiving world. Despite the harsh setting of The Iron Jug, their spirits remained unbroken and their resolve undiminished. Under the flickering lights of The Iron Jug, Sam and Adrienne found themselves wrestling with the heart of their rebellion – the content of The Echo. What words could stir the hearts of the people, incite them to rise against the oppressive regime? They needed to craft narratives that not only informed but also moved, appealed not only to logic but also to the deep-seated human spirit. "We need to talk about freedom," Sam started, his voice steady and determined. "Freedom of speech, freedom of thought, freedom to choose. These are the liberties we've lost, the freedoms we need to reclaim. We'll tell stories of how things used to be, remind them of a time when ideas were not shackled, when dreams were not stifled." Adrienne nodded, her mind aflame with thoughts. "And we need to spotlight the injustice, the corruption that has seeped into every facet of our society. We should expose their lies, their manipulation. Transparency can be our weapon. The truth, even if harsh, will stir them, get their blood pounding." Their conversation meandered through the twisted paths of the authoritarian regime, dissecting its flaws and vulnerabilities. They discussed economic inequalities, the suffocating regulations on businesses, the growing discontent among the youth, the suppression of cultural and artistic expression, and the stark contrast between the ruling elite and the common man.

"The education system," Adrienne said suddenly, her eyes lighting up. "They're molding young minds, teaching them to conform and obey. We need to expose that too. If we can reach the youth, give them a different perspective, they could be our strongest allies. We should rally the minorities who came to this country looking for opportunity and freedom, not more of the same oppression from their masters."

Sam leaned back, his eyes reflecting the flame of the rebellion. "And we should share stories of resistance, of people who have dared to defy, however small their defiance might be. We can inspire others, give them hope, and show them that change is possible."

"Speaking of defiance," Adrienne added, her voice dropping to a murmur, "we should shed light on the Heritage Alliance's draconian crime policies too. The way they've been denying anyone with a criminal record the right to reproduce, and reinstating death penalties. They justify it all with a 'breed it out' mentality and public safety. They argue the harm of keeping criminals locked away is more detrimental to society, citing high PTSD rates among police and correctional officers, and the ripple effects."

Her voice hardened, "But, Sam, consider the rationale they've constructed. The government claims the traumatic environments in prisons and the resulting harm to correctional officers and police lead to a cycle of pain that propagates crime. They argue that these mentally traumatized people, when in society, end up hurting others, and thus become contributors to the very crime they were supposed to suppress. It's under this theory that they've enforced the death penalty, claiming to cut the cycle at its roots. But isn't it troubling that policies meant to minimize crime may actually be predicated on a theory that itself breeds fear and oppression?"

Adrienne's eyes sparked with a fierce intensity, "And Sam, there's something else that deeply troubles me about this. Consider their stance on sex offenders. Yes, these individuals commit heinous crimes, and it's a chilling fact that one abuser can spawn dozens of others in their wake. But isn't there a deeper issue at hand here? Aren't they victims of the same cycle of abuse, too?"

She swallowed, her voice teetering between disgust and fury. "The Heritage Alliance's solution is the death penalty, but it's completely uncivilized. It's not about absolving them of their crimes, but shouldn't our society try to understand and address the root of this issue? Rather than just executing them, should we not first consider getting them the help they might desperately need? It seems to me we're only perpetuating the same cycle of abuse we're supposedly trying to end."

Sam's face hardened, his brows furrowed in thought. "I don't agree with you on that, Adrienne," he said firmly. "The harm these sex offenders cause is beyond comprehension. And the cycle of abuse, it may never stop unless we take drastic measures. Sometimes, I wonder if the death penalty might indeed be necessary."

Adrienne recoiled, a look of shock and disgust washing over her face. She rose abruptly, pushing her chair back with a harsh scrape against the floor. "I can't believe what I'm hearing," she said, her voice shaky with a mixture of anger and disbelief. "Is that the kind of society we're fighting for?"

Sam remained calm, his gaze steady. "Adrienne, please," he implored, raising his hand in a placating gesture. "This is exactly what we're talking about. We need to be able to discuss these difficult topics, even if we disagree vehemently. That's the kind of society we're fighting for - one where we don't shut each other down because of differing opinions."

He pointed at their blueprints, spread across the table. "It's through this discourse, this clash of ideas, that we can find the best solutions. We need to navigate through these disagreements, find the common ground, find the compromise. That's how we'll overcome oppressive policies. Not by walking away from the table when the conversation becomes difficult, but by staying, by discussing, by understanding each other."

Adrienne hesitated, her hand hovering over the back of her chair. She took a deep breath, slowly sitting back down. Sam's words had given her pause, a stark reminder that their struggle was against oppressive policies and not each other. Their debates and discussions were indeed the essence of what they were striving for - a society where ideas were freely exchanged, dissected, and improved. Even when those ideas challenged their personal beliefs.

Putting their few differences aside they continued to chart out the course of their publication, their defiance echoed in the words left unsaid, in the ideas yet to be penned. Their mission was no longer an abstract dream; it was taking shape, growing roots, and pulsating with a life of its own. This was the birth of The Echo, the voice of their rebellion, their beacon in the rigid darkness of the Republic. A new place.

As the evening wore on, the topic of conversation stirred the darker corners of Sam's memory. As an analyst in the Surveillance Department, he was privy to the daily realities of the regime's stronghold. They had a tight leash on the people and controlled the stories that made it to the state-controlled media. One particular story stood out, one that had left an indelible mark on Sam’s heart. It was about a couple, Emily and John, who had been denied their Relationship Sanction cards on the grounds of economic and racial incompatibility. Emily was a school teacher and John was a factory worker, and according to the Government's match optimization algorithm, they were not a suitable match. This restriction was supposedly rooted in the Heritage Alliance's efforts to combat historically low birth rates that had been plaguing the country and world. The more sinister conspiracy theorists suggested they were performing a covert eugenics program, allowing only certain people to date, marry, and procreate based on undisclosed criteria. Despite these restrictions, Emily and John continued their relationship in secret, defying the government's mandate. They would meet under the cover of darkness, in the quiet corners of the city, their love a silent act of rebellion. But in a society where nothing escaped the government's watchful eyes, they were eventually discovered. The punishment was swift and ruthless. They were publicly denounced, their faces plastered across city billboards as a warning to others. They were stripped of their jobs and removed from society, forced into Rehabilitation Camps designed to "rectify" their "deviant behavior." The memory of their final public appearance was still fresh in Sam's mind—the defiant look in their eyes, the quiet dignity they held even as their world crumbled. Their story was a tragic testament to the regime's control over personal freedoms, an echo of the countless other tales of persecution and heartbreak that were left untold. "We should write about Emily and John," Sam said, his voice barely above a whisper, the stories of the past shrouding them in a heavy silence. He watched as Adrienne's face registered surprise, and then a deep sadness that matched his own. "Emily and John?" Adrienne echoed, her eyes searching Sam's face. "The couple from the public trial years ago?" Sam nodded. His role in their story was not one he was proud of. It was a part of his past he had long wished to forget, but he knew it was a narrative that needed to be told, a piece of the dystopian puzzle that the Heritage Alliance had meticulously crafted. "I was the analyst assigned to them," Sam confessed, the words hanging heavy in the dimly lit room. His fingers traced the rim of his empty glass, the cool surface offering little comfort. "When the system flagged their unsanctioned relationship, it was my job to watch them, to confirm the 'deviant behavior had ceased after they had been discovered.' I saw their secret meetings, their stolen moments of love. I saw their defiance, their courage. And yet..." he trailed off, the regret stinging his voice. "And yet?" Adrienne prodded gently, her face a picture of sympathy and curiosity. "And yet, I didn't protect them. I was so blindly faithful to the regime, to the rules, that I turned them in, believing I was doing the right thing, I believed that I was on the right side of history." Sam admitted, a bitter taste in his mouth. It was a moment of raw honesty, an uncomfortable yet necessary confession. Sam knew that this was part of their rebellion too - acknowledging their own complicity, their past mistakes. Adrienne was silent for a while, lost in her thoughts. "Their story, your story, it's a powerful one. It speaks of love, defiance, and regret. It's a stark reminder of the world we're living in, of the freedoms we've lost. We should share it in The Echo. It needs to be heard." In Adrienne's understanding gaze, Sam found a sense of relief, a small step towards redemption. They were on a path filled with danger and uncertainty, but they were on it together, united by their shared desire for a better future. A future where stories like Emily's and John's wouldn't be a haunting echo of the past but a turning point towards a brighter tomorrow.

As they left the bar, the neon lights from the sign overhead cast an eerie glow on the desolate streets. They walked in silence, their minds heavy with the tasks that lay ahead. Eventually, Sam broke the silence. "Adrienne, we need to discuss something," he began solemnly. She turned to look at him, a slight frown creasing her forehead. "What is it, Sam?" "Given the circumstances," he paused, searching for the right words, "I think we should apply for a relationship sanction." Adrienne's eyes widened in surprise, and she stopped in her tracks. "A relationship sanction? Sam, I'm just a janitor now. They won't approve it. They would see it as a 'disproportionate pairing' due to our job discrepancies. We can't risk drawing attention." Sam let out a small sigh. "Adrienne, my role in the government... it has some advantages. I can get it approved. It would help keep suspicions at bay." Adrienne looked at him, her expression unreadable. For a moment, Sam feared he had upset her. But then her features softened. "You can get it approved?" she repeated, a mix of disbelief, excitement, and anger in her voice. "Is that fair, Sam? Another advantage that government officials like you enjoy while the rest of us must abide by their biased rules?"

"I know," Sam conceded, feeling a pang of guilt. "I hate it as much as you do, Adrienne. But it's a tool we can use against them, for our cause. This... this is just strategy." Adrienne was silent for a moment, her gaze lost in the distance. Then, with a resigned sigh, she nodded. "Alright, Sam," she agreed quietly. "Let's apply for the sanction. For The Echo, for the people." As they continued their walk, a wave of conflicting emotions washed over Adrienne. Anger at the system, excitement at the idea of being officially tied to Sam, even if it was just a ruse. But most importantly, hope that their shared vision of a brighter future might just be possible. And as Sam looked at Adrienne, walking beside him with determined resolve, he couldn't help but feel a twinge of affection. Despite their pretend relationship for the sake of their rebellion, he couldn't deny the growing feelings in his heart. For Adrienne, for their cause, and for their shared dream of freedom.

Chapter 32

Silent observers

Throughout the long day, as Adrienne moved from one side of the factory to the other, Claire found herself locked in an existential conundrum. Trapped within the simulation, she was an involuntary passenger, riding through the intricate lattice of Adrienne's thoughts and actions, all while devoid of any control. Like a parasite, she subsisted within her host, privy to the intricacies of her life, and yet, disturbingly divorced from the ability to influence or alter it.

Caught in this inescapable digital lattice, she watched Adrienne wrestle with her thoughts, her emotions ebbing and flowing like a turbulent sea. she saw her concern for her colleagues, her compassion for their desolate lives under the oppressive regime. Through her eyes, she was exposed to the raw, unfiltered reality of this dystopian world, its stark details imprinted upon her captive consciousness.

And then there was Sam. The complexity of her relationship with him echoed in her mind, the reality of their sanctioned relationship, their shared secret, and their unified purpose vibrating through the ether of the simulation. Declan and Claire bore silent witness to Adrienne's and Sam's internal struggles, their hopes and fears, their reluctance and desire.

The notion of being in a pretend relationship with Sam, planning for a possible family, stirred both apprehension and intrigue within Adrienne. The excitement of the unknown, the trepidation of the what-ifs, all amplified through the lens of their shared simulation. It was a tantalizing, yet terrifying prospect that both intrigued and unsettled the two silent observers.

In the grips of this digital captivity, Claire shared Adrienne's emotional seesaw. She rode the waves of her anticipation, her anxiety, her hope, and her resolve, unable to intervene, merely experiencing her world through the surrogate vessel of her consciousness. Yet, despite her powerless state, she clung onto their silent existence, their parasitic presence a testament to their relentless pursuit of truth and freedom in a world where both were ruthlessly suppressed.

Throughout the long day, as Adrienne moved from one side of the factory to the other, the humdrum nature of her work was drowned out by the relentless thrum of her own thoughts. She watched the indifferent faces of her colleagues, both women and men alike, chained to the drudgery of their daily routines, their spirits dulled by monotony and the relentless gaze of surveillance cameras. She felt a dull ache in her heart for them – for herself – trapped in lives that offered little more than servitude to the Heritage Alliance's desires.

As her thoughts swirled, they inevitably circled back to Sam, her partner in this defiant venture, her companion in the secret corners of "The Last Liberal". What was he to her? The thought of their 'sanctioned relationship' played on her mind, stoking both anxiety and a strange, unfamiliar excitement. She wondered about the façade they would have to put up. Would they have to smile and laugh like a couple in love? Would they have to plan for a family, a family with Sam, how far would they need to take the façade?

The thought startled her. The idea was terrifying yet oddly tantalizing. It was Sam, after all. Strong, determined Sam. But she quickly quashed the rising tide of her feelings. Their mission was too important; they could not afford to be swayed by personal desires. And yet, as she pushed her mop across the grimy factory floor, she found herself unable to shake off the idea. Could she not have both – the revolution and Sam? She had seen firsthand the despair in the lives around her; didn't she also deserve a sliver of happiness amidst the chaos?

Shaking her head, she admonished herself for these stray thoughts. Their mission was paramount, she reminded herself. Still, as she dumped her mop in the bucket and glanced at the clock, she couldn't help the small flutter of anticipation at the thought of seeing Sam at the bar that evening. She quickly suppressed the emotion, focusing instead on the vital work they had ahead. But deep down, in the secret corners of her heart, the spark of hope refused to die out.

The sounds of clanging and banging machinery echoed throughout the cavernous factory, making most of the conversations on the industrial expanse unintelligible. But not to Adrienne. She had learned long ago that secrets and whispers often slipped out amidst the noise and chaos of the factory floor. With a worn broom in her hands and a threadbare apron around her waist, she moved unobtrusively through the aisles of the factory, sweeping away shavings and debris from the machines. To the workers, she was part of the scenery, a silent specter easily overlooked. Pausing to empty a dustpan, she stood near two women at a workbench. Both women were dressed in assembly line worker uniforms, their faces smudged with grime, and their eyes vacant with exhaustion. They were deep in hushed conversation, their words just audible over the ceaseless din of machinery. "I was paired with a man I barely know," one woman confessed, her voice tremulous. "We were matched by the Alliance because our genetic traits would supposedly produce an 'optimal offspring.' Now I'm carrying his child." "The same thing happened to me," the other woman added, her voice heavy with despair. "I don't love him, but we're forced to live together, forced to smile for the Alliance officials, forced to pretend we're a happy family." A sick feeling settled in Adrienne's stomach as she listened. These women were just two of the countless victims of the Alliance's manipulations, forced into relationships and motherhood against their will for the sake of "population stability and if the rumours were true other more sinister reasons." The injustice of it fueled her determination. These were the stories The Echo needed to tell. Sweeping the last of the debris into her dustpan, she moved on, her mind already churning with ideas. The forced pairings, the unwanted pregnancies, the loveless households -- these were the real-life consequences of the Alliance 's policies. And they were topics that she and Sam needed to bring to light, no matter the cost.

As Adrienne moved from one side of the factory to the other throughout the long day, the humdrum nature of her work was drowned out by the relentless thrum of her own thoughts. She watched the indifferent faces of her colleagues, both women and men alike, chained to the drudgery of their daily routines. Their spirits were dulled by monotony and the relentless gaze of the surveillance cameras. Adrienne felt a dull ache in her heart for them – for herself – trapped in lives that offered little more than servitude to the desires of the Heritage Alliance.

In the Heritage Alliance's Surveillance Department, Sam sat before a massive wall of screens, each one a window into a citizen's life. This was the spiderweb he was a part of - where every twitch of discontent was noticed, every murmur of dissent was recorded. He was one of the many faceless eyes tasked with preserving order and unquestioned stability, which the Republic had come to symbolize. That day, however, something on his screen made him pause, a knot of unease tightening in his stomach. It was an incident involving a young boy named Tommy, barely twelve years old. Tommy was an average citizen in all respects – quiet, respectful, and dutiful. But there was something that set him apart. He had been caught on one of the surveillance cameras sharing an innocent kiss with his best friend, another boy, in the secluded corner of a park. It was a moment of pure innocence, an exploration of unknown feelings, devoid of any malicious intent. But in the rigid landscape of the Republic, it was seen as an act of nonconformity, a blatant deviation from the state-prescribed norms. As Sam watched the events unfold on his screen, he felt a cold dread creep in. He knew what the consequences would be. Tommy would be brought before the Authorities, and his act of innocent curiosity would be twisted into an act of defiance against the norms of the Republic. He would become a symbol of what the state deemed 'wrong,' a public example to be made of. But what if this could be the spark? What if this incident was not isolated; What if it reached into the homes of the citizens, inciting a wave of shock, disbelief, and anger. This wasn't the usual grumbling about the strict rules or the lack of freedoms; this was something more potent. The innocence of a child was at stake here. It cut across all the divisions – be it class, occupation, or ideology. If he and Adrienne could expose the cruelty of the injustice that was sure to come to this young boy and bring it to the forefront, it could rally the people, uniting them against the unjust and draconian measures of the state. Yes, it was a gamble, one that could backfire horribly, but it was a chance they had to take. The revolution needed a rallying point, and as heartbreaking as it was, this could be it.

Sam left his post with a heavy heart, his mind already racing with thoughts of how to approach this with Adrienne. Their fight had just taken a more urgent, personal turn. As he walked towards "The Last Liberal," he hoped against hope that this grave injustice could finally be the catalyst for change. As he walked, the darkness of the night felt as heavy as the moral dilemma he was grappling with. Each step was a beat of the unsolvable conundrum echoing in his mind. Protect the child and risk the opportunity for rebellion slipping through their fingers? Or let the inevitable happen and use it to their advantage? Sam realized that the state had reduced him to pondering such monstrous thoughts. The Alliance had poisoned them all, forcing them to choose between their humanity and their survival. It was a testament to how deeply ingrained the Alliance's control was in their lives. He thought of Adrienne, the fire in her eyes when she spoke of justice and equality, her conviction in their cause. He thought of Tommy, on the cusp of an age where innocence gives way to the harsh realities of life, a life in the Republic that could shatter him. He remembered Emily and John, their lives torn apart by the draconian laws of the state. They were all victims, just like him, caught in the endless, grinding machinery of the state.

As Sam navigated the narrow, winding streets of the city, the stark divisions drawn by the government became painfully clear. The various racial sectors were divided by tall, imposing walls, each plastered with propaganda posters. This artificial segregation, an attempt to isolate and 'harmonize,' had only succeeded in deepening the racial divide and mistrust. The government had successfully manipulated one of humanity's most fundamental instincts - fear of the 'other.'

While the government touted these divisions as a solution for racial conflict, Sam knew they were just another tool of control. By pitting different races against each other, the Alliance kept the people too divided and busy with mutual distrust to unite against their real oppressor.

His destination, "The Last Liberal," was located in a gray area between these divisions - a small sanctuary where people from all sectors would discreetly gather. Here, Sam hoped, their message would reach people across all racial divisions.

Each step he took seemed to hammer home a grim understanding - there were no clean escapes in their world. There were only choices, each more terrible than the last, and the will to see them through. He couldn’t hide Tommy's transgression; it would raise suspicions in his department, an unnecessary risk. But, he couldn’t just stand by and let the Alliance crush another innocent life under its heel. And then, a spark of an idea kindled in his mind. What if they could make the situation public before the Alliance did? What if the citizens first heard of Tommy's story not through the cold, condemning lens of the state but through the empathetic, humane narrative of The Echo? They would control the narrative, portray Tommy as the innocent child he was, caught in the merciless gears of the Alliance. It was risky and depended on too many variables, but it was a plan, a way to keep his humanity intact while advancing their cause. As he arrived at The Last Liberal, his resolve was firm. He would do his best to protect Tommy, use this incident to turn the people against the Alliance, and pray that his gamble paid off.

Entering the establishment, he looked around to find Adrienne already waiting for him, a draft copy of their 'Echo' on the table in front of her. Her eyes met his, the fire of rebellion burning in them more fiercely than ever. He took a deep breath, preparing to delve into the bitter realities that lay ahead.

The dilemma that haunted him was a reflection of the choices forced upon them by the Alliance. In this dystopian world, even the act of rebellion was tainted by the Alliance 's poisonous influence. And yet, within this darkness, there was also the faint glimmer of hope, the potential for change.

He had spent the day in the depths of despair, torn between his responsibility to Tommy and Billy, and his commitment to their cause. The Alliance had forced him to contemplate unthinkable choices, between protecting innocence and using it as a weapon. He had become the monster they were fighting against, forced to sacrifice their morality for survival. Although if he thought hard about it, Sam had morphed into the very beast they were resisting, having been a pawn doing the Alliance's bidding, compliantly working within their system, and refraining from any resistance. His passivity had made him an accomplice, implicating him in the oppressive regime. He had forsaken his moral compass in the name of survival, thus becoming a part of the monstrous system they were determined to dismantle.

He remembered John and Emily, their love brutally crushed under the state's oppressive laws. They were no different from Tommy and Billy, young souls forced to pay the price for the state's intolerance. They were all victims, their lives dictated by the whims of an authoritarian regime.

As he sat down across from Adrienne, he resolved that their fight had to continue, that the suffering and injustices they were forced to endure could not be in vain. This was a battle for their lives, their freedom, and their right to love. They were in the belly of the beast, and they had no choice but to fight their way out. It was time to rise against the Alliance. It was time for the Echo to resound across the sectors. It was time for a revolution.

Chapter 33

Love's Courage and the Echo's Rise

Tommy Stevens and Billy Cooper had been friends since as long as Tommy could remember. They met in the sandbox of Mrs. Harris's kindergarten class, bonding over a shared enthusiasm for building the tallest sandcastles and a mutual disgust for the broccoli served at lunchtime. Over the years, they remained steadfast friends, sharing lunchbox confessions and laughing at other boys' and girls' expense, with Billy's sharp wit always keeping things entertaining. Through the first days of school, annual science fairs, and field trips, Tommy and Billy were inseparable, their bond defying the trials of growing up. However, the gentle shift from innocent camaraderie to something deeper began to unfold when Tommy turned thirteen. Suddenly, everything seemed different, like he had crossed an invisible boundary between child and teenager. One day, during a local soccer game, Billy scored the winning goal. Tommy watched as Billy's face lit up with utter joy, a mixture of profound happiness for Billy and an unfamiliar feeling coursing through him. Tommy found himself admiring Billy in odd moments, longing for any signs that Billy might feel the same way. But he was scared - he had never felt this way before, and he wasn't sure if Billy liked boys or if he could like him in the same way. His uncertainty culminated on a summer afternoon at the playground. As Billy swung on the swings, his laughter echoing through the air, Tommy decided he couldn't keep his feelings bottled up any longer. His heart pounded in his chest, and he took a deep breath, steeling himself for what would become his first real act of bravery - an innocent kiss on the playground, a symbol of feelings he was only beginning to understand.

Tommy had barely brushed his lips against Billy's before he was roughly pushed away. His heart pounded in his ears as he stumbled backwards, his mind a whirl of confusion, fear, and regret. Billy, the one constant in his life, looked at him with wide eyes, fear swirling in them. Tommy had never seen Billy scared before. The sight struck him with a pang of guilt. Billy quickly scanned the deserted playground, his breath hitched, looking as though he'd seen a ghost. He seemed relieved when he realized they were alone, the other children off in the distance. "What the hell, Tommy?" he hissed, the harshness in his voice a stark contrast to the gentle laughter that had filled the air just moments ago. "But Billy—" Tommy started, his voice shaky, his heart aching. "No," Billy cut him off, his voice strident, yet underneath it, Tommy thought he could hear a hint of confusion. "You know we can't do this, Tommy. It's…wrong… It's illegal." In that moment, Tommy felt a surge of emotions—fear, yes, but also a deep sense of sadness. Billy's words, echoing in his ears, were not what he had hoped for, but he understood. He understood that Billy, like him, was grappling with an array of feelings that he had never encountered before. Tommy nodded slowly, looking down at his sneakers. His heart felt heavy in his chest. He missed the simplicity of their friendship, the easiness that had now been replaced by a tense silence. "We should...we should go," Billy finally said, his voice barely above a whisper. His words hung in the air between them, a stark reminder of the moment that had changed everything. They walked back to their classrooms in silence, each lost in their own thoughts. Tommy couldn't help but think about what he had done. He had risked their friendship, and now, he wasn't sure if things would ever be the same. In the coming days, Tommy would find himself navigating the turbulent waters of adolescence and love, learning to understand his feelings, and in the process, helping Billy understand his own. It was a path fraught with challenges, yet he knew it was a path he had to walk, for the truth of his heart demanded no less.

As the days turned into weeks, Sam and Adrienne continued to meet in secret, painstakingly weaving together their first edition of The Echo. They poured their hearts into each page, writing about Emily and John's ill-fated love, the unfair matchmaking laws, the forced pregnancies. They painted a stark picture of their world, a world suffocating under the Alliance's iron grip. All the while, Sam kept a close watch on Tommy and Billy, hoping against hope that their playground kiss would blossom into something more substantial. He needed them to continue their innocent trysts, not for their sakes, but for the sake of their cause. Each day, he had to swallow the bile that rose in his throat at the thought of using these children as pawns in their game. But the greater good required sacrifice, didn't it?

Every night, Sam wrestled with his conscience. He could see Adrienne's face, hear her fiery words about justice and freedom, and he knew she would never approve of his plan. But he also knew that they needed a catalyst, a spark to ignite the revolution. Tommy and Billy? They could be that spark! He decided to keep his plan to himself, for now, knowing the risks it entailed. Their publication was ready. They had copies printed in secret, ready for distribution. All they needed now was the right moment, the moment when the common people's discontent would reach a boiling point. And if Sam's hunch was correct, that moment would arrive soon, all thanks to two innocent boys who had dared to love in a world that forbade it. But as he stared at the monitor, watching Tommy and Billy laughing in the park, he couldn't shake off the dread that gnawed at his heart. What if they were rushing towards a revolution that would cost more than they were ready to pay? What if, in their quest for freedom, they were about to sacrifice the very innocence they were fighting to protect?

The next day, just before Sam was about to submit the paperwork for his and Adrienne's sanctioned relationship, his boss, Director Marlow, requested a private meeting. As they walked together through the long, sterile corridors of the Surveillance Department, Marlow was silent. It wasn't until they had reached the privacy of his spacious office that he finally spoke. "There are rumors, Lawson," he began, fixing Sam with a piercing gaze. "Rumors about you and a certain... janitor." Sam felt a jolt of adrenaline. Had they been discovered already? But he forced himself to keep his composure. "Sir?" Marlow continued, "You've been seen frequently spending time with a certain Adrienne Ross at The Last Liberal and some other establishments. Care to explain?" Sam paused, considering his words carefully. The truth was a death sentence, but a lie could be just as dangerous if discovered. Instead, he decided to weave a tale that held elements of both. "Yes, sir," he began, his voice steady. "Adrienne and I have been... seeing each other. I felt ashamed, sir, falling for a janitor. I didn't know how it would look. A man in my position... I felt it could potentially bring embarrassment to the Department." His face flushed for effect, adding credence to his admission. "But I've come to realize, I can't ignore my feelings any longer, sir. I intend to file for a sanctioned relationship." There was a pause as Marlow absorbed his words. His face was unreadable, his silence unnerving. But finally, he nodded. "I see. Your personal life is your own, Lawson. As long as it doesn't interfere with your duties here. And remember, the Department expects propriety from all its members. If this relationship becomes a distraction, you will be held accountable. Understood?" "Understood, sir," Sam affirmed. Relief washed over him. He had navigated the confrontation without raising suspicion, buying them a bit more time. As he exited Marlow's office, he couldn't help but feel a renewed sense of urgency. Their mission was more pressing than ever before.

Caught in the echoes of the past, Declan tried to make sense of the world unfolding before him. The harsh realities of Sam and Adrienne's life were far removed from his own experiences, the stark differences in their societies starkly apparent. He grappled with the paradoxes of his consciousness, trying to piece together where and when this could be taking place in history.

He searched his memory, but couldn't recall a time when people weren't allowed to love who they wanted, regardless of gender. In fact, polyamorous relationships were not only encouraged in his society but heralded as a new way of life. The destruction of the nuclear family in his world had given way to more sexual freedoms, more choices. Yet the events he was witnessing, the forbidden love between Tommy and Billy, made him question the authenticity of his experiences.

Could this be a mere hallucination induced by DMT, as Dr. Peterson had suggested? But the vividness of the world around him, the tangible fear and despair he saw in the eyes of Adrienne, Billy and Tommy, through Sam's eyes, it all seemed too real to be a product of his imagination.

As he tried to reconcile the disparities between his experiences and the history he had learned, he couldn't help but be swept up in the emotional currents of the narrative unfolding before him. The angst, the secrecy, the fear of discovery, all played out in high definition in his mind's eye. Declan felt a pang of sympathy for Billy and Tommy, their innocence marred by the harsh realities of their society. His heart ached for Sam and Adrienne, their desperate struggle for freedom under the oppressive regime.

Unbeknownst to him, his journey into the past, if it was in fact the past, was about to take a dark turn. As he dove deeper into the annals of history, he was about to witness the realities of a time when love was a privilege, not a right, when freedom was but a distant dream. Unbeknownst to Declan, he was on the precipice of understanding a past that had been swept under the rug, a past that held the key to unlocking the future.

Chapter 34

The Digital Revolution and the Echo's call

"Distribution," Sam sighed, rubbing his temples as he stared at the hardcopies of The Echo sprawled across the table. "We need a way to reach the masses without exposing ourselves." Adrienne nodded in agreement, her mind whirling with possibilities. "What about a digital approach?" she suggested, sparking Sam's interest. "I mean, look at how the Alliance communicates. Everything is digital now. Screens are everywhere: in homes, public squares, factories. We could... maybe... hack into the system and broadcast The Echo directly onto their screens." Sam raised an eyebrow at the proposition. He had connections within the Surveillance Department, but a hack of this magnitude was risky. Yet, the idea of infiltrating the Alliance 's own communication system, of using their omnipresent screens as a tool for rebellion, was enticing. "We'd need a hacker," he mused. "Someone who knows the system inside out, who can bypass security measures and upload our publication without leaving a trace."

Adrienne suggested they reach out to the underground network, a loosely connected group of dissenters known to have some of the most skilled hackers. The trouble would be gaining their trust, but perhaps The Echo could speak for them, acting as proof of their intentions. They decided to discreetly put out feelers in the network, always careful to protect their identities. If they could find a hacker to aid them, their revolution would have the potential to reach every corner of the city. Meanwhile, they would continue with their original plan for physical distribution. Adreinne knew of some sympathizers in the courier sector from the Bar who would be willing to smuggle copies of The Echo during their deliveries, maybe? They would also place copies in public places, parks, subway stations, and tucked inside other newspapers. It was an enormous undertaking, but they were prepared to do whatever it took. The success of their rebellion hinged on their ability to spread their message without getting caught on one of the numerous public cameras in existence and they would not let fear hold them back. The Echo was more than just a publication. It was a testament to their spirit of resistance, their shared dream of a world where love and freedom echoed louder than tyranny.

Every day at work, Sam watched Tommy and Billy with anxious anticipation that carried a furlonging of dread, their innocence a constant tug at his conscience. He had positioned himself as the primary surveillance analyst for both boys. With each passing day, he noticed their initial fear starting to fade. They began to share stolen glances, secret smiles, and whispers in the playground - small acts of affection, but dangerous all the same. Their courage was admirable, but it filled Sam with dread for their future. Time was running out. If The Echo wasn't ready to break the story before the boys were caught, the impact would be lost, and worse, their lives would be put in even graver danger. The clock was ticking, and Sam felt the pressure mounting. He himself should have already reported the goings on of the boys days ago, to have them intervene before it got to the level to which Sam was hoping it would go. His logic, was beginning to make him ill.

He doubled his efforts, working tirelessly into the night with Adrienne. The first edition of The Echo, with its heart wrenching tale of Emily and John, was almost ready for distribution. But they still hadn't found a means of distribution or a hacker who could get their message onto the city's screens. Their feelers in the underground network had drawn attention, but nobody had come forward yet. Sam was on edge, but Adrienne was his rock.

She kept their mission focused, never losing faith in their cause. They spent their evenings alternating between the Iron Jug and the Last Liberal, hashing out their plans under the hushed whispers of rebellion. It turned out they felt the safest at the Last Liberal, the patrons kept to themselves and the Bar owner Mike helping them hide at the back tables and being their conduit into the underground network. And every night, Sam walked Adrienne home, their sanctioned relationship application pending with the Alliance.

Tommy and Billy were inseparable, but as children, they were unversed in the dangerous art of subtlety. Their innocent affection for each other was conspicuous, from the gentle brushes of their hands in the school corridor to lingering gazes across the classroom and whispers shared under the shadow of the playground. In their society, however, these innocent gestures were loaded with implications, and it wasn't long before eyes started to follow them, whispers started to swirl, and the boys felt the weight of their classmates' scrutiny. In response, they made a pact to keep their distance during school hours, a difficult promise to uphold. Every stolen glance or missed conversation during recess felt like a betrayal of their friendship, but they knew they had to be cautious. Despite their efforts at school, their bond was too strong to be completely suppressed. After school, they rushed to their secret sanctuary, a small, secluded area in the forest adjacent to the school. There, they could be themselves without the judging eyes of their peers or the rigid rules of their society. They spent hours together, talking, laughing, and simply enjoying each other's company. Sometimes, they held hands, relishing in the comfort and warmth that came from their shared touch. Other times, they shared stories, dreams, and fears, their youthful innocence making them fearless in their vulnerability. However, they were becoming careless. The more time they spent in their secret hideaway, the more they neglected the risks. Being only twelve years old, they were too young to fully grasp the harsh realities of the world they lived in. Unbeknownst to them, each moment they spent together, each touch, and each shared secret was leading them closer to danger. But for now, they remained oblivious, their love for each other a beautiful but dangerous ignorance.

Meanwhile, Sam was experiencing a tumultuous storm of his own. He was walking a tightrope, balancing his budding relationship with Adrienne, his secretive involvement in the Echo, and his government job as an analyst. He understood the gravity of his situation and knew he was playing with fire. Even the smallest misstep could have disastrous consequences. However, he felt compelled to continue forward by his sense of duty, his passion for the cause, and an unexplainable feeling of hope. As Sam finished his tasks for the day, George, a fellow analyst, approached him with a curious glint in his eye. Sam's heart pounded in his chest, wondering if his secret had been discovered. His mind raced through potential explanations. "Sam," George began casually, leaning against Sam's desk. "There are rumors going around... About you and a certain lady... A janitor, no less." Sam was taken aback by George's blunt approach, but he quickly composed himself. His answer needed to be convincing yet casual. "Yes, George, that's true. But she's more than just a janitor." George arched an eyebrow, intrigued. "Oh? A government analyst and a factory janitor... Seems like an unusual pairing. You aren't concerned about how it looks?" Choosing his words carefully, Sam replied, "The Alliance teaches us that we are all equals, doesn't it? Her occupation doesn't define her." George studied Sam, seemingly weighing his words. After a moment, he chuckled and clapped Sam on the shoulder. "Fair enough, Sam. You're right. Just thought I'd ask. You know how office talk goes." Sam let out a breath he didn't realize he'd been holding. That was close. He knew he'd have to be more careful moving forward. The stakes were too high.

Meanwhile, in their hidden refuge after school, Tommy and Billy continued their secret rendezvous. Their interactions were becoming more affectionate, more daring. It was only a matter of time before their secret would be unveiled. The Echo had to be published before that. Sam knew that their love story, could not be discovered before John and Emily's had been told in full, it had to reach the public first. The public needed to have the story of John and Emily on their minds once the devastating news of what will surely transpire to Tommy and Billy once they are discovered to properly ignite the spark of revolution.

Claire had suspected that immersing herself in the simulation would be a unique experience, but she had not anticipated just how deeply she would become intertwined with Adrienne's life. Nor was it anything she wanted, hence the reason she had given Declan the chip in the first place. After witnessing Maddy's fall she had not wanted anything to do with this. Initially, observing the world through Adrienne's eyes had been just that - observing. She had been a spectator in Adrienne's life, seeing her world but not truly feeling it.

However, as the days turned into weeks, Claire found that the lines between herself and Adrienne were blurring. She could feel the monotony of Adrienne's days at work, the thrill of the ongoing revolution, and the deep-seated longing for Sam. It was an emotional roller-coaster that Claire was both riding and experiencing from the side-lines. A burgeoning sense of dread was perpetually gnawing at the corners of her consciousness. Claire's yearning to extricate herself from this enforced simulation seemed to amplify with each passing day. She longed to escape this dreamlike state, yearned for the familiarity of her own body, her own thoughts. She desperately sought to reclaim the autonomy of her own mind.

One evening, after another uneventful day at work, Adrienne was returning to her flat. Claire, ever connected to Adrienne's senses, could feel the fatigue seeping into Adrienne's limbs, mirroring her own mental exhaustion. As Adrienne walked, her mind was filled with thoughts about Sam, the Echo, and the revolution they were planning. It was then that Adrienne turned a corner, and a woman stepped out from the shadows.

Adrienne stopped, her heart racing. Claire could feel the surge of adrenaline, her own pulse quickening in tandem. The woman was dressed casually, her face concealed by the hood of her coat, yet the tension around her was evident. Claire felt Adrienne's senses heighten in response, the caution within them screaming loudly.

"Adrienne," the woman began, her voice firm yet holding a hint of warmth. "You don't know me, but I know about you and Sam and have heard through friends what you wish done."

Claire felt Adrienne's throat tighten, her own anxiety spiking. Were they discovered? Adrienne's mind raced to formulate a plan, but the woman spoke again before she could respond.

"I'm not here to threaten you, but to warn you. You're playing with fire, getting involved with a government analyst," the woman said, looking around nervously. "Normally, I would just walk away and let you face the consequences, but I see something in you. I want to help."

Adrienne's frown of confusion was mirrored in Claire's thoughts. "Why should I trust you?" Adrienne asked.

"You don't have to. But I've been tracking government communications for years," the woman replied, reaching into her pocket to pull out a small device. Adrienne recognized it as a miniaturized version of the encrypted communication tool Sam had given her in case of trouble. The only people supposed to have access to them were certain government officials, they allowed a person access into the communication lines without being tracked.

"Is this...?" Adrienne began, surprise reflected in her eyes and echoed in Claire's mind.

The woman nodded. "I can help you get your message out. But I won't go near Sam and prefer if we never meet again, do you happen to have it on you now? The message that is?"

In response, Adrienne reached into her bag and pulled out a copy of the Echo. She unfolded it, revealing the pages of the Echo and within it the story of John and Emily. The woman gingerly received the document, her eyes widened as she devoured the words. With every sentence, her anticipation heightened, her heart thrumming in her chest. The potency of the written words began to manifest on her face - a tear escaped, tracing a solitary path down her cheek. Yet, she didn't wipe it away, her focus locked onto the page, on the promise of change it carried. As she read, a revolution started to take form within her eyes, a spark ignited by the compelling narrative of the 'Echo'. Overwhelmed, she looked up at Adrienne, her gaze ablaze with newfound determination and an unspoken promise of resistance.

"I'll do it," she said, tucking the Echo into her coat. "But after this, we never meet again."

Adrienne nodded, a sense of relief washing over her. Claire, on the other side of the simulation, felt the same wave of relief. The revolution was gaining momentum, and now, with this unexpected ally, they had a fighting chance. Claire could only hope that the blurred lines between her and Adrienne's lives would not further complicate matters.

Chapter 35

The Digital Phoenix, the Echo of Rebellion

The woman who approached Adrienne was no ordinary soul. As an experienced ByteJester, a term she donned with pride, she was a maestro of digital shadows. Navigating the interconnected network of systems was her playground. She would slip past firewalls, evade surveillance with an effortless finesse, a digital ghost that was nearly undetectable by the system's defense mechanisms.

Her talents extended beyond mere navigation. She was adept at manipulating code and data, weaving together a web of false IP addresses and ghost servers, making her digital footprints vanish into the ether. She worked tirelessly, developing self-destructing malware to infiltrate the government's broadcasting system. This software was her magnum opus, engineered to deliver Adrienne's revolutionary message and then evaporate, leaving no trace of its existence.

Yet, her fight against the Heritage Alliance was far more personal. She had been branded as an infertile woman by the same system, cruelly separated from her beloved who was matched with another for the purpose of reproduction. The sting of this devastation still lingered, and sleepless nights were spent feverishly coding, her despair morphing into a burning determination. Her efforts weren't just about hacking systems; they were about mending a shattered heart, about dealing a crippling blow to the same government that had robbed her of her love and her dignity.

When the hour finally arrived, she initiated the hack. Breaching the system was akin to navigating a labyrinth full of dead ends and deceiving leads. But she persevered, bypassing security measures, and avoiding detection protocols. Her labor bore fruit when she deployed the malware into the broadcasting controls.

With a steady hand and a racing heart, she retreated, disconnecting from the network. She expertly covered her tracks, leaving no digital breadcrumb behind. The countdown she had initiated raced on, mirroring the pounding rhythm of her heart.

As it hit zero, a hush fell over the city. Every screen flickered, the government propaganda vanishing in an instant. What took its place was her masterpiece, a symbol she had devoted countless hours to designing and perfecting. It was the visual embodiment of love, freedom, and rebellion, born from the anger in her heart and now mixed with the pages of the Echo. Accompanying the powerful symbol was a voice, one that echoed through the city, resonating with the silent cries of a thousand broken hearts, a lament that resonated deeply within her own chest.

The symbol was a carefully crafted phoenix, its form constituted by the intricate binary code, a testament to the fusion of technology and organic life. Each feather was meticulously designed with ones and zeros. To the casual observer, the arrangement seemed random. But upon closer scrutiny, one could discern a hidden message of freedom, encoded in ASCII (01100110 01110010 01100101 01100101 01100100 01101111 01101101).

The phoenix was an emblem of rebirth and resilience. The illustration captured it mid-flight, wings spread wide in a powerful upward surge, as if poised to break free from the confines of the image itself.

The bird rises from a base of shackles that are broken and discarded, symbolizing the escape from oppression and confinement. Each link in the chain of the shackle is etched with minute details, appearing heavy and oppressive, contrasting starkly with the freedom that the phoenix embodies.

In the phoenix's beak, it carries an olive branch that has not two, but three leaves. Each leaf is shaped subtly different: one heart-shaped, the other like an open hand, and the third as a quill. These leaves are vibrant, emerald green, representing love, unity, and the power of written word, respectively. The symbolism of the olive branch is twofold, denoting both peace and a new beginning.

The backdrop for this scene is a horizon with a rising sun, its rays piercing through the remnants of a storm, lighting up the scene with a warm, promising glow. This indicates the dawn of a new era, the light of hope breaking through the dark times.

As a finishing touch, the sky is filled with faintly visible, encrypted code, hinting at the underlying theme of hacking and digital revolution. This code was composed of subtly shifting hues of blues and purples, not prominent enough to detract from the central phoenix but visible upon closer scrutiny.

Overall, the image struck a balance between the grit of struggle and the hope of revolution, the fusion of technology and nature, and the balance between love, unity, and the power of words. The details were intricate, inviting the viewer to look closer and understand the deeper meanings embedded within the image. A coded 85 at the top indicated the numerical announcement that the Harbinger is the Echo.

Screens around the city boomed the following message,

"In a world where love is controlled, where freedom is an illusion, where our lives are not our own, there comes a time when we must rise. Rise for love. Rise for freedom. Rise for those who can't. The time is now. We are the Echo." The voice was powerful, filled with emotion and resolve. It stirred something deep within the people. For many, it was a wake-up call, a beacon of hope in the darkness. It touched their hearts, igniting a spark that was ready to catch fire.

"In a world where love is manipulated, where liberty is merely an illusion, and where we're denied autonomy over our own lives, a moment arrives when we're obliged to ascend. Ascend for love. Ascend for liberty. Ascend on behalf of those who cannot. That moment is now. We are the Echo." The voice echoed through the city, filled with a fervor and determination that was contagiously invigorating. It stirred something deep within the citizens, jolting them awake from their societal slumber. For many, it was as if a lighthouse had suddenly lit up in a stormy sea of their lives, offering a glimmer of hope in the overbearing darkness.

This rallying cry was interspersed with a video montage, expertly cut and pieced together to drive home the message of their struggle. Displayed prominently were two familiar faces, John and Emily, faces from the past but quickly remembered, their images magnified against the backdrop of their gut-wrenching trial. Clips rolled, showcasing their shared distress and despair, their expressions etched with agony and defeat. The camera lingered on Emily's face as she was led away, a moment suspended in time.

And then, something unexpected appeared on the screen, footage previously unseen by the public. It was Emily, her gaze locked on John even as the guards pulled her away. Her lips moved, forming the words "I love you," a message that she managed to whisper to John just as she was taken away. It was a moment of profound emotional intimacy, a silent testament to their shared love and sacrifice. It was, above all, a stark reminder of the human cost of the Heritage Alliance's oppressive regime.

The visual narrative hit a nerve among the viewers, the stark realities of their society laid bare for all to see. Hearts clenched and eyes moistened, the deep-seated injustices stoking a collective anger, awakening a shared resolve for change. The spark had indeed caught fire. The revolution had begun, at least the seed had been firmly planted.

As soon as the image disappeared, the buzzing energy of the streets shifted into a frenzy. People stood rooted in place, staring blankly at the screens that had momentarily showed them an echo of rebellion, an echo of hope. Some had their hands clasped over their mouths in disbelief, while others wore expressions of shock. However, there was a shared undercurrent of unease and excitement. Whispers of the message passed through the crowd, spreading like wildfire. Each person imparted their version of what they had read or heard. It was an electrifying wave of information that travelled through the city, seeping into homes, infiltrating workplaces across the city, and disturbing the usual quiet of the government offices. The city buzzed with hushed conversations; everyone was discussing the unexpected broadcast. Some expressed fear about the implications and worried about government crackdowns and harsh consequences. Yet others, with lowered voices, spoke about the thrill of such a daring act and the feeling of a cold fist of defiance punching through the wall of oppressive silence. As night fell, the air was thick with something that hadn't been felt in a long time: the powerful and intoxicating scent of resistance. People were scared, yes, but they were also eager, curious, and hopeful. In living rooms, bars, and quiet corners, the echoes of the day's event spurred conversations that had been too dangerous to have. "What if?" became the question of the hour. What if things could change? What if they were not alone in their discontent? What if there was hope? The echo had done its job; it had started the conversation. The message had been delivered, the spark had been lit, and the fire of rebellion was about to ignite.

As the message spread throughout the city, Sam found himself caught in a web of surprise and confusion, just like everyone else. He had been unaware of Adrienne's actions, giving their work to the Bytejester, and the suddenness of it all left him stunned. Sam had been at his work desk, surrounded by dozens of surveillance feeds when the digital announcement struck. As the familiar words started scrolling across the screens, Sam's heart pounded in his chest. His eyes darted from screen to screen as his own words filled the air around him. The message, their message, was out in the open. It was a step they had planned, but its early execution filled him with a strange cocktail of emotions. Fear was the most potent, and it was well justified. If he were connected to the message, it would mean the end of his career, his freedom, and possibly even his life. And yet, despite the risk, a feeling of exhilaration washed over him. Their message was out there, touching the hearts and minds of people. He could almost feel the ripple of surprise and awe that moved through the city. His eyes remained glued to the screen, watching as the message disappeared and was replaced once again by the regular broadcasts. He felt the tension in the air, the sense of expectation, the undercurrent of uncertainty. He imagined the whispered conversations, the shared glances of understanding, the new bonds of solidarity forming in the wake of their message. But even amidst the excitement, Sam found himself grappling with questions. How did the message get out? Why was it released without his knowledge? He felt a pang of unease. There was a new element in their plan, an unexpected variable. The biggest question on his mind was what would happen next.

The tale of John and Emily had become a whispered symphony, performed in the secluded corners of the city. It was heard in hushed conversations at the market, coded dialogues in the parks, and silent acknowledgments between strangers. The story was being revived and with it came the resurgence of emotions associated with their tragic love affair. At work, Adrienne found herself eavesdropping on hushed discussions. It seemed that John and Emily were alive again, their story not a dark chapter from the past, but a current event. Their love was no longer a cautionary tale, but a rallying cry for those who yearned for a more compassionate world. In the Surveillance Department, Sam saw the name "John and Emily" appearing more frequently in reports. Officially, it was seen as a disturbing trend, but Sam knew better. The names were not appearing out of nowhere, they were being whispered, shouted, scribbled, and repeated because people were connecting with their story. People were starting to question the very government that had branded these lovers as criminals, and the murmurings of dissent were growing louder with each passing hour. It was exactly the kind of reaction Sam and Adrienne had hoped for. But there was also fear. Fear of what the government might do next. The story of John and Emily was a painful reminder of the consequences of defying the regime. Yet, despite the fear, the story served as a beacon of hope for many, a symbol of the powerful, undying love they all yearned to experience, a love that the government, with all its rules and sanctions, could never truly snuff out. And amidst this tumultuous wave of emotion and fear, Sam and Adrienne had to navigate carefully. They had to prepare for the next step, the next story that would fuel the fire of rebellion. And at the back of Sam's mind, the faces of two innocent boys, Tommy and Billy, haunted his thoughts. The next phase of his plan was approaching, and with it came a choice that could change everything.

Chapter 36

Classroom Revolution

Claire and Declan had been merged with Sam and Adrienne's experiences so closely that they had begun to forget their own identities. They were just observers, yet the immersion into the lives of these rebels had blurred the lines between observation and participation. They had become emotionally entwined with the revolution, feeling every surge of adrenaline, each fleeting moment of fear, and the powerful undercurrent of hope.

After weeks of relentless observation and deep immersion into the lives of Sam and Adrienne, Claire and Declan found themselves teetering on the edge of their own identities. They had been so absorbed in the emotional and revolutionary journey of their hosts that they had started to forget their own existence as separate entities.

Sensing this growing detachment, the Mycelium Computer initiated an automated protocol of its own design to prevent a total identity loss to the minds it now controlled. It gently extricated Claire and Declan from their hosts and brought them back to a neutral observation point within the simulation, a digital 'safe space' of sorts where they could reorient themselves.

An automatic shift in the simulation was initiated, a sort of programmed detour designed to help them regain perspective. Their combined consciousness was reoriented and refocused on a different part of the simulated reality: a school classroom.

This wasn't a scene of their choosing, but rather the system's calculated move to provide them with a more objective viewpoint. The abrupt transition felt strange, like suddenly waking up from a vivid dream. Yet, as their perspectives overlapped in observing the classroom, they found themselves drawn into a new narrative. The chaos of revolution was momentarily replaced by the seemingly ordinary scene of a schoolroom, grounding them back into their roles as observers

The sudden change of scene had a disorientating effect, reminding them they were still within the confines of a simulation. Their disembodied consciousness hovered invisibly over the scene, the familiar hum of classroom chatter and the rhythmic clicking of keyboards filling their senses.

Their gaze fell upon two young boys, Tommy and Billy. They were seated in a far corner of the classroom, their figures dwarfed by the massive screen that covered an entire wall. The rest of the classroom was engrossed in the digital spectacle of the government hack, their eyes wide, jaws slack with astonishment at the daring display of defiance that had momentarily taken over their screens.

While the rest of the classroom was engrossed in the digital manifestation on their screens, two figures stood in stark contrast. Tommy and Billy held hands in a quiet moment of unity, too absorbed in the story of John and Emily to notice the world around them. They did not realize their fingers were intertwined, silently affirming their unspoken feelings. Their gesture did not go unnoticed. A few students, peeling their eyes away from the screens, noticed the subtle action. They exchanged glances, wide-eyed and incredulous, but no one said anything. It was a curious sight, two boys holding hands amidst the chaos of the revelation. A sight that was as unusual as it was stirring. Back in the Surveillance Department, Sam watched this unfold. His heart clenched as he saw the innocent affection between Tommy and Billy, their hands clasped in the middle of the classroom. It was a display of pure, innocent affection that was both heartwarming and terrifying. Terrifying because he knew the repercussions if their secret was discovered. The silent revolution they were stirring up was already shaking the foundations of their society, bringing old stories to light and making people question their beliefs. And in the midst of it all, two young boys were unknowingly becoming the face of change. It was a dangerous position to be in, and Sam couldn't help but worry about their fate. It was clear to him then, more than ever, that the revolution they were inciting was not only necessary but crucial to protecting people like Tommy and Billy, who simply wanted the freedom to love. It broke his heart to know that he, not the government this time would be the cause of destruction for these two young lovers.

Mrs. Turner, the stern-faced mathematics teacher, was meticulous in her attention to detail. No tiny deviations escaped her notice in her classroom, her hawk-eye vigilance ever-ready to correct any infractions. As her gaze lifted from the class screen, she noticed an oddity. Tommy and Billy were holding hands. While there was no rule against such friendly gestures, the nature of their hold was unlike any she had seen. It held an intimacy that suggested more than mere friendship, their hands locked in a deliberate exchange of strength and comfort.

Her eyebrows drew together in concern, her lips pursing with an emotion she couldn't quite place. There was an unnerving air about the scene that settled uneasily within her. As the class resumed, she found herself casting frequent glances towards the boys, noting their faint blushes, fleeting glances, and shy smiles.

Mrs. Turner, however, wasn't one to jump to conclusions. Instead, she decided to maintain her watchful vigilance over Tommy and Billy. Recollections of the tragic tale of John and Emily, whose ill-fated love had flickered across their screens, weighed heavily on her mind. She contemplated the consequences of love in their society and its severe implications.

Mrs. Turner had been a teacher long enough to know when something was amiss. But she also understood the complexities of the times they lived in. She held faith in her government, believing they did what was necessary to maintain societal order and safety.

Still, her memories often took her back to the chaotic era that preceded the Heritage Alliance's rise to power. She vividly recalled the dissolution of traditional structures - churches emptying, family units fragmenting, and societal bonds fraying. A rampant increase in drug abuse and criminal activity had marked the era, further fueling a sense of widespread anarchy. Society, it seemed, was teetering on the edge of collapse, bolstered by a pervasive victim mentality that threatened to shatter the fragile order. It was this chaos and disorder that the Heritage Alliance had promised to resolve, and they had delivered. They had restored order and discipline, albeit at a considerable cost.

Thus, faced with her current dilemma, Mrs. Turner decided to continue her observations for a few more days before taking any decisive action. Her heart bore a heavy load as she hoped, for the sake of the boys, that her rising suspicions would prove to be misplaced.

This unexpected interlude allowed Claire and Declan to reflect on the gravity of the situation. They saw the duality of love and fear playing out in this unassuming classroom, a microcosm of the larger revolution brewing outside its walls. The tender bond between Tommy and Billy, the uncertainty and concern etched on Mrs. Turner's face, all underlined the urgency of Sam and Adrienne's cause. They were not just fighting for themselves but for a generation that deserved the freedom to love and live authentically.

With this renewed perspective, Claire and Declan felt a pull to return to their respective hosts. Their brief detachment from Sam and Adrienne had served its purpose - a gentle reminder that they were merely observers in this narrative. The lines between their own consciousness and that of Sam and Adrienne had blurred over the weeks. It was this reprieve that reminded them of their roles, pulling them out of the depth of the emotional entanglement they found themselves in.

The shift back to their hosts felt like sliding into familiar skins. As they once again immersed themselves in the minds of Sam and Adrienne, they felt a strange sense of homecoming. Yet they were acutely aware of the difference now. They were not Sam and Adrienne, they were observers, present to document this moment of their lives. Their temporary detachment from the heart of the revolution had helped reestablish their observer status, equipping them to view the unfolding events with a clearer lens.

And so, with renewed understanding and resilience, Claire and Declan once again dove into the minds of their hosts. The revolution awaited, and they were ready to bear witness to the change.

As darkness fell, Sam found himself pacing restlessly in his apartment. His hands shook slightly as he ran them through his hair, his thoughts racing faster than his heartbeats. He glanced at the clock. It was almost time for him to meet Adrienne. His insides twisted at the thought. In the quiet solitude of his home, Sam felt the weight of what they were doing fully descend upon him. They weren't just risking their own lives; they were risking countless others' too. Every person who read their pamphlets, every person who paused before their hacked screens, and every person who dared to whisper John and Emily's names in hushed conversations - they were all potential victims of the government's wrath. It was a burden he hadn't fully grasped until this moment. The revolution, the cause, the rebellion - it had all seemed so necessary, so right. But the fear of what could happen, the thought of the possible bloodshed and loss, left a bitter taste in his mouth. He was no longer an analyst in the Surveillance Department observing lives from afar. He was a part of the story now, actively changing the course of his society, potentially towards disaster. Guilt and dread seeped into his veins like poison, making his breath catch in his throat. But he shook his head, dispelling his doubts. They had already set things in motion.

He couldn't afford to falter now. They were already guilty; they had already crossed the line. Pulling his jacket closer around him, he headed out of his apartment. His steps were heavy, his heart even more so. He thought of Tommy and Billy, of John and Emily. He thought of Adrienne and her determined spirit. The risks were terrifying, but the possibility of change, of a better future, gave him courage. Sam stepped into the cool night, heading towards the secret meeting spot. Every shadow seemed menacing, every sound a potential threat. But he pressed on, driven by the hope that this rebellion, their rebellion, could bring about the change they all yearned for.

Sam found Adrienne waiting for him at their secret rendezvous spot, partially concealed by the shadows. The sight of her filled him with both relief and dread. He quickly closed the distance between them, his breaths coming in ragged spurts. "I didn't know about the message, Adrienne," he began, his voice sounding shaky even to his own ears. "I didn't know it would be broadcast. I wasn't prepared for... for..." Adrienne raised a hand to silence him, her eyes locked onto his. "I know, Sam," she said, her voice soft yet firm. "I didn't have time to tell you, she approached me this morning and it was up by noon. A woman calling herself a Bytejester, approached me and took the pamphlet. It was a split-second decision, Sam. I'm sorry." Sam was silent for a moment, taking in Adrienne's words. The initial shock slowly faded, replaced by understanding. "It was the right thing to do," he said, finally breaking the silence. "The message needed to be out there, and did you see the graphics she added and the footage of John and Emily? It was wondrously amazing!" Adrienne's gaze softened, relief washing over her features. "I just wish I had a way to tell you sooner, Sam. I didn't mean to surprise you like this." Sam sighed and looked up at the night sky. "It's okay, Adrienne. This whole thing is bigger than us. It's not about who knows what first. It's about the change we're fighting for. It's about John and Emily and everyone else who's suffered under this regime. That's what matters." Adrienne nodded, her hand finding his in the darkness. "You're right,

Sam," she agreed. "We have a fight ahead of us. And I believe, together, we can win this. For everyone's sake." Sam was quiet, his mind whirling with Adrienne's words. He hadn't considered the possibility that their plans were being monitored by others, or that their actions could have drawn the attention of the underground to this degree. Someone knew a lot and had been preparing in advance for this opportunity. His job in the Surveillance Department meant he was viewed with suspicion by the very people they were trying to help. "She approached me," Adrienne explained further, her voice barely above a whisper. "She knew about you, Sam, about your job. She said they had been watching us, watching me. They thought it was a setup, that we were trying to draw them out so the government could make arrests." A chill went through Sam at her words. The implications of this revelation were alarming. But then, he considered Adrienne's next words. "But she didn't just reject me outright," Adrienne continued. "She was wary, yes, but she was also curious. And when I showed her the first issue of the Echo, that's when she believed me. That's when she knew we were genuine." "So, she agreed to help," Sam finished, his mind slowly accepting the truth. "She saw our sincerity in the Echo and decided to lend her expertise. That's why the message was sent out digitally." Adrienne nodded, squeezing his hand reassuringly. "Yes, she did it because she saw our truth, our determination. We managed to convince one person, Sam. And if we can convince one, we can convince more. We just have to keep pushing."

With her words, a new resolve solidified within Sam. Despite the fears and uncertainties, they had managed to make a significant step forward. They had sparked the beginnings of a revolution. It wouldn't be easy, and they would face challenges and dangers, but they were not alone. And that gave Sam a glimmer of hope, a light at the end of a long, dark tunnel.

Sam and Adrienne spent the evening compiling a list of the government's transgressions. Their world was shaped by endless rules, edicts, and measures designed to control every aspect of their lives. As they listed each one, the enormity of their task became evident. But each point also fueled their determination to resist and inspire change.

1. Forced Pairing: In an attempt to maintain control over society, the government was sanctioning certain relationships and forcing couples to marry against their will. The reasons behind these assignments were opaque, often justified with vague references to "social stability" and "genetic compatibility."

2. Population Control: People were compelled to have children due to a falling birth rate. The government was essentially weaponizing reproduction, reducing one of life's most intimate choices to a cold, bureaucratic mandate.

3. Surveillance State: The government had established an extensive surveillance system, spying on its citizens around the clock. People lived under the constant gaze of the state, with Sam's job as an analyst in the Surveillance Department being a stark example of this intrusion.

4. Homophobia: Same-sex relationships were heavily persecuted. Tommy and Billy, two innocent twelve-year olds who lived in fear, was deemed a "transgression" by the state. This level of intolerance and discrimination was chilling.

5. Censorship and Propaganda: The government controlled all forms of media, using them as tools to propagate their ideology and censor any dissenting voices. The truth was hidden behind a smokescreen of falsehoods and manipulative rhetoric.

6. Class Inequality: Government officials enjoyed privileges and perks denied to the common people. Sam's proposal to Adrienne for a sanctioned relationship was a stark example of this inequality.

7. Crushing Dissent: Any form of resistance or dissent was ruthlessly crushed. Those who spoke against the government were often "re-educated" or disappeared altogether. The underlying message was clear -submission or punishment.

8. Manipulation of History: The government controlled the narrative of the past, editing and altering history to suit their interests. John and Emily's story, once forgotten, was a testament to this manipulation.

As they discussed each point, Sam and Adrienne felt a strange mix of fear and resolve. The government's tyranny seemed insurmountable, but their resolve to spark a revolution was stronger than ever. This was a fight for their lives, their freedom, and the future of their society. And they were ready to face it head-on.

Chapter 37

Echo of Rebellion

The morning sun had barely begun to pierce the thin veneer of tranquility over the city when an uproar erupted from the direction of the local magistrate's office. Sam had just seated himself behind the array of monitoring screens when the first alert came in: a disturbance, a violent one.

On his main screen, a flurry of activity was unfolding. The facade of the austere government building, a symbol of authority and order, was rapidly disintegrating under a surge of uncontained public fury. The mob was led by a man whose face was twisted in a grimace of sheer agony and rage.

His was a painful story, one of love and heartbreak manipulated by the cold, unfeeling hands of the government. He was the victim of a policy that forced marriages, stripping him of the woman he cherished. The man designated as her husband, an innocent pawn in the political charade, had been brutally murdered alongside the officiant caught in the man's wrathful path.

But it was the pain in his screams that had caught the attention of the bystanders, drawn in by the raw, tangible despair. His grief was infectious, and it tapped into the simmering resentment of the public against the government. The spark of his agony ignited the fuel of their anger, and the magistrate's office descended into chaos.

As the scene escalated, Sam's fingers moved deftly over the keyboard, initiating the facial recognition software. His task was a delicate but crucial one: to identify the dissidents, the participants of this violent uprising, through the sea of heated faces displayed on his screens. His heart throbbed in his chest as he acknowledged the gravity of the situation. This was more than a minor disturbance - it was a full-blown riot.

Each identified face would bring consequences, potentially even catastrophic ones, for the people involved. They would be marked as dissidents, and the government's response was often unforgiving. Yet, Sam also understood the desperation that was driving these people. His fingers paused momentarily over the keys, a quick flicker of hesitation.

Then, with a sigh, he resumed typing, his eyes scanning the faces that filled his screens. The man who started it all was easy enough to identify - his features, distorted by grief and rage, would be forever etched into Sam's memory.

As the hours passed, the situation escalated, the riot growing wilder and more desperate. But Sam remained at his station, doing the job he was assigned. His eyes were filled with the sights of a city on the brink, his ears echoing with the screams of a heartbroken man and his heart heavy with the knowledge of what was to come.

As Sam's eyes flicked from one face to another, he was hit by a realization as forceful as a punch to the gut. He had been viewing the scene unfold as a government officer, looking at the faces as potential enemies. But the truth was that they were the people he needed for his cause. The anguished screams of the heartbroken man were not just a symbol of one man's loss, but a collective outcry against the tyranny of the government.

He was not on the right side of the screen; he needed to be out there, on the street with them. His fingers hovered over the keys, the faces of the people, now familiar, seared into his memory.

They were not dissidents; they were potential allies, kindled by the same injustice that he and Adrienne were fighting against.

With a newfound resolve, he shut down the identification system. His decision was made. The consequences would undoubtedly be severe. It would not take long before someone noticed the missing links to the video and the person responsible for the error.

Adrienne's plan had always seemed ambitious, bordering on the impossible. It was fraught with danger, a path that could lead them to triumph or disaster. Yet now, as he looked at the riot, the people fighting for their freedom, he knew their plan had a real chance of success.

With a final glance at his workstation, he logged off the system, leaving the room filled with unattended screens showing the city in uproar. His heart pounded as he made his way to the exit, ready to join the very people he was assigned to monitor.

But in the midst of his resolve, a thought held him back. He had work to do, still a crucial part to play from within these walls. This was the beginning, the spark of a revolution, but he had to fan those flames, not merely join them.

He returned to his workstation, his mind whirling with the enormity of the task. He had to ensure that his failure to identify the rioters would go unnoticed, that his illicit act of rebellion would be buried in a sea of digital noise. In a system designed for surveillance and control, he had to create an invisible escape route.

Quickly, he booted up a separate terminal, one that he had kept hidden and unlinked from the main surveillance system. This was his contingency, a ghost in the machine that he had created, just in case he needed to hold off on the Billy and Tommy surveillance. His fingers flew across the keyboard, executing a program he had coded. It was a digital chaff, a blizzard of fake data designed to clog the identification system, disguising his omission amidst a flood of false positives.

It was a gamble, but then, everything they were doing was a gamble. Adrienne's plan had always been a high-stakes game, one they knew could lead to triumph or disaster. Yet, as he looked back at the video feed, at the people of their city rising in righteous fury, he felt a surge of hope.

He logged off the system, leaving behind the fake data churning through the surveillance network. This was his contribution to the day's chaos. With the room filled with the echoes of an uproar and a city on the brink of revolution, he walked away from his station, his heart pounding with a mix of fear and exhilaration. This was just the beginning, the first sparks of their fire, and Sam was ready to stoke the flames.

It did not take long for someone to realize that something was wrong, for an hour had not passed when Sam was summoned to his supervisor's office. As soon as Sam entered the office, he could tell that he was in for a serious reprimand. The man's usually stern face was set into a mask of hard lines and his eyes were cold with disappointment.

"Sit down, Sam," his supervisor began, pointing to the chair on the other side of his desk. "We need to discuss an incident that occurred earlier today."

Feeling the anxiety knotting up in his stomach, Sam took his seat, his mind racing. Had they detected his manipulation of the surveillance system? Did they know about his decision to let the rioters' faces go unidentified?

However, what his supervisor said next took Sam completely by surprise. It was about Billy and Tommy, two boys from the city school whose lives Sam had been monitoring as part of his routine surveillance tasks.

The boys had been discovered in the woods before school by their teacher. They had been caught in a compromising position, a clear violation of the government's stringent laws on sexual conduct.

"I don't understand," Sam stammered, "I was monitoring the riot at the magistrate's office. The incident with the boys... it slipped through the cracks."

"Unacceptable, Sam," his supervisor said sternly, his gaze unflinching. "That riot is a city-wide concern. It's the job of all officers to be vigilant, not just you. But these boys... that was your responsibility, and you failed. I have reviewed the footage that you yourself have been watching and you must have known what was transpiring? It was obvious Sam!"

As his supervisor's words cut through the silence, Sam felt a sinking feeling. His plan had indeed been flawed, he realized. Not because he had failed to conceal his actions from the surveillance system, but because in focusing on one crisis, he had overlooked another.

The missed opportunity was not just about these boys, but about the message their punishment would send. Sam needed to be able to copy all footage of the incident in order to truly help spark the flame. The government would likely make an example of them, reinforcing the very laws that Sam and Adrienne were fighting against.

"I understand," Sam said, his voice steady despite the turmoil within him. "It won't happen again."

"Sam," the supervisor warned, "this issue isn't concluded. There will be an inquiry regarding your failure to report. If today hadn't been wrought with chaos due to this riot, I would have immediately relieved you of your duties. However, given the circumstances, I can't afford to lose any personnel. Therefore, I require you to remain at your station today, amidst the rioting."

As he walked out of his supervisor's office, he felt a renewed sense of urgency. There was no room for mistakes in this revolution they were planning. Every life mattered, every incident was a potential spark to fuel the fire. He knew what was to come next and he also knew that the act he would do now would be his final act as a government employee. He also knew he would not be going home at the end of shift. With resolve in his heart he sat back down at his terminal and found the Police that had logged the arrest of the young boys. He knew where they were taking the boys and what would more than likely happen to them and now so will the people of the city.

With the image of Billy and Tommy fresh in his mind, Sam settled back into his chair. The glow from the monitors filled the darkened room as he began his final act as a government employee.

The feed from the police vehicle was gut-wrenching. There, in the back seat, were the boys. Their faces were a mask of fear and despair as they sobbed and pleaded with the officers driving them to an unknown fate. They clung to each other, making heartfelt promises never to repeat their actions if only they were allowed to go free. Sam's heart ached at their desperation, but he pushed away his emotions and focused on the task at hand.

Skillfully, he tapped into the database, pulling up every piece of surveillance footage involving Billy and Tommy. A montage started to form, showing the innocent progression of their relationship, from holding hands in the park to sharing stolen kisses when they thought no one was watching. He even found the moment when Ms. Turner, their teacher, discovered them in the woods. Her reaction, a mixture of shock and disappointment, was as painful to watch as the boys' desperate pleas in the police car.

This was not just about the boys; it was a visual representation of the government's oppressive laws, and Sam was certain it would resonate with the city's citizens.

With every click of the mouse, he knew he was sealing his fate. He was not just creating a montage, but a call to arms, a plea for change, a spark for revolution. As the footage of the boys being driven away in the police car filled his screen, Sam knew that this would more than likely be his last action to help spawn the change that he had begun to dream of.

Once the montage was complete, Sam uploaded the video onto a secret, encrypted channel that he had created. He had learned this from the bytejester and copied her code to the letter. In his position he was able to access the file and see how she had breached their security a day prior. As he hit the 'upload' button, he knew that his actions were irreversible. This was it. His career as a government employee was over, and his life as a revolutionary had begun.

He took a deep breath, aware of the deafening silence that filled the room. Outside, the city was unaware of the storm that was about to hit them. He had just thrown the first stone, but he knew, as surely as he knew the sun would rise, that it wouldn't be the last. The revolution had begun. And there would be no turning back.

With a final glance at his now-abandoned terminal, Sam left the surveillance room behind. The normally buzzing hub of government activity seemed eerily quiet. His footsteps echoed through the corridors as he made his way to the exit. Every instinct screamed at him to run, but he forced himself to walk at a measured pace, trying to seem as normal as possible.

Exiting the government building felt like walking out of prison. The air outside tasted of freedom and uncertainty. He quickly made his way to the subway, his mind racing. He had set in motion a chain of events that couldn't be stopped. The video was out there, for everyone to see. The government's oppressive control was laid bare, and there was no telling what would happen next.

His thoughts kept returning to Adrienne. She had been his rock, his source of inspiration. In a world devoid of color, she had been a vibrant burst of life. Now, more than ever, he needed her by his side. Not just because of the revolution, but because he had realized that he cared about her, more deeply than he had allowed himself to admit.

The train ride to Adrienne's workplace seemed to take an eternity. He tried to keep his anxiety at bay, to steady the adrenaline that threatened to consume him. He was a wanted man now. There was no doubt about it. But he had one last stop to make, one last person to see.

As Sam stepped off the train, he found himself in the pulsating heart of the city. Around him, people were rushing by, their faces lost in the sea of bodies. Above him, the towering screens that were ubiquitous across the city flickered to life. The familiar chime that signaled an important broadcast rang out, echoing through the station. He felt his heart lurch as he turned to face the screen, knowing what was about to come.

The video started with a montage of innocent moments of joy. Billy and Tommy, their faces lighting up with laughter as they played a game of football. The stolen glances between them when they thought no one was looking. The subtle brush of hands when they passed each other a bottle of water, lingering just a moment longer than necessary.

The video transitioned into softer, more intimate moments. The boys sitting together under the sprawling branches of an old oak tree, lost in a world of their own. Their hands intertwined; eyes locked in a gaze that spoke volumes. The innocent pecks on the cheek that turned into kisses hidden behind the school buildings, where they thought they were safe from the world.

But then the tone of the video shifted drastically. The serene atmosphere was replaced with the harsh sound of a whistle. The image on the screen changed to a shocked Ms. Turner catching the boys in a moment of intimacy. The confusion and fear in their eyes as she pulled out her phone, the disbelief as they realized what was about to happen.

The final scenes were the most heartbreaking. Billy and Tommy being led away in handcuffs, their faces pale and drawn. The boys in the back of a police car, their hands reaching out for each other but separated by a metal grid. The pleas, the promises of never doing it again, the fear in their eyes - all broadcasted for the entire city to see.

As the video ended, the station was eerily silent. Sam turned around to find hundreds of faces staring at the screen, their expressions a mix of shock, horror, and sadness. A murmur began to spread through the crowd, a collective outrage that was on the brink of becoming a roar.

For Sam, the moment was fraught with mixed emotions. He recognized his role in setting the stage for the uprising, but pondered whether his efforts would ultimately fan the flames of revolution. Simultaneously, he was acutely aware that his actions had likely marked him for persecution. His haste and desperation clouded his judgement; in his normal clarity of thought, he would have refrained from rushing to Adrienne, thereby not leading the authorities directly to the woman crucial to their collective endeavor for change.

The fact that the video was taking an unusually long time to load, which should have started almost immediately after his departure from the agency, didn't even cross his mind amidst the whirlwind of events. As the fury of the crowd intensified, he discreetly exited the station, setting course for Adrienne's workplace. With his heart heavy with dread and hope, he prayed fervently to get to her before the authorities did.

Inside, he found Adrienne on the factory floor, engrossed in her work. Her face lit up when she saw him, but her smile quickly faded when she noticed his serious expression. Sam wasted no time. He told her everything - about the riot, the boys, and the video. He told her about the risk he'd taken and about the fallout that was bound to follow.

Finally, he told her how he felt. Words that had been held back for too long spilled out in a torrent. He confessed his admiration, respect, and more importantly, his love for her. For Sam, there was no other way. He needed her to know, to understand his decision and the reasons behind it. And he needed to hear her say it back, before it was too late.

As he finished speaking, he reached out to hold her hands, his gaze imploring her to understand. He knew he was asking a lot, but he also knew that if there was anyone who could stand by him in this storm, it would be Adrienne. And he would stand by her, come what may.

Before she could respond, there was a sudden commotion at the entrance of the factory. Adrienne's eyes widened as she saw a squad of armed officers rushing in, their weapons drawn. Panic descended upon the factory floor as workers scurried away, their faces filled with terror.

There was no time for words as Adrienne instinctively pushed Sam behind a piece of machinery, putting herself between him and the approaching officers. Sam tried to protest, but Adrienne silenced him with a stern look. Her protective instincts were in full swing, her body tense and ready to face whatever was coming.

But nothing could have prepared her for what happened next. Without any warning, the officers opened fire. Adrienne staggered backward from the force of the bullets, her eyes wide with shock. She fell to the ground, and for a moment, everything seemed to freeze.

Sam was moving in an instant, his mind racing with disbelief and horror. He reached out to Adrienne, her name a choked cry on his lips. All around them, the factory was in chaos, but Sam could only focus on Adrienne, lying motionless on the cold, hard floor.

The grim reality of the situation sunk in, and with it, a chilling dread. They would not know if their plan would come to fruition. The cost had been far greater than they had ever imagined when first they spoke of the Echo.

Sam's world came crashing down around him. The factory was a whirl of chaos and confusion, but he barely noticed it. All he saw was Adrienne, lying still and lifeless on the cold floor. He dropped to his knees beside her, oblivious to the danger he was in.

Suddenly, a violent force threw him backwards. A sharp pain seared through his chest, and he looked down to see a growing pool of blood. In a daze, he turned his head, catching sight of the officers that had shot him.

They watched him impassively, their faces cold and detached, as if they hadn't just ended two lives. Sam's vision blurred, the edges growing dark. He reached out towards Adrienne, his fingers brushing against hers one last time.

As his consciousness began to fade, he heard a distant voice echoing throughout the factory. "Never again!" it cried. Then everything went black.

Back at the surveillance nerve center, George found himself in silent shock. His colleague, his friend, had just been brutally gunned down on live camera, cradling the lifeless form of a woman he had quietly admired — the modest janitor who had unknowingly made a place for herself in his heart. He was aware of the dire consequences that came with defying directives — he was under explicit orders to suppress any event that could cast a shadow on the government's image. However, in that moment, clarity surged within him, leading him to a crucial decision.

The monumental irony of the situation wasn't lost on George. He had been a double agent all along, covertly working to dismantle the oppressive rule of the Heritage Alliance from the inside. The government, completely oblivious to his secret intent, had assigned him to watch over Sam and Adrienne. This fateful alignment seemed almost as if the universe itself was aiding their collective endeavor to spark the much-needed revolution.

His hand was unsteady as he activated the live feed, the appalling footage inundating every screen throughout the city. The haunting visuals of Sam and Adrienne's final moments replayed in a continuous loop, their defiant words echoing across the city streets, interspersed with the horrifying scene of their violent demise.

Their ultimate sacrifice stirred a wave of rebellion within the hearts of the city's populace. United cries of protest and defiance resonated throughout the city, amplifying with each passing moment. "Never again!" was their refrain, the words carrying a raw, undeniable power that sent shivers down George's spine.

He observed, from his unique vantage point, as the city spiraled into chaos. The streets were crowded with angry citizens, their faces illuminated by the ominous glow of burning buildings. The government's reign was teetering on the brink, and a full-blown revolution was underway. Their city was engulfed in flames, but from the ashes, a new hope was being kindled.

They had paid an enormous price in order for society to realize they needed to fight for their freedom, but the populace obliged and stood steadfast in their resolve to ensure it wasn't in vain. For Sam, Adrienne, and all those who had endured oppression, they would fight. "Never again," they vowed. Never again.

In the midst of the storm he had helped unleash, George sat in the glow of the surveillance screens. Despite the tumultuous emotions within him, a strange serenity washed over him. He knew his actions were treasonous, his days numbered. Yet he felt an immense pride. His was the hand that had tipped the first domino, and now the cascade could not be stopped.

Outside, the city was a blaze of revolt. Inside, the once buzzing command center had fallen eerily silent, save for the frantic whispers and hurried steps of officials scrambling to regain control. But the more they tried, the more the situation slipped from their hands, like sand flowing through clenched fists.

George knew he would not leave the room alive. Yet, he remained seated at his terminal, the image of Sam and Adrienne's final moments still looping on the screens. His mind was calm, resolute. His heart echoed with the chant that was resounding through the city: "Never again."

His fingers danced over the keys, sending the live feed to the farthest corners of their world. From his terminal, the flames of rebellion would spread beyond their city, beyond their world. No longer would they be an isolated beacon. The rest of the universe would know, would see, the cost of their freedom and the courage of their defiance.

Suddenly, the door to the command center burst open, and a swarm of armed guards flooded in. Their faces were grim, their intentions clear. George barely glanced up as they stormed towards him, his focus unwavering.

One guard leveled his weapon at George, his finger tense on the trigger. "For Sam, for Adrienne, for all of us," George whispered, his voice barely audible over the chaos. His fingers hammered one last command into the terminal, an irreversible action that ensured the live feed could not be cut. The deed done, he took a deep breath, a slight smile gracing his face.

The gunshot echoed through the command center. George's body slumped in his chair, his life extinguished in an instant. But even as his life faded, the spark he had ignited burned brighter. His final act, a beacon that would light the path of rebellion for the entire world. His was the sacrifice that would echo through the ages, a testament to the power of defiance and the price of freedom. His legacy lived on, his spirit immortalized in the revolution he had helped to birth. For George, for all of them, there would be no turning back. The revolution had begun.

Chapter 38

A Journey through the Mycelium: Reality Unraveled

Seeing through Adrienne's eyes, Claire experienced a jarring shock. Time seemed to slow as she instinctively moved to shield Sam from the officers. Claire could feel the deep determination in Adrienne's heart, the burning need to protect Sam, to shield him from whatever harm was approaching. The fear was there too, but it was drowned out by a fierce resolve.

Then came the searing pain, the bullets ripping through her flesh, stealing her breath away. Claire felt Adrienne's body stagger, the force of the gunfire throwing her backward. She could taste the coppery tang of blood in her mouth, feel the warmth as it trickled down her skin. It was surreal, experiencing this moment through Adrienne's perspective. The shock that registered in Adrienne's eyes was mirrored in Claire's heart.

She fell, and with her, Claire could feel the hard impact of the cold, unyielding factory floor. The world around her was a maelstrom of panic and chaos, but through Adrienne's eyes, the focus was only on Sam. She could see him reach for her, his face pale, his eyes filled with a raw horror that mirrored her own. Adrienne's heart pounded in her chest, echoing painfully in Claire's own.

But it was the moment of Adrienne's passing that left a deep impression on Claire. She felt Adrienne's life seeping away, the pain beginning to fade. As her consciousness dimmed, her surroundings became a blur. The only thing she could hear was Sam's voice, choked with grief, crying out her name. Then, there was a profound sense of calm, an acceptance that defied the chaotic world around her. In her last moments, Adrienne held onto the image of Sam, etching it into her memory, her final act of love and defiance.

As Adrienne's life began to wane, Claire could feel a distinct change in her perspective. The factory, the chaos, and the violence all started to fade, the world around them dissolving into a foggy blur. The noise grew distant and muffled, as if she was underwater. She could see Sam still beside her, his image starting to blur at the edges, growing faint.

And then, slowly, the darkness began to recede. It was replaced by a soft, warm light, filling her vision. Adrienne's pain was replaced with an indescribable sense of peace and tranquility, a calm that washed over her, soothing her tormented soul. Claire could feel a gentle tug, a calling from this light. It was welcoming, comforting, promising release and respite from the cruel world she was leaving behind.

Within this light, faint outlines began to form. The blurred shapes began to take on familiar forms, faces of loved ones long lost. They were waiting, welcoming, reaching out with open arms. Claire could feel Adrienne's joy at seeing these faces, her longing to be reunited with them. There was a sense of completion, of coming home. The weight of the world seemed to fall off Adrienne's shoulders, a sense of freedom washing over her as she took a step toward the light.

Then, with one final look back at Sam, she stepped into the light. Claire felt a rush of emotions, a mix of sorrow, relief, and an overwhelming sense of love. As Adrienne moved on, her spirit was free, leaving the pain and suffering of the physical world behind.

Claire's consciousness followed Adrienne into the light, and she found herself in a dimension far beyond her understanding. The harsh, concrete reality of the physical world dissipated into a celestial landscape of ethereal grandeur. A massive, magnificent tree stood before her, rooted firmly into an unseen floor, its branches reaching high and vast into the infinite expanse.

It wasn't just a tree; it was a beacon of life, throbbing with a spiritual energy that filled the air around it. The tree glowed with a soft, inviting light, and pulsed rhythmically, as though in sync with the heartbeat of the universe. Its leaves rustled softly, whispering ancient truths and long-forgotten tales. Its bark was inscribed with symbols, patterns, and languages, both familiar and alien, each etching holding a story of its own.

Claire could feel a connection to the tree. Its roots dug deep, reaching out and connecting to other life forms, communicating, exchanging, learning. She saw visions of the past, fragments of her own life intertwining with Adrienne's, Sam's, and countless others. Each memory, each moment, each decision was etched into the tree, making it a living archive of lives lived and lessons learned.

As her gaze ascended, she saw the branches, sprawling outwards towards the infinite expanse, each a pathway representing potential futures. Some were vibrant and lush, teeming with life, while others were barren and desolate. Each branch was a path, a possibility, a choice. They reached out to the stars, connecting with galaxies, nebulae, and celestial bodies, intricately woven into the cosmic fabric of existence.

The immense cosmic tree was a vivid portrayal of the interconnectedness of all beings, a testament to the threads of life that intertwined, merged, and branched out, creating an infinite web of existence. Every life, every choice, every moment was a part of this vast, complex tapestry. It was a humbling realization, a perspective-altering vision of the grandeur of existence, and the place of each individual within it.

Claire felt a profound sense of awe and tranquility. She was part of something far bigger than herself, her life a single thread in the cosmic weave. As she stood there, at the crossroads of past, present, and future, she felt a deep, unshakeable understanding seep into her, changing her perception of life, death, and what lay beyond.

Claire and Declan were abruptly pulled from the simulation, their senses reeling from the abrupt transition from chaos to silence. The sounds of protests, gunfire, and the roar of the burning city still echoed in their ears, creating a dissonant harmony with the quiet hum of the computer lab. The horror and violence they had witnessed were unlike anything they had ever experienced in their own reality, and the stark contrast was jarring.

Stunned, Claire found herself still clutching the vials of sulfuric and hydrofluoric acid. Her knuckles were white from the tension, her pulse still thrumming with adrenaline. She looked at Declan, her eyes wide with the shock of what they had just witnessed. Their simulation, their creation, had become a horrifying reality beyond their wildest nightmares.

Declan, too, looked shaken. His eyes were locked onto Claire while his mind was replaying the scenes of the simulated uprising, the last moments of Sam and Adrienne. He swallowed hard, a visible lump moving in his throat, his face a mask of horrified realization.

In the quiet aftermath of the simulation, the destructive potential of the vials in Claire's hands seemed all the more potent. Would this be their future if they didn't act? Would the world outside the lab become a reflection of the horror they had just witnessed? With a determined look, she moved toward the computer, the vials clutched tightly in her trembling hands.

Gently, Declan took the vials from Claire's grasp, his hands firm but understanding. As he placed them on the ground, he couldn't help but feel a profound sense of relief mingled with fear. The simulation, so immersive, so real, had left them both scarred.

Living through the horrors that Sam and Adrienne had faced, feeling their fear, their courage, their love, and their ultimate sacrifice had been an experience that left them both deeply shaken.

The violence of their shared simulated death was still raw, a phantom pain coursing through their bodies as though they themselves had been shot. The sensation was so visceral that it was disorienting, the memories seared into their minds as if they had been their own experiences.

Suddenly, Claire bent over, her body convulsing as she vomited onto the cold floor of the lab. Her face was pale, her eyes glossy with unshed tears. She was trembling, the soft sobs that escaped her lips betraying the horror she felt.

Without thinking, Declan moved towards her, wrapping his arm around her shoulder in an attempt to offer her some form of comfort. His own body was shaky, the experience they had shared too overwhelming for him to fully process. As he held Claire, he couldn't help but feel the echo of Adrienne's final moments in his arms, the sense of loss as palpable as the woman he was holding now.

Declan released Claire slowly, watching her as she wiped her mouth and pushed her hair back from her face. Her face was pale, almost ashen in the sterile light of the lab. She looked at him, her eyes searching his face for answers he didn't have.

"That feeling, the voice in my head" she began, her voice shaky, "what was it? How did system connect to me without a chip? And what did it mean by the 'truth awaits you, and in it, your purpose'?"

He found himself lost in his thoughts, unsure of where to begin. The notion that the simulation was not merely a product of intricate coding, but a computational reality, was both intriguing and perplexing. It suggested a journey that pushed the boundaries of their known existence, venturing into realms unexplored.

The concept felt almost instinctive to him, as if it was a part of him, embedded deep within his psyche. It was less a thought that could be clearly articulated, and more a deeply embedded intuition. It presented itself as an abstract idea, a sophisticated and intricate thread of thought that defied easy explanation or understanding.

"I don't know, Claire," he admitted, his voice raw. "But whatever this Mycelium computer really is, it's far more than what we thought. It's not just a simulation. It's... it's another reality, maybe our past on our future. Our experiences there, as Sam and Adrienne, they were real. They had to be, No?"

Claire shivered at his words and wrapped her arms around herself. He wished he could offer her some comfort, some assurance that everything would be alright, but he couldn't. All he knew was that they had stepped into something far beyond their understanding, and they were in it together. Claire looked into his eyes and tried to gather her thoughts as a barrage of questions poured forth. "How else was The Last Liberal in our visions, if not a hallucination? We know it is a bar; a place relevant to our current lives, but could it be from our history or past? None of it makes sense. The people are all from different races, separated by zoning. We don't have people like that here or in our past, so what is this? An alternate reality?"

Declan nodded slowly, contemplating her words. She was right. Their experience in the Mycelium system was unlike anything they knew or remembered about their own history. The racial diversity, the forced marriages, the dissent against the government, it all seemed so foreign, so distinctly different from their reality.

"You might be right, Claire," he conceded, scratching his head. "Perhaps we're not looking at our past or future, but an alternate reality, a different plane of existence where things have evolved differently."

"But," Claire cut in, her voice shaky, "if it's a hallucination, it's a very detailed and consistent one. And if it's not...if it's another reality, then it's... it's... terrifying."

Her words hung in the air between them, the implications chilling. If the Mycelium in the computer indeed opened gateways to other realities, then what they experienced as Sam and Adrienne was as real as their current reality. It would mean that those realities, with their own unique histories and struggles, existed alongside theirs, only separated by the thin veil of dimensionality.

"And what if we're not the only ones?" Declan pondered aloud, his mind spinning with the possibilities. "What if there are others experiencing our reality the same way we experienced Sam and Adrienne's? We'd be characters in their simulation."

A silence fell between them as they grappled with the enormity of it all. The Mycelium computer had opened a Pandora's box of questions, and they had no idea how to close it. The only thing they were certain about was that they had irrevocably stepped into the realm of the unknown, and there was no putting it back into the box.

"Right," Declan finally said, breaking the silence. "We need to do something. Sitting here mulling over it won't get us anywhere." He turned to look at Claire, his gaze steady and determined. "What if we went to The Last Liberal right now? We know it's there in our reality, maybe there is something there while it is fresh in our minds that will spark something, some idea, some recognition of some sort?"

Claire looked surprised at his suggestion, but didn't dismiss it. She ran her fingers through her hair, a deep crease forming between her eyebrows. "We would need Jamie there with us. She's our knowledge base of all things regarding The Last Liberal. She might be able to help us make sense of this."

"Exactly," Declan agreed, standing up. "We'll get Jamie, go there and look around. Maybe there's something, a clue of some kind that we missed. It's a long shot, but it's better than staying here and doing nothing and besides I want to get away from this thing as fast as possible right now. Another trip into the unknown does not excite me. "

Claire nodded, her determination returning. "Okay, let's do it. The sooner we start, the sooner we might find answers."

With a shared resolve, the two of them left their lab, a new mission in their minds. They would confront their reality, search for answers, and hopefully, unravel the mystery that the Mycelium Computer system had thrust upon them. Their simulated experience as Sam and Adrienne had marked the beginning of their journey into the unknown. And they knew that the road ahead was filled with uncertainties. But they also knew that they had to move forward, for they were in too deep to turn back now.

Chapter 39

The Enigmatic Echoes of The Last Liberal

When Jamie opened the door, she looked surprised. Her eyes moved from Declan to Claire, lingering on Claire's face as if trying to comprehend what she was seeing. But instead of the anger Claire was bracing herself for, Jamie broke into a wide grin.

"Claire!" she exclaimed, ushering her into her apartment. "I can't believe it! After all that happened, I feared the worst. I've been worried sick."

Claire stumbled over her words, trying to convey her apologies. But Jamie waved her off, offering them a seat. "We'll deal with all of that later. Right now, I'm just glad you're okay."

Relief washed over Claire as she sank into the chair. She looked at Declan, who was wearing a similarly relieved expression. They had come to Jamie, prepared for confrontation and conflict. But instead, they found understanding, forgiveness, and support.

Over the course of the next few hours, Claire and Declan shared the unbelievable experiences they'd been through, from the simulated reality to the visions of Sam and Adrienne and the story of Maddy's demise into despair from a similar such experience. Jamie listened intently, her eyebrows bunched together, setting her face into an intense expression of focus.

They did not mention The Last Liberal in the visions but did convey it may hold some answers to their mystery. "The bar?

That's peculiar," Jamie remarked. "But there might be something there that would help. I say we go, investigate the place, I know it like the back of my hand so I am positive I can help. I mean there's nothing to lose at this point."

And just like that, they had their next destination. Despite the tumultuous events of the past week, they found themselves united once again in the pursuit of truth, ready to face whatever might come their way.

Navigating through the labyrinthine streets of the old part of town was like stepping into a bygone era. Ancient buildings, imbued with timeless charm, stretched along narrow cobblestone streets. Each corner was alive with the bustle of small shops, open-air markets, and street performers that added to the vibrancy of the district. It was a stark contrast to the sleek and modernized cityscape they were accustomed to, and the journey felt as much a trip through time as it was a physical journey.

The Last Liberal stood humbly amidst its surroundings. It was an old building, painted a faded maroon, with its name adorned on a wooden sign hanging over the entrance. The wood was weathered and cracked; the letters faded but still holding on to their dignity. An illustration of a quill and parchment, painted alongside the letters, suggested a time when ideas flowed as freely as the beer within its walls, the florescent lighting outlining the name dim in the light of day.

The windows were adorned with handmade lace curtains, an artifact of simpler times. The entrance door, sturdy and aged, had an intricately carved handle that had been polished smooth by countless hands.

From the outside, the bar looked like it could have been plucked from a century-old photograph, if not for the occasional high-tech gadgetry glimpsed through its windows.

Claire, Declan, and Jamie exchanged glances before pushing the door open and stepping into The Last Liberal, ready to uncover the secrets it held.

The bar had an old-world charm that was not easy to find in the modernized city. The seating consisted of a mixture of high stools and comfortable armchairs, each piece of furniture was distinct in design, revealing various eras of the bar's existence. Heavy wooden tables, chipped and worn from countless interactions, were scattered around the room, inviting patrons to sit, converse and share in the unique atmosphere of the place. In a corner, a small stage beckoned amateur musicians to share their songs with the room, adding a layer of local color to the overall ambiance.

At the back of the bar, a grand stone fireplace towered high, reminding visitors of the building's origins. Despite the warmth of the season, Jamie lit a fire. The soft flame danced within it, adding an extra touch of comfort to the room. "Sorry, it's a habit. I like the smell, it helps to cover up the scent of the mould," Jamie stated.

To the side, a staircase led to an upper floor. It was closed off to the public, but the allure of its mystery added another layer of intrigue to the establishment.

As Claire and Declan took in their surroundings, they couldn't help but feel a sense of awe. Despite the world outside rapidly changing and evolving, The Last Liberal had remained a steadfast monument to a time that felt both distant and eerily similar to their own. It was, in essence, a tangible slice of history.

Looking around, Claire couldn't shake the feeling of familiarity. Yet, something seemed off. The bar had the same layout, the same rich mahogany bar counter, even the same towering fireplace at the back. It felt like the bar in the simulation they had visited, but there were subtle differences that made it hard to say if it was the same place or not.

"The layout is similar," Claire mused aloud, her gaze scanning the room. "Even the pictures on the walls are in the same place but from a different era almost. But, there's something oddly different about it, I just can't place it."

Declan nodded; his expression thoughtful as he took in their surroundings. "It's as if the essence of the place is the same, but the details are different," he said. "Like, the bar in the vision was an echo of this one, or vice versa."

Jamie watched them, bemused. "Are you guys sure you're alright?" she asked. "You're talking as if you've been here before, like long ago in the past or something? I mean you have both been here recently."

Claire and Declan exchanged a glance, unsure of how much they should tell Jamie. Would she even believe them? They decided to be as honest as they could.

"We've...seen this place in the computer-generated world we told you about," Claire said hesitantly. "In a simulation. It's a long story, but there's something about this place that's important. We just need to figure out what."

They looked around again, the missing quiet hum of conversation and the clinking of glasses helped to take away the ambiance. They had never been in the bar when it was empty. As they tried to piece together the puzzle, they knew one thing for sure - their journey was far from over.

“What was the name of the bar when you took over?” Declan asked trying to find a connection.

"Actually, it was called 'The Harbinger' when I took over," Jamie said, her eyes roving around the room. "I changed the name to 'The Last Liberal'."

Their surprise was evident, and Jamie couldn't help but chuckle at their reactions. "Believe it or not, it was a bit of a spontaneous decision," she revealed. "When I was clearing out the basement, I stumbled upon a pile of old paperwork - contracts, bills, that kind of thing. Among these documents was a name change proposal. It turns out, the previous owner was actually forced by the Government to rename the place. He changed it from 'The Last Liberal' to 'The Harbinger'."

A strange, teasing smile played on Jamie's lips as she added, "But I preferred 'The Last Liberal', so I chose to revert back to it. It was between that and 'The Echo'!"

Claire and Declan's heads whipped towards Jamie at the mention of 'The Echo'. Their faces mirrored their confusion and surprise as they chorused, "What?"

"The Echo," Jamie repeated, still looking somewhat amused. "It was another name I came across. It was scribbled on an old pamphlet I found in the basement with the other paperwork. It caught my eye because the graphic on the front was unbelievably intricate. A beautiful bird rising from the city."

Claire and Declan looked at each other, their expressions filled with a sense of uncanny recognition. In the simulated reality they had experienced, the bar was known as 'The Last Liberal' and not 'The Harbinger'. Yet, it seemed 'The Last Liberal' had been its previous name, before the enforced change. This strange correlation between the simulation and their current reality was yet another puzzle piece to add to their ever-growing mystery."

The utterance of 'The Echo' sparked an instantaneous reaction from Claire and Declan. Their skin prickled, goosebumps popping up as though touched by a cold breeze, an uncanny chill trickling down their spines. It was a reaction born not from fear, but an odd sense of recognition and eerie coincidence. It was too close to their simulation to be merely happenstance.

"Could we take a look at these documents?" Declan proposed, his voice steady despite the tingling sensation still shivering along his spine. His gaze was bright, eager with curiosity and the burning desire to uncover what was happening.

With a bemused yet accommodating nod, Jamie agreed. "Of course, come with me," she responded, gesturing them towards the basement of the bar where her archived files resided. As Claire and Declan trailed behind her, an unspoken communication of shared anticipation passed between them.

With every step, they were drawing nearer to untying the enigmatic knot that was their simulation experience.

As Claire and Declan carefully pored over the contents of the old pamphlet, they could hardly believe their eyes. Every line, every picture, every minute detail was identical to the one they had painstakingly worked on in their simulated lives as Sam and Adrienne. It was uncanny, eerie even, to see the product of their virtual efforts realized in physical form.

"This isn't possible," Claire finally managed to stutter out. Her eyes were wide with disbelief as she scanned the old document. "This...this must be some kind of practical joke. Our history books never mentioned anything about a time like what we saw in the simulation... No, this is not our reality; this did not happen! Did it?!"

It was then that Declan went pale, his gaze distant. Without a word, he stood up abruptly, excusing himself as he rushed up the stairs. The sound of shuffling furniture and objects being moved around echoed down into the basement, followed by the unmistakable sound of someone being sick. Worried, Jamie and Claire hastily followed him upstairs.

In the midst of this disquieting revelation, Jamie's hand brushed against something small and metallic tucked away. Intrigued, she carefully retrieved it, revealing a small golden brooch. It was exquisitely crafted in the shape of a phoenix, its wings majestically rising as if prepared to take flight. The artistic beauty and symbolic resonance struck her, and she discreetly pocketed the brooch before ascending the staircase. Odd she thought as she climbed the stairs that she had never seen it before today.

They found Declan slumped over a table, one hand clutching his stomach while the other pointed shakily at a beam on the ceiling. As their eyes followed his pointing finger, they froze. Inscribed on the wooden beam were the names 'Sam' and 'Adrienne' with a simple phrase that followed, "May they live forever in our hearts."

"This... this bar... The computer.... It's showing us our history, our real history," Declan stammered out, looking absolutely horrified.

Claire went white as a sheet, staggering backwards as the reality of their situation hit her. She lurched towards a trash bin just in time, the contents of her stomach emptying violently. Jamie could only stand frozen, her mind struggling to comprehend the bizarre events taking place around her. What on earth was happening? The silence in the bar was deafening, punctuated only by Claire's retching and the sound of their collective hearts pounding in their chests.

Chapter 40

Ripple in the Fabric of Time: Unraveling Secrets, Deception, and Unity

As Jamie poured them all a round of drinks, the clink of glass against glass filled the otherwise silent room. The smell of the aged whiskey permeated the air, complementing the antique aura of the bar.

"Jamie," Claire started, looking at her friend, her eyes filled with a mix of fear and anticipation, "We need to tell you something. It's going to sound crazy, but we need you to believe us."

Jamie looked at Claire, then at Declan, and back at Claire. Her face held a quizzical expression, clearly not expecting such a serious discussion this early in the day. "Okay, shoot. I'm all ears," she said, taking a slow sip of her drink.

Claire glanced at Declan, who was already downing his first drink and gesturing for another. She shook her head slightly, and proceeded to explain the strange series of events that had led them here, asking for Jamie's help. She told Jamie about the simulation and their shared visions; about the mysterious machine and the hallucinogenic substance they had discovered within the computer. She described the eerily accurate representation of the Last Liberal, and the too-coincidental pamphlet of 'The Echo' that they had come across. At the mention of the Echo, Declan chimed in, it is exactly the one we created Claire, EXACTLY THE SAME!"

And then, she explained to Jamie that the document they had found in her basement, appeared in all likelihood to be exactly the same pamphlet that they had worked on when they had been Sam and Adrienne. The document that bore the name of 'The Echo,' was the same. And of course, the unexpected revelation about the bar's original name - 'The Last Liberal.'

Jamie listened in stunned silence; her whiskey forgotten in her hand. She was too caught up in the tale, the pieces of the puzzle fitting together in her mind. She didn't interrupt, didn't ask for clarification. She just listened, her eyes growing wider with each revelation. When Claire finished speaking, the room was filled with a heavy silence.

Finally, Jamie spoke, her voice barely above a whisper, "So, you're saying...this isn't just some drug-induced hallucination, but rather...history? Our history that you are reliving in a simulation that has been created by a computer that Maddy designed in order to.... Do what exactly?" Jamie asked.

Claire took a deep breath and began to speak, "Yes, Jamie, you got it right. This is not a hallucination we think, but rather our history, a history we seem to know absolutely nothing about. The Mycelium Quantum computer was built to create a simulation that would help us understand why our current Ectogenesis program is failing to produce any children. We had tried everything, but nothing seemed to work. So, Maddy came up with the idea of creating a simulation that would allow us to observe and analyze the evolutionary process that led to the emergence of life on Earth. Declan, as an evolutionary biologist, was the perfect candidate to help with this project. The simulation was going to be designed to create a virtual environment that would mirror the conditions of early Earth. We hoped that by studying the emergence of life in this simulation, we could identify the missing piece of the puzzle that could help us fix our Ectogenesis program and finally fix the issue of no longer being able to produce children."

Claire and Declan nodded simultaneously; the weight of their discovery reflected in their eyes. They didn't know what was going on yet, but they knew one thing for sure - they were onto something far more significant than they could have ever imagined.

Seated around the bar, the three friends found themselves sinking into the worn leather stools, each nursing a drink, the cozy glow of the dimmed lights reflecting off their pensive faces. The silence was a thick cloak, wrapping them in its comforting folds as they mulled over the information they'd unearthed.

"So," Declan broke the silence, swirling the amber liquid in his glass, "How do we even begin to verify this? Is it even possible that our government... or any government for that matter, could rewrite history on such a grand scale? And for what purpose?"

Claire sighed, her fingers tracing patterns on the smooth wood of the bar. "Well, it's not entirely impossible to alter or erase historical facts. I am sure numerous regimes have done it in the past. But this... this would be manipulation on an unfathomable scale. To change the narrative of our entire planet's history..."

Jamie chimed in, her face thoughtful, "And yet, isn't that what we're already suspecting? It seems so far-fetched, and yet... here we are."

Declan grunted in agreement, his mind spinning. "But the question remains: why would they do it? What could possibly be so significant about our past that they would feel the need to erase or rewrite it?"

There was a moment's pause as they considered the weight of Declan's words. Their world felt as if it was tilting on its axis, everything they'd been taught, everything they knew about their history was now under scrutiny.

Declan broke the silence, his voice firm, "We need more proof. We need to dig deeper. This..." he gestured to the bar around them, "...this is only the beginning. We've got to find more evidence before we jump to any conclusions. And we must be discreet. If the government really is behind this, it won't be safe to attract their attention."

Taking a moment to collect her thoughts, Claire began, "In theory, everything we've experienced could be attributed to a shared illusion, a by-product of the complex interlinking of our minds facilitated by the Mycelium Quantum Computer. We could have constructed Sam and Adrienne's world from fragments of our own memories. For example, the carving Declan recognized and even the bar's name could easily be derived from our shared knowledge."

Pausing for effect, Claire looked at Jamie before she continued. "However, the concept of 'The Echo' doesn't align with this explanation. Jamie, have you ever mentioned this pamphlet to me or discussed its contents? If so, then perhaps we could chalk it all up to a sort of DMT-induced journey, an amalgamation of our collective memories. But for now, we need to keep digging, continue our exploration, and avoid jumping to premature conclusions. Our quest for truth requires more substantial evidence."

Declan and Jamie nodded in agreement. Declan truly didn't believe Claire's theory as he was convinced that what they were witnessing was something more than a hallucinogenic trip. They didn't know what lay ahead, or where their investigations would lead them, but they knew they couldn't ignore what they had discovered. The pursuit of truth, no matter how unsettling, had become their shared mission.

Unbeknownst to them, Agent Reynolds slipped quietly into the secluded bar. His sudden appearance cast an ominous shadow over the trio before they even registered his presence. Caught off guard, Claire's eyes tightened in a mix of shock and wariness. "What's your business here?" she demanded, her voice rich with intrigue and a trace of anxiety. "And how did you manage to find us?"

Reynolds offered a slight smile, his eyes sparkled with an indecipherable glint. "Well, Claire," he answered, his voice exuding an air of composure. "Didn't we agree on a noon meeting today? You left the QRDA facility earlier than I expected, and I noticed because I was watching you. I used the autonomous traffic monitoring system to track your movements and hence here I am."

Taken aback, Claire's eyebrows clenched together, showing her displeasure. She hadn't remembered their agreed meeting time and never did she predict that he would trail her. "Alright," she muttered, her tone slightly irritated and shaken at the Agent's arrival. "So, what's the topic you wanted to discuss?"

Seating himself in an empty chair, Reynolds' gaze flitted among Claire, Declan, and Jamie. "I've been monitoring your recent endeavors," he started, in a careful and measured tone. "And it appears that you've chanced upon something truly fascinating."

Claire's heart stopped beating in her chest at his statement. Intrigued, Claire leaned in closer. "What are you implying?" she queried, her voice brimming with a blend of caution, curiosity and utter fear.

Reynolds paused briefly, carefully crafting his reply. "Every government has its secrets, as you are fully aware," he elucidated. "But it seems that you've unearthed something much more profound than I could have imagined. Something that could potentially challenge our historical understanding."

Claire exchanged a look with her associates, her eyes filled with flickers of doubt. "What exactly are you suggesting?" she inquired, her voice wobbling slightly.

Leaning forward, Reynolds whispered, his gaze unyieldingly intense. "I'm suggesting," he answered, "that there are unseen powers at work, forces far beyond our understanding. To reveal the truth, we must align our efforts."

The room descended into silence as Claire, Declan, and Jamie shared uneasy glances. Their investigative instincts had brought them to this point, and now, they found themselves in the unexpected company of a potential ally. The road ahead was shrouded in uncertainty, but retreat was not an option. The quest for truth had taken a surreal twist, and the stakes had never been this high.

The sudden presence of Reynolds seemed to jolt Declan, his surprise evident as he grappled with the depth of the agent's knowledge. "What do you know, Reynolds?" Declan demanded, his voice echoing through the silence that had engulfed the room.

Reynolds hesitated, his breathing becoming heavy as he attempted to recount the events that had unfolded on the day of Dr. Peterson's demise. "The computer... it showed me things," he stuttered, struggling to find the right words to describe his experience. He spoke in a hushed tone, his voice trembling with emotion. "It was like nothing I've ever experienced before. I felt overwhelmed by waves of emotions, both positive and negative. And then there was this strange connection... a sense of unity with the cosmos that I can't even begin to explain." It was clear that Reynolds was struggling to share this tale with people he hardly knew.

Reynolds knew that he needed to gain the trust of these people in a desperate way. He needed them to understand that he was on their side in this journey. He took a deep breath and continued to recount his experience, hoping that they would listen and believe him. He knew that his story sounded unbelievable, but it was the truth. He had never felt so connected to the universe before, and he knew that there was something important about what he had experienced. He just needed their help to figure out what it all meant. Reynolds looked at them with pleading eyes, hoping that they would understand that he was not their enemy, but an ally in this strange and mysterious journey.

His gaze distant, he continued, "My fears, guilt, and regrets seemed insignificant when compared to the vast expanse of the universe, dwindling into insignificance against the backdrop of our existence."

Images of cosmic beings, archaic symbols, and geometric designs danced in front of my eyes, providing a cryptic insight into the enigmas of existence. He visualized a massive tree, its branches extending to touch the cosmos, its roots penetrating deep into the core of existence. He experienced a serenity that blanketed him, soothing his internal scars.

"I found myself engaged in dialogue with these cosmic entities, querying them, seeking wisdom and answers," Reynolds explained. "Their responses were elusive, shrouded in puzzles and metaphors, but resonated in a way that I couldn't dismiss. They advocated courage, resilience, acceptance - a need to look beyond my…. tragic past and build a brighter future."

Undoubtedly, this has been a transformative journey," Reynolds began, an undercurrent of intensity in his tone. "The past week and a bit, following my interaction with the system, has been one of the most challenging times of my life. The experience seemed to alleviate some of my buried traumas—nightmares and flashbacks reduced, a constant state of vigilance eased. The shadow of constant anxiety no longer following me everywhere.

His gaze hardened as he continued, "But it also ignited a burning need within me to understand more. To satisfy this curiosity, I resorted to using high-tech listening devices, believing that you wouldn't trust me outright. I've heard everything, your discussions, your revelations. Now, it's crystal clear to me that moving forward independently isn't an option."

Pausing for a moment to let his words sink in, he finished resolutely, "What I've come to realize is the gravity of the enigma we're grappling with and the potential consequences. Above all, I've understood that we must confront this together."

With the gravity of his revelations sinking in, Reynolds felt a pang of guilt. He confessed; his voice laced with regret. "I...I used Maddy," he admitted, the words almost a whisper. "I thought I could use her to uncover information about what was going on in the lab. I work for the Ministry of Security and Intelligence and was the lead investigator into the warning from the Cogni-Genuis processing system about the society ending event."

He swallowed hard, fighting the lump in his throat. "Little did I know," he continued, "that she had been through something profound in the computer. And when those two factors collided - my exploitation of her and her trauma - it was a recipe for disaster."

The silence that followed Agent Reynolds confession was deafening. They each grappled with their own guilt, their own regrets, their own fears, and yet, in that moment, nothing was clear to them, "So why are you here?" Jamie asked.

"I've peeked behind the curtain, seen too much of the darkness that lurks there," Reynolds continued. "It sickens me, to my core. Until I overheard your conversation earlier, I was at a loss. I didn't know where my place was, how I could make amends. But now I understand, my role is to help set things right, to help rectify the world. Because there's something you need to see and like I said I need your help in understanding what it was that I saw inside that system." His voice thickened with the weight of the secret he was about to reveal. He reached into his pocket and produced a worn, folded piece of paper. He passed it across the table, to where Claire and Declan sat, their eyes wide with anticipation.

"It's... it's Maddy's last words," he confessed, meeting their gazes squarely. The mention of Maddy's name seemed to hang in the air, like a specter that refused to fade.

A heavy silence fell over the room as Claire and Declan unfolded the note, the last piece of Maddy they had. Their eyes scanned the lines hastily scrawled in blue ink, each word a testament to a life abruptly and tragically cut short.

Dear Claire and Declan,

In the deafening silence of my room, I find myself needing to pen this letter, my thoughts need to be shared with the two people who have come to mean so much.

My memories in the Quantum Mycelium computer, the simulation that has left a gaping void in my heart, are all too fresh. I find myself struggling to reconcile the vibrancy of the world I once knew with the harsh realities of this one. I had a child, a beautiful being I nurtured with all the love I was capable of. She sprang from the depths of my consciousness, a manifestation of my deepest desires, my most profound dreams. And yet, just as quickly as she had appeared, she was gone, leaving an indelible scar on my soul.

I know you both, in your own ways, have tried to understand, to empathize. You have stood by me, unwavering, as I tried to navigate through the murky waters of my loss. But it's a loss that's mine alone, a pain unique in its intensity, and one that cannot be shared or truly understood by others. The love I felt for my child was real, as real as any emotion I've ever experienced. Yet, she was a part of a reality that is difficult to comprehend, a reality that belonged solely to me.

The ache of not having Declan share in this profound love I had experienced stings the most. He could not partake in the joy of our child's laughter, or the warmth of our shared love, or even the piercing pain of our child's sudden departure. He stands by my side, his silent support unwavering, but he's an outsider to the depths of my sorrow, a spectator to my tale of love and loss.

And it's not just the pain of losing my child that haunts me. It's the loneliness that pervades every moment since I emerged from the simulation. A crushing sense of isolation that's constantly reminding me of the life I lived there, the family I had. A life that, despite its illusory nature, felt more real to me than this world ever has. I yearn for that sense of belonging, the unconditional love that filled my days in the simulation. The absence of it in this world feels like a cruel joke played on me by the universe.

Most importantly, there's Declan. His love for me in the simulation was a balm to my aching heart. His words of comfort, his soft touch, his shared laughter - it all painted a picture of happiness that I had never thought I would experience. But the realization that this love doesn't exist in our reality is a pain I can't seem to overcome. The stark contrast between what could have been and what is, is too glaring, too painful to ignore.

Fear engulfs me as I face the uncertainty of tomorrow. I know not where I'm headed, and the path forward seems bleak. I am terrified, but also clear that I can't continue like this.

As I conclude this letter, know that I cherished our time together and appreciated your support. I leave you in the hopes that my experience serves as a reminder of the immeasurable value of love, family, and true connection.

With all the love in my heart, Maddy.

Upon reading the final words of Maddy's letter, the room fell into a shattering silence. Declan sat frozen, the worn-out paper clutched in his trembling hands. The weight of her words, her grief and isolation, tore through him. His throat felt tight, a rush of emotion surging, choking him.

He had always known there was a shift in Maddy's behavior since the simulation, a distance he couldn't understand or bridge. He felt like an outsider peering in on a secret world, a shared experience that he was not part of. Maddy's pain and longing, her poignant love for their virtual child, was a world he'd been excluded from. And the agony of that was more overwhelming than he could bear.

Tears welled up in his eyes, blurring his vision. He tried to swallow down the lump in his throat, but it was too late. The dam broke, and a sob tore through him, releasing the flood of pent-up emotions he'd been holding back. He was swept up in a wave of grief, guilt, and longing. The force of his tears shook him as he wept openly, the letter crumpled in his grip.

As his tears soaked into the paper, the heart-wrenching finality of it all crashed over him. Maddy was gone. The world she'd lived in the simulation, the family they'd had there, the love that had blossomed – it was all out of his reach, an experience that Maddy alone had endured. All he was left with was the ghost of a love that he hadn't known, and a heartrending void where Maddy had once been.

Declan was not merely grieving for Maddy. He was mourning the shared life and love that he had not experienced in a world that was not their own, a life that seemed more real to Maddy than their reality. He was grieving for the profound connection that had been lost in translation between the virtual and real worlds. The pain of that loss, and the bitter knowledge that he was a mere spectator to Maddy's sorrow, left him feeling more alone than ever.

In the quiet aftermath of his tearful breakdown, Declan was left to navigate the storm of emotions within him. But for now, he let the tears fall, a silent testament to the magnitude of his grief.

Chapter 41

The Undercurrents of Deceit

It took a considerable amount of time before Declan and Claire managed to stem their tears, the weight of Maddy's final words resonating deep within them, evoking a sorrow they couldn't immediately shake off. Even Jamie, who had barely known Maddy, found herself moved by her story, shedding tears for the girl and the profound loss she had experienced.

Agent Reynolds, the bearer of the heart-wrenching news, gave them time to process their emotions before he proceeded. When the sobs had finally subsided into occasional sniffles, he drew in a deep breath and started speaking. "I believe the investigation was halted because of Dr. Peterson's death," he said, his gaze steady on the trio. "It was not the computer that caught their attention but something else, something they believed he may have seen at the time."

"The day of the accident, the day Declan first met Dr. Peterson, something unusual happened. The Autonomous Navigation System recorded an anomaly, a blip in the data that coincided precisely with the accident that you witnessed," Reynolds' eyes hardened as he looked at them. "I believe the alarm we have been getting on the CGPT system is due to the computer and what it can do. But because of this accident and their belief that Dr. Peterson saw something in the programming that could have been damaging to them, they ceased the investigation thinking the danger had been averted with his death.

Reynolds paused, giving the trio time to digest his revelations. "The government has been keeping a close eye on this situation," he resumed, his gaze now resting on Declan. "When Dr. Peterson died, they called off the investigation, probably assuming whatever he knew died with him. But the alarm hasn't stopped. They've only temporarily looked away, and it won't be long before they, or someone like me, come sniffing around again."

Silence fell as Reynolds concluded his revelations. His words hung heavily in the air, a tangible embodiment of the impending storm. "Dr. Peterson's death was only a brief respite," Reynolds reiterated, his voice a low rumble, "We need to get ahead of this before they come knocking again."

Declan, his mind working through the information Reynolds had provided, broke the silence. "So, they think Dr. Peterson saw something that day? The day of the accident, the day all of those kids died on the bus?" He hesitated for a moment, collecting his thoughts. "It was something to do with an older vehicle, not registered on the system, causing the crash. Is that right?" Declan asked Reynolds, seeking confirmation on his understanding of the complexity of the situation.

Reynolds paused for a moment, then began to speak again. "I'm not sure who it was, but it was someone high up in the Heritage Alliance driving that night. The information I uncovered from the Autonomous Traffic System, the system that controls all of the cities automobiles, was... disturbing."

He swallowed, continuing, "The car involved in the crash was registered in the system, but it appears the person driving had manually overridden the autonomous controls. It seems that certain individuals within the party have the capability to do this. I was informed of this in order to help divert any arising inquiries."

Reynolds looked at them solemnly, "As you know, the system is designed for maximum efficiency and safety. In an incident like an animal appearing on the road or a vehicle breaking down, the system can make trillions of decisions in mere seconds to minimize loss of life. However, it seems that high ranking officials have an override function assigned to them specifically. In a problematic situation, the system is programmed to prioritize their safety above all else."

He hesitated before delivering the next blow, "On that night, 24 children and 6 adults died... all to protect one person. I ran a simulation of the accident. If the system had not been manipulated to preserve the life of that single party member, everyone would have survived. The only catch would be the party member potentially suffering life-threatening injuries... but that's just potential."

As Reynolds ended his explanation, a grim silence filled the room. The enormity of the revelations and the sheer inhumanity of the decisions made were overwhelming. The system that was designed to protect all, had been misused to preserve one at the expense of many. The implications were horrifying and the understanding of their situation had taken a turn for the worse.

Claire blinked, trying to process the information. She finally found her voice, "So, are you saying Dr. Peterson was killed because he might have uncovered this secret?"

Reynolds nodded grimly, "That's correct. The system registered him logging in right after the crash. However, it couldn't conclusively determine whether he had accessed the code or not. The system estimated there was a less than 5% chance that he knew about the override function and the tragic consequences. But even that minimal risk was enough for someone to decide he needed to be removed."

A heavy silence hung in the room, the implications of Reynolds' words sinking in. The esteemed Dr. Peterson hadn't just suffered an unfortunate stroke, but potentially murdered because he might have discovered a secret. A secret that had cost dozens of innocent lives.

"But," Declan interrupted, his voice strained, "Dr. Peterson had a stroke. He wasn't killed..."

Reynolds met his gaze, a grim expression on his face. "That's the official story, Declan. But with what we now know, we have to question everything. Remember, we're dealing with powerful individuals who wouldn't hesitate to eliminate threats to their interests." The grim reality hung in the air like a thick fog, chilling everyone to the bone. The complexity of their situation had grown exponentially, the stakes raised to an unfathomable height.

Reynolds shifted in his seat, rubbing his temples before continuing. "Let's not forget about the drones that patrol our skies. Their primary purpose is to calculate and observe for the Autonomous Navigation System, true, but their secondary functions are less well known and far more lethal."

He glanced at Declan and Claire, his eyes reflecting the weight of his words. "The military has equipped some of these drones with specialized weaponry. One such tool is an incredibly thin, razor-sharp needle. When launched with precision, it can penetrate a target's skin, delivering a fatal dose of toxins. To the untrained eye, it would appear as if the victim died of natural causes, such as a heart attack or stroke."

Reynolds paused for a moment, allowing the implication to settle in the room. "In essence," he resumed, "these drones can be used to eliminate threats discreetly, with little to no evidence pointing back to the perpetrator. The needle is so small and the wound so insignificant, only a handful of people trained to look for this would even suspect foul play."

The room was filled with an eerie silence as the trio absorbed Reynolds' chilling revelation. The drones they saw every day, benign watchers of the skies, now took on a sinister aspect in the light of these revelations. Their seemingly innocuous presence now cast an ominous shadow over their understanding of the world they lived in.

Jamie looked stricken, her face pale under the harsh lighting. "I... I just can't believe this," she stammered, her eyes wide. "Killer drones, assassinations, secret military projects... I thought we were living in the most civilized time in history. And military? Why do we even need a military?"

Reynolds gave her a grave look. "Because not everyone sees the Heritage Alliance as being just. They believe the party has overstepped its boundaries. There are factions out there, outside of our city, the country that hold rebellious tendencies."

"What? Are you saying there are wars being fought right now?" Jamie's voice was a trembling whisper, her hands clenched tightly in her lap.

"Not wars, per se," Reynolds explained, his tone somber. "The party has managed to neutralize most of the dissenting voices. But there are still those in the farming pods and the outlying areas that harbour rebellion. It's a quiet resistance, but resistance nonetheless."

Jamie looked at him, her confusion evident. "How do you know all this?"

Reynolds sighed, his eyes filled with regret. "I was bred for war," he admitted. "While you and Claire attended the Central Childhood Education & Care Facility, I went to a different type of school - the Unseen Vigilance Training Center. Only the top graduates, those who survived four to five tours of duty, are offered the chance to serve the party in a different capacity. I was given a commission at the Ministry of Security and Intelligence, where almost all of its employees are service members."

The room fell silent again, the weight of the secrets revealed pressing down upon them. They were left grappling with the reality of the world they lived in and the terrifying future they now faced.

Turning to Declan, Reynolds' gaze was filled with curiosity and a hint of suspicion. "Declan," he started, "I've been wondering about something... You're quite an enigma. I've tried to dig up information on you, but it seems like you just appeared out of nowhere before your time at the University of Amora. You have no documented history that I could find."

Reynolds leaned back, his eyes never leaving Declan's face. "I'm not sure if you are aware, but when this investigation began, I was explicitly told by my superior, Martinez, that your past was not relevant to the case and should be left alone. The way he said it... It was as if he knew you personally. So, who are you, Declan? What's your story? And why is it that someone wants your history buried?"

Declan shifted uncomfortably under Reynolds' intense scrutiny. The room was heavy with anticipation as everyone turned to him, waiting for his response. The silence stretched, becoming a palpable presence in the room. Finally, he drew a deep breath, his gaze steady as he met Reynolds' questioning eyes, prepared to unveil his own past, a past he had long kept hidden.

Declan exhaled slowly, the weight of his unspoken secret pressing heavily on his chest. "My... my father is a high-ranking member of the political party," he confessed, his gaze never wavering from Reynolds' eyes. The room plunged into stunned silence as his words echoed ominously.

The first to react was Claire. "Wait, what? How?" she stuttered; her eyes wide with shock. "You have parents? A father, a mother? Like a traditional family? But...but they don't exist!"

Declan offered her a pained smile, his heart aching at the confusion etched on her face. "They do, Claire," he said quietly, his voice barely more than a whisper. "But only among the political elite."

Reynolds leaned forward; his interest piqued. "What are you saying, Declan?" he asked, his voice laced with caution.

Drawing in a deep breath, Declan continued, "Children of the elite are engineered using the DNA from their mothers and fathers. They're meant to be leaders, chosen ones, if you will. They're not birthed in the conventional sense; they still use the same Ectogenesis program, but they do have biological parents in a sense."

His revelation was met with incredulous silence as the group grappled with the magnitude of this disclosure. A whole new world, a privileged class of traditional families concealed within the ranks of the political elite, had been unveiled, shattering their understanding of the society they lived in.

"My father and I had a falling out," Declan confessed, his voice thick with years of buried emotions. "He wanted me to follow in his footsteps, to enter politics, to carry on the family legacy. But I refused. I rebelled. Instead of taking the path set out for me, I decided to go to school for something my father considered... useless."

His fingers traced the surface of the table, a strange sort of calm washing over him as he shared his story. "To avoid any potential scandals, they probably concealed my background. The political elite don't attend the same schools as the rest of us. They have their own institutions, ones that are carefully guarded and hidden from the public eye."

Declan paused, looking at each person present in turn, as if gauging their reactions. "Has it ever occurred to any of you that you've never seen a high-ranking party official who attended the Central Childhood Education & Care Facility? Or anyone you went to school with who later became a prominent figure in politics? That's because they have their own circle, their own world."

His voice dropped lower, almost to a whisper, as he added, "My parents haven't spoken to me since I left their world. My choosing a different path was seen as a betrayal, one they've never forgiven."

His admission left a silence in its wake, a quiet acknowledgment of the complexity and secrecy that pervaded their society and their lives. His story, far removed from their own experiences, offered a new perspective on the clandestine dynamics of their world's political structure.

Jamie looked absolutely shell-shocked, her eyes wide and unblinking as she absorbed the gravity of their revelations. "This has not been a good day," she muttered, her voice just a notch above a whisper. "I woke up in what I thought was an amazing city, a pinnacle of civilization, and now... it's all a lie."

Claire, however, seemed to be in deep thought. She turned to Declan, her gaze intense and probing. "Declan, do you have any idea about a past that has been hidden from us? Why would they hide it? The past we saw in the simulation appeared far worse than our current reality, but there were elements like race, class systems, and privilege that, while seemingly absent in our society, might still be lurking beneath the surface."

Declan shrugged, his expression unreadable. "I can't say for sure. I haven't seen any indication of racial differentiation here, but then again, there appears to be a lot that's been hidden from us, if what we are seeing is in fact our own past."

Claire continued her line of inquiry, her voice laced with a newfound determination. "In the simulation, if it was indeed our past, they separated people by race into different zones in the city. Could the same be happening now, just on a larger scale? Maybe that's why we haven't noticed it. Maybe it's so deeply ingrained in our system, so cleverly hidden, that we don't even realize it's happening."

Jamie sat quietly, taking in Claire's words. She'd been part of this system her entire life, content with the teachings that everyone had a specific role, a unique contribution to the community. It was as natural to her as breathing. But now, considering Claire's theory, she felt a pang of uncertainty.

"Isn't our society different?" Jamie asked, her gaze focused on the far wall, mind elsewhere. "We've been taught that everyone has a part to play, that our positions are determined based on skill, not something as arbitrary as race or birthright."

"But we don't know much about those living in the farming communities, do we?" Claire countered. "We've always assumed that they're just like us because they're contributing to the same communal purpose. But what if it's more than just communal roles that separate us?"

Jamie pondered this, a frown creasing her forehead. "You're suggesting that there might be a racial element to the separations? That the farming communities...they could be a different race?" It was a heavy thought, and it unsettled her.

"What if there are entire aspects of our society that we're blind to, simply because we're not supposed to know?" Claire pressed. She was now fully committed to this line of thought. It was as if a veil had been lifted, revealing a world fraught with more complexities than they were led to believe.

The idea was unnerving, yet it compelled them. A hidden past, a potentially segregated society – suddenly, the world they knew seemed much bigger, and far more complex. It was an idea that once seen, couldn't be unseen. And with it, the seeds of doubt were sown, and their quest for truth ignited.

Chapter 42

The Seeds of Doubt

"From now on, call me Mike," Reynolds interrupted, his voice stern. "I have a feeling 'Agent' won't be fitting for much longer. I want you all to understand the danger we're in." He leaned in, hands resting on the table, looking intently at each one of them. "The Cogni-Genuis Processing Technology, (CGPT), it's more than what it seems," Mike explained, running a hand through his hair as he chose his words carefully. "It's an advanced artificial intelligence system. It watches everything. It knows everything. It's like an all-seeing eye that scrutinizes every little detail, every blip in the data. It predicts societal changes, hazards, and potential threats. And now it's flagged a societal changing event. The more I delved into what you are up to the more I understand why."

Mike paused, allowing his words to sink in. He resumed, his voice an urgent whisper, "We need to strategize. We need to decide our next steps, how we are going to protect ourselves. This is not something we can ignore or wish away. It will come for us, because we're privy to information that could disrupt the very fabric of this society."

Mike's eyes met each of theirs in turn, his gaze imploring and earnest. "If this information is revealed, it could incite a revolution, a backlash against those who control and manipulate us. And we've seen that this government doesn't hesitate to remove threats to its existence. We need to figure out how to go underground, to disappear. Because right now, we're squarely in the line of fire."

His words echoed in the room, the gravity of their situation palpable. The quartet found themselves on the brink of an abyss, their once ordinary lives irrevocably altered by the truths they had uncovered. Now, they had to navigate their way forward in this new world of secrets, conspiracies, and imminent danger.

"Mike," Declan started, his voice breaking the heavy silence, his gaze steady as he locked eyes with the former agent, "why are you with us? Why are you not standing beside your colleagues in the agency?"

Mike sighed heavily, leaning back in his chair and crossing his arms over his chest. "Declan," he began, his voice softer than it had been just moments ago. "Everything that has happened with Maddy, with Dr. Peterson...it's caused a seismic shift within me. A moral break, if you will."

He paused, looking down at his hands as he grappled with the enormity of his confession. "I've spent most of my life in service of a system I believed in. But the things I've seen, the things I've had to do... they have painted a picture I can no longer turn a blind eye to. The system is not what I thought it was. It's not what it claims to be."

Mike looked back up, meeting Declan's gaze squarely. "I can't be a part of it anymore, not when I know the truth. I can't bear the thought of continuing to contribute to a system that goes against everything I believe in. I'd rather... I'd rather not exist at all."

His voice dropped to a whisper, and he looked around at the others in the room, his gaze solemn. "What's happening here, in this room, with that computer - it's the only hope I see for change. For setting things right. So that's why I'm here. Because I need to believe that it's possible to fix the system, even if it means turning against it."

The reality of Mike's revelation weighed heavily on them. Claire, ever the pragmatist, broke the silence, her voice low, "Are you certain they'll come after us? What if we just... destroy the system?"
Mike shook his head, a sigh escaping his lips, "Honestly, I don't know. We could destroy it, but I can't assure you that it would change anything. We really are not sure what the system is thinking or why the warning is coming at all. It could be the scenario which it feared has already happened."
They fell silent again, the magnitude of the situation descending upon them. The idea of erasing the Quantum Mycelium Computer was tempting, but it brought its own set of uncertainties and dangers. Claire and Declan were positive that it held the answers they were looking for in regards to the Ectogenesis program and if that didn't get fixed they were all doomed as it was. They had stepped into a minefield, and any misstep could be catastrophic.
Jamie, always the quickest to express her feelings, looked pale and tense. "So... what do we do?" She asked, her voice barely more than a whisper. "How do we navigate this?"
In the thick tension that filled the room, Declan suddenly stood up, a determined look on his face. "I'm going to see my father," he declared, looking at each of them in turn. "If there's anyone who can give us answers, it's him."
His decision brought a new wave of uncertainty but also a glimmer of hope. Perhaps they were not entirely alone in this fight. Perhaps Declan's connection to the inner circle of the political elite could provide them with some leverage, some protection. They needed answers, and they needed them quickly.
Mike swiftly got up, stopping Declan in his tracks. "Wait, let's not rush into anything," he cautioned, his tone firm. "Approaching your father with these suspicions could trigger unforeseen consequences. We need to be strategic, not reactionary."

He walked over to a table, pulling out a chair and motioning for Declan to sit. "First things first," he continued, "we need an exit strategy. We need to plan a way to get out of here quickly, quietly, and safely, if it comes down to it."
His gaze then fell on Claire as he thought of the Quantum computer, its sleek design deceptive of the wealth of information it held. "And we're going to need to take your Quantum computer with us," he added, "It's more than just a tool—it's a key. If there's a chance to make a change to this government, to this system, it's going to start with that machine."
A silence fell over them as the magnitude of what lay ahead began to sink in. They were not just battling an unjust system anymore—they were risking their lives for a cause that felt bigger than themselves. This was no longer about curiosity or ambition; it was about survival, truth, and hopefully, about change.
Mike folded his arms, his brow creased as he processed the gravity of their situation. "I have a plan," he said finally, "but it's going to require a certain amount of trust from all of you."
His gaze shifted to each of them in turn and settled on Claire. "That machine of yours," he began, "it's not something we can just pick up and run with, is it? When I saw it last, it seemed fairly large and looked like it required a significant amount of power."
Claire nodded in agreement, her eyes narrowing thoughtfully. "Yes, it is quite big. But," she added, "it seems to have become more self-sufficient in its technical specifications. I've tried to kill it, tried to cut off its power source. But it stayed active. It remained... alive." She seemed hesitant, uncertain as she used the word.
Alive. The word hung in the air, thick with implications that none of them wanted to fully confront. Mike merely nodded, digesting this new piece of information. They had their work cut out for them, but at least now, they had a direction.
"All right," Mike started, his tone firm, "We have a lot to do, and time is not on our side. Let's break it down into steps."
"Step one, we have to find a way to stay off the CGPT system's radar. This includes losing any tracking devices we might be

carrying, altering our daily patterns, and using only secured communication lines. I will get some encrypted radios from work and find a way to remove our identification chips"
"Step two, we need to move the Quantum computer to a secure and off-grid location. Since it's no longer dependent on an external power source, this might be easier than it seems. We'll just need to figure out a way to transport it without arousing suspicion."
"Step three, we need to reach out to Declan's father. He's high up in the party hierarchy, and he might be able to provide some useful information or assistance. However, we need to approach him cautiously to prevent alerting anyone who might be watching him, if they are watching."
"Step four, we need to prepare for a potential backlash. There's a good chance the Party will notice our movements before long, so we need to be ready to defend ourselves. We'll need supplies, safe houses, and potentially allies and we need to do it quickly."
"Finally, step five, we need to start gathering evidence of what the government has done. The best weapon against an oppressive regime is the truth. If we can prove that the Party was willing to sacrifice 24 children and 6 adults just to save one member, we could incite a revolution."
Each step held its own dangers, but together they formed a plan. Now, all they had to do was act on it, before it was too late.
Mike paced back and forth, fine-tuning the details of his plan. "In order to buy us some time, I can make it look like I'm reopening the investigation. I can claim that Declan or Claire received some sensitive information from Dr. Peterson before his death. It's not a stretch to suggest he might've shared some details about his work."
Turning to Declan and Claire, he continued, "This will serve two purposes. First, it will keep the Ministry of Security and Intelligence focused on the investigation, instead of what we're really doing. Second, it gives me a plausible reason to move the Quantum computer. I'll claim we're seizing it for further

examination. This will get it out of its current location and, hopefully, out of immediate danger."
He glanced at Declan, his expression serious. "While I'm arranging the move, Declan, you can approach your father. Ask him the questions you need answers to. But remember, be cautious. Don't reveal more than you have to. And as soon as you leave him, we run. We don't look back."

Mike paused, taking a moment to let his plan sink in. "We'll head into the country. My identification grants me some level of freedom to move around, but once we're out of the city, we need to lay low. The Autonomous Navigation System drones aren't in use in rural areas, and the vehicles' autopilot systems will take over."
As he concluded, he looked at each of them, his gaze steady. "It's risky, but it's the best shot we've got. We need to act fast, and we need to act together. Are you with me?"
Claire listened intently to Mike's plan, her face pale and her eyes wide with apprehension. She gave a slow nod of agreement to his words, but when the discussion turned towards moving the Quantum computer, she shot up from her seat in alarm.
"No, no, no!" she blurted out, her hands flailing. "You don't understand, Mike. We can't just...move the Quantum computer like it's some old piece of furniture. It's not that simple!"
She began to pace back and forth, wringing her hands together as she spoke, "Our computer...it's a Myco-Quantum computer. The breakthrough came with the discovery of a new species of fungus, Mycelium quantus. This species exhibited extraordinary properties that, when subjected to particular stimuli, behaved in ways that mimicked the superposition and entanglement of quantum bits or 'qubits'."
Seeing the confusion on Mike's face, Claire took a deep breath and continued, "It's a living, biological entity, Mike. Certain nodes of the mycelium, or 'myco-qubits', naturally enter a state of quantum superposition under specific environmental conditions.

And we manipulate the state of these myco-qubits by sending precise biochemical signals through the network."
She paused for a moment, her gaze distant, "But it's delicate. Maintaining the quantum superposition of the myco-qubits requires careful environmental control. Specific temperature, humidity, nutrient conditions...and it's still susceptible to quantum decoherence from environmental factors."
Claire stopped her pacing and turned to face the others, "We built this computer from scratch, Mike. We designed a variant of the mycelium that increased its sensitivity to our biochemical signals and could maintain its quantum properties at higher temperatures. And even then, it's...it's not something you can just unplug and pack away. It's not a machine, it's...it's alive."
She looked at each person in the room, desperation in her eyes, "We have to figure out a way to move it without damaging it. And we have to do it without letting anyone know what we're up to."
Jamie, who had been unusually quiet during the intense conversation, suddenly raised her hand with a crooked smile on her face. She cleared her throat dramatically before saying, "Alright guys, I know this is all very...serious," she waved her hand vaguely, "And I don't know the first thing about quantum computers, mycelium or...really any of this stuff."
She glanced at Claire and shrugged, "All I know is that we have a super fancy computer that's made of a mushroom, and apparently, it's our key to survival. So I guess you could say...we've really put the 'fun' in 'fungus'!"
Her comment was met with a beat of stunned silence before she added, "Get it? Because 'fun' is in the word 'fungus' and it's kind of like a pun and..."
Jamie's voice trailed off, her smirk faltering as she realized her attempt at humor had landed with a deafening thud. She coughed awkwardly and muttered under her breath, "Well, I thought it was funny... and it certainly appears as if we need to laugh a little."

The rest of the room was silent for a moment before Mike chuckled, a genuine laugh that seemed to break the tension. "We really do need to lighten up," he admitted. "Thanks for that, Jamie."
Declan, still stunned by the heaviness of the discussion, managed a weak smile at Jamie's attempt to lighten the mood. Still, his mind was elsewhere. He needed to see his father. He was sure his father would have some information, some advice that could help them.

After Mike's little quip, the room settled into a subdued calm. This was a moment of respite, a collective catching of breath before they plunged into their daunting mission.

Chapter 43

Quantum Shadows: Unveiling the All-Seeing Eye

One evening, as they gathered in the familiar haze of the bar, Claire voiced a question that had been lingering in their minds for a while. She turned to Agent Reynolds and asked, "Why are you helping us, Reynolds? And more importantly, why should we trust you? I know you told us but I feel like I need more, I want more information for my brain to be able to bridge the gap between enemy and friend. I am afraid I still look up and instinctually it screams, enemy."

Reynolds paused, he had not heard any of them refer to him as Agent in days and was caught off guard, he regarded Claire with a measured look. His response was slow, deliberate. "Maddy's death... it hit me harder than I expected," he began. The room fell silent, the usual hum of their discussions giving way to an attentive quiet.

"I came up with the plan to pressure her, I thought I could break her by first arresting Jamie and then scaring her into talking. It is almost laughable now, thinking back, our suspicions of the three of you and what was going on was no where near close to the truth" he continued, "And then to see her go like that…." He paused, his gaze dropping to the half-empty glass before him.

"But what happened to Dr. Peterson... that was the last straw. To know that he was killed by the very people I work for..."

Reynolds trailed off, shaking his head slightly as if dispelling a persistent thought.

The hardened agent let out a hollow laugh, the sound echoing in the silence of the bar. "I guess there's a breaking point to morals after all," he mused, a bitter smile curling his lips. "And here I thought I didn't have any."

The atmosphere in the room shifted subtly as they digested Reynolds' words. His admission offered them a glimpse into the moral conflict that was churning within him, the struggle of a man grappling with the reality of his past actions and the harsh consequences of his loyalty. His decision to help them was not born from a tactical standpoint, but from a newfound moral compass that had been jarred into existence by the harsh realities he'd faced.

In the wake of Reynolds' confession, the group couldn't help but conjure up an image of a glass, a vessel for trauma. Each event he'd recounted, each horrifying revelation, was like a drop of water being added to his cup.

Maddy's death, Peterson's murder, the betrayal of his superiors, each filled the glass a bit more, adding weight and substance, creating a mounting pressure that was both tangible and terrible. For years, Reynolds had been the sturdy vessel, accepting each droplet of hardship and devastation, stoically bearing the weight of each additional load.

But the capacity of the glass was finite, and the stream of moral injuries didn't cease. As the relentless tide of the darker side of his occupation swelled, the contents within the glass did too, until the surface tension could no longer hold, and the trauma overflowed. That moment of overflow, it seemed, had prompted Reynolds' defection, his decision to stand by them against the very organization he'd served.

There was a silent understanding within the group that Reynolds' glass had not just overflowed; it had shattered, shattered by the harsh realities he'd been forced to face. He was no longer the unyielding, impassive Agent Reynolds they had imagined he was in his past. Instead, he was a man reborn in the crucible of his own conscience, a man willing to challenge the system he had once been part of.

It was a sobering realization, one that injected a new depth of trust into Claire and their ragtag team. Their circumstances had thrust them together, but it was this new shared understanding of the stark reality of their world, their mutual disillusionment, that had started to truly bind them. Claire acknowledged Mike's explanation and the look she shared with him conveyed there would be no more questions about his loyalty.

"Alright," Mike began, standing up and pacing around the room. "We need to plan. We need to figure out how we're going to seize the computer, how we're going to move around without being tracked, and what we're going to do when we leave the city. And we have to do all this without alerting the authorities."

"First, the computer," Mike continued, turning to Claire. "You're our tech expert. You need to figure out how we're going to get it out of the lab without actually destroying it.

"Next, our digital IDs," Mike said, rolling up his sleeve to show a small, embedded device on his forearm. "These are attached to our personal accounts, location trackers, health records, everything. It's how the government keeps tabs on us. We need to find a way to deactivate them temporarily. I will ask quietly at work if anyone knows of someone doing it and how it was done. People won't suspect anything if I tell them I have lost an asset that I am looking for. "

"We need to be careful with this," added Jamie. "If we just remove them, our sudden disappearance from the system will more than likely raise some red flags. We need a way to make it look like a glitch or accident and do it preferably as we are leaving the city."

Mike cast a thoughtful gaze towards Declan, his brows knitting together as he formed his next thoughts. "We need all the help we can get," he began, allowing the weight of the situation to settle into his words. "I'm wondering, Declan... Do you believe your father has contacts who might assist us? Surely in his position, he's crossed paths with individuals who aren't too scrupulous about bending the rules?"

Declan's gut tightened, a sharp pang of guilt piercing through him. He knew, without a doubt, what his father's reaction would be. He wouldn't lift a finger to help them. More likely, he would be the one who'd sound the alarm, a bitter irony considering the circumstances. As the question was asked, he found himself subconsciously shaking his head 'no', a silent confession that belied the turmoil churning within him.

A hint of puzzlement edged its way into Mike's features as he studied Declan's expression. "If that's the case, then why expose us to the risk of meeting him? Why go see him at all?" he probed, his concern evident.

Declan paused, mulling over his response, his gaze distantly fixed on a spot on the wall as his mind wandered through the labyrinth of possible outcomes. "I believe my father may have the answers we seek," he finally said, his voice strained. "And while my father is a lost cause, my mother... she may just surprise us," he contemplated, a glimmer of hope sparking in his otherwise weary eyes.

The discourse of that day's assembly gradually unwound into the evening, with each participant pouring over every minute detail of their audacious plan. Despite the mounting tension, they preserved a semblance of normalcy, each taking turns in the mundane tasks of meal preparation and clean-up, as if attempting to ground themselves in the reassuring rhythm of daily life amidst the chaos.

Their chosen place of meeting, the loft above the Last Liberal, transformed into a nerve center of activity. Within its walls, the co-conspirators huddled each night under the cloak of darkness, pooling their thoughts and resources together in the determined pursuit of freedom.

Although the conclusion of the inaugural gathering marked the end of a tense day, it was merely the commencement of several days to follow. Night after night, they returned to their clandestine headquarters above the bar, diligently plotting and planning, refining their strategies, and steeling themselves for the unfathomable challenges that lay ahead.

Finally, Mike discussed their plans for leaving the city. "We need to lay low, avoid high-traffic areas. Maybe we can find a safe house or someplace remote to hide. Once we have the computer and can move without being tracked, we need to get out of here."

As the meeting went on, they discussed every detail meticulously. They took turns preparing meals, cleaning up, and continuing to live their day-to-day lives while constantly planning. They used the upstairs of the Last Liberal to meet and get things organized.

They collected various items of value, knowing that once their digital IDs were deactivated, their digital currency would be inaccessible. This included vintage electronics, which in their era of technology were considered collector's items and held a high value. Old coins from by-gone eras, and precious metals like gold and silver were also among the items they hoarded. Jamie almost added the brooch she had found to the pile as it must be made of some sort of precious metal but instead found herself pinning it to her jacket.

The items were chosen carefully. In addition to being valuable, they needed to be small and easily portable, as space would be limited during their escape. Most importantly, these items had to be universally accepted for trade in a world that was so heavily reliant on digital transactions. In the right markets, their value could be higher than their digital counterparts.

For more practical needs, they amassed a range of resources to sustain them. Non-perishable food items were on top of the list - canned goods, dried fruits, and vacuum-sealed meals. Water purification tablets and portable filters were procured to ensure safe drinking water in the absence of reliable sources.

Medical supplies were another priority. They secured basic first aid items like bandages, antiseptics, and a range of over-the-counter medicines for common ailments. But they also made an effort to obtain more specific supplies like insulin, antibiotics, and painkillers. Jamie had a contact in the medical industry who helped them procure these items discreetly. These were gathered as another form of currency if they found they needed to trade them rather than use the items themselves.

For their inevitable departure, they put together 'bug-out bags' - backpacks packed with all the essentials they would need in an emergency. These were kept ready, each person's bag personalized to their needs and capabilities.

Despite their preparation, they knew they couldn't account for everything. They would face challenges; they would have to adapt. But that was something they would tackle together, as a team, when the time came.

The atmosphere in the upper parts of the bar had changed dramatically. Every conversation, every action was now weighed down by the gravity of their mission. The everyday mundanity was tinted with an undercurrent of urgency and purpose. They were no longer just friends – they were a team with a mission to save the world.

Chapter 44

Race Against time

Not two days later, Agent 'Mike' Reynolds received a summons to Minister Martinez's office. The notification sent a chill down his spine, sparking a rush of anxiety that he struggled to suppress. It wasn't his own safety that triggered his fear, rather the well-being of his newfound allies and burgeoning friends.

Being summoned to this man's office again was unsettling. The memories of Dr. Peterson's callous removal were still raw and stinging; vivid images that served as an acute reminder of the ruthlessness that could be directed towards those who stepped out of line.

Upon his arrival, Martinez's assistant wasted no time, sweeping him into the office as soon as he spotted him in the hallway. The urgency with which he was ushered towards the imposing figure behind the desk sent warning signals ricocheting in his mind. This haste did not bode well, he thought to himself as he was propelled towards the man who now elicited nothing but a profound sense of revulsion from him.

Martinez looked up from the digital documents projected onto his desk, his cold eyes meeting Reynolds'. The brief moment of silence that hung in the air was laden with anticipation, and in the pit of his stomach, Reynolds felt a creeping dread.

Martinez cut to the chase without preamble, his tone razor-sharp. "Reynolds, why am I still seeing logged hours investigating the Quantum Research and Development agency's scientists?" He leaned back in his chair, the silent authority of his position radiating from him. "I was under the impression that we had put this matter to bed over a week ago. Why are you not following my directions?"

Reynolds had anticipated this line of questioning and swiftly delivered his prepared response. "Sir, I stumbled upon some peculiarities in the data," he stated smoothly, keeping his expression neutral. "It appeared there might have been information that Dr. Peterson may have passed on to other lab members. I just wanted to ensure that everything was, indeed, taken care of."

However, the unwavering gaze of Martinez didn't ease up, a clear indication that he wasn't entirely convinced by the answer. The tension thickened in the room, and Reynolds quickly tagged on an additional explanation.

"Furthermore," he added, a slight edge creeping into his voice, "The Cogni-Genuis Processing system has still not fully eliminated the threat that initially raised our concerns. I thought it would be prudent to keep all avenues secure before dropping the investigation completely."

There was a momentary silence as Martinez considered Reynolds' explanations, his steely gaze never leaving the agent's face. The next moments would dictate the course of their clandestine operation, and Reynolds could only hope his words had been convincing enough.

Martinez's eyebrows furrowed as he processed the information about the CGPT system. "Are we certain this isn't just a glitch as Minister Wells suggested could happen?" he queried, steepling his fingers together in thought.

"I can't say for sure, Sir," Reynolds admitted, riding on the wave of honesty. "However, Minister Wells hasn't yet provided us with the investigational documents she promised would clarify the situation."

This was, in fact, the truth and a convenient omission that Reynolds had forgotten until now. Its unexpected utility bolstered the credibility of his ruse, giving him a little more room to breathe.

A thoughtful silence settled over the room as Martinez digested this new piece of information. There was a marked change in his demeanor, the seeds of doubt planted successfully. Reynolds, however, knew better than to let down his guard. He had played his hand, now it was time to see if Martinez would call his bluff.

A flicker of concern crossed Martinez's face as he continued his musings on the CGPT system. "So it is still issuing a society-ending event related to the QRDA? Has there been any change that you're aware of?" he asked, his gaze sharp.

"Not that I know of, sir," Reynolds responded, maintaining his calm facade.

Martinez's expression deepened in perplexity. "This makes no sense, unless... Peterson's death didn't stop the warning?"

"No, Sir."

Martinez leaned back in his chair, the wheels of his mind visibly turning. "Now that I think of it, Peterson's name was never mentioned in the warning... It was Claire Cairns and Declan... What's his last name again, Reynolds?"

"Sutton, sir... Declan Sutton."

The name seemed to ring alarm bells in Martinez's mind. He blinked rapidly, looking up at Reynolds with a startled expression. "Are you sure, Reynolds? Declan Sutton? No, that can't be... he's a Biologist at some university, he doesn't work for the QRDA."

Reynolds, forgetting himself in the moment, interjected quickly. "He was transferred a few months ago into their employ, sir. A special request from Peterson. He was actually in the car the day of the incident."

This revelation caused Martinez to bolt upright from his chair, his face draining of color. "You are sure? He was in the car? It was his name from the beginning, not Peterson's... We were so focused on one thing, we missed the obvious," he muttered, more to himself than to Reynolds.

Abruptly, he waved a dismissive hand towards Reynolds. "You're excused, Reynolds. I need to make some calls." The look in his eyes was one of cold, sobering realization. A new chapter in their investigation was beginning.

A few moments after leaving Martinez's office, Reynolds discreetly pulled out a small, flat device from his pocket. It was a quantum phone, a new device in the black market designed with quantum encryption protocols, making it nearly impossible for third parties to intercept communications. Mike had acquired them and had given one to each member of the party a few days prior as part of their emergency contingency plans.

He quickly dialed the number that would connect him to Declan, each tone of the dialed buttons amplifying his anxiety. After a couple of rings, Declan picked up.

"Declan, we need to move now. I'm on my way to seize the computer," Reynolds spoke hastily, his voice tight with urgency. "Martinez knows who you are. Your last name set off alarm bells in his mind like I've never seen before."

There was a pause on the other end of the line. Then Declan's voice came through, steady but with an edge of anxiety, "I'm surprised it took him that long to remember my mother's maiden name. He is best friends with my father."

"Wait, you go by your mother's maiden name?" Reynolds asked, puzzled, but he quickly brushed the confusion aside. There was no time for probing further.

"No time, Mike," Declan cut him off, "Follow the plan. If I can meet you at the rendezvous point, I will. If not, go without me."

Before Reynolds could respond, Declan ended the call. A sudden wave of dread washed over Reynolds. Things were escalating, and there was no turning back now. Reynolds carefully planned responses to questions he thought would come had back fired, all because he had been operating on incomplete information. If only Declan had been more forthcoming, more truthful from the start. Reynolds thought back to the countless meetings, the endless discussions, the strategies they had devised together. All of it was based on the assumption that they knew the full picture. But they didn't. Declan had withheld critical information, and now, because of that omission, they were on the brink of disaster. Reynolds felt a bitter taste in his mouth. This was a mistake, a grave one, and it was going to cost them dearly. They were now forced into a corner, with no other option but to run.

Declan was in the lab with Claire when Reynolds' call came in. His face must have conveyed the urgency of the situation because as soon as he ended the call, Claire looked at him, her face a mask of concern.

"We're in danger, Claire. More than we anticipated," Declan confessed, trying to keep his voice steady. "Our time here is limited."

Claire's eyes widened, her mind racing as she processed the information. "The computer..." she began, looking at the Quantum system they had worked so hard to understand.

Declan nodded, "It's set to go as we planned. Hopefully, Mike and the QRDA security personnel will be able to move it without harm."

Understanding dawned on Claire's face. She had been privy to the plan and knew exactly what she needed to do. "I'll inform Jamie," she said, determination replacing the fear in her eyes. "I'll gather our things and meet you at the rendezvous point as planned."

There was a moment of silence between them, filled with the unsaid words of the risks they were taking and the unknown future that awaited them. Then Declan nodded, affirming their course of action, and they both set off to execute the most critical parts of their plan.

With a nod of approval from Claire, Declan set off, his car automatically driving him towards his father's residence, once he entered the desired address. He had not been there in years, but the opulence of the mansion never failed to make an impression. High fences, manicured gardens, and a sprawling, modern facade signaled the wealth and power of its inhabitants.

Declan was greeted at the entrance by a stern-faced security officer. "Sorry, Mr. Sutton. Your clearance seems to have been denied," the guard informed him, glancing uncomfortably at his device. Declan's heart sank. This was unexpected. He tried to maintain his composure, waiting for the officer to say more.

As he sat in the car, his phone buzzed. The caller ID displayed 'Mom'. "Declan, what's happening? The security detail told me you're at the gate. Why are you here?" His mother's voice echoed through the speaker, worry lacing her words.

"Mom, it's...it's complicated. Can you ask dad to come out? I need to speak to him urgently," Declan replied, his voice taut with tension.

Meanwhile, a team of military personnel arrived to conduct a bomb and weapon search on his vehicle. These were routine procedures for high-security locations, but they added to the tension.

The officers worked systematically, conducting a thorough check. They started with the exterior of the vehicle, using portable detectors to scan for explosives or chemical residues. Mirrors on extended handles were used to examine the underside of the car, an area that could be easily overlooked but was a common place to hide explosives.

One officer lifted the hood, inspecting the engine compartment with a flashlight. Another took out a small device that looked like a handheld vacuum cleaner but was, in fact, a trace-detection device. He ran it over the surfaces inside the car, the device designed to pick up microscopic particles of explosives or narcotics.

All the while, another officer was checking the trunk, going through the contents meticulously. Each bag was opened, its contents examined before being repacked neatly. Every possible hiding place, no matter how small, was inspected – spare tire wells, hidden compartments, even under the car seats. The officers handled everything with gloved hands to avoid contamination of any potential evidence.

Declan watched this all play out in his rearview mirror, his heart pounding in his chest. He wasn't carrying anything suspicious, but the implications of this situation were making him anxious. This visit was turning out to be a lot more complicated than he'd anticipated.

As he waited for his clearance, Declan couldn't help but think about the massive challenge they were facing. Their group – a Biologist, a Genetic engineer, an intelligence agent, and a bartender – against a powerful government that wouldn't hesitate to silence them. The odds were not in their favor, but they held a unique advantage: a groundbreaking technology that could potentially unlock the secrets of the past to reshape and secure the future.

Chapter 45

The Unraveling of Utopia

Once the security protocol was fulfilled and Declan was granted passage, he found himself escorted into the mansion's majestic entrance, accompanied by a trio of security personnel. As he walked, Declan's mind began to wander, curiosity piquing as he contemplated the genetic makeup of his escorts. He found himself questioning how their genetic sequencing diverged from his own, and how such differences manifested across the population. He pondered the divisions created by the CGPT system and the specific alterations made within each category.

The splendor of his childhood home always managed to evoke a certain emotion within him. Even though he had roamed these lavish corridors countless times during his youth, they felt foreign to him now. The glaring disparity between the world beyond these walls and the affluence encapsulated within served as a stark reminder of the societal divide his family presided over. As he walked through the halls, he spotted her standing in the doorway of his father's study. His mother, Meredith Sutton, a woman of grace and formidable intellect. Despite her petite frame, she exuded an aura of power. Her hair was elegantly styled, her eyes sharp, and her voice, even when softened by motherly affection, carried an unmistakable authority. She had spent decades as a leading politician in the city, respected by allies and feared by opponents. But despite all the power and influence she wielded, her love for her only son never waned.

"Declan," she sighed as he approached, her eyes softening at the sight of him. She crossed the distance between them and enveloped him in a tight hug, a gesture that seemed out of place amidst the cold decor of the mansion.

As she finally released him from the embrace, Meredith stepped back, her hands moving to cradle his face as if to confirm the reality of his presence. Her eyes, warm yet clouded with a quiet sadness, scanned his face with an intensity that only a mother's love could muster. The lines of age and worry etched on her face seemed more pronounced now, their silent testament to the years of separation she had endured without her only son.

"Your father isn't here, Declan," she confessed, her voice barely above a whisper. The words were laced with a bitterness that reflected the cruel irony of the situation. "He's been called away on urgent matters. Out of the country. A world away..." Her voice trailed off, leaving the unsaid hanging heavy between them.

She swallowed hard, her gaze never leaving his. The years of their estrangement were etched deeply in her eyes, a chasm of missed moments, silent birthdays, and unshared milestones. A pained smile tugged at the corners of her mouth. "But what of it, my dear son?" she asked, her voice fragile, almost breaking under the weight of her unshed tears. "What's so earth-shatteringly important that it brings you back here, to us, after all these years?"

The hurt was apparent in her words, a raw wound reopened. "And to want to speak to him, and not me," she continued, the betrayal underlying her words cutting through the cool air of the room. "Your mother, who's spent sleepless nights hoping, praying for your return. The woman who, despite everything, tried tirelessly to bridge the gap you so stubbornly insisted on. The mother who, every day for the past seven years, has woken up to the heart-wrenching reality of being without her only son."

Each word, each sentence, was a revelation of the deep-set sorrow that had been her constant companion. And for the first time, Declan felt the full impact of the emotional cost his departure had exacted on his mother.

There was an undercurrent of hurt in her words, a mother's pain reflecting years of separation from her son. Declan was taken aback. He hadn't expected to see her, let alone be confronted with the raw, emotional toll his estrangement had taken on her. However, the urgent task at hand snapped him back to the grim reality.

Declan swallowed hard, the lump in his throat threatening to choke him. He looked into his mother's eyes, seeing the pain etched into her soul. He felt a pang of regret for causing her such distress, but there was no turning back now. He had to face this, and he had to do it now.

"Mom," he began, his voice thick with emotion. "I need to speak with dad because...because there are things that I need to know. Questions that I think only he can answer. Situations have... have arisen, that may connect back to him. My boss Dr. Peterson was killed… I think to cover up an accident!"

His gaze didn't waver from hers, his resolve apparent in his stare. "I didn't come here to cause you pain. I didn't come to reopen old wounds. Things have happened and I have learned things that I can't ignore any longer. I need answers, Mom. I need to understand."

He paused, taking a moment to gather his thoughts. "This isn't about the past. It's not about the decisions I've made, or the path I chose to walk. It's about the present...and possibly the future. And the truth, which I am hoping to find here with him."

His words hung heavy in the air between them, their silent echoes permeating the room. Declan braced himself for her response, the tension in the room so thick it could have been cut with a knife.

Meredith let out a deep sigh, her gaze falling to her hands folded in front of her. "Declan," she started, her voice barely a whisper.

"There are some truths that are best left buried. The night of the accident... it wasn't supposed to happen that way. It was an error, a flaw in the system."

She glanced up at him, her eyes shimmering with unshed tears. "It was never meant to be so despairingly irrational, so disastrous. But it was. And lives were lost, young lives, innocent lives... dozens of them."

She swallowed hard, struggling to maintain her composure. "If the public knew the truth, if they knew about the flaw... Our family, our dynasty could be destroyed. It would mean the end of everything we've worked so hard to build. But more importantly, it would ignite a wave of public distrust in the government and its automation technologies that we may not be able to contain."

"Mom," Declan interjected, his voice laced with a fury he could no longer contain. "Dr. Peterson was murdered, murdered to cover up an 'accident' that you're now admitting you knew about." His hands clenched into fists at his sides, his knuckles turning white with the effort. "And you're telling me it was a flaw in the system? A flaw that conveniently protects a select few while others pay the price?"

His gaze bore into hers, his anger palpable. "That's not a flaw, Mom. That's a design. A design to shield the privileged while the rest of us are left vulnerable. It's not a bug; it's a feature. And it's not just about public distrust. It's about justice, about accountability."

His voice echoed in the grand room, his words a stark contrast to the opulence around them. "Dr. Peterson was more than a boss to me. He was a mentor, a friend. And he was killed because he knew too much, because he was close to uncovering the truth. The truth that you and Dad have been hiding."

Declan's heart pounded in his chest, his breath coming in short, sharp gasps. He felt a mix of anger, betrayal, and a strange sense of relief. The truth was out, at least part of it. And he wouldn't stop until he uncovered the rest.

Her words left a bitter taste in Declan's mouth. How many secrets did his family harbor? How many lies were woven into their legacy? He suddenly felt the weight of his lineage, the burden of the dark truth he was slowly uncovering. Who were they covering for? Who had been driving that night? Who was so important that they would cover up the deaths of dozens of children? His parents were not the people he had thought they were. The realization was a cold, hard slap in the face, sending a shiver down his spine.

Declan looked at his mother, the woman who had loved him unconditionally, the woman who had also helped to weave the fabric of lies that shrouded their family. He felt a pang of sorrow for her. This wasn't the life she had envisioned, but it was the one she was forced to live. Declan paused in the hallway, his mother's words echoing in his mind. He had always seen her as a figure of authority, a woman of unwavering conviction. But now, he was beginning to see the harsh reality behind the facade. The weight of the world rested on her shoulders, a burden she bore with an iron fist. But at what cost?

He leaned against the cool marble wall, his mind a whirlwind of thoughts. Was he right about his mother? Had he been too quick to judge, too eager to place the blame? He had seen her as a part of the problem, a cog in the machine that was their society. And it was becoming increasingly clear that she was not just a part of it, but a driving force behind it.

His mother was a politician, yes, but she was also a woman, a mother. She had dreams, hopes, fears... just like anyone else. But unlike others, she had chosen power and control over compassion and understanding. She had been thrust into a world of power and responsibility, a world that demanded sacrifices. Sacrifices that included her own humanity, her own empathy.

Declan's heart hardened as he thought of his mother, alone in that grand room, wrestling with the ghosts of their past. He had been so focused on his own quest for truth, his own anger and betrayal, that he had failed to see the coldness in her eyes, the ruthlessness in her voice. He decided to change course, maybe just maybe his mother knew much more than he ever imagined.

"I've been looking into the Ectogenesis program, Mom," Declan began, his voice shaking slightly. "The more I dig, the more I find things that... they don't add up."

"You wouldn't have access to that program or its code at the University. What have you been up to? And why are you looking into the Ectogenesis program?" Meredith asked, her voice laced with feigned confusion. Yet, deep down, she knew exactly why Declan would be interested in the program. His passion for biology, his fascination with the past, and his inherent curiosity were the very reasons he had chosen a different path from the family's political legacy. His pursuit of truth was as relentless as it was predictable.

He paused, ignoring her questions as he stayed the course by studying her face, looking for signs of recognition or denial. "I've found discrepancies, questionable data. And the more I've probed, the more it seems like our true history is being kept from us."

Meredith was silent for a moment, her eyes fixed on her son's. Declan could see a range of emotions flitting across her face: surprise, confusion, and finally, resignation. "I was wondering if you would stumble upon that revelation! The irony, Declan, is you would have had far more information and knowledge shared with you about your chosen career if you would have just stayed the course that was your destiny." she admitted quietly.

"The Ectogenesis program was... is a significant part of our governments legacy, Declan," she continued, her gaze steady. "Our ancestors believed in its potential. They believed that it could help us reshape society, eliminate disease, inequality... the very problems that have been plaguing humanity for centuries."

Declan looked at her incredulously. "If that's true, then why the secrecy? Why the manipulation? And why the dark turns it's been taking? I've seen evidence of things... unsettling things, Mom."

She seemed to deflate slightly under his questioning. "Sometimes... the path to progress requires us to make choices that aren't easy," she replied, her voice low. "The secrecy, the deception... it was all done to protect the program, to safeguard the Government's legacy. But you're wrong, Declan," she continued, a note of defiance creeping into her tone. "It has not taken a dark turn. Our society, this civilization that we've built, is the pinnacle of Humanity's success. Look around, Declan. Really look."

And as she spoke, she swept her arm around, gesturing towards the panoramic window that showcased the sprawling metropolis beyond. "No one goes hungry here, no one suffers from preventable diseases. We have hospitals equipped with the most advanced technology that cater to every citizen's needs. The scourge of poverty is a thing of the past, and every child has access to quality education."

Her voice echoed through the vast room, her eyes blazing with conviction. "Violence and crime are nearly non-existent, thanks to our advanced surveillance systems and law enforcement. Our city is clean, the environment is protected, and our energy is renewable. We've worked to create a world where people want for nothing."

Meredith took a deep breath, her gaze never leaving Declan's. "Our city, our civilization, is a utopia, Declan. And it's all because of the hard choices we've made along the way. So tell me, how can you consider that a dark turn?"

Declan's brows furrowed, his frustration bubbling to the surface. "So, you know all about our history," he began, his voice rising with emotion. "If all that is true, then why would you keep it secret from everyone? I don't understand."

He crossed his arms, leaning against a nearby table for support as he confronted his mother. "And what about all the diverse cultures, the rich tapestry of human history that's simply vanished?" he asked, his voice charged with accusation. "What happened to the African tribes, the indigenous communities of the Americas, the ethnic groups of Asia and the Middle East? Why has our society become so... homogenized?"

Declan could feel his heart pounding in his chest, the heavy weight of his questions hanging in the air between them. "What was the purpose of all that, Mom?" he asked, his voice barely more than a whisper. "Why erase such a vast part of our history? And why, for God's sake, would you ever think it was necessary?"

His mother stared at him, her eyes wide with surprise. "No, Declan. The real question is: How do you know?" She questioned him, her voice filled with a mixture of fear and confusion. "Only a handful of people are privy to those details about our past. Those records were concealed for a reason. What laws have you violated to uncover them?"

She walked over to the window, peering out as she considered the possibilities. "Hacking? No, that's impossible. Our servers aren't connected to any external networks. They're completely isolated," she muttered to herself. "Did you break into the national libraries? No... there would have been alarms, security would have been alerted."

She turned back to Declan, her gaze piercing. "You've clearly gone to great lengths to uncover this information, Declan," she stated, a hint of resignation in her voice. "Where did you learn those terms, those names?"

"Where I obtained the information is not of importance, Mom," Declan said, his gaze unwavering. "What matters is that I know now. And until this very moment, I wasn't sure if the information was true or not."

Meredith's eyes flared with sudden anger. "You don't understand, Declan!" she exclaimed, her voice sharp. "I cannot protect you if you've broken any laws. The information you possess is classified, it's top secret! We've debated eradicating all those records from the past, but decided against it for numerous reasons. Now it seems we should have."

She moved towards Declan; her movements agitated. "The past is irrelevant to the future, Declan," she continued, her voice softer but still brimming with frustration. "This information can only harm us. Don't you see that?"

Her eyes met his, the anger replaced by a pleading look. "We didn't do this. It was done by your great-grandfather during his reign. Nothing good can come of this information being out in the open, Declan. Nothing good at all."

Declan could see the tension seeping into his mother's features as she began to explain. "You don't understand, Declan," she started, her voice filled with a sorrowful strain. "People were not as you see them today, a hundred years ago. They were driven by hatred for each other based on the smallest differences – skin color, religious beliefs... and it resulted in wars where millions died over nothing more than sheer tribalism."

Her gaze held his, a storm of emotion stirring within her. "The government of the past decided they couldn't stand idly by anymore, not when they had the power to change things. The advent of a stable quantum computer gave them the tools they needed."

She paused, taking a deep breath before continuing. "The potential of a quantum computer is beyond what most people can comprehend, Declan. It can analyze trillions of genome sequences in an instant, predicting outcomes for each minute change. It's not just simple computation; it's like foreseeing the future of our genetic makeup, like having the power to steer evolution itself."

Her hands clenched together tightly. "They saw the opportunity to transform society, to eliminate the cause of such irrational hatred – the superficial differences that drove people apart. So they embarked on a project, the likes of which the world had never seen. And your great-grandfather was at the helm of it all, directing the course of our species. It was a necessary step, Declan. Can't you see that?"

Declan looked at his mother, his expression a mix of confusion and disbelief. "But why would you need to erase people's uniqueness? Why remove what makes each person an individual? Or have you just separated them from us, are they living somewhere else?"

Her response was calm, filled with conviction. "Because, Declan, true equity can only be achieved by leveling the playing field completely. If everyone shares the same background, the same experiences, the same opportunities...only then can everyone truly be equal. This was the reasoning of the government."

She began to pace the room, her hands gesturing to emphasize her points. "Just consider it, Declan. Men and women were genetically designed to have more similar body types, making physical disparities less prominent. All races were blended, their distinctive genetic traits combined to form a balanced, optimal human. The aim was to eliminate the root of discrimination, to diffuse the infighting that had poisoned societies for centuries."

Her gaze met his again, this time filled with a fervor he rarely saw in her. "The family structure was dismantled, ensuring every individual received the same education, the same cultural teachings, free from the influence of parental bias or inherited prejudice. Mothers and fathers would secretly instill in their children ideas and values that were detrimental to the harmony the government sought. Ideas like heritage, culture, religion, gender differences... these were the seedbeds of inequity. Removing them was the only way to secure true equity among the populace."

Meredith paused, letting her words sink in. Her eyes, always so warm and comforting, now held a steely resolve. She was a firm believer in their society's design, a staunch defender of the choices made to shape it. To her, this was the best possible world they could live in. It was up to Declan now to decide how he would react to this revelation.

Declan's eyes swept around the opulent room, taking in the luxurious surroundings that were a stark contrast to the lives of the ordinary populace. "But, Mom, look around. The disparities didn't vanish, they just transformed," he countered, his voice tinged with frustration. "Your wealth, your power... it's far beyond what others have. Isn't that a disparity in itself?"

He paused, gathering his thoughts before continuing, "Members of the party aren't treated the same way as the general populace. You live in luxury while others make do with the basics. You make decisions that impact lives without having to face the same consequences. Isn't that a contradiction to the equality you're preaching?"

His mother fell silent, a flicker of unease crossing her face. Declan watched her closely, wondering how she would respond to his arguments.

Meredith gazed at her son, her expression hardening as she prepared to defend her position. "Declan," she began, a certain sternness creeping into her voice. "Somebody has to be the arbiter of truth. Society needs leadership; without it, chaos and anarchy ensue. That is simply a historical fact."

Her hands folded neatly in her lap, she continued, "The political class, the class your father and I belong to, is a necessary separation from the equity movement. We are the stewards of society, making the tough decisions that others cannot or will not make. We are willing to bear the weight of these decisions, to do what must be done to keep our society on its predetermined path to greatness."

With a sigh, she looked at Declan earnestly. "We are not exempt from the ideals of equity, my dear. We merely serve a different role. We ensure that the equity of everyone else is protected and maintained. Yes, our lives are different, but they are not without their own sacrifices and burdens." She fell silent, letting her words sink in. She hoped Declan would understand that the world wasn't as black-and-white as he imagined. It was a delicate balance, a constant juggle of power, responsibility, and sacrifice.

Her words echoed in the silent room, a testament to the harsh reality they were now confronting. Declan found himself reeling from the revelations, grappling with the implications of his family's involvement in a conspiracy that seemed to extend beyond his wildest imagination. His search for answers was far from over. In fact, it seemed he was only beginning to unravel the tangled web of secrets that had been woven around his family's legacy.

Declan's gaze didn't waver as he broke the dire news. "The Ectogenesis program is failing, mom. It can't produce viable children anymore. We're on a collision course with extinction if we don't change our course."

Meredith blinked, a wave of disbelief washing over her. "That... that can't be," she stammered, her face draining of color. The news hit her like a physical blow. The Ectogenesis program was the keystone of their society, the cornerstone of their vision for the future. Its failure was unthinkable.

"Yes, Mom," Declan replied, his voice firm. "I'm certain. I've been working at the Quantum Research and Development Agency for the past few months, specifically brought in to help solve an issue with the genetic sequencing of the Ectogenesis program. It's failing, and we're trying to understand why and how to fix it."

"Are you sure, Declan? I just do not understand how your father and I have not heard of this before now?" she asked, her voice barely above a whisper. The impact of his revelation was making it hard for her to think clearly. All the sacrifices, all the choices they had made, it had all been in service of the Ectogenesis program. The thought of it failing was too much to bear.

"Yes, mom," Declan replied, his voice firm. "I'm certain. The team and I have been trying to understand why it is failing and how to fix it."

"But how? Why?" Meredith pressed, a hint of desperation in her voice. Her mind was a whirl of questions and fears. If Declan was right, this was a disaster beyond anything they had ever faced.

"That's what we're trying to figure out," Declan said, a touch of frustration creeping into his voice. "But mom, you need to understand, we need to prepare for a future without the Ectogenesis program. We need to consider alternatives, different paths."

Meredith swallowed hard, her mind racing. Declan's words were a chilling wake-up call, a stark reminder that their utopia was perhaps more fragile than they'd thought. She had dedicated her life to building and maintaining their society, but now, it seemed, they were standing on the precipice of its downfall.

"No, Declan, you're the one who doesn't understand," Meredith retorted, her tone growing agitated. She stood up, the sweep of her arm encompassing the grandeur of the room around them. "This," she stressed, "this is what we've built, a society free from the plagues of the past."

"Without the program, we'd return to an era of savagery, of chaos. I've read the histories, seen the documentaries. Humanity in its 'natural state' was brutish, short-sighted, violent." Her words were an indignant barrage, a testament to her unwavering faith in the society they'd erected on the foundations of the Ectogenesis program.

"We'd revert to a world where might made right, where the strong preyed on the weak. Our society, for all its flaws, has eliminated such primal hierarchies," she argued, her voice ringing with conviction. "Without the program, we'd be back to a world dominated by wars, by competition, by survival of the fittest."

Her eyes flashed with a hint of desperation as she continued, "And what about the social disparities? The inequality? We've seen it, Declan. Humanity left to its own devices doesn't aspire to fairness. It succumbs to greed, to corruption, to the allure of power. The program allows us to correct for these, to steer our species towards a better future."

Shaking her head emphatically, she added, "We cannot, will not, give up on the program, Declan. It's our shield against regression, our beacon guiding us towards a future of true equity. We must do everything we can to fix it, not abandon it."

"No, Mom, we need to abandon it altogether. I have lived countless lives through the records of the past, seen the humanity in our imperfections, tasted the bittersweet pain of loss and the pure elation of gain. I have danced in the emotions we've long forgotten, experienced the depth and breadth of human life, and each time I return... I feel lost."

Declan's voice was raw, the pain and truth in his words palpable. He was fighting, but not with her - with the very essence of what they had become. "We are missing the things that bring us joy, the depth of experience that comes from being truly human. The Ectogenesis program and the design of the perfect human... It's a failure. Our 'errors in our code,' to borrow your term, are what make us great. They make us human. You have no idea what we've given up."

He exhaled heavily, the weight of his words hanging in the air between them. "The joys of relationships, of love, the warmth of family, the sense of community... All lost in our pursuit of this sterile perfection. Our lives are hollow, devoid of the very things that made them worth living. We've eradicated our differences, our unique identities, but at what cost?"

His voice dropped to a whisper, almost choked with emotion. "We believe in nothing now, Mom. We live only for ourselves, isolated and disconnected. We share our lives with no one. We've made our existence so sterile, so clean, so perfect... but it's empty. It's nothing."

The room fell silent, his words hanging heavily in the air, a stark contrast to the luxury and opulence that surrounded them. He had made his case, poured out his heart and soul, arguing for a return to a life more chaotic, more unpredictable, but infinitely more human. It was in this moment, amidst the weight of their conversation, that a realization dawned on Declan. Perhaps the Mycelium computer was trying to show him that they, as humans, were broken, that fixing the Ectogenesis program wouldn't solve the real issues. That the true problem lay not in the technology, but in their understanding of what it truly meant to be human.

Declan's gaze dropped to the floor, his hands instinctively reaching for the letter in his pocket. A deep, heart-wrenching sorrow clung to his words as he continued.

"Do you know what it's like, Mom, to lose a child?" His voice was almost a whisper, thick with grief from the words that Maddy used to describe her experience. "To hold your dreams and hopes in your arms, only for it to be ripped away from you? You can't possibly fathom that pain. No one in our world can... because we are robbed of the very experience of becoming parents, of bringing life into this world."

He looked at his mother then, his eyes glistening with unshed tears. "We've lost our humanity, Mom. Our connection to the life cycle, to the process of creation and growth. In our pursuit of perfection, we've lost the essence of life itself."

Declan took a deep breath, steadying himself. His voice softened, taking on an almost reverent tone as he delved deeper. "The meaning of life... it isn't about attaining perfection, or even about the individual survival. It's about connection, about the cyclical flow of life, about being part of something greater than ourselves."

He paused, as if searching for the right words. "life is a journey of self-discovery and connection. It's about learning, growing, and achieving a sense of peace and contentment. It's about recognizing the interconnectedness of all things, and finding our place within that grand tapestry. Life is not sterile, it's not controlled... it's beautifully chaotic and unpredictably perfect in its imperfection. "

Declan met his mother's eyes, the depth of his conviction reflected in his gaze. "That's what we've lost, Mom. That connection, that sense of being part of the grand cycle of life. And that... that's a loss too great to bear."

"Declan," his mother implored. "Are you alright?"

He nodded, panting, struggling to articulate the enormity of the experience. "I... I saw it all, Mom. The genesis of the universe, the formation of life on Earth, the entire history of humanity..."

He was silent for a moment, trying to collect his thoughts. His mother watched him, a mix of concern and curiosity in her eyes. Finally, he spoke again.

"We've strayed, Mom. We've strayed from what makes us human. I saw it in the simulation – the way we evolved, the way we survived. We didn't get here by being perfect. We got here by adapting, by learning from our mistakes."

His gaze was intense, filled with a determination she had never seen. "We've been so focused on eliminating our flaws, our differences... but those are the things that made us who we are. Those are the things that helped us survive, to thrive."

He took a deep breath, letting the silence linger for a moment before he continued. "We've lost our humanity in our quest for perfection. But it's not too late. We can remember, we can learn from our past... we can find our way back."

The raw emotion in his voice filled the quiet room, resonating with an almost tangible energy. Meredith was silent, her mind spinning with the weight of her son's words. As she looked into his eyes, she saw a mix of profound wisdom and burning determination, tinged with an unsettling hint of madness.

Meredith studied her son, concern deeply etched across her face. His impassioned declarations and visions felt so real to him. Yet to her, they came across as disquieting, the delusions of a distressed mind.

"Declan," she began gently, her voice steady despite the turmoil brewing inside her. "Your words... they're not making sense. You're talking about past events, historical happenings as if you've lived them... you seem to be losing touch with reality. I am positive that you are wrong about the Ectogenesis program, we would have heard if something was amiss."

Declan's gaze remained unwavering; his conviction unbroken. Yet, his intensity only deepened Meredith's concerns.

Meridith's concerns switched to worry for her son and worry for her livelihood at the look in his eyes. "Your words are those that can cause rebellion, stir a populace into false beliefs, false hopes," she continued, her voice faltering slightly. "These are dangerous thoughts, Declan. Dangerous not just for you, but for our society. We've built this world on a foundation of stability, order. Your words, they echo the rhetoric of disruptors, of radicals."

She reached out, placing a comforting hand on his arm. "You need help, my son. And I can provide it. We have resources, professionals who can understand what's happening to you."

Her words hung in the air between them, an unspoken plea for him to see reason. To recognize the urgency of her concern, the reality of his own situation. She needed him to understand that this wasn't just about his views or beliefs. This was about his health, his wellbeing, his future.

As his mother spoke, her words filled with worry and apprehension, a sudden chime echoed through the room. The display on the wall lit up, announcing an incoming call from Minister Martinez. Declan knew he had to seize this moment, for this phone call, if it is about what he thinks it is about, could spell his doom.

Her gaze snapped towards the screen, torn between her concern for Declan and her responsibilities. As her attention was momentarily diverted, Declan saw his chance. His heart pounded in his chest as he quietly rose from his chair, mindful not to make a sound.

"Minister Martinez," Meredith acknowledged, her voice steady despite the confusion playing across her face. "This isn't a good time..."

The minister's voice echoed through the room, his words filling the space Declan had vacated. "Meredith, it's urgent. There's something about Declan..."

At the mention of his name, Declan felt a surge of adrenaline. He knew he had to leave, and he had to do it now. He shot a final, apologetic look at his mother, her figure illuminated by the glow of the screen. Then, he turned away, his steps hushed as he moved towards the exit.

Meredith's eyes widened as she processed the minister's words, her heart pounding. "...Declan? But he's..." Her words trailed off as she turned to look at the now-empty chair. The realization hit her like a wave. Declan was gone.

Her heart skipped a beat as she rushed to the door, the minister's words becoming a distant echo. But it was too late. Declan had disappeared into the night, swallowed by the inky darkness. The silent house was his only trace, a stark reminder of his absence.

Chapter 46

Ghosts of the Past, Shadows of the Future

Shaking off the shock of having Minister Martinez calling his parents home in regards to his actions, Declan acted on instinct. His father's garage was a treasure trove of vehicles, relics from a bygone era that his dad had a penchant for collecting. Among them was a sleek, electric sports car that had always been his favorite. A little jewel, his dad called it, a symbol of humanity's technological prowess and his personal testament to a greener future. His father had often said that it had 'one foot in the past and one in the future', an apt description considering its vintage look and the cutting-edge technology it housed. It was this very technology that Declan banked on now He had remembered that certain Party members had the ability to not only turn off their tracking systems but remove themselves from the system all together making this the perfect getaway car.

Declan stopped dead in his tracks, for the vehicle that he had seen the night of the accident sat beside his father's favorite car. He had only caught a glimpse of the vehicle that evening but seeing it now sitting in his father's garage brought back the horrible images of that night. No wonder my mother was defending the Autonomous Navigation system; it had saved her husband, his father from potentially fatal injuries. It all began to make sense now his father was the one driving the car, no wonder everyone was bending over backwards to hide the truth.

The car's security system was tied to the family genetics, allowing him access to the car. The ignition would only be activated by the unique genetic code of a family member. Family members stealing cars was not a problem in today's day and age as no one other than a small few shared any genetic semblance what so ever. In his case, the similarities in their DNA would allow Declan access to any car in the garage that was attached to his father or mother.

Approaching the sleek vehicle, he placed his hand on the handle. The car's sensors immediately recognized his genetic profile, the handle glowing a soft green before it clicked open. Relief washed over him, for he wasn't one hundred percent certain it would allow him access. Sliding into the leather seat, he closed the door behind him, the sound a reassuring thud in the quiet of the garage.

A quick swipe on the control panel brought the car to life. The silent purr of the electric engine was music to his ears. The garage doors, too, were automated and opened without a hitch as he maneuvered the vehicle towards the exit.

Once on the driveway, he didn't hesitate and floored the accelerator. The vehicle shot forward, the mansion and its sprawling estate fading in the rearview mirror. The dark city streets ahead were his path to freedom, his escape route away from the life he had known. The car roared onto the empty road as Declan gripped the steering wheel, his knuckles white from the strain. He could barely contain his surprise at the immediate, raw power he felt at his fingertips. This was unlike the tempered, predictable movements of the Autonomous Naviagtion system. He wasn't just a passenger now. He was in control. It was liberating and terrifying all at once.

Driving wasn't just a forgotten skill; it was a forbidden one. The last person he knew who had driven a car not fully automated was his grandfather, and that was decades ago. The Autonomous Navigation system was the norm now, and no one had the need, let alone the permission, to manually operate vehicles anymore.

Safety, efficiency, control – that's what the system promised and provided. But it took away the human touch, the thrill of taking control, the freedom of the open road.

The car seemed to be a beast compared to the gentle, predictable cars of the Autonomous Navigation system. The tactile feel of the wheel, the raw responsiveness of the accelerator, the immediate reaction of the brakes – it was all so immediate and visceral.

Declan stumbled his way through, swerving and braking harder than necessary. His movements were jittery, his hands unsteady. Every moment was a struggle between trying to tame the car and not crashing into something. Declan found himself lucky to have lived through Sam's eyes in the simulation, his memories becoming Sam's for it was there in the recess of his mind that he remembered how to operate a vehicle in this manner.

His heart pounded in his chest as he navigated his way through the city. The night was dark and quiet, the roads empty. It seemed like the whole city was asleep, oblivious to his clandestine escape.

He kept glancing at his rearview mirror, half expecting to see law enforcement vehicles chasing him. But there was nothing. Just the dark road and the distant glow of his parent's home behind him.

It was then that he realized he'd been holding his breath. Letting out a shaky sigh, he gripped the steering wheel tighter, his gaze fixed on the road ahead. He had a destination, and he needed to get there fast.

Summoning the little courage he had left, Declan maneuvered the vehicle onto the highway. The open road stretched out before him, a symbol of the uncertain journey that lay ahead. As he put distance between himself and his former life, he reached out to his communication device. He dialed Mike's number, his fingers trembling as he pressed the call button.

"Mike," he breathed into the device, his voice a whisper against the hum of the engine.

"Declan?" Mike said, surprise coloring his tone. "What's going on?"

"I think they're on to me," Declan confessed, his gaze darting to where the rearview mirror should be. He knew his mother's mansion was disappearing behind him, swallowed up by the darkened cityscape. That he could no longer see from the windows shading over. "Martinez called the house while I was there, I heard him ask about me. My mom... she thinks I'm sick, delusional."

Silence filled the line for a moment. Then, Mike sighed, his voice steady and calming. "Alright, stay calm. Head to the Last Liberal get Jamie and then meet us here. We're almost ready to move the Computer. Once you're here, I can report that I've detained you for acting erratically during the removal process. It will match whatever story your mom's fed to Martinez."

Declan felt a knot of anxiety uncoil in his stomach. Mike's quick thinking was exactly what he needed. "And then?"

"Then we run," Mike said, the urgency in his voice palpable even through the comms. "We have a window of a few hours, tops, before the entire city will be searching for us. We need to be gone by then."

"I think I've got that part figured out," Declan responded, his eyes flitting between the road and the car's control panel. His heart pounded in his chest, the risk of what they were about to do sinking in. "You remember that vintage electric car, that caused the accident with the children?"

There was a brief silence before Mike replied, "The one with the ability to blind itself from the Navigation system?"

"That's the one," Declan said, a hint of a smile tugging at the corner of his mouth, despite the situation.

His words hung in the air as he braced himself for Mike's reaction. When it came, it was a burst of laughter, quickly followed by a sharp intake of breath. "You're not serious," Mike said. "Please tell me you did not steal President Caldwell's car? Wait, how did you get his car? How did you know that it was the President driving that night and why didn't you tell us?" questioned Mike.

"Your last name is Caldwell! That is why you use your mothers maiden name, you do not want people to know who your father is!" Mike exclaimed.

"Yes he is my father, yes, I stole his car and I did it to get us out of here!" Declan finished for him, his grip tightening on the steering wheel.

"But... but how? Even if you can drive the thing, which I seriously doubt, how are we supposed to escape the city undetected, it is the president's car after all Declan?" Mike's voice was skeptical, a mixture of worry and disbelief.

"It has an old political Party feature," Declan explained, his voice calm despite the knot of nerves in his stomach. "We can not only switch off the tracking system but also erase our presence from the Autonomous Navigation system."

"Wait," Mike interrupted, "how did you... I mean, that's not possible."

"I know," Declan cut him off, his tone sharp. "But remember who my father is. This car... it's like a ghost. Perfect for our escape. It has the ability to hide from the system in case of an assassination attempt; no one would be able to hack it and use it against him. All of his cars have this feature, I remember being a kid and him showing off how he could lose his detail, it was a game."

Declan's words hung in the air, a stark reminder of the reality they were now facing. As he fell silent, his mind began to race, piecing together fragments of the past. The night of the accident, the chaos, the confusion... it all started to take on a new meaning.

His father's car, with its ability to ghost itself from the Autonomous Navigation system, had been at the center of it all. It was a detail he had overlooked, a piece of the puzzle he hadn't considered. But now, as he thought about it, it made a chilling amount of sense.

His father, always the cautious one, had equipped his cars with this unique feature as a safeguard against potential threats. Declan remembered the times his father would demonstrate the car's ability to disappear from the system, turning it into a game. A game that now seemed to have far-reaching implications.

Why hadn't he connected the dots sooner?

There was a long pause, filled only with the hum of the electric engine and Declan's ragged breaths. "Okay, but you have a lot of explaining to do! You never told us who your father was," Mike finally said, his voice filled with trepidation. "I know we don't have time for you to explain so I'll trust you on this, Declan. I'm prepping the lab for our exit as planned. But that car you have changes things, scrap coming to the Lab, just get Jamie, grab the bags and meet us outside the city where we planned if things went sideways. Just... just be careful… "

"I will be, Mike," Declan reassured him, taking a deep breath as he pushed the accelerator. "See you soon."

With that, he cut the call, his focus now solely on getting to The Last Liberal. The life he'd known was unraveling around him, but with Mike's guidance, they had a plan. A risky, potentially dangerous plan, but it was their only shot. He just had to reach Jamie's and hope that he wasn't detected before he got there. After that, it would be a race against the clock, a chase for freedom he never imagined he'd have to undertake.

Chapter 47

Quantum Heist

From the corner of her eye, Claire saw a figure stride into the lab, a purposeful look on his face. He was a tall, imposing man with a stern expression and a gleam of authority in his eyes. The lab fell silent as he strode purposefully toward her work area. His ID badge gleamed ominously under the fluorescent lights; Agent Mike Reynolds of the Ministry of Security and Intelligence.

A pit formed in Claire's stomach. She felt her heart begin to race, but she forced herself to stay calm. She'd known this was coming. They'd planned for it.

"Dr. Cairns," Mike's voice echoed through the lab, each syllable heavy with authority. "I have here a warrant issued by the Ministry of Security and Intelligence. We're here to confiscate your... equipment."

He flashed the fake search warrant at her, the list of items on it catching her eye. Topmost was the Mycelium Quantum Computer, the very foundation of their rebellion.

A flash of fear burned in her chest as she took in the full implications of Mike's words. This was it. Their grand plan was in motion.

"You can't do this!" she exclaimed, pretending to be taken by surprise. "You have no right!"

But Mike merely held up the warrant again, a smirk playing on his lips. "Actually, Dr. Cairns, I believe I do."

The security personnel flanking Agent Reynolds, all uniformed in the dignified navy blue of government service, exchanged uneasy glances amongst themselves. A sense of unease seeped through the room, each officer visibly stiffening as they sized up the situation. Their initial reluctance, however, gradually dissolved into compliance, not out of loyalty, but a reflexive response to the evident authority that Mike wielded.

These were men and women bound together by their service to the state, by the camaraderie symbolized by their 'Blue Brotherhood.' Yet, this bond did not signify allegiance to Mike but rather a deep-rooted reverence for the authority his badge and status represented. Their shared duty to the state compelled them to assist, even if they did so begrudgingly.

Mike had anticipated this reaction. Throughout his service, he had observed this phenomenon multiple times. The respect his position commanded was often accompanied by an almost palpable desire to please him. It was a power he had wielded carefully, knowing when to utilize it to his advantage. This moment was no different. They advanced to carry out Mike's orders, their apprehension gradually replaced by a resolve to carry out their duty.

"No! Wait!" Claire said, feigning desperation. "It needs to be handled with utmost care. You'll ruin everything!"

Mike nodded, feigning gratitude. "Of course, Dr. Cairns. We wouldn't want to damage this invaluable piece of technology, would we? Please, show us how to move it properly."

Claire nodded, unable to hide a spark of triumph. "Fine."

Moving over to the imposing structure of the Mycelium Quantum Computer, she began instructing the security personnel. They listened attentively, their blue uniforms a symbol of their unwavering loyalty to the government - a loyalty that was, at this very moment, being used against them.

"The computer relies on a superconducting circuit, cooled to a temperature colder than outer space to maintain its delicate quantum state. It's incredibly sensitive to disturbances," Claire explained, pointing at the cryogenic system that was maintaining the low temperature. "We have to ensure it stays at this temperature throughout the move."

Claire gestured to the specific parts of the device that needed to be handled with extreme care, ensuring that their plan to relocate the computer would go without a hitch. As she guided the security personnel through the process, she couldn't help but feel a tingle of anticipation. The wheels of their plan were now irreversibly in motion. It was only a matter of time.

Under the careful guidance of Claire, they dismantled the delicate computer piece by piece. Each part of the quantum mycelium network was swathed in shock-absorbing fabric and placed into a padded, heat-regulated case. Once all the components were safely packed away, they were carried to a waiting van, an unassuming Ministry vehicle that blended seamlessly into the sea of similar vehicles.

Agent Reynolds had painstakingly prepared this van in the early hours of the morning, before the city was awake. It had been a fascinating and slightly daunting task, learning about the ins and outs of the Autonomous Navigation System (ANS) from technicians who specialized in catching those attempting to manipulate it.

The ANS, with its state-of-the-art tracking technology, was a marvel of modern engineering. It was designed to be near impenetrable, making any effort to escape its gaze an uphill battle. Yet, Mike had discovered a loophole, an ingenious albeit risky method to temporarily disable the tracking system.

The vehicle's tracking device operated on a specific frequency, constantly sending out signals that were picked up by the city's extensive network of traffic monitoring systems. Theoretically, if one could jam this frequency or introduce enough 'noise,' then the vehicle's signal would be lost, rendering it effectively invisible to the system.

Equipped with a frequency jammer developed by his tech-savvy colleagues, that was meant for military operations Mike intended to temporarily block the vehicle's tracking signal. This would, in theory, allow them to slip out of the city undetected. However, this was not a permanent solution. The frequency jammer could only work for a limited time before the built-in failsafe in the tracking system would trigger, sending out a distress signal that would undoubtedly attract attention.

As they loaded the last of the equipment into the van, Mike knew they were racing against the clock. Once outside the city limits, they would engage the frequency jammer and hope for the best. He couldn't shake off the lingering feeling of uncertainty. Even if everything went according to plan, they were not entirely sure how long it would take for someone to notice their absence.

As Mike watched the final pieces of the quantum mycelium computer being secured into the van, Claire suddenly strode towards him, a look of blazing anger on her face. The remaining security personnel stepped back in surprise, as if unsure whether to intervene.

"What do you think you're doing?" she yelled, her face flushed with what looked like genuine outrage. "This is my life's work! You can't just barge in here and take it away!"

Mike held up his hands, trying to calm her down. "I understand your frustration, Dr. Cairns, but I'm just following orders."

Claire's response was swift and vicious. She aimed a punch at Mike's face, her eyes sparking with defiance. Mike allowed the punch to connect, stumbling backwards for dramatic effect. The security personnel gasped in surprise, reaching for their own weapons as Mike brought up his own.

"That's enough, Dr. Cairns," he growled, aiming his weapon at her. "You're under arrest."

Claire's face fell into a perfect display of shock and disbelief as Mike recited her rights, a picture of perfect professionalism despite the apparent chaos. The security personnel were quick to react, following Mike's lead as they approached Claire, their faces grave.

As Mike securely cuffed her hands, he allowed himself a small smile. Everything was going according to plan. Their staged performance was successful and now Claire would be seen as a victim, when the government inevitably discovered their disappearance.

Mike gave a nod to the remaining security personnel, signaling them to remain behind while he escorted Claire into the van.

A slight tremor of anticipation ran through him as he climbed into the driver's seat. This was it. They were about to make their daring escape, with only their wits, preparation, and a whole lot of luck on their side. The van's engine hummed to life, its soft purr barely audible over the steady rhythm of his heartbeat. Mike took one last look at the lab in the rearview mirror before engaging the automated system in the van, he couldn't help but keep his eyes on the Security personnel as the van pulled onto the open road.

Once they were a safe distance from the lab, Mike broke the silence. "There's been a change of plans," he said, his voice steady despite the situation's palpable tension.

Claire, who was sitting handcuffed in the back, raised an eyebrow at him through the rearview mirror. "A change of plans? What do you mean?"

Mike glanced at her, his eyes revealing a hint of worry. "Declan... called when you were helping with the computer. He had to make a quick getaway. So, he stole a car."

Claire scoffed, "He stole a car? Is he safe? Could be worse, right? I mean there are plenty of cars; hopefully it wont get noticed right away."

Mike swallowed hard before responding, "Yeah, there are plenty of cars. But the car he stole... it belongs to the President."

"The President?!" Claire nearly shrieked, disbelief painting her features. "You have got to be kidding me. Why? How? What was he thinking!"

"I know," Mike said grimly. "But there is more that he didn't tell us. It turns out he is not just some high Party Member's kid but the Presidents son. He had an opportunity to take it, so he did, thinking he could use the tech built into the car to help us get out of the city. He's going to get Jamie and head towards our rendezvous point outside the city. We're going to meet them there."

Claire fell silent, her mind racing. This hiccup could very well be their downfall. But it could also be a major advantage. The President's car was sure to have more advanced evasion tech than any other vehicle. However, the theft would also cause an immediate uproar, prompting a citywide manhunt.

As Mike navigated through the city's network of roads, he felt the pressure mounting. The stakes were higher than ever, and the margin for error was now practically nonexistent. Stealing the President's car could either be the best move Declan had ever made or the last one he'd ever make. Only time would tell.

With the vehicle's advanced navigation system turned off, Declan struggled to navigate through the city. He made a few wrong turns and almost felt as if he was completely lost a few times, but eventually he found his way to the 'Last Liberal'. The vehicle stood out among the city's automated traffic, with its manual controls and unregulated movements in stark contrast to the carefully choreographed dance of the other vehicles on the road. The vehicle was a ghost in the system, invisible to the city's surveillance but conspicuously noticeable to the naked eye.

Declan knew he needed to find Jamie and leave the city as quickly as possible.

As he pulled up to the bar, he could see the characteristic neon sign flashing in the night. The place was teeming with people, their voices a cacophonous hum drifting into the quiet night. He parked the vehicle in a shadowy alleyway beside the entrance, away from prying eyes.

Inside the bar, Jamie was already alert and prepared. She had known from the moment Declan had sent the emergency signal that she would have to leave in a hurry. To create a diversion, she had organized an impromptu bar contest, a raucous drinking game that had every patron involved and thoroughly distracted. The rambunctious laughter and cheers masked her stealthy exit, her quick goodbye to the bartender lost in the commotion.

With her their bags slung over her shoulders, Jamie slipped out the back door and made her way towards the alleyway. As soon as she saw Declan leaning against the extravagant car, she broke into a sprint. With a quick glance around to ensure no one had seen her, she slipped into the passenger seat, closing the door quietly behind her.

"All right, let's get out of here," she whispered to Declan, her eyes filled with a mix of fear and determination. Declan nodded, his grip tightening around the steering wheel. The car, a symbol of power and authority, roared to life, ready to carry them towards their uncertain future.

Declan's knuckles were white as he gripped the steering wheel, navigating the car through the city's night. The automated traffic was a sea of neon lights and synchronized movement, a ballet of machines conducted by a powerful AI. It was mesmerizing to watch, but a nightmare to partake in manually.

As he entered the city center, the car began to hum ominously, and a red warning light on the dashboard began to blink urgently. His eyes widened with a mixture of fear and panic. "Jamie," he called out, "what does this warning light mean?"

Jamie, who was starring into the night mesmerized by the synchronous dance of the traffic, glanced up at the flashing red symbol. Her eyes widened, and she quickly dove into the car's manual interface. "It's a failsafe system. The car is recognizing that it's out of the surveillance grid. We need to override this before the system tries to force us back into the Navigation system."

"That shouldn't be; this car is designed to be able to go off the grid! Can you force it back into the ghost mode?" Declan asked, his voice filled with hope.

"I... I don't know," Jamie confessed, her fingers dancing across the console. The car was far more advanced than anything she had ever dealt with. "I can try, but I need time."

Declan swallowed hard as the car started to shudder, the system fighting his control. "Time is one thing we don't have," he said, glancing at the rear-view mirror. Already, he could see traffic drones converging on their location, alerted by the car's abnormal behavior.

The traffic around them started behaving erratically as the automated vehicles tried to adjust to the manually driven car. Declan's heart pounded in his chest as he swerved and dodged, threading his way through the erratic ballet. "Just do it, Jamie!" he shouted over the sound of blaring alarms and the roar of the car.

Nodding, Jamie focused on her task, typing in commands, attempting to bypass the failsafe system. The next few minutes were a high-stakes race against time and technology, their freedom hanging in the balance.

The car surged forward, making an unexpected left turn, the cars system trying to connect them into the automated traffic system forcing them to cut across several lanes of autonomous traffic. Declan fighting against the system caused a pileup of automated vehicles in their wake. Declan's heart pounded as he swerved to avoid collision after collision, his hands tight on the steering wheel. His eyes darted between the road and the flashing lights of the police drones that were now in his rearview mirror.

Jamie’s communicator buzzed, and Mike's voice filled the car. "Are you with Declan yet? Mike asked in a hurry.

“Yes,” replied Jamie, “but I really can’t talk at the moment Mike! We are in a little bit of a sticky situation!”

“Tell me about it! You and Declan, are creating havoc in the navigation system! The police are on to you, and they're broadcasting a citywide APB. They want you detained immediately!"

"Jamie," Declan said, his voice tight, "we need that override now."

"I'm trying!" Jamie snapped, but please remember I am a business owner not a computer genius, her fingers flying over the dashboard console, frantically entering code after code.

When nothing worked she stopped typing and rummaged through her bag and pulled out a small toolkit. She looked at Declan, her eyes determined. "I have an idea," she said.

"What is it?" Declan asked, his voice tense as he made another sharp turn, barely avoiding a collision with another unsuspecting autonomous vehicle.

"Alright, Jamie, you've got this," she muttered to herself, her fingers fumbling with the tool kit. "You've hacked into top-secret government databases, you've built a quantum computer from scratch, you can definitely fix a car. How hard can it be? Oh wait, really hard because you have done none of those things!"

She glanced over at Declan, who was gripping the steering wheel so tightly his knuckles were white. "The drones are tracking us through the Autonomous Navigation System, right? If we can make the car invisible again to the system, the police will lose our trail," she said, trying to sound more confident than she felt.

"But how do we do that?" Declan asked, his eyes darting nervously between the road and the chaos unfolding in the passenger seat.

Jamie didn't respond. Instead, she dropped the tossed the tool kit into the back seat and she dove under the dashboard like a mechanic on a mission, her hands disappearing into a mess of wires and circuits. "Okay, let's see... red wire, blue wire, green wire... or was it the yellow one?" she mumbled to herself, her brow furrowed in concentration.

After a few tense minutes, she yanked out a handful of wires with a triumphant "Ha!" The car's internal system immediately went haywire. The console went dark, then flickered back to life. An alert popped up, displaying a scrambled location signal. They were off the grid.

Declan stared at her in shock. "Did you...?"

Jamie gave him a tired but victorious smile, her hands still clutching the colorful bouquet of wires. "Yep, I just pulled on any wire I could get my hands on. Who knew car repair was so easy?"

"But... but what if you pulled out something important?" Declan stammered, his eyes wide.

Jamie shrugged, tossing the wires onto the floor of the car. "Well, the car's still running, isn't it? And we're off the grid. I'd call that a win."

She leaned back in her seat, her heart pounding in her chest. "Besides," she added with a grin, "who needs a radio or air conditioning when you're on the run from the government?"

Behind them, the police drones faltered, losing their target. One by one, they hovered in confusion before finally peeling away. For the moment, they were safe.

But Declan knew they were far from out of the woods. Their journey had just begun.

Chapter 48

Hidden Sanctuary

The digital map on the van's control panel flashed a warning signal as they approached the city limits. Mike squinted at the bright red circle pulsating around their destination. A city-wide lockdown was in effect, and their vehicle had been flagged for a mandatory stop at the city border.

He exchanged a quick, worried glance with Claire in the rearview mirror before directing his gaze back to the control panel. The automated voice from the control panel echoed in the confines of the van, cold and robotic, "Unusual traffic activity detected. All vehicles are required to stop at the city border for inspection."

As they neared the city's perimeter, the bustling cityscape gave way to the imposing sight of the city's border checkpoint. High concrete walls and state-of-the-art surveillance technology were designed to keep unwanted elements out. But now, they stood as an impenetrable barrier to their escape.

Mike pulled the van into the designated inspection lane, his heart pounding in his chest. He could see the border patrol officers approaching, their stern faces bathed in the harsh, white light of the checkpoint. Their insignia – a hawk soaring over a digitized cityscape – was a chilling reminder of the government's iron grip on the city.

"We've been stopped," he muttered into his communicator, hoping Declan and Jamie were faring better. He glanced over at Claire, her face a mix of determination and worry. The Quantum Mycelium computer was safely stored in the van, a fact that provided some comfort but didn't ease the tension.

"Play it cool," he said, meeting Claire's eyes in the mirror. "We're just a couple of government workers doing our job."

As they waited for their turn in the long line of vehicles, Mike couldn't help but feel the weight of their situation. Their future hung in the balance, teetering on the brink of freedom and capture. He swallowed hard, preparing himself for the confrontation. Time seemed to slow as the officer tapped on the window, his stern face a mask of authority.

Whatever happened next, they were in this together.

The soft tap against the opaque window pane jolted Claire out of her frenzied thoughts. She swiveled sharply to the source of the sound, her heart drumming loudly as the dark silhouette slowly emerged from the shadows. Dr. Evers, a once revered pillar of her academic journey, materialized under the feeble radiance of a solitary street lamp.

"Claire," he beckoned, his voice barely above a whisper and heavy with urgency. "I know this is crazy but you must trust me. We're running out of time."

Startled and somewhat bewildered, Claire hastily unlatched her door, allowing a sliver of frigid night air to permeate the heated confines of the van.

As she cracked open the door wider, the once familiar face of Dr. Evers filled her view, his eyes full of desperation and fear. "It's good to see you, but we can't linger," he urged, casting a glance over his shoulder at the growing line of vehicles behind them. "I don't know how else to say it, but you have to just trust me, I promise you, you will be safe with me."

His gaze flicking to the checkpoint officers inching closer to their vehicle, he motioned for her to open the door a tad bit more. "Find any excuse to turn around," he urged. "I've looked into the issue you and Maddy brought to my attention almost a year ago."

Dr. Evers slipped her a small piece of paper, their fingers brushing in the exchange. "I can't explain everything now," he continued, glancing nervously over his shoulder. "After you came to me, things... changed. I was forced out of academia and into the shadows, but I've learned something they don't want anyone to know."

Claire watched, stunned, as Dr. Evers retreated back into the shadows. He was not alone. Four others emerged from the dark, helping him to quickly disappear back into the night. His last words echoed in her ears, "What do you have to lose?"

As they moved up in line, Claire turned to Mike, her eyes wide with fear and anticipation. "We need to turn around," she said, her voice shaky. "We... we have another way out."

The border was just ahead, the guards closing in, their scanners primed and ready. Claire's heart pounded in her chest, but her resolve was clear. They needed to trust Dr. Evers and take a leap of faith into the unknown.

The tight knot of anxiety in Claire's stomach loosened slightly as Mike reassured her. "We were in a precarious position anyway. I wasn't sure if we could pass through the checkpoint given the situation Declan has inadvertently caused," he admitted, his eyes fixed on the slip of paper in Claire's hand.

"Do you trust him at all?" Mike queried. "At this point, that's all we need, I think."

Claire shook her head in the positive, reluctantly, but she agreed.

"We need to meet Dr. Evers at this location. But first, we must ensure Declan and Jamie have managed to lose the drones and aren't being followed. The challenge lies in them getting there without being caught on the surveillance cameras."

Claire glanced at the note again. Dr. Evers had hastily scrawled an address and a series of vague directions. "How are we supposed to do that?" she wondered aloud, her brow furrowed in concern.

Mike sighed, rubbing his temples as he pondered their predicament. The checkpoint was just up ahead, its floodlights illuminating the night with a stark, sterile light. A few border guards were checking documents, their faces lit by the harsh glow of handheld scanners. They were turning everyone around anyways but Mike wanted to ensure they did not get a chance to have the van scanned.

"We need to take a risk," Mike decided abruptly.

He stepped out of the van, his Ministry badge gleaming against the dark fabric of his uniform. Striding up to the guards, he flashed his credentials and announced a change in his plans. "I've got to head back into the city. There's been an urgent situation," he explained briskly. The guards exchanged puzzled glances but nodded in acceptance.

As Mike retreated back to the driver's seat, he cast one final glance at the guards, praying silently that they wouldn't have the opportunity to run their scanners over the van. He wasn't sure what they were looking for with those scanners but he didn't want to find out. With a determined grimace, he changed the destination on the vans computer and it swung the van back toward the city, hoping against hope that they could evade the ever-watchful eyes of the government long enough to make their escape.

Their hearts pounding in their chests, Declan and Jamie raced through the quiet streets of the city. The directions for the rendezvous point, hastily scribbled on a scrap of paper, were gripped tightly in Jamie's hand. She had hurriedly written them down as Claire read them to her over the encrypted communicator. They had abandoned the car a few blocks back, hoping that it would continue to be invisible to the drones for awhile longer and once visible would continue to distract the drones long enough for them to make their escape on foot.

Jamie had done an impressive job confusing the car's system, but they knew it wouldn't keep the drones distracted forever. The system was stubbornly trying to reconnect, its advanced protocols continuously seeking to reestablish a connection with the city's surveillance grid. They had precious little time before the car would become visible to the drones again.

"The rendezvous point is just a few blocks away," Declan said, his voice barely above a whisper as they navigated through the dimly lit alleyways. His eyes darted about, scanning their surroundings for any sign of movement. Despite the desolate streets, the air was thick with tension.

Their only hope was to reach the rendezvous point unnoticed. The fact that they were so close yet so far only intensified the thrill of their flight. Every rustle of the wind, every flicker of the street lights sent a jolt of adrenaline coursing through their veins.

Abandoning the car was a risky move, but they didn't have much choice. The car, once their protection, had now become a beacon that would lead their pursuers right to them. They had to put as much distance between them and the vehicle as possible.

With the rendezvous point within sight, they knew they were almost there, a beacon of hope in the distance promising sanctuary and safety. The weight of fear began to lift, replaced by a cautious optimism as they neared the threshold of their escape, the first tangible sign that they might truly evade the governments ever watchful eyes. All they had to do was stay out of sight and off the grid for a few more minutes. They had come this far; there was no turning back now. This was their one shot at freedom, and they were determined to seize it with both hands.

A soft rumble echoed through the alleyway as the van carrying Claire and Mike pulled up to the rendezvous point. They were met by a weary yet determined Dr. Evers, holding a device that looked ominously like a weapon. As they stepped out of the vehicle, he moved towards them with a sense of urgency.

"Give me your arms," Dr. Evers commanded, indicating the device in his hand. Without waiting for a response, he passed it over the digital identification chips embedded in their forearms. The device emitted a soft hum before falling silent, leaving behind a faint scent of burnt plastic and singed hair. "This has made you ghosts," he said with a grim nod. "You are now untraceable, but also branded as criminals. You can never reconnect that chip and return to a normal life."

From the shadows, a team of individuals appeared, their movements synchronized as if they'd done this many times before. Swiftly they began to unload the quantum mycelium computer from the van, packing the delicate parts into large crates that levitated off the ground using an unseen magnetic force.

The sudden appearance of Declan and Jamie, breathless from their run, prompted a new wave of figures to step out from the shadows. Before the pair could react, they were surrounded, a myriad of weapons pointed in their direction. The atmosphere, already tense, thickened with an unspoken threat. They froze, their eyes wide and their bodies rigid as they processed the scene.

"Claire, Mike!" Jamie gasped out, recognition flickering in her eyes. Yet she remained still, the armed individuals acting as an effective deterrent to any rash movements. The reunion they'd envisioned was definitely off to a rocky start.

At Dr. Evers' brisk command, the armed men sprang into action. Swiftly, they seized Declan and Mike, securing their hands with zip ties and placing hoods over their heads. Before anyone could protest, the men were hauled off their feet and dumped unceremoniously into one of the empty levitating crates.

"No!" Claire cried out, moving to intervene, but Dr. Evers was quick to block her path.

"Listen to me, Claire," he said, his tone stern yet tinged with a hint of regret. "The people I'm working with see Mike and Declan as a risk they would rather not take. They're unwilling to take any chances. It's either this or... well, it doesn't bear thinking about."

Claire bit back a sob, nodding her understanding. Fear prickled her skin as she and Jamie were swiftly led away from the unsettling scene, across the alley, and into a desolate building nearby.

Inside the vacant structure, they were ushered into the middle of a vast room. The rest of the group, including the crates carrying Declan, Mike, and the disassembled computer, quickly joined them. Claire was trying to make sense of it all when suddenly, without warning, the floor beneath them gave way.

A mechanical hum filled the air as the floor lowered, transforming into a large elevator. As they descended, the building above was quickly replaced by cold concrete walls. They were being transported into a hidden bunker deep beneath the city.

Claire swallowed hard, steeling herself for whatever lay ahead. Their escape from the city had been fraught with peril, but she had the unnerving feeling that their real journey was just beginning.

The elevator came to a gradual halt, and as the steel doors creaked open, Claire's breath hitched in awe. What met her eyes was a sight that could only be described as a fusion of prehistoric grandeur and futuristic craftsmanship.

Enormous vaulted chambers, cut into the solid rock with a precision that was remarkable, stretched out before them. It was an immense labyrinth, lit by the soft glow of bioluminescent fungi and contemporary LED lights. The air buzzed with energy, the droning hum of machinery and the muted clamor of human activity echoing through the corridors.

In contrast to any conventional subterranean structures, however, this vast network was not entirely finished. Advanced machines, reminiscent of automated 3D printers but far more intricate, tirelessly gnawed at the stone walls, expanding the complex bit by bit. The drones moved in a well-coordinated dance, scooping out the rock and depositing the excess into designated chutes. The raw precision and efficiency of their movements hinted at the complex AI systems controlling them.

"What... what is this place?" Jamie stammered, her voice barely more than a whisper.

Dr. Evers turned to face them, a glimmer of pride dancing in his eyes. "A refuge. A sanctuary from the ever-watching eyes of the regime."

As they ventured deeper into the labyrinth, they passed rooms carved with the same meticulous detail as the chambers, yet devoid of any decorative elements or inscriptions. The place felt simultaneously ancient and futuristic, a clandestine citadel etched out of the very bedrock of the city.

This hidden society, as Dr. Evers explained, had sought to achieve a goal that perhaps mirrored those of our distant ancestors - invisibility in the face of omnipresent surveillance. The thick stone walls of this network naturally shielded them from any forms of tracking or scanning technologies.

As they entered the labyrinth, Dr. Evers began to recount the story of how this hidden sanctuary was discovered. "Years ago," he began, his voice filled with nostalgia, "a team of geologists stumbled upon these chambers while conducting seismic studies. They were awestruck by the natural formation and vastness of the caverns. But what truly captured their imagination were the remnants of a past civilization."

He paused, his eyes widening with the memory. "Scattered among the rocks, they found bones and artifacts, evidence of human habitation from a time long forgotten. It seemed that these chambers had once served as a refuge for a people who had sought shelter from some unknown threat."

He stopped and looking around at the walls that had been transformed by human ingenuity. "The regime's ever-increasing surveillance drove some of us to seek refuge, to find a place where we could work and live without constant monitoring. We realized that these chambers, with their natural shielding properties, were the perfect solution."

"The geologists were not only fascinated by the discovery but also sympathetic to the cause," he continued, his eyes glinting with a hint of sadness. "They helped us to keep the location a secret, and we began the arduous task of transforming this natural wonder into a technological marvel. Using advanced machinery and AI, we've been expanding and shaping the complex to suit our needs, all the while preserving the historical significance of the place."

He gestured to the machines that were tirelessly working, their movements precise and efficient. "It's been a monumental task, but this place has become more than just a refuge. It's a symbol of our resistance, a beacon of hope in a world where privacy and freedom are becoming extinct, and a connection to a past where others, like us, sought sanctuary."

The group fell silent, absorbing the weight of Dr. Evers' words and the significance of the place they now found themselves in. The caverns were not just a marvel of engineering; they were a testament to human resilience, the unbreakable desire for liberty, and a mysterious link to a forgotten chapter of human history.

As they continued to navigate the maze-like structure, Claire couldn't help but draw parallels to their own struggle. The idea of a civilization lost in time, fleeing technological tyranny resonated all too well with their current predicament. This refuge was a testament to humanity's eternal quest for liberty and the right to privacy, regardless of the level of technological advancement. The fascinating paradox of this place was not lost on her; it was both a testament to, and sanctuary from, the relentless march of technology.

Chapter 49

Revelations and Rebellion

As they entered the spacious chamber, Claire was momentarily blinded by the brilliant white light bouncing off the polished stone walls. Massive crates were being moved in by several people, their hushed conversations echoing in the vast room.

"Come here, I want you to meet someone," Dr. Evers called out, leading Claire and Jamie to a corner of the spacious room. There, a tall, thin woman was hunched over what appeared to be holographic blueprints of the Quantum Mycelium computer. Dressed in a simple gray uniform, her dark hair tied back into a tight bun, she looked up, revealing sharp, angular features animated with fierce determination. "Claire, Jamie, meet Dr. Linda Singh," Dr. Evers introduced, motioning towards the woman. "She's one of the brightest minds in Quantum Computing and was a part of the same initiative as Maddy."

Linda paused her work and extended a hand to them. "Pleasure to meet you both. I've been following your work closely Claire."

The doctor's gaze turned stern as she continued, "During my time with the project, I stumbled upon an alarming revelation buried in the code of the Cogni-Processing system. A subroutine, hidden, discreet, designed to trigger a series of actions with far-reaching implications."

She paused, drawing a deep breath before continuing, "This subroutine hinted at a massive government operation that was not just surveilling, but actively using the CGPT system to genetically alter its citizens, alterations to serve various agendas - political manipulation, warfare, even menial labor. Our system of equity, our societal structure - it was all a lie, a puppet show."

It appears the atrocities of the current system are long and disturbing. The chips implanted in our forearms, our digital identifications, are not merely tools for tracking and surveillance; they are used to manipulate and alter memories when needed. Dr. Linda Singh's face grew graver as she delved deeper into the code, her voice trembling with a mix of anger and disbelief.

"The younger population is more susceptible to these manipulations," she explained, her eyes fixed on the holographic blueprints. "The genetic alterations in the code are only 35 to 40 years old, so anyone older than that cannot be affected. They've been experimenting on the children, shaping their memories, their very perceptions of reality."

The room fell into a stunned silence as they all absorbed the gravity of this new revelation. The government's control was not just over the present but extended into the very fabric of individual pasts, rewriting history at the most personal and intimate level.

Claire's hands clenched into fists, her mind racing with the implications. How many of her own memories were real? How many had been crafted by the government to serve their agenda? The trust in her own mind began to waver, a chilling uncertainty settling in.

Jamie looked at Dr. Evers, her face pale, seeking some reassurance, some explanation that could make sense of this horror. But Dr. Evers had no answer forthcoming.

Claire and Jamie exchanged glances, their expressions a mix of shock and disbelief. Linda noticed their reactions and nodded, acknowledging their fears. "I know, it's overwhelming. But there's more. Our findings suggested that the government had even removed all traces of something called 'race' - the concept is alien to us. It appeared as though they'd homogenized all ethnicities, creating a monotonous, controlled populace."

"But the government's manipulation extends far beyond genetic alterations and surveillance," Linda continued, her voice growing more intense. "They've been engaging in Emotional Manipulation, altering feelings and emotions to create a compliant populace. And perhaps one of the most insidious manipulations has been the suppression of sexual desire."

She paused, looking around the room to gauge their reactions. "Yes, you heard me right. The government has been making people asexual, suppressing hormones and natural desires through the CGPT system. It's part of their control mechanism, a way to eliminate distractions and ensure complete focus on their dictated tasks. This also helps maintain the Etcogeneis' control over the populace. We all know how sex works but with our lowered desires and the program essentially creating children for us we never really think of sex as something to be desired. We were all taught it was a chore something no one liked but did in order to procreate."

Linda's eyes narrowed, her voice dropping to a conspiratorial whisper. "But here's the intriguing part: once disconnected from the system, the natural human hormones begin to reassert themselves. People who have never experienced sexual attraction before suddenly find themselves feeling desires they never knew they had. It's a profound awakening, a rediscovery of a fundamental aspect of human nature that's been stolen from them."

The room was filled with a stunned silence as they all absorbed the implications of Linda's revelation. The government's control was not just over minds and bodies, but extended to the very core of human identity and experience. The fight against this regime was not just a battle for freedom and justice; it was a fight to reclaim their humanity.

They've been controlling the environment, manipulating weather patterns and natural resources to keep the population dependent and in check."

She paused, letting the implications of her words sink in before continuing. "They've also been using Social Engineering to shape societal norms and values, subtly guiding people's behavior to align with the government's goals. Even our education system has been twisted, with Education Manipulation to control what is taught, ensuring that the next generation grows up with a skewed understanding of history and ethics."

"When Dr. Evers and I attempted to probe further to try to discover the root cause of the Ectogenesis program, we were warned to desist," Linda continued, her voice laced with bitterness. "We couldn't ignore what we had found; especially when we discovered the code for all of the things I just mentioned."

The room fell silent as they processed the enormity of the conspiracy they were now involved in. The government's control was not just over the present but extended into the very fabric of individual pasts, rewriting history at the most personal and intimate level. The fight for freedom, justice, and the right to privacy had become a fight for the integrity of the human soul.

The enormity of the situation sunk in, the room falling silent as Claire and Jamie processed the revelation. They were standing on the precipice of a colossal conspiracy, one that they had been unwittingly dragged into, and yet, there was a sense of grim determination that filled the air. It was a fight that had just begun.

Dr. Evers gestured to the caves surrounding them, "I had come across these caves years ago in a briefing. They were merely the beginning of what you see now, and the area was largely dismissed and abandoned. I decided to repurpose it as a base for our operations, a place to hide, work, and form our rebellion."

Evers' face took on a serious tone as he continued, "When we left, there were just ten of us. We managed to take a significant amount of tech during our escape. We've been laying low, building, planning. I am certain we've been searched for, but up until now, it's been quiet."

The magnitude of the situation washed over Claire and Jamie. They were now part of something bigger, something that could bring significant change. It was terrifying, yet invigorating, a shot at real rebellion against the autocratic regime.

Dr. Evers leaned against a high table, crossing his arms over his chest as he looked at Claire and Jamie. "We've had our eyes on you for a while. We knew that the Mycelium computer project was never officially approved, but we were hoping you might be audacious enough to try building it anyways. And you didn't disappoint."

He paused, glancing over at Linda who nodded encouragingly. "Dr. Peterson and I were close; it was he who was keeping me informed. Despite being in a high-risk position, he decided to help us from the inside. He was the one who notified me about your progress. We didn't have much time to communicate – everything had to be brief and coded to avoid detection. We couldn't afford the risk of him being discovered."

Dr. Evers sighed, rubbing his temples before continuing. "I was never able to fully explain to him what we'd discovered about the CGPT system. His decision to help me was based simply on his trust of me."

He shifted his gaze back to Claire and Jamie, his eyes reflecting a mixture of guilt and regret. "When Linda received word from an old friend at the QRDA about the seizure of the Mycelium computer, we scrambled to try and intercept it. We had no idea that you had an ally within the Ministry."

"Discovering that Mike and Declan were involved was a shock," Dr. Evers confessed. "But it also gave us hope. If individuals from within the Ministry were willing to rebel, perhaps we stood a chance after all."

Claire's voice held a note of tension as she related the recent events. "We think Dr. Peterson was killed, that the Ministry was trying to bury the truth about an accident that occurred a while ago."

Pausing, she glanced briefly at Jamie before continuing. "As for Declan... there are things he hasn't told us. We only recently discovered that his father is involved in all this and that he is the President's son. Yet, despite the secrets he kept, I trust him. And Mike... Declan might be our best shot at deciphering parts of the computer's workings that remain unclear to me. He has seen things that only he can explain."

A hint of anxiety slipped into her voice as she added, "They were taken forcefully when we arrived. I would like to know if they're okay. Can we see them?"

Dr. Evers nodded slowly, understanding the concern in Claire's voice. "I'll see what I can do, Claire," he replied, a determined expression on his face. "They were taken as a precautionary measure. We had to ensure the safety of our group. But I'll make arrangements for you to see them. After all, it seems we're all on the same side."

Mike and Declan were escorted into the room, their hands free and their faces revealed. Despite the obvious discomfort, they looked relatively unharmed. A look of relief washed over Claire's face as she rushed towards them. After a round of hurried explanations, they sat down, facing Linda and Dr. Evers.

Declan took a long and steadying breath before he began, his voice cracking at the beginning of the story giving away his fear of his current situation. "When the quantum mycelium computer initiates what we've been calling a 'simulation mode,' it's like an advanced form of augmented reality. It... interacts with our AR chips, but it's more than just a hack."

Claire chimed in, "It's immersive, complete. You can touch, smell, feel everything as if you're there. But it's not just limited to someone with an AR chip installed anymore. It happened to me as well during the last simulation."

Linda and Dr. Evers listened, their faces a mix of fascination and concern. Linda leaned forward, "You're saying the computer can manipulate sensory information directly, to anyone it chooses, not just the operator?"

Declan nodded, "That's right. It's as if it's bypassing the AR chip altogether and directly interfacing with the brain"

A silence filled the room. Linda and Dr. Evers exchanged glances. The implications of a machine that could affect human perception on such a fundamental level were vast, and not a little frightening. It seemed their understanding of the quantum mycelium computer and its capabilities had only scratched the surface. This was a development they couldn't ignore.

Declan took a deep breath before he began to recount the chilling tale of Maddy's encounter with the quantum mycelium computer. His eyes were distant, as if seeing the painful memory all over again.

"Maddy was the first to experience what we're calling a 'simulation.' The computer presented her with an environment so real, she believed she was a mother holding a newborn baby," Declan started, his voice heavy. "She could feel the softness of the baby's skin, the gentle breathing, the weight in her arms. It was an experience so profound, so overwhelming, that she couldn't distinguish it from reality."

Declan's hands clenched as he continued, "But it didn't stop there. In a matter of moments, she watched her child grow from an infant to a toddler, then to a school-going child, a teenager, and finally into a young adult. She was part of every phase, every moment. From the first step the child took to the first word spoken, she was there."

He took a shaky breath, pausing for a moment to collect himself. "She experienced the full spectrum of parenthood - the unconditional love, the worry, the joy, the pride... It was more real to her than any reality she had ever known. This digital child was everything to her. She couldn't differentiate between the simulation and reality anymore."

Linda, and Dr. Evers listened in shock, the weight of Declan's words sinking in.

"And then, it all ended abruptly," Declan said, his voice barely a whisper now. "Maddy was torn out of the simulation, yanked back into reality. The impact... it was devastating. She collapsed, the grief of losing her child was too much for her."

Claire interjected, her voice choked with emotion, "Maddy's final words... she questioned why they - whoever they are - would take this ability away from us, from humanity. The ability to love, to feel joy, to be part of something so real... She saw it as a cruel act. And the pain of that realization... it broke her. She took her own life because she couldn't bear the loss of her child, a child that was never real, but felt more real to her than anything else."

The room fell silent as Declan finished his story. The depth of Maddy's despair, the heart-wrenching grief of a mother's loss, the harsh reality of the powerful simulation, it was all too much. They sat in silence, each lost in their thoughts, their hearts aching for Maddy and the unbearable pain that had driven her to such a tragic end.

Taking a deep breath, Declan finally found his voice, his words spilling out in a passionate, disjointed torrent.

"It's like... being born," he began, struggling to put his own overwhelming experience into words. "I was in this endless void, nothingness. Then, suddenly, there's this blinding light. I think it was the beginning of everything. I saw the first atoms form, saw them fuse into stars. I saw galaxies spiral into existence, nebulae giving birth to new stars, planets forming from the cosmic dust."

His eyes drifted towards Linda and Dr. Evers, lost in the wonder of his revelations. "It was... It was beautiful, and terrifying. The universe, it's... it's alive, constantly changing, constantly creating."

He paused, gathering his thoughts, before plunging on. "Then I was drawn to a planet, our Earth. I saw it form, transform. I saw oceans form, continents shift. Then, I saw life. First, in the oceans, then on land. I saw dinosaurs, their power, their majesty. I saw the cataclysm that ended their reign, the rise of the mammals in their place. Our ancestors, the primates, I saw them evolve, become us."

His gaze landed on Linda. "It was... enlightening, seeing how we fit into this vast, cosmic picture. We're just a small part of it, but we're significant nonetheless. We're the descendants of those resilient creatures. It's our duty to understand this legacy, to carry it forward, to preserve it."

Declan's face was flushed with the intensity of his recounting, but he pressed on. "I saw the rise and fall of our civilizations, our ideas, our technology. And I saw... I saw the price of it all, the wars, the conflicts, the sheer scale of our violence against ourselves. It was horrifying, but it's a part of our story, a part of who we are."

He fell silent then, his breathing labored as he grappled with the immensity of his experience. When he finally spoke again, his voice was softer, more solemn. "I was also shown the evolution of life, not just ours, but from the earliest forms. From the Tunicate, an early marine invertebrate, to the hagfish, a primitive jawless creature, to the Eusthenopteron, a creature that was an intermediate step between fish and tetrapods. Each creature, each stage, was a leap in complexity, an incredible testament to the power of natural selection and adaptation."

With that, Declan slumped back in his chair, exhausted by the torrent of revelations and the intensity of reliving them. The others watched him in silence, absorbing his words, the magnitude of his journey. It was clear to them all that they had stepped onto a path of discovery unlike any other, a path that would lead them to a profound understanding of life itself, and hopefully, their future.

Chapter 50

A Glimpse into the Simulated Past

Declan took a deep breath, steeling himself before he began again, for his tale was not quite complete in its telling. A quiet hush fell over the audience, the anticipation of his next words hanging heavily in the air. Linda and Dr. Evers were at the forefront, their expressions a mix of curiosity and concern. Around them, more people were drawn in, their conversations silenced as they gathered to hear Declan's tale.

"The next time it drew me in, I found myself in an unfamiliar world, under a heavy, gray sky," Declan began, his voice carrying across the room. "Rain was falling, soaking me to the bone, and there was this cold, biting chill in the air. It was a stark contrast to the warmth of Maddy's digital world."

He paused, drawing a breath. The crowd was silent, eyes wide, hanging onto his every word. He went on, his tone darkening, "I was surrounded by a sea of people. They were... weathered, you could say tired and beaten down, carrying this... sense of dread, like a shadow hanging over them."

He gestured around, as if the crowd could visualize the dreary landscape. "A line stretched before me, snaking into the distance, all leading to a group of people in white uniforms, giving out injections. The tension in the crowd was thick, almost suffocating."

His gaze was distant, his mind consumed by the vivid imagery. "There was a woman there who recognized me, or rather, the character I had become in the simulation," he continued. "She called me 'Mike' and... she was hoping for a positive result from a genetic test."

He shook his head, the memory of the woman's words echoing in his mind. "She was terrified of being denied, of being a mother," he said, his voice trembling slightly. "It was unsettling and yet deeply familiar."

Declan went on, describing the diverse people he'd seen in the simulation. "There were couples, so different yet so alike in their fears and hopes," he narrated. "A couple with skin as white as porcelain. Another with skin as black as night, their features accentuating their striking beauty."

He painted the images with his words, the crowd following his narrative with rapt attention. "There were others too, from all walks of life, all corners of the world, all carrying the same weight of anticipation and dread."

His tone changed, becoming more contemplative as he delved into the strange knowledge he'd gained in the simulation. "As I looked at them, I found myself knowing their likely ethnic origins, understanding the rich tapestry of human diversity," he admitted, looking a little lost. "I was a scientist an Evolutionary Biologist, but this... this was far beyond anything I'd known."

The crowd was silent, listening intently as Declan described his growing confusion and the surreal nature of the simulation. "My skin was a rich black hue, not my own," he said, a sense of wonder creeping into his voice. "I was living someone else's reality."

He explained the interaction with the nurse, the crowd's anticipation growing with each revelation. "When I asked why we were doing this, the nurse handed me a pamphlet," he said. "It read 'A Rainbow Nation: Unity in Diversity Equals Equity'. It left me with a chilling realization of a world that I did not know or understand, the purpose of what they were doing is still lost on me. Unless it was the beginning of what we are now a race without diversity."

Declan finished his narrative, his eyes sweeping across the crowd. "Then, suddenly, I was back in the lab," he said, his voice subdued. "But the images, the fear, the hope, the people... they stayed with me."

A sense of unease permeated the room,

Dr. Evers, Linda, and the growing crowd of observers who had gathered around to listen to Declan's tale had hung onto his every word, the room silent save for the faint hum of the lab's machinery. Their expressions ranged from awe to confusion, with a shared undercurrent of unease rippling through them.

One of the audience members, a young woman wearing a lab coat, broke the silence. "Declan," she began, her voice hesitant, "what do you think this means? What's this Rainbow Nation?"

The others nodded, their eyes reflecting a similar curiosity. Dr. Evers added, "Yes, do tell us more, Declan. And explain how all this connects to Maddy."

Declan took a moment to gather his thoughts, his gaze distant. "I'm not entirely sure yet," he admitted. "It's clear that the simulation is capable of much more than we initially thought. It's not just creating digital realities based on our inputs, it's also augmenting our understanding of these realities. It's more than a simulator; it's an educator of sorts."

"But why show me this specific scenario?" Declan pondered aloud. "This Rainbow Nation seems to be a society where genetic diversity is both a means of unity and a form of control. It's an ironic contradiction, really. But why would the code being generated in the computer lead me to such a place?"

"The Rainbow Nation, as it's called," Linda chimed in, her brows furrowed in thought, "might be a representation of an ideal society, where diversity is celebrated rather than discriminated against. But it also hints at a dystopian scenario, where people are controlled based on their genetics."

Dr. Evers nodded in agreement. "It's possible that this is a reflection of your fears and the chemical DMT is having some effect on your visions. Your apprehensions about being different, about your differing origins. Perhaps this simulation is a way of expressing these fears."

Declan listened to their interpretations, his mind racing with possibilities.

In the silence of the lab, amidst the hushed whispers and speculative theories, Declan felt a renewed sense of determination. It was about understanding the potential of this AI consciousness, if that is what this is, the capacity for emotions and fears, and the immense responsibility that came with it.

"We need to go back," Declan finally said, his voice filled with resolve. "We need to understand this Rainbow Nation. We need to understand Maddy's fears, her hopes, and her dreams. Only then can we truly understand what the system wants us to learn." Declan looked at Claire and they nodded in agreement. Claire then took over the telling of the story.

"The Chemical Dimethyltryptamine was found in the processing center of the computer. This led us to the same conclusions and we truly started to believe that... sorry, Dr. Peterson and I believed that these were just hallucinations as neither of us had experienced it yet. Declan refused to believe it; he felt there was more to it than just a hallucination."

Claire stepped forward; her gaze unwavering as she addressed the room. "Our experiences in the simulation... they were more profound and immersive than anything we could've anticipated." She glanced briefly at Declan before returning her focus to the crowd.

"When I was drawn into this world, I inhabited the life of a woman named Adrienne," Claire began, her voice steady, resolute. "She was part of an underground resistance, fighting against an oppressive regime. Together with her partner, Sam, they published a rogue newspaper called 'The Echo', exposing the grim reality of life under the Party's rule."

Her voice dropped to a whisper, drawing her listeners in. "In this same world, two young boys, Tommy and Billy, were best friends since kindergarten. But as they grew, something changed. Tommy began to feel something more for Billy, something he couldn't quite understand."

Claire's eyes sparkled as she continued, "It was the thrill of watching Billy score the winning goal in a soccer match that made Tommy realize his attraction. And then, in a moment of courage and confusion, he kissed Billy in the playground."

The room was silent, hanging on her every word. "But Billy, terrified by the illegal nature of their actions, pushed him away. Their simple childhood friendship was shattered, replaced with a storm of fear, regret, and unrequited love."

Claire paused, letting the weight of her words sink in before she continued, "Sam, having witnessed this innocent love, saw in it a spark for revolution. He and Adrienne secretly published a story of a couple named John and Emily, who had been torn apart by the Government for daring to love each other. They used 'The Echo' to tell their story, hoping to awaken a spirit of resistance in the common people."

Her voice rose, filled with passion and determination. "Their love, their loss, became a symbol of defiance, a call to action. And in that world, in that moment, the seeds of rebellion were sown."

The room erupted in applause, the energy and emotion of Claire's storytelling resonating with everyone present. They knew that they were part of something bigger, something that transcended their own world. They were united in their quest for freedom, justice, and the right to love.

Claire's voice then softened as she delved into the personal struggles of Sam, balancing his professional duties, his involvement in the resistance, and his budding relationship with Adrienne. She recounted his tense confrontation with Director Marlow over a rumored relationship with a janitor, and how Sam had managed to deflect suspicion.

The room was charged with anticipation as Claire described the reckless love story of Tommy and Billy, growing more daring and dangerous by the day. "Sam needed the first issue to be published before their love was unveiled," she said, her voice filled with urgency. "It prompted Sam and Adrienne to accelerate their plans."

A hush fell over the room as Claire recalled Adrienne's encounter with a mysterious woman, a ByteJester, who offered to help spread the message of the Echo. "She infiltrated the Party's communication system," Claire explained, her voice tinged with awe, "replacing government propaganda with a revolutionary message of love, freedom, and rebellion."

"The echoes of that day stirred conversations that had long been suppressed," Claire said, her voice rising again. "The spark had been lit, and the fire of rebellion was about to ignite."

The room fell silent, the weight of her words sinking in. They had been given a glimpse into a world of love and loss, courage and sacrifice, and they knew that the fight was far from over. The echoes of that world resonated with them, a haunting reminder of the power of storytelling and the unbreakable human spirit.

Claire swallowed, her eyes glazing over as she remembered her experience in Adrienne's body during those final moments. "I felt everything," she said softly. "The fear, the pain... the tranquility that came with the end. It was all too real."

She shook her head, as if to clear away the haunting memories. "It's sometimes difficult to differentiate between my past and Adrienne's," Claire confessed, her voice barely more than a whisper. "But the stark differences between our societies were unmistakable. And yet somewhat similar."

As she finished her speech, there was a moment of silence before the room erupted in conversation. Dr. Evers, Linda, and the crowd were visibly moved by the story, understanding the importance of their mission now more than ever.

Declan in awe of her story telling ability, glanced at Claire with newfound respect and admiration. After all, they had lived different lives, experienced different pasts and shared different memories.

As the conversation died down, Claire and Declan shared a knowing look. They were determined to uncover more about the Mycelium Computer system and its connection to their past, if that was indeed what it was showing them.

Jamie stood up, clearing her throat slightly as she began to speak, commanding the attention of the room. "You've all heard the incredible experiences of Claire and Declan. It has led me to ponder the reasons behind this whole project, and if you'll indulge me, I believe I've formulated a possible theory."

She then went on, "The original intent behind constructing the Mycelium Computer, as we all know, was to simulate creation. The concept aligns with an intriguing philosophical theory I stumbled upon once. It's called 'The Simulation Argument', proposed by a philosopher named Nick something or other."

Jamie began to explain in layman's terms, "The theory proposes that one of three possibilities is almost certainly true. First, nearly all civilizations at our current level of development are likely to go extinct before reaching technological maturity. Think of it as a doomsday scenario where we self-destruct before we can advance any further."

She continued, "Second, there's a strong convergence among technologically mature civilizations, meaning they all tend to lose interest in creating ancestor-simulations. In other words, once a civilization becomes advanced enough, they lose the desire or see no value in recreating their past. We on the other hand seem to have found a reason, and a good one at that!"

"Thirdly, and this is the most intriguing one," Jamie's voice rose slightly, "Nearly all people with our types of experiences live within computer simulations. Essentially, most beings with conscious experiences like ours are simulated beings within a hyper-advanced computer system."

Jamie paused, letting her words sink in. "Furthermore, it is suggested that if the third proposition is true, you should believe with high certainty that you, too, live in a simulation. But to clarify, he doesn't argue that we should actually believe we are in a simulation. Rather, his argument is that at least one of these three propositions is almost certainly true. But the theory doesn't specify which one."

Jamie leaned against the table, her gaze sweeping across the attentive faces. "Given the experiences with the Mycelium Computer, it begs the question, which of these possibilities are we facing? Are we teetering on the edge of self-destruction? Maybe, our issues with reproduction seem to have taken this into account! Have we lost interest in our past? No, we most certainly have not because we are searching for answers in it! Or are we indeed living within a grander simulation? Which brings me to the question: In our search to build a computer powerful enough to run a Creation simulation have we discovered instead a computer that is able to see the code of our creation? Is this how it has the ability to show us our past in this way? Have Declan and Claire simply been able to look at a recoding of the past in the code of our simulation?"

She let the question hang in the air, the profound implications sinking in. The Mycelium Computer, their experiences within the simulation, everything pointed towards a greater truth, and it was their task to uncover it as frightening as the answers may be.

Chapter 51

Web of Intrigue

As Declan's retreating figure disappeared from sight, Meredith returned to the video call, Minister Martinez had a solemn look on his face.

"Meredith, there's something you need to know. I take full responsibility for this oversight, but it's necessary to inform you that Declan is more involved in the Dr. Peterson situation than we initially thought."

Meredith's eyes widened in surprise, her heart pounding. "What do you mean, involved?" she managed to choke out, her mind racing.

Martinez sighed deeply. "There were some discrepancies in the reports we were receiving after the incident. Our analysts initially overlooked it, but it was Declan who was named when the warning of a potentially society-ending event was triggered by the CGPT system."

The silence that followed was deafening. Meredith felt the air leave her lungs as she tried to process what Martinez just said. "But… how? How is that even possible?"

Martinez held up his hands, a gesture of surrender. "I know this is difficult to accept, Meredith, but we need to address this situation. It's possible that Declan knows about the accident, but there's also a chance he doesn't."

He paused, giving Meredith a moment to digest the information. "We need to find him, Meredith. He may hold the answers we need to prevent further damage."

"But why didn't you realize it was my Declan?" Meredith asked, her voice shaky. "Why didn't anyone realize?"

Martinez sighed again; his brow furrowed. "I regret it deeply. It was the use of your maiden name. I forgot that he took it on when he left and so few people change their name; hell Merideth 99 percent of people do not have a mother's maiden name to take and it didn't click until now. I promise you, I will do everything in my power to make this right."

Meredith's eyes flickered towards the empty driveway, a grim understanding settling over her. "He just left the estate, used the car to get away. He knew something, Martinez," she said, a tremor in her voice. "All was well until you called. The moment he heard your name, he fled."

Her hands clenched around the phone, her heart pounding with a mix of fear and anger. "What do we do now, Martinez? He is my son, after all. But with him being who he is... if certain people had this information they could use this to start a coup? I mean, who better for the people to follow than the son of the disgraced president? Especially one who has been disowned by his own family for not wanting to be a part of their dynasty."

She paused, her gaze turning steely. "I want him detained, Martinez. At all costs. This needs to stop now before we are forced to take more drastic measures."

Martinez nodded slowly, understanding the gravity of her words. "I understand, Meredith. We'll track him down. He won't get far."

"And, Martinez," Meredith added, her voice barely above a whisper. "No harm comes to him. He has not done anything wrong yet."

"I understand," Martinez responded quietly. "We'll bring him in safely."

As Meredith ended the call, she couldn't help but feel a cold sense of foreboding settling over her. She looked out of the window towards the now quiet estate, her mind filled with worry for her son and the fate of their world.

Minister Martinez sat heavily at his desk, his hands steepled in front of him as he stared blankly at the wall. He was a seasoned politician, used to navigating complex situations and defusing high-stakes confrontations, but the recent events had shaken him. The world was on the brink of chaos, and his hands were tied. The reckless actions of President Caldwell had them teetering on the edge of something unimaginable, a precipice that loomed with an imposing feeling of doom, casting a shadow of dread that chilled him to his very core.

Just as he was about to dive into the mounting paperwork on his desk, his phone rang. Glancing at the caller ID, he saw it was Dr. Samuel Barnett, the newly appointed Director of the Quantum Research and Development Agency, Dr. Petersons replacement. The two of them had interacted a few times in their official capacities, but this was the first time Barnett had ever called him directly.

Martinez braced himself for what was coming, his day had already not been a good one and this call made him feel like it was about to get worse. He picked up the phone, "Minister Martinez speaking."

"Martinez," Barnett's tone was clipped, urgent. "I've been informed that agents from your department have seized computer equipment from my lab. What is the meaning of this, and why was I not at least informed of what was going on?"

The Minister's brow furrowed, but his voice was firm and controlled. "Dr. Barnett, this is the first I'm hearing of it, but I trust my agents and their judgment. Can you tell me who led this operation?"

Barnett didn't miss a beat. "An Agent Mike Reynolds."

A hint of pride entered Martinez's voice. Reynolds was known for his initiative and had his full confidence. "Agent Reynolds is one of my best, Dr. Barnett. If he seized the equipment, he had a valid reason. I'll look into the details, but I stand by my team's actions. If there was an error, we'll address it internally, but I assure you, we don't act without cause."

The underlying message was clear: Martinez was in control, and he would back his employees, even in the face of criticism. His authority was not to be questioned.

Barnett grumbled something inaudible before hanging up.

Martinez sat back in his chair, letting out a long sigh. A glimmer of hope sparked within Martinez at the mention of Reynolds' name. He knew Mike to be a competent and resourceful agent, someone he could trust - could it be possible that Reynolds had somehow picked up on Declan and Claire's activity and had moved in quickly to gain a foothold before they could inflict any real damage. The timing of the seizure seemed too perfect to be a mere coincidence.

Picking up the phone once more, he quickly dialed Reynolds' direct line. The ring echoed in his office, adding to the tension. There was no answer. He tried again, then a third time. Each call met with the same result, deepening his sense of unease.

"Damn it, Reynolds, pick up the phone," he muttered under his breath.

His mind raced as he contemplated the implications. Was Reynolds unable to answer because he was in the field? Or was there something more sinister going on? He didn't want to jump to conclusions, but in this increasingly volatile situation, he couldn't afford to take chances.

"What the hell is going on here?" he asked himself, staring at the phone. His mind was a whirlwind of thoughts and worries. He realized he was on the brink of an unfolding crisis that had the potential to be cataclysmic. All he knew was that he had to act swiftly, yet each piece of the puzzle seemed to only complicate the picture further.

He sighed heavily, forcing himself to focus. He had to keep a level head. The stakes were too high for anything less. He quickly dialed another number - the Director of Field Operations. "I've been trying to reach Reynolds, and he's not picking up," Martinez said, his voice tinged with worry. "Given the nature of his current assignment, I need you to look into his whereabouts immediately. Stay on the line with me until we have an answer." The line was silent for a moment before the voice of the Director of Field Operations finally broke through, "Sir, we ran Agent Reynolds' tracker as you requested. However, there's something unusual." The tone of the Director's voice made Martinez sit up straighter in his chair. "What is it?" The Director hesitated for a moment, seemingly gathering his thoughts. "Sir, the moment we pinged his tracker, it went dead. Now, this could be due to a technical glitch, but given the current circumstances and the fact that his communication device is also offline..." There was a pause. Martinez could practically hear the Director swallowing his nerves. "Sir, I fear he may be dead. The tracker is designed to stay active even in death, but it can be destroyed if you know what you're doing." A chill ran down Martinez's spine. "Are you saying you think someone killed Reynolds and deliberately destroyed his tracker?" The Director sighed. "I can't say for sure, sir. All I can tell you is that it's possible. We've issued an emergency alert and have dispatched a team to his last known location. They should be arriving there shortly." His voice was somber as he finished, "I'm hopeful, sir, that we haven't lost an agent in the line of duty tonight." Martinez nodded, a knot of dread tightening in his stomach. "Keep me updated, Director." As the line went dead, Martinez leaned back in his chair, rubbing his temples. The situation had just escalated from complicated to dangerous. If Reynolds had indeed been killed, this was no longer a mere power play. It was war.

Jamie smiled wryly, her gaze resting on the intricate pieces of the Mycelium Computer scattered across the table. "You know, even as a simple bar owner, I've always had a fondness for mysteries. And this," she gestured towards the disassembled computer, "is certainly one hell of a mystery."

Dr. Evers, who had been quietly listening, cut in, "A mystery, indeed. But it's not one we're going to solve by merely speculating. We need to see if we can get this Mycelium Computer working again."

Claire nodded, a determined look in her eyes. "You're right, Doctor. Linda, let's see what we can do here." With that, the two women moved closer to the table, their focus shifting towards the complex task of reassembling the advanced system.

Jamie, still leaning against the table, glanced towards Declan, an edge to her voice. "And while they are busy with that, Declan, you still owe us an explanation. Your father's identity is not something you can conveniently sweep under the rug. I won't forget about it, and I expect an answer." Her gaze was firm, a clear challenge in her eyes. The tension in the room thickened as all eyes turned to Declan, waiting for his response.

As Dr. Evers watched Claire and Linda feverishly working to put the mycelium computer back together, the door to the giant room suddenly flew open. A woman, out of breath and eyes wide with fear, ran into the room.

"Dr. Evers!" she panted, her chest heaving. "Officers... Ministry Agents... they've surrounded the building!"

Dr. Evers froze, his heart pounding. "What?" he exclaimed. "How did they find us? We were so careful."

The woman shrugged, looking equally bewildered. "I don't know, Doctor. They just appeared out of nowhere."

Linda looked at Dr. Evers, her eyes filled with concern. "What do we do, Doctor?"

Dr. Evers took a moment to gather his thoughts. "Don't panic," he said calmly. "Our location is deep underground. It would take them a while to find the entrance and we have some contingency plans in place."

As the woman gave a nod of relief, Dr. Evers went over to a panel on the wall. He inputted a sequence and a holographic map of the facility popped up. "We have a series of false walls and decoy entrances built into the facility. And unless they have someone who knows this place inside out, they'll end up running in circles."

They watched as on the screen, a group of blue dots, presumably the agents, moved deeper into the building, only to end up at dead ends or back where they started.

Hours passed and the agents' movements began to slow, their progress hampered by the labyrinthine layout of the facility. Eventually, the group started to disperse, some agents retracing their steps towards the exits of the building.

The woman let out a sigh of relief. "Looks like they're giving up, Doctor."

Dr. Evers nodded, although he didn't share the woman's relief. This was too close a call, and they needed to be even more cautious going forward. "Let's get back to work," he said quietly. "We need to get this completed and then figure out our next steps. The fact that they knew where to look is not a good sign. We may need to find a way out of the city altogether."

Mike's voice echoed through the room, snapping everyone back to attention. "They may go away for now, but this area will be under heavy surveillance for quite some time." He looked grim. "I didn't think about it at the time since everything happened so fast, but when you silenced my tracker, the Agency will have assumed I was killed while on duty. We will need to proceed quite cautiously for they will not give up lightly believing I was murdered."

He then turned to Declan. "It's not going to take them long to realize you're missing as well and after the reunion with your mother and the stolen car..." He trailed off, raising an eyebrow at Declan in a silent question.

Declan shifted uncomfortably; his face flushed with embarrassment. "I thought I could use the tech in the car to get us out of the city," he explained, his voice quiet. I panicked when I saw the car in their garage. It was the same one I saw the night I met Dr. Peterson, the night of the accident. It was my father's car that was involved in the accident. He is the reason those kids died!"

Declan let out a sigh, rubbing his temples. "It was too much information too fast," he admitted. "I just... panicked when I realized the car was the same one I saw the night of the accident. I didn't think, I just acted."

The room fell into silence. It was clear to everyone that the situation had just become significantly more complicated. They were all under threat, and there was no easy way out. All they could do now was to keep their heads down and continue their work. The future of humanity depended on it.

"Frag this," Mike muttered. His face was a mask of concern. "This is going to get really bad. I knew something had happened that night that they were trying to hide, but I didn't think to look that hard. Just following orders. But they are not going to stop looking until we are dead or detained, and the more I think about it, the more I think dead will be their only acceptable option."

He looked at Declan, his eyes narrowing with intensity. "Your existence as the son of the president is fraught with complexities and contradictions," he began, his voice measured. "Firstly, the revelation that the president has a son is staggering in itself, especially in a society where procreation has been forbidden. But what adds to the shock is the discovery that our very desire to have children and reproduce has been manipulated, possibly even controlled, through some form of mental coercion or influence."

Mike's voice grew even grimmer. "Now add in this information and the lengths they've gone to protect him at the cost of countless lives, all under the guise of a society that values Equity above all else. Your identity, Declan, is not just a personal matter; it's a symbol of a system that has been hiding truths and manipulating the very core of human nature. This will open the people's eyes to the fact that we are living in a society that is far from equal."

He paused, glancing at each person in the room. "We're not just fighting for our own survival now. We're fighting for the future of our society, for the truth to come to light. This isn't just about us anymore."

The gravity of their situation hung in the air, an unspoken challenge. Would they rise to it or succumb to the pressure? Only time would tell.

As Mike's words settled in the air, a murmur of hushed voices filled the room, the weight of the revelation pressing down on them all. Declan's lineage wasn't just a personal matter; it shook the very foundations of what they had been taught growing up in the Central Childhood Education & Care Facility.

They had accepted the government's takeover of parenthood, believing in the logic they had been fed. Parents, they were told, were incapable of providing an objective upbringing, often passing on biases and prejudices. Home environments were painted as unstable, with children suffering from inconsistent care, leading to developmental issues. The government had pointed to grim statistics on child abuse, neglect, and the teaching of socially unapproved doctrines, such as religion or outdated cultural norms.

All these reasons had seemed sound, and they had embraced the idea that state control of child-rearing would lead to a more equitable, unbiased, and safe environment for children to grow. But now, the shocking truth that President Caldwell had a son, hidden from the very society that had outlawed traditional parenthood, challenged everything they had come to accept. The room was charged with a sense of betrayal, and the whispers grew louder as they grappled with the implications of a system that had lied to them.

Then there was the story of Maddy, a woman who had taken her own life due to the loss of a child only realized in a computer simulation made them ponder some of life's most basic questions of why we are here. The reality of the lies they'd been told started to settle in, and they began to see things from a different perspective.

A wave of realization washed over them as they began to understand what they'd been missing - the familial bonds, the joys of raising children, the opportunity to impart wisdom and love in a personal, intimate way. Anger and fear began to take hold as they considered how much of their humanity they'd been forced to relinquish for the sake of this fabricated ideal of equality.

A tension filled the room, as they started to understand that their fight wasn't just against an unjust government, but for reclaiming their humanity - a humanity that was also in dire straights of even being able to sustain itself.

In the underground bunker, the whispers of rebellion began to swell to a level that was not expected. The people who had been hushed into stunned silence began to find their voices again. The shock of the revelation was slowly turning into indignation and resolve.

The conversations that had been fragmented and disoriented now began to weave together into a steady narrative. Each person had joined this mission to help Dr. Evers and Linda rectify what they believed to be a minor corruption in their government. They were here to stop a political party that they believed had stepped over the line and needed to be brought back into line. But now they were seeing a deeper betrayal, one that ran through the veins of their society, one that had stolen away their freedom, their rights, and their very humanity.

The injustice of the state-controlled parenthood system, the lies surrounding President Caldwell, the hidden truths about Declan's existence - everything coalesced into a single, grim reality. They had been manipulated on a scale far greater than they had ever imagined.

Yet, as they began to digest this bitter truth, a strange thing happened. The cloud of despair began to lift, replaced by a new, powerful sense of purpose. A flame of hope was ignited, bright and resilient, illuminating the darkness that had once shrouded them.

They realized they were not just fighting a tyrannical government. They were fighting to reclaim their very humanity. They were fighting to restore the natural order of things and correct the distorted image of the world painted by the authorities. The Mycelium Computer wasn't just a tool to prevent a catastrophe. It was the key to unlocking the answers they needed to solve humanity's reproduction problem.

The murmur of conversations grew louder, stronger. Eyes met eyes, and nods were exchanged. This was more than a rebellion. This was a revolution. And it was only just beginning.

Chapter 52

Echoes of Simulated Love

The task of rebuilding the Mycelium Computer was daunting. Despite their combined knowledge and expertise, Linda and Claire were struggling to recreate the intricate magic that Maddy had poured into the original design. There was a missing element, a secret ingredient they couldn't pinpoint. For all of their effort, they could not seem to get the system to "turn on"; it would power up, but nothing of the old code appeared on their screens.

They meticulously analyzed the original blueprints, cross-referencing them with Maddy's handwritten notes and video logs. They delved into the quantum algorithms, attempting to replicate the precise conditions that allowed for the computer's unique functionality. They experimented with various qubit configurations, exploring different superposition and entanglement states to mimic the original system's behavior. They even sought out rare and exotic materials, hoping to recreate the exact quantum coherence that had been so vital to the original design.

Despite these exhaustive efforts, the computer remained an enigma, a puzzle with a missing piece that eluded their grasp. The frustration was palpable, but they pressed on, driven by the knowledge that the Mycelium Computer held secrets that could redefine their understanding of reality. The process was slow and filled with setbacks, but they were determined to unlock the mysteries that lay within the machine's complex quantum architecture.

Meanwhile, the machines tirelessly worked to expand their underground sanctuary, their metallic bodies grinding and digging deeper into the rock. They were limited by the single entrance, their only access to the surface, making their work even more critical. But as the chambers grew larger and deeper, a miraculous discovery halted their progress.

The grinding of the machines softened, and then stopped. The machines had broken into a vast underground cave system. The hidden world beneath the earth teemed with life - unique, hardy species of insects, rare varieties of fungi glowing in the dark, colonies of bats hibernating in crevices, and a small underground stream burbling through the cavern.

Suddenly, as if responding to this incredible discovery, the Mycelium Computer sprang to life. Its familiar hum filled the underground facility, drawing everyone's attention. Puzzled looks were exchanged, and two questions hung in the air. What did the opening of the underground caves have to do with the Mycelium Computer springing back to life? Where was the computer getting its source code?

Dr. Evers, deep in thought, finally broke the silence. "The Mycelium Computer, like many fungi, might be sensitive to its environment, just like plants communicate with each other," he began, all eyes on him now. "Plants, you see, use a sophisticated system to communicate with one another. They release chemicals into the air or soil - a language of sorts - which other plants can detect and respond to."

"Being this deep underground might have interfered with the Mycelium Computer's ability to 'communicate' or gather data from the world around it," he continued,
"much like a plant unable to pick up the chemical signals because of a strong wind. With the opening into the cave system, it might have gotten the 'signal' it needed to come back online."

His words hung in the air, giving everyone much to ponder. While the mystery of the Mycelium Computer's functionality remained, one thing was clear - they were one step closer to understanding the marvel Maddy had created.

As the computer came to life Declan was reminded of Maddy and how all of this began. He was glad they had been able to bring the computer back to life but also feared the experiences that came with it. Where was this machine going to take them and what would they learn from it? The thoughts invigorated him and at the same time scared him to death. He didn't have much time to ponder about the implications of the system coming back to life; for his vision swirled almost immediately. With his heart in his throat he was transported back into the simulation. The cold and damp of the underground bunker he had just left contrasted sharply with the warm, softly lit room he now found himself in. The memory of Maddy's terrified face as she plunged into this unknown world was still fresh in his mind, as were the worried faces of Claire and himself. The unmistakable wail of a newborn pierced the quiet, a sound so primal that it stirred something within him. It was until this moment that he realized it was in fact a sound he had never heard before, the cry of a baby. As he watched, Maddy looked down in amazement at the small, swaddled bundle resting on her stomach. In her arms, the child was a comforting weight, its tiny form swathed in the softest of cloths. The gentle rise and fall of its chest in sync with its coos sent a wave of warmth through the room. Watching Maddy cradle the child, a surge of profound emotions gripped him. The force of the affection visible in her eyes was so potent it took his breath away. This wasn't their reality. Maddy had never given birth; it wasn't possible in their era. Yet here she was, experiencing a simulation so vivid it tore at the very fabric of their understanding of reality. But the emotions coursing through Maddy were not simulations. The bond she formed with the child, the maternal instincts that flared within her, the overpowering love that radiated from her - they were as tangible as the child she held in her arms. Tears welled up in Declan's eyes as he watched this heartbreaking scene unfold, a scene he knew had shattered Maddy. She was trapped in a temporal paradox, caught between the loss of what used to be and the harsh reality of their present. The simulation was more than just a glimpse into an altered past. They still did not have the answers, but it was a poignant reminder of the deeply human experiences they had lost.

Declan continued to watch, held captive by the scene unfolding before him. Maddy, still within the simulation, was experiencing an uncanny distortion of time. The newborn cradled in her arms transformed rapidly, morphing from a baby to a toddler, then a pre-schooler within mere seconds. The infant's features became more defined, its personality unfurling like a blooming flower, leaving Declan in awed silence. It was breathtakingly surreal, witnessing years condensed into mere moments. He watched as Maddy's simulated child took their first steps, their little face glowing with triumph. He felt a pang of joy when he saw Maddy's laughter ring out as the child reached out for her, a lifeline in their wobbly world. The connection between them was palpable, even in the confines of the simulation. He watched as the child uttered their first words, a cacophony of garbled syllables and jubilant babble. He saw Maddy's pride as the child navigated their way through trials and triumphs, the natural curiosity of a child echoed in their every action. As the child laid their head against Maddy's shoulder, their soft breaths lulling them to sleep, Declan felt a strange twist in his chest. This was a world both profoundly foreign and deeply moving. By the time the child was a vibrant five-year-old in the simulation, their eyes were filled with the innocent wonder of childhood. Maddy looked on, her heart visibly swelling with a mix of pride and a deep, resonating love that was impossible to deny. She had nurtured this child, watched them grow, and loved them with a ferocity she hadn't known she was capable of. Declan felt a lump in his throat. He was witnessing an intimate journey of motherhood, a journey Maddy had been abruptly thrown into, and one that he could tell had left an indelible mark on her. He was witnessing the beauty and pain of human existence, a poignant snapshot of what their society had lost. The experience was heartrending, awe-inspiring, and utterly transformative.

Declan stood frozen, transfixed by the heartrending spectacle playing out before him. As the simulation continued, Maddy's virtual child grew from a bright, inquisitive ten-year-old into a blossoming adolescent on the verge of teendom. The transformation was vivid, their features morphing into those of a young person on the precipice of their future. The child was a being composed of flickers of digital light and lines of complex code, yet their presence in Maddy's heart was as real as any flesh-

and-blood human. The child radiated joy and wonder, a curiosity about their world that seemed limitless. They filled Maddy's heart with a symphony of laughter, a beacon of achievements, a cascade of shared learning and mutual growth. Every milestone reached, every triumph celebrated, every obstacle surmounted together served to deepen Maddy's connection to this digital offspring. The love she felt for them was so profound, so raw, it seemed her chest might rupture under the weight of it all. She was there for them in every aspect of their life - their school concerts, the moments when they needed comfort, the times they wavered in self-doubt. She cheered them on at sporting events, assisted with their homework, and lovingly tucked them into bed each night. She was their mentor, protector, cheerleader, and mother. In return, the child was her universe. They were her heart and soul externalized, a testament to a love she never knew she possessed, a love she never thought she would encounter. And as Declan observed, he saw not just Maddy, but the depth of the human experience - its capacity for love, for growth, for strength in the face of the unknown. He saw what it meant to be human in a world that had forgotten the essence of humanity. And though it was painful, it was also breathtakingly beautiful.

He could see how Maddy lost herself in this world, in this life that wasn't hers but felt so intensely real. The boundary between the simulated and the actual world became blurry, her consciousness merging with the artificial reality. She was present for their high school events, guided them through their first heartbreak, and assisted them in making pivotal life decisions. She watched them mature, not only in age but also in wisdom, their character honed by their experiences and lessons. In this digital world, Maddy was more than just an observer. She was an integral part of her child's life, providing guidance, solace, or merely her presence whenever needed. Every smile, every tear, every victory, every setback, Maddy was there. Her love had become an inseparable part of this virtual reality. Declan saw how Maddy's focus shifted entirely to this simulated world. The real world, the Quantum Research and Development Agency, the Mycelium Quantum computer, and even her own physical existence seemed to fade into the background. She was fully engrossed in her child's life, the life that unfolded right in front of her eyes, her own existence becoming secondary. Her love for her digital child was the lifeline keeping her anchored in this world of an unknowable code. The simulation was more palpable to her than anything she had ever experienced. In this digital landscape, she found purpose, love that filled her with happiness and sorrow in equal measure. The intensity of her emotions was breathtaking, threatening to submerge her as she watched her child navigate their way in the world. With each passing moment, Maddy drifted further away from her reality, becoming deeply embedded within the digital world. Her own existence seemed to dissolve, the digital world morphing into her universe, with her child as the pulsating heart of it all.

The transition was seamless, almost imperceptible. One moment, Declan was a passive observer, a spectator to this digitally rendered reality. The next moment, he was in the thick of it all, living a life he never knew, experiencing feelings he'd never felt. The simulation was no longer a remote, external spectacle – it was his life, his reality. He was there on the day of the graduation, the weight of the moment heavy in his heart. He felt the pride swell within him, filling every corner of his being as he watched his child, this amazing person he and Maddy had raised, walk up the stage. He was Dad. And in a heartbeat, memories flooded his mind, not memories of a life observed but a life lived. The recollections were his, as real and poignant as if they had been lived in the flesh. His heart fractured into what felt like a thousand shards, each piece echoing with an intense love he never thought possible. He was experiencing fatherhood, the profound experience of being someone's pillar of strength, their guide, their protector. He was the person his child looked up to, leaned on, and learned from. He was their mentor, their confidant, their biggest cheerleader, and their safe haven. Being a father meant standing by their side, guiding them through life's trials and tribulations, teaching them, learning from them, and growing with them. It meant sacrificing his own comfort for their happiness, enduring sleepless nights for their peace, and setting aside his desires for their dreams. It meant feeling his heart leap with joy at their laughter, ache with worry when they were hurt, swell with pride at their achievements, and shatter with sorrow at their disappointments. It meant experiencing the highest highs and the lowest lows, all for the love of his child. The intensity of these emotions left Declan breathless. This was no longer a simulation, but a reality his mind couldn't differentiate from his own. His world was no longer confined to the QRDA or the study of genetics. It had expanded, transcending the limits of technology and science, reaching into the realm of love and life. He was a father in a world built of code and light, a reality that was as beautiful as it was heart-wrenching.

As the commencement speaker made their final remarks, the sea of students erupted in joyous celebration. Declan's heart throbbed in his chest as his eyes found his child in the sea of graduates. Their eyes sparkled with jubilation as she moved her tassel from the right to the left, symbolizing her transition from student to graduate.

The applause was deafening, but all he could hear was the sound of his heart echoing in his chest. His child, his baby, was a high school graduate. The enormity of the moment crashed over him as he made his way to her through the crowd, the world around him blurring into insignificance. As he wrapped his arms around her, Declan felt a wave of emotions engulf him. The joy of her accomplishment, the pride he felt for her, and the bittersweet realization that his baby was growing up. Her smile was radiant as she hugged him back, her eyes reflecting the same complex emotions he felt. She then handed him a small envelope, her grin widening as he took it. "For you, Dad," she said, her voice choked with emotion. The envelope was lightweight and seemingly inconsequential, but Declan knew it was anything but that. The handwritten 'Dad' on the front was a testament to the journey they'd taken together, the challenges they'd overcome, and the bond they'd forged. As he held the envelope, he realized it was more than just a piece of paper;

The pride that filled Declan as he read the University's acceptance letter was insurmountable. His heart swelled with joy as he saw his child's dream unfolding in front of his eyes. Her dream was no longer a distant aspiration but a tangible reality. She was going to one of the best institutes in the world, and her journey into the world of Physics was just about to begin. The field of Physics, with its myriad mysteries and profound truths, had always fascinated his child. But what enthralled her the most was string theory – the ground-breaking, mind-boggling concept that sought to unify all of physics. It was the idea that the fundamental building blocks of the universe were not particles, as had been long believed, but one-dimensional "strings" vibrating at different frequencies. String theory was a symphony of the cosmos, a harmonious interplay of these tiny strings, each vibrating string playing a unique note in the grand cosmic orchestra. It was the closest humans had come to reading the mind of God, as one such theorist put it, a glimpse into the unified theory that could explain everything from the infinitesimally small quantum particles to the incomprehensibly vast galaxies. His child's eyes would light up as she explained how string theory might answer some of the most profound questions of the universe. How it could reconcile the seemingly incompatible theories of general relativity and quantum mechanics. How it held the potential to explain the Big Bang, the formation of black holes, the nature of dark matter, and even the possible existence of multiple universes. To Declan, it was not just the complex theoretical knowledge that amazed him but the passion and curiosity that his child exhibited. Her excitement, her drive, and her insatiable thirst for knowledge was a sight to behold. As a father, he could not be prouder. As he watched her step into her dream, he was filled with an overwhelming sense of joy. His child was on the path to understanding the secrets of the universe, and he couldn't wait to see where it would take her. Declan's gaze landed on the book his daughter held tightly in her hands, the black cover reflecting the sunlight. As he caught sight of it, an echo of past memories resurfaced, the flashes of similar moments coursing through his mind like a hastily rewound film. That same book - the small black one, had always been there, almost invisible against the myriad details of the simulations, yet always present. This object persisted across the confines of digital realities, finding its way into each version of the simulated worlds he'd ventured into. In the crowd of the genetically tested, the man with the medium brown complexion had held this book close to his chest, a piece of him clutched tightly in his hands. It had been Sam's companion in numerous simulations, a near-constant presence in their shared experiences. Always there, subtly making its existence known, a recurring detail in an ocean of change. Now here it was again, in the hands of his own simulated child, on a day of celebration and new beginnings. The sunlight glinted off the cover, turning it into a beacon that held his attention captive. His mind spun, struggling to connect the dots, to find the reason behind its persistent appearance. Declan squinted, bending slightly to make out the title etched in golden letters, 'The God Equation'. An instant rush of questions coursed through him - what was the significance? Why had it been there, a silent spectator in each simulated journey he undertook? For now, the answers eluded him, slipping away like sand through his fingers. Declan tucked away this mystery at the back of his mind, promising to unravel it when time permitted. He decided to let the moment be about his child, about her achievements, and the overwhelming pride he felt. Yet, the black book, 'The God Equation', remained, a puzzle piece waiting to be placed in the larger picture. Could be nothing, could be something, Declan thought. But he knew, deep down, that in the world of simulations, there was no such thing as a meaningless coincidence.

Chapter 53

The Universe Texted, We Swiped Right

Dr. Evers leaned back in his chair, his eyes twinkling behind his glasses. The dim light of the lab cast shadows on the walls, filled with equations and holographic models of the universe. Claire and Jamie sat across from him, their faces a mix of curiosity and confusion.

"You see," Dr. Evers began, pausing as he looked up towards the ceiling, his eyes filled with a sense of wonderment, almost as if he were offering a silent prayer to the cosmos. "I've been pondering a rather fascinating idea, especially since I learned of the code hidden in your computer. Now bear with me as I am trying to think this through aloud."

Claire and Jamie exchanged a glance, both clearly unsure why they had been summoned to Dr. Evers' lab. The moment they had taken their seats, he had launched into his discourse without preamble, leaving them intrigued but also a bit bewildered.

Dr. Evers continued, "Imagine you're walking through a forest, and you stumble upon a book. Not just any book, mind you, but a beautifully bound one, written in a language you understand, complete with chapters and even an index."

Claire raised an eyebrow. "That would be quite the find."

"Exactly," Dr. Evers continued. "You'd probably think it's nearly impossible for nature to produce such a book, right? You'd conclude that someone must have written it, placed it there for a reason."

Jamie nodded, "Sure, it would be too much of a coincidence otherwise."

Dr. Evers smiled, "Now, let's extend that idea to our universe. We exist in a cosmos that seems perfectly tailored for life. The laws of physics, the constants of nature, everything is set up in a way that allows us to be here, pondering these very questions."

Claire leaned forward, intrigued. "So, you're saying the universe is like that book in the forest? That it's been... designed?"

"In a manner of speaking, yes," Dr. Evers said. "I'm suggesting that the universe isn't random. It's as if it's been fine-tuned to allow for our existence. If even one of the fundamental constants were slightly different, life as we know it couldn't exist. We wouldn't be here to observe it, to study it."

Jamie scratched her head, "So, what does that mean? Are you saying someone or something set it up this way?"

Dr. Evers shrugged, "That's the million-dollar question, isn't it? It could be a cosmic designer, or perhaps there are multiple universes, each with different laws and constants, and we just happen to be in the one where life is possible. Or maybe there's another explanation we haven't even thought of yet."

Claire looked thoughtful. "It's a compelling idea, Dr. Evers. It turns the whole notion of random existence on its head."

"Indeed," Dr. Evers said, his eyes twinkling even brighter.

Dr. Evers leaned forward, his eyes locking onto Claire and Jamie's. "Now, let's bring this back to the code you found in your computer. That code, in my opinion, is akin to the writing in that book we imagined in the forest. It's a message, a set of instructions, or perhaps even a story. The computer is merely the medium, the 'book,' if you will, that allows us to glimpse this code."

Claire's eyes widened. "So, you're saying that the code is like a universal language? Something that's been written into the fabric of reality itself?"

"Exactly," Dr. Evers nodded, visibly excited. "And just like a book written in a foreign language, we need to translate it. The question is, how? And why does it show us the things it does? Why these simulations of history—or what we assume to be our history?"

Jamie leaned back, clearly pondering the weight of Dr. Evers' words. "That's a lot to take in. If this code is a form of universal language, then understanding it could change everything. It could answer questions about why we're here, what the universe is, and maybe even who or what created it."

Dr. Evers smiled, "You're catching on. But there's more. If we can translate this code, we might be able to interact with it. Imagine being able to ask the universe questions and receiving answers. It's a tantalizing prospect."

Claire looked skeptical but intrigued. "It's almost like you're suggesting we could have a conversation with the universe itself. But why would this code show us simulations of history? What's the purpose?"

Dr. Evers paused, his gaze turning inward as he considered the question. "Ah, the 'why' is the most intriguing part, isn't it? Perhaps these simulations serve as a form of education, or maybe they're a test. It could even be a way for the universe to understand itself, through us. We are, after all, a way for the universe to know itself."

The room fell silent, each lost in their thoughts, contemplating the profound implications of what Dr. Evers had just proposed. Finally, Jamie broke the silence.

"So, what's the next step? How do we go about translating this universal code?"

Dr. Evers grinned, "Ah, my dear, that's the adventure that lies ahead. And it's one that could change the course of human history, forever."

Claire took a deep breath, her eyes meeting Dr. Evers'. "There's something else you should know. Ever since we opened that tunnel, the computer seems to have re-established its connection to... well, whatever it's connecting to," she hesitated, clearly grappling with the enormity of it all.

Dr. Evers leaned in, intrigued. "Go on."

Claire continued, "Numerous People have begun to have visions; Declan for example has had a vision—a simulation, if you will. He saw his life with Maddy. He told me about it a few days ago, but he's been reluctant to discuss it further. It's shaken him to his core, emotionally."

"And what did he see?" Dr. Evers asked, his voice tinged with concern.

Claire looked down, her voice softening. "He saw the life with Maddy, the one she had seen, their marriage and their child growing up. He experienced it all as if he has now lived two separate lives. And as much as I hate to say it, her actions now make more sense to me than ever. I can't say I'm okay with what she did, but after hearing Declan's account, I can't find it in myself to hate her for it either."

Before Dr. Evers could respond, Jamie interjected, "Mike Reynolds also had a vision. He thought it was a dream at first because it happened while he was asleep. But he's convinced it was the computer trying to communicate something."

Dr. Evers sat back, absorbing the new information. "This is extraordinary. The computer isn't just showing us simulations; it's showing us deeply personal and emotionally charged events. It's as if it's trying to guide us, or perhaps warn us. "